HARD LAND TO RULE

<<<<<<<<<<<<<<<<<<<<<<< • >>>>>>>>>>>>>>>>>>>>>

A novel

by

Anthony Whitt

Published by Anthony Whitt
Austin, Texas
www.anthonywhitt.com

ISBN-13: 978-0-9898868-0-2 (softcover)
ISBN-13: 978-0-9898868-1-9 (ebook)

FT
Pbk

Hard Land to Rule is a work of fiction. Although actual locations are mentioned, they are used in a fictitious manner, and any resemblance to persons, living or dead, or to places, events, or locales is purely coincidental. The characters are productions of the author's imagination.

Cover design by Philip Whitt, www.philipwhitt.com
Cover image copyright @ Shutterstock/27454459
Editing, interior design and layout by Lana Castle, Castle Communications, www.castlecommunications.com

This book is dedicated to my wife, Cathy. She knows the true value of family. Without her support, this story would not have been possible.

ONE

A feral danger brimming with intelligence inhabits the Texas hill country. This native menace awakens the deepest primordial fears of all the frontier settlers he encounters. He, like the land, knows no kindness. He gives no mercy. His cunning and ruthlessness are legendary. Moving with incredible stealth, he stalks his quarry, often catching it totally unaware. The blood he spills flows freely over the white limestone rocks, staining them umber in the drying sun. Watching the pall of death cast its shadow over his victim satisfies his savage instinct. A lustful trance of ecstasy intoxicates him after his conquest. Retribution is his. He does not kill to satisfy a hunger in his belly. He kills for vengeance.

These were *his* hills, *his* hunting lands. This is where he formerly made his life. This was where he raised his family. He mourns the theft of the cut-up canyons and rugged hills where he used to roam in freedom. Resentment and anger fill his soul with the need to quell the bitterness at any occasion that presents the chance.

Opportunity knocked on this damp night, faintly lit by a moon sliding behind a solid layer of cloud cover. A wet blanket of fog smothered the woods and obscured his furtive movements. His supple body crept forward, long and lean as a mountain lion, an undefined apparition gliding from one cluster of brush to the next. The rocky terrain was slippery from the moisture but offered little challenge to his catlike movements. He was adept at traversing unfamiliar territory. His eyes were accustomed to travel at night and provided him an advantage in the somber conditions. At home in this element, he knew no fear. He was confident in his ultimate conquest.

His other companions, secluded at the end of a ridge overlooking this small group of cabins, depended on him. They would hold the horses secure until his return. Then, they would make their getaway and bask in the glory of their raid. Their desires for continued raiding against these white intruders depended upon his success during this predawn raid.

Closing in on his target, he paused to take in details of the unfamiliar terrain. The line of dense cedar currently providing concealment would get him to within fifty feet of his intended target — a detached shack of weathered cedar logs. Inside the crude enclosure was the food his party would need to continue their incursion amongst these despised trespassers. Since leaving the village on the high plains a month ago, their provisions had dwindled to nothing. The smoked meat and corn stored in the log building was a temptation he could not pass. This should be an easy theft with the white men safely secured in the main cabin, deep into their dreams. He did not respect the poor fighting skills of the loosely organized bands of pale intruders.

A short lapse of time passed as he finished acquiring the final details of the surroundings. All that remained was a quick dash to the closed door of the shack. Crouching behind the fog-shrouded brush, he gathered his courage and offered a prayer to his guiding spirit. He prayed for clear thinking and protection during his coming actions. He would begin with a stealthy exit from the brush when the fog gathered its thickest. Concealment of his movements from the main cabin was a necessary precaution, but he felt there was little to fear if discovered. White men seemed hesitant to respond to unexpected events they did not understand. He had learned this during past raids that had left the men with hair on their face bewildered.

After completing this theft, he would rejoin his brothers on the ridgetop. Together, they planned to ride to the adjoining valley to raid another cabin at a previously scouted location. This cabin, apparently inhabited only by women, would be their destination just after sunrise. Once there, it would be a simple matter to overpower the undefended occupants. Then the soft bodies of the white women would satisfy his powerful animalistic needs. His loins began to stir while considering the prospect of several helpless females at his lustful disposal. After they served their purpose for pleasure and degradation, the blood spilled from the bellies of these unworthy squaws would briefly appease his long-standing resentment. He missed his former home.

He missed his old hunting grounds in the violet-crowned hills outside of the town the white men called Austin.

Finally, the fog rewarded his patience with a floating haze that provided maximum concealment. War club at the ready, he uttered a final plea to his spirits for their protection, now and later. He cautiously rose from his crouch and darted towards the shack in a stooped trot. His soft buffalo moccasins made contact with the ground in well-placed steps that mimicked a deer's ability to travel with no disturbance, no sound. The distance to the door closed rapidly until he stood motionless at the entryway.

Taking a moment for observation at this close proximity uncovered nothing disturbing. He could detect no movement or white man smell. The only odor was from the mesquite-smoked meat hanging tantalizingly close, just inside the door. He salivated at the thought of tasting the richly flavored meat. No alarm from within the shed or the nearby cabin indicated any detection of his movements. All that remained was to push the door open. The time had arrived to enter and take the hard-earned reward of plunder. Pride in his quest swelled in his heart and filled his head with confidence. He would be triumphant here, and in the upcoming raid at dawn. Success was ordained by the spirits and meant to be. He was a warrior. He was a Comanche!

Hiding to the side of the door, he cautiously pushed it inward. A drawn-out creak broke the silence as the door slowly swung open. The enticing aroma of smoked meat spilled out the gap, filling his senses. His mouth watered; he had to have the meat. He stepped into the open doorway, pausing to acquire details of the darkened interior.

The blinding blast met him with the heat of searing fire and the roar of a dozen enraged bears. His body rippled with shock waves tearing through his left breast. The intense concussion of hot lead ripping through flesh spun him from front to back and threw him to the ground with the force of a charging buffalo. His eyes burned with the bright orange flash of the gun's violent explosion. An undeniable power had shattered his success at point-blank range. Pain was immediate, and deeper than any he had ever known.

The jarring impact on the damp soil awoke every survival instinct instilled since his youth. To remain on the ground meant surrender, and acceptance of the death that would surely follow. Summoning his catlike reflexes for evasion, he used the ground contact to ricochet back to his feet in a stumbling escape to the nearby treeline. Running with his vision blurred in agonizing pain, his left arm dangling useless, he bolted into the woods in an adrenaline-induced panic. With tree limbs and underbrush tearing at him, the foliage and fog wrapped a cloak of concealment around his retreat within moments of the dreadful blast. Dazed and confused, he disappeared quickly with but one thought on his mind: to make it to the hilltop where his brothers waited. Survival depended on his companions and the horses they held for a hasty escape. They had to ride like the wind to reach a safe distance from the tricky white men. His spiritual medicine was weak compared to the unexpected strength of the weapon that roared like a bear.

TWO

Matt eased out of the confines of the smokehouse a little stunned from the thunder of his Colt in such a small enclosure. His head throbbed with the booming resonance of the pistol. Peering around the doorway, he caught a fleeting glimpse of the prowler making a remarkable exit into the pool of blackness, albeit with a definite droop to his left side. Matt was amazed at the swift response he had just witnessed. This nighttime intruder had tumbled to the ground from the impact of the bullet, but he wasn't fast enough to get a follow-up shot. All he saw was the back of an Indian vanishing into the fog-shrouded murkiness of thick woods. Damn all the luck! He wanted results. He wanted a dead Indian on the ground. Now, the uncertainty of tracking a wounded and dangerous foe faced him. Failure mocked his efforts.

Hesitating outside the door, Matt ran his fingers through his rumpled hair, contemplating the new problem. His mind worked on the numerous angles when he realized the risk he was taking. His low voice seemed loud in the silent darkness, "I could end up shot out here in the open. Be a helluva way to take one."

Instinctively, he ducked back inside the shed.

He felt disgusted by the circumstance brought on by his poor aim. It had been startling to wake to the sight of an Indian buck silhouetted in the door less than ten feet away. But that was no excuse. He would not forget the mistake that was his alone. His lips curled up in contempt as he muttered, "It's what I git for snoozing."

He could not detect any movement outside as he peered through the doorway, but he knew Indians could be sneaky. He continued to grumble under his breath, "Best git back to the cabin. They'll be jumpy."

His thoughts were racing with all the possibilities as he stepped out into the damp night. Near the door, he found the war club that had flown from the intruder's hand after he took the hastily aimed bullet. This definitely identified the prowler as a marauding Indian. Apache or Comanche was hard to tell, but it didn't matter much to him. All Indians were the same, a nuisance, and a hindrance to his efforts to make the land productive. All of the tribes were better off far removed from the settlers, or just plain wiped out. Just get the hell out of the way.

He felt the same way about carpetbagging Yankees as he did about Indians. He spent four years fighting the blue-bellies in that cursed land to the east. Now, he had heard of a few of them showing up in Austin. Those scoundrels were down here to suck the life out of honest Southerners. Yankees and Indians! To hell with any of them that stood in his way. He had a life to maintain in these hills and failure was not an option his family would understand. The complexities of the current situation were enormous without a body on the ground.

Cautiously, he backed his way up to the steps of the main cabin. The woodline faded into the dreary shadows without any sign of danger emerging. Matt mounted the steps of the porch and cracked open the door. He sensed movement inside the darkened room. From the depths of the cabin came the murmurs of the women worked up in nervous chatter. Matt could hear his younger brother Lee, and his nephew Travis shuffling around the darkened interior groping for their clothes. More importantly, he hoped they had their guns.

Through the cracked door Matt hissed, "Lee! Git your ass out here."

Lee quickly appeared at the door. He was half dressed, with his long hair badly tangled, but armed and wide-awake. He stepped outside to face the criticism Matt's voice conveyed.

"Hell, Matt, I was comin' fast as I could."

"I might've been dead by the time you got your slow-movin' ass out here. I told you to expect something tonight!"

Lee hung his head and kept quiet at the truth of Matt's words. Death in these hills came suddenly, and the reports of Indians thieving food from the neighbors had just hit home.

Matt spoke with agitation, "We got ourselves a situation here that's gonna take some attention. Got a wounded Indian trailed off in the direction towards Tucker's Ridge. I reckon he'll leave some sort of sign. Be light enough in about thirty minutes to follow him."

Lee absorbed the context of Matt's comment and wasn't at all pleased with the implications it carried. What could be gained from following a wounded Indian? Not much, but a lot could be lost.

Lee knew it would do no good, but he said it anyway. "Uh, Matt, who all is goin'?"

"Just you and me, brother. Travis can stay with the women and kids in case more trouble comes around."

"What are we gonna accomplish? Did he git anything?"

"No, he didn't. But I'll not be havin' attempts on my land."

"How bad was he hurt?"

"Left arm drooped a little, was all."

"Could be more of 'em?"

"Yeah, there could be. But I aim to finish business. Git your carbine and rustle up some food. I'll git some water and saddle up the horses. Make sure Travis is squared away with the scattergun. Women and kids stay inside until we git back."

"When will that be?"

"After our business is finished. However long it takes. Best git a move on."

Lee slouched back inside the cabin to do as directed. The women moved aside to let him enter when he reached the door. Their worried glances surveyed the gloom outside the cabin before they ducked back in to assist Lee in his efforts to get ready.

Matt moved cautiously to the side of the cabin where the sturdy corral fence secured the stock. He felt a little uneasy moving about in the open with such low visibility, but the woodline was set back a ways on this side of the cabin. Most likely, no sneaking Indian would cross the open area around the corral. Besides, after suffering one of theirs wounded, most Indians would make for the hills. Too damn cowardly to take any loss.

Not at all like his boys with the Rebel cavalry. He'd left behind a lot of brave men on those forlorn fields of battle. They'd followed him wherever he asked them to go. Through dense thickets, or across open meadows. They had followed him suffering, bleeding, and far too many, dying. In the end it was all for naught. Their sacrifice had accomplished nothing. Just a lot of long, hard miseries, day after day. And now, back home, the tough fight to survive continued relentlessly.

He mumbled in the damp air, "Don't need no damn Indians prowlin' 'round."

Matt knew Lee didn't want to come along, but that was just too bad. He needed somebody for his backside and another gun if more Indians were about. Lee was not an aggressive sort, but he could handle a carbine well and generally remained cool in hot situations. Lee would do. He was all Matt had at the moment. Travis was a little too young at seventeen, and somebody needed to stay with the women.

The women. What a subject! Cora had been with him quite a while. She knew what was up. She'd come with him to these hills when they both were a lot younger. Together, they'd built up their spread until it could produce a suitable living for a family. A good woman to have. Good for the kids. Kept the cabin running smooth. She worked hard. Here lately, that was where it ended between them.

Disgruntled with the situation, Matt quickly filled the canteens with water and had the horses saddled. He checked the action on his Henry repeating rifle. The smooth-loading lever action he took off a dead Union soldier would serve well against mobile Indians. Satisfied with the rifle, he confirmed that the trailworn saddlebags contained extra boxes of .44 caliber ammo. By the time Lee got the grub and gear organized, Matt had the horses in hand and was anxious for a start. The first signs of dawn were glowing orange through the mist that hung stubbornly in the air.

Lee rushed out to his mare, Midnight, slid his Spencer carbine into the scabbard, and then secured the rations of beef jerky, pemmican, and hardtack in the bags. Always wanting sweets, he also included some hard cinnamon candy that he kept easily accessible.

With his final preparations completed, Lee finally looked at Matt and asked, "What's your plan?"

"We'll lead the horses to start with. You follow a little distance behind me. Go ahead and git your carbine out right now. You be ready to cover me while I look for sign. I'm sure we can pick up some sort of trail over by the shed door. Just about enough light to follow if the trail ain't too puny."

"You gonna say goodbye to Cora before we go?"

"We got to git goin' and take advantage of daybreak. Not much time for long goodbyes. She knows what's expected."

A sad family watched from the cabin porch as their men left for an undertaking that could be their last. Worried expressions laced with frowns spoke of their uneasiness at this departure. They called out words of concern to be careful, mixed with pleas to return home soon. Cora, in particular, knew what Matt was capable of. She did her best not to show any outward signs of the fear she felt swelling up in her chest. This scene had become all too frequent in her life.

Matt looked her way until their eyes met. His cold gaze did nothing to bridge the emotional chasm growing wider between them with each passing day. He nodded slightly at her before shielding his eyes with the brim of his hat.

The dirt around the smokehouse showed clear signs of the encounter. A fresh pockmark in the damp soil gave evidence of a body tumbling to the ground. The shallow indentations in the dirt held faint bloodstains, providing proof of the damage done to the Indian. The moccasin footprints led into the thick underbrush that flourished beyond the smokehouse. Fog continued to hang heavy in the air, obscuring the canopy of oak trees and the knot of brush below their arching limbs. Matt grimaced at the thought of following a trail in these conditions. Despite their propensity to flee, they were still Indians, and an ambush was one of their favorite methods of attack. The buck could be slightly wounded, and as ready to pounce as a cornered mountain lion.

Matt mulled over these thoughts while gazing at the trees standing somber in the pale gray mist. The bloodstain was evidence of a wound, but that didn't count for much. The injury could be fatal, or simply a nick that quickly dried up. Damn his poor shooting! The buck should be dead on the ground instead of running off. No sense in delaying any longer; it was time to move out.

"Lee, take the horses and work your way around the treeline to meet me on the other side. I'm going straight in, but it will be slow trailin' until I git a feel for what's going on. Give me a little lead-time. I suspect the bastard cleared out, but he might be laid up in there. Keep your eyes peeled. I want to be first out of the trees on the other side. Hang back some. I'll whistle when it's time for you to come around."

Lee held the reins in his left hand, while cradling the Spencer in his right, ready for action. He watched as Matt trailed off with his Henry, disappearing as silently as a hawk gliding overhead.

Matt kept his eyes roving from ground to treetop, moving cautiously into the brambles the Indian had crashed through earlier. It was difficult to see far into the mess. The brush seemed undisturbed, with no broken limbs, and the soil was too rocky in this area to show much sign of anything. Working along, no blood trail showed up. Matt realized that catching the Indian might not come easy. He fought to control the anxiety building with the prospect of tedious trailing.

Easing forward, he thought like the fugitive he was pursuing. I would go this way. It is easier that way. Help is just a short distance away. They might be following.

Knowing what lay on the other side of this grove of trees, it was no problem for Matt to contemplate a band of warriors waiting for him or Lee to make an easy target. Searching thoroughly, he finally reached the edge of the woods. He paused to survey the exposed hill rising before him while he hid under the cover of limbs sagging with the weight of moisture. Water dripped from the overhanging oak and rolled off the brim of his hat onto his back. The cool water chilled his skin and sent shivers to his stomach, knotted up with tension. Violence could erupt at any time.

The gray murkiness of the hill loomed before him, strewn with blackened stumps and littered with fallen limbs. Charred remnants of burned-out cedar trunks resembled beasts sulking behind the suspended wisps of fog. The atmosphere seemed permeated with an evil premonition. Matt had to shake his head clear of the menacing images that burrowed into his mind. It was becoming hard to distinguish real danger from imagined.

Collecting his thoughts, he calmed his overactive imagination to realize nothing of danger stirred among the limestone ledges. Easing up to the outside border of the trees that concealed him, Matt paused a moment before he let out a soft whistle.

Lee materialized as a ghostly image at the far end of the obscured treeline, trailing the horses behind him with a racket of shoe scraping against stone.

When Lee came up shoulder-to-shoulder, Matt confessed in a whisper, "Didn't find any sign in there. Didn't really think I would."

Lee was jumpy. He searched for directions in Matt's eyes and asked in a hushed voice, "Where to now?"

He knew the answer would spell out difficulties not pleasant to consider.

"That's a good question," Matt replied vaguely as he continued to analyze the lay of the hill, working out his plans.

Lee's eyes darted around the hillside, imagining Indians lurking behind every stump and tree.

Matt calmly continued with his answer, "If I was makin' a raid, I would want a fast getaway. The best spot to rendezvous around here would be on top of the hill. Then they could take Tucker's Ridge. Connect up with any number of trails to head off anywheres they wanted to. It all seems clear from down here, but you never know. There's some cover up there on top."

Lee gazed up the hill with apprehension.

Matt nodded his head toward the open hillside ledges as he said, "Tell you what. Tie off the horses and let's separate a little. We'll ease on up to the top and have a look."

Lee tied the horses off and they both crammed extra ammo in their vest pockets before heading up. The slope was rock strewn and a little steep, but they carefully picked their way through the weeds hiding rocks slick with moisture. Maintaining thirty feet of separation from each other, they reached the top within minutes to find all the evidence they needed. The water puddles on top of the limestone slabs still had mud in them. Hoofprints mixed together in a jumble of confusion on the damp soil. Bent and tromped down grass was everywhere. It was plain to see where moccasin prints pressed into the soft mud when the Indians mounted up. Matt took in the details of the site. The implications of the evidence sent the hair on his neck erect.

"Three or four of them red devils is what I'd say. They held the horses and waited for the thief to meet 'em back up here. Just as I expected. He took a bullet, and they didn't like that one bit. No siree. Didn't like it at all. Bunch of no good bastards. Boy, do I want 'em."

Matt stomped around, soaking in all the sign. He was hardly able to contain his excitement. He rushed over to a point of evidence that interested him.

"Look over here. You can see where they trailed out. Tracks narrow a little as they git into a line. Probably just three from the looks of it. Got a pretty good head start though."

Lee followed the prints of the hasty exit the Indians had made. He realized the trail receding into the distance would transform Matt into a bloodhound on the scent of a coon. Matt would not stop until the masked bandit was treed.

Behind Lee's back, Matt had already spun on his heels and headed out in a straight line down the hill to retrieve the horses at the bottom. Lee had to put it into a run or face being exposed and alone on the ridgetop. Matt led the way in a rush and rapidly descended to the base of the slope. He loosened the reins on Midnight and flipped them to Lee just as he awkwardly slid to a stop.

Mounting up, Matt was a blur of motion calling out to Lee, "Git yourself saddled up! They got nearly an hour on us, but by God, we will close that down on 'em. They'll soon regret their mistake."

Lee mounted without hesitation. He raked his mare to stay in sight of Matt's swift ascent up and over ledges, around cedars, and under low-hanging limbs in a superb display of riding. Matt created a memorable sight for Lee, riding low, just off the saddle, absorbing the impacts, leaning forward, shirtsleeves flapping in the breeze. Matt was intent as an eagle diving from the heavens, tucked in and ready to release his latent power upon contact with the target.

Reaching the crest, Matt pulled to his right and made his way to the beginning of the pony tracks, with little slacking in pace. Lee fell in behind Matt a short gap to the rear, taking up his unspoken duty to scan for signs of danger while Matt concentrated on following the path of the Indian ponies. The land flattened out on the hilltop and the vegetation opened up, but vigilance was still called for to avoid the frequent areas from which an ambush was possible.

Matt set a blistering pace with an easy trail to follow. The low-hanging vapor in the upper meadows started to dissipate with the piercing beams of early morning warmth. Dense patches of haze occasionally rolled over them, but their pace never slackened. Lee contemplated the recklessness of such speed. They could stumble into the fleeing warriors in an instant and uncover more fight than they could handle. It didn't matter; he knew it would do no good to speak up when Matt was on a fresh scent.

For half an hour, they pressed on with a pause now and then to relocate the tracks when they crossed solid rock. Matt was determined to make contact with the raiders as soon as possible, for he knew time was on the side of the Indians. He knew the Indians were as good as lost if dusk overtook their pursuit before they brought them to engagement.

His desire burned deep to punish those that intended harm to his family or to his place on the Colorado River. Trespassing Indians were at the top of his list. Too many times, he had witnessed the aftermath of their handywork. Homes burned to the ground. Cattle scattered about, riddled with arrows. Women lanced to the ground and left for dead. Men sliced up and tortured until death finally lifted them away from their torment.

Worse yet, the images of brutality inflicted on children and babies stoked the fire that raged in his heart. Innocence ravaged. There was no need for the wanton destruction of young life. The despicable acts of the red man made no sense to him.

And he required justice. If the scales were out of balance, it was his duty to right them. He would pursue the Indians to hell and back to deliver his preferred method of reparation.

The trail unfolded beneath his mount, veering to the north. The change in direction began to strengthen his suspicions of its ultimate destination. It could all come together if they pushed hard enough. Retribution would be at hand, and the expectation of its deliverance radiated from his steel-gray eyes.

Thoughts of a different nature consumed Lee. The winding tracks of the Indian ponies were leading them to the proximity of the Ellis homestead. This fact seriously concerned Lee for the safety and well-being of the Ellis women. Frank Ellis had recently taken a nasty fall from a horse that had temporarily left him an invalid. The fall came near to killing him. He suffered severe head injuries that required confinement to a bed for recuperation. This situation left his wife and daughters alone to run his spread. The family had adapted and done well enough to keep their place running while he recovered. But the thought of Indians about with no men to protect the women produced disturbing images in Lee's conscience, impossible for him to ignore.

They were now riding on a ridge directly above the Ellis place and Lee knew it would be very disruptive, but he wanted to get this thorn out from under his saddle.

"Hey, Matt," Lee hollered into the wind.

Matt showed no signs of hearing, his focus on the Indian trail and the drumming of horseshoes drowning Lee's voice. Lee spurred his mount to close the distance to Matt and repeated his hailing in a shrill voice. Shocked, Matt pivoted to glare back at Lee. He pulled up on the reins and slowed his buckskin until Lee rode up beside him.

"Matt, I been thinkin' about the Ellis place. They might need to be looked in on."

Matt gave Lee a hard once-over that had weakened many a Confederate soldier who'd served under his rank of sergeant during the recent war.

"Ain't got time."

"We have to make time. Could be those bucks paid them a visit too last night."

"Slow us down too much."

Matt continued to stare at Lee with an expression of annoyance. The slackening of their pace didn't rest well with him. Lee could see color beginning to flush Matt's face. Matt could be single-minded to a fault, but Lee decided to press on.

"Not much, Matt. We can swing by their place and won't even lose sight of the trail."

"Damn, Lee. I hate to lose any ground we might've gained. This here trail is awful fresh. And I want them Indians dead."

"We'll make it up. Won't take long, and them bucks can't travel too fast with one bein' hurt. I can cut down to their cabin while you keep an eye out up here on the ridge. If everything's fine, great! If it's not, how would you feel about it if we kept on ridin' by and not stop? You'd have hell livin' with that. Won't take long, and besides they need to know there's Indians about."

A flush of realization came over Matt's face. He should have thought of it and probably would have if Frank had been an able body. It would have been worth picking Frank up just to have another gun. Matt mulled it over, chastising himself for not considering the women down on the Ellis place. Lee was right. They needed to check in on them. He nodded to Lee to acknowledge his younger brother was correct. At the same time, he reined Whiskey to the left, heading towards the rocky overlook above the Ellis ranch.

Arriving in short time, Matt halted his buckskin at the scenic outcrop above the well-kept cabin and corrals that made up the homestead built by Frank and Mary Ellis.

"I'll watch from here. It'll give Whiskey a breather. Things appear fine, but go on down. Be quick about it and find out if Frank is any better."

Matt watched Lee work his horse down the cactus-strewn hillside before he dismounted to stretch out his legs. Whiskey put his head down and began to work on the sparse bluestem growing amongst the honeycomb rocks scattered along the ridgeline. Matt felt his back muscles tightening from the pounding of the early morning ride and the all-night vigil in the smokehouse. He bent at the waist to grab his ankles and stretch the taut muscles. Holding his ankles brought some relief to his aching back but allowed the other pains of his abused body to be recognized. Knees that cracked and chafed as if packed with sand reminded him of the many twists and turns of negotiating the rough terrain of the hill country. He also remembered the Yankee who'd delivered a hot round to his leg in the backwoods of Virginia. The muscle around the bullet wound never healed properly and served as a painful memory of his service in the war of independence from the Northern states.

Ignoring these ailments was a necessity he had learned and accepted as a man's role in dealing with the struggles of life on the frontier. The gnawing hunger in his stomach was another matter. He rose from the bending position and pulled some venison jerky from his beat-up saddlebag. The meat, seasoned with pepper and spices in the proper mix, made a satisfying breakfast out here on the trail. Cora was responsible for the satisfaction he received from his meals while in the woods. She had the right skills to bring an acceptable level of comfort to this unforgiving land.

Matt's mind started to wander at the thought of female companionship, and in particular, the woman directly below him in the little cabin. He could not help but reflect on the ability of Frank's wife to soften the harshness surrounding this remote location subject to such intolerable extremes. Mary was a pleasure to think of, in contrast to the woes that normally bedeviled Matt. She had a pleasing influence on him with her long blonde hair cascading over her shoulders. Her eyes, clear blue as a pool of cold spring water, always invited him to peer into their mysterious depths. Like any man, Matt was susceptible to seduction in their promise of sensual charms. Mary's stylish manner of dress accented her voluptuous feminine curves. Unforgettable memories of her beauty danced across his mind, dimming the urgency of the current task at hand.

For years, he had watched her at the frequent social gatherings that brought neighbors together for special occasions. She always outshone the other women with her attractiveness. All of the frontier men held Mary up on a pedestal, but she remained unaware of their idolatry. This was part of her charm. Despite her fine appearance, she remained modest at heart, except for one occasion that Matt remembered well.

Mary had accidentally brushed against him rounding a blind corner at a community celebration. Facing each other, isolated and alone, his hand had slipped around her waist to help catch her balance. He was surprised as she willingly fell into his embrace and leaned immobile in his firm grasp.

Now, he vividly remembered her warm softness under the thin material of her dress. Purposely, he had let his hand linger in the pleasure of touching her far longer than fitting. She didn't try to break free of his caress, but gave him a yearning look that flushed her face with impassioned desire. As if it were yesterday, he recalled how his pulse quickened at the realization she could be his for the taking. The mesmeric attraction sizzled between them. In that short moment, imaginary thoughts of lovemaking bound them together as one. Time had slowed as his focus narrowed on the tantalizing possibilities tempting him.

Eventually he had mumbled an apology as the fascination of her feel lengthened to the point that he feared they would be stumbled upon. But she insisted there was no need to make an apology. She seemed willing to accept the consequences if they were discovered.

The want in her eyes from that day haunted him still. Matt dwelt on the spark that moment had produced many times, but this was an indulgence the current dilemma spoiled. He peered down the hill and saw Lee stepping briskly up to the cabin door.

Before Lee could make it to the door, it swung open, and out stepped Mary. She was a vision of loveliness powerful enough to capture Matt's appreciation, even at a distance. Lee had his hat in his hand and stood before her explaining the morning's events with hand gestures that Matt could easily follow. When he pointed up at Matt, her attention turned to him with a gaze lasting longer than necessary. Matt met her distant stare and held it in his grasp until her focus returned to Lee standing by reverently. She finished her explanations to Lee and he backed up from her, placing his hat on his head before turning to remount.

Mary took the opportunity to glance up at Matt, shaking her head in answer to her private thoughts before she melted back into the shadows inside the door. The scene on the porch was suddenly much less interesting.

THREE

Matt remained standing, chewing on a last bit of jerky as Lee rode up beside him. Raising his canteen, Matt washed down his thirst and said, "Go ahead and step on down, little brother. A few more minutes is all we got. Give your horse a rest while you give me the news. All seems to be fine from here."

Lee grunted as he lifted his leg and slid off the saddle. He plopped to the ground and said, "She says all's well. They didn't hear a thing last night, except the coyotes howlin' it up. Haven't seen or heard anything to be alarmed about. Mary is keepin' the guns on hand, just in case. Says the stock is secure as can be. Frank is showin' some improvement and might be up and movin' in a day or two. Thinks we're foolish, goin' off, just the two of us."

"She did, huh? Think she'd prefer we did nothin'? Maybe let them pay her or our other neighbors a visit after they finish lickin' their wounds? No, we got a job to do and not enough time to raise a posse. I want to catch 'em now. Before they git out of reach. We just gotta be careful of an ambush or them joinin' up with more of their kind."

Lee pulled some jerky out of his bag and chewed slowly while listening to Matt expound. His mare chomped at the grass near his boots, nudging him out of the way of the sparse offerings. Off in the distant head of a brush-choked ravine, a turkey let loose with a coarse rattling gobble. Another tom hidden in the woods nearer to the Ellis overlook answered him with fervor. Valley fog continued to blanket the wood-lined creek bottoms that meandered down to the river. Cottontails fed along the distant edge of moisture-soaked bee-brush while overhead a red-tailed hawk was sizing the rabbits up for an early breakfast. All around them, the early morning atmosphere seemed refreshed from the overnight cleansing of fine mist.

Lee felt moved by the serenity cast by the receding ridgelines that gradually faded off into the distant hills. He said, "You know, it can be nice and peaceful at times out here. That's why I hang on. Times it seems worth it to be on our own."

Matt nodded in agreement and said, "Wouldn't want to work for another man or live in the city packed together like a bunch of sorry rats."

"Not that it's easy being so far out," Lee replied. "Damn red man raising hell. No doc. Supplies so far off."

"Sure not easy," Matt drawled after another long pull on the canteen.

"Don't bother you too much, does it?"

"Been near men long enough, I guess. Don't always like what I see."

"Can't argue that point. But this here trackin' ain't my idea of a good time. We could end up dead, or worse."

"Losing your faith?"

"No, I still got it. It's just the thought of somethin' more than we can handle is a real possibility. I don't want to be in their hands and have to take what they could dish out."

"We'll do the dishin'."

"Don't know how you can be so sure."

Matt didn't reply while he watched Lee, sizing him up and once again wondering how he would do in a pinch. Lee had never faced a man in a life-or-death situation. Matt's hard stare pierced deep, searching for an answer. Lee became uncomfortable with the obvious scrutiny and felt compelled to break the momentary silence.

"That Mary sure is a looker."

"My, oh my," Matt cracked his first smile of the day. "The obvious just now hittin' you? I've already dealt with enough of them thoughts tuggin' at me. Don't need you remindin' me of her fine qualities. Let's head it out. Wasted enough time already."

Quick as snakebite, Matt swung back up into the saddle, turning Whiskey to the direction of the fresh pony trail. Lee fell in behind as Matt quickened the pace, intent on making up for lost time. The trail weaved in and out of sparse stands of live oak that cast their long shadows on grasslands tinged burnt orange in the shorter days of fall. Scattered thickets of dark green cedar trees created large areas capable of hiding horse and rider alike. The trail was fresh, with grass flattened and muddy rocks overturned in the Indians' haste to put distance behind them. They never veered to the handy concealment available. Matt didn't have to slow his pace to stay on top of such obvious signs of passage. The riders were not trying to mask their escape.

Matt began to understand they just wanted to put distance between them and their potential pursuers. This knowledge inspired him to maintain a reckless pace. He wanted to push the Indians up against the wall. He sought a violent conclusion. Anticipation began to rise within him as the passing ground took them both further from home. A strong metallic taste filled Matt's mouth with the unpleasant reminder of the brutality men inflicted upon one another in their disputes over who ruled the land. He intended to tear into his red quarry like a wolf ripping into the soft underbelly of a deer.

The chase began to seem endless to Lee. They had covered many miles in a rough pounding gait that chewed up the distance. The advancing morning warmed up nicely with only a few of the deeper valleys continuing to hold remnants of the heavy fog. Terrain was occasionally familiar to him, but they were approaching areas Lee had never traveled through. In his apprehension, he realized they were not well prepared for an overnight stay. They possessed only the most basic necessities packed during the dark hour before dawn. Overnight camping was becoming a distinct possibility when he considered their increasingly remote location. Camping deep in the wilderness with savages about! Cold camping. Cold food. Noise in the night that could be man or beast. Hell of a situation, he thought, while pulling out hard candy and nervously popping it into his mouth.

<<<<< • >>>>>

Up ahead at a high ridge, the Colorado River bottom was visible for the first time since leaving the home place. Matt was slowing, peering down intently at the trail and leaning out of the saddle to his right when Lee loped up behind him.

"Lee, come see what you think."

Lee pulled up beside Matt, looked down, and saw signs of where several horses had churned the soil at the juncture of two trails. One trail headed west. The other turned north into the broken-up headlands that rose above the river bottoms covered in heavy stands of ancient pecan trees. The mixture of hoofprints was haphazard in the mud-strewn intersection, proving that the fugitives had spent some time in the area. Several table-sized, flat limestone rocks rested in the area. One in particular caught Matt's eye.

Lee observed, "Looks like they headed north, to them draws leadin' down to the pecan bottoms."

"Yeah, they headed out on the old Comanche trail, no doubt about it. But check the sign on that rock and tell me what you see."

Lee sized up the rock and shook his head no. Matt had always trailed like he was part Indian. Lee often felt inadequate in his presence.

"Looks like they dismounted here and maybe our friend had to lie down for a while," Matt said. "See the dark spot? Not much blood. But enough that it hurts a bit too much for him. Seems to me like they got a little rest, and then those moc tracks show me they helped him back up on his pony. Judgin' by what I see, it wasn't too long ago neither. We're gittin' close. I bet they know we're trailin' 'em by now."

Lee frowned. "I don't like that too much."

"Just got to be careful is all. They're Indians. Always sneaky devils, wherever they're at."

Lee's frown deepened as Matt gazed in the direction the trail led. It melted away into thick brush. Matt stood in his stirrups to get a better view while speaking his mind. "I like it. We're catchin' up. Got enough day left to press 'em 'til they show. They'll make a mistake if we apply pressure."

Matt's chest swelled at the thought of closing in on his target.

The frown Lee wore turned into a look of fear.

"Matt, they may show all right. With a couple of shots to the head. Think of that?"

Matt gave Lee a hard stare as he said, "You go ahead and hang back a little further for right now. Could be they won't git us both at the same time."

His brother paled at the comment.

Matt grinned and then said, "If they git me, you can take care of 'em, and git all the glory."

Lee was having none of it. "You ain't helpin' one bit, smart ass."

Matt's grin faded. A veil of serious intent spread across his face turned hard as granite.

"Fall in a little behind me and keep a sharp eye out. Carbine at the ready. Watch for hand signs. If I see somethin', you'll know. Coo like a dove if you see somethin'. This hunt just changed. Be ready for anything."

Matt reined Whiskey onto the fresh tracks, leading them off the break of the ridge. They rode down the rock-covered trail used by past generations of Comanche hunting in the hills outside of Austin. The trail declined steeply at first, and they worked the horses gently off the highlands, facing the risk of sliding on the slick limestone ledges topped off with fist-sized rocks. While leaning back in his saddle, Matt kept his eyes roving, searching for danger concealed in the thick brush that flanked the trail. The slower pace irritated him but was necessary.

Lee did as directed and cradled his Spencer in his left arm, a short distance behind the imposing buckskin Matt rode. At times, Matt held his hand up to halt Lee while he gave a troubling area a thorough search before proceeding. They slowly lost elevation as the river bottom faded from sight, blending into a distant tangle of treetops that glowed with the golden light of the late afternoon sun.

Seldom did Matt venture this far out on the old trail. He continued to make occasional slowdowns to absorb the unfamiliar surroundings. Reaching level terrain, he reined to a stop below a low rise that the trail made its way over before entering the river floodplain. The fertile black soil supported a forest of massive pecan trees littered with fallen limbs and thick underbrush. Matt motioned for Lee to pull up beside him to his left. They sat silent for a short time, taking in the feel of the claustrophobic woods.

The hill rose before them and blocked the view of where the trail would eventually lead them. Off to the right, a pair of fox squirrels chased each other round and round the coarse bark of a dead pecan tree. They chattered loudly as the pursuit carried them to the top splintered limbs and a death-defying leap to a neighboring tree. Crows cavorted in the upper canopy and called out warnings of a nature understood only by them. Aloof in their high perches, they looked down upon the earthly events of men with scorn. A passing cloud cast a gloomy blanket of shadow over the scene when off in the distance, past the intervening hill, a faint but unmistakable whinny of a pony floated through the trees.

Matt turned to find Lee's face contorted in a wide-eyed expression.

He whispered, "Now, Lee. It's action time. These woods close in thick on this trail with a helluva lot of places to hide out. The risk is up. I don't know if they got guns, arrows, or what. Might be both, but we are damn close to 'em. This trail is real fresh and that pony sure ain't far off. They could be anywhere up ahead."

Lee focused on Matt with all of his attention. This was a new experience for him and he depended on Matt to lead him through it safely.

Matt continued in a subdued voice, "Best to go on foot from here. I got a feelin' they're holed up, waitin' on us. They don't like lookin' over their shoulders, and maybe even seen us. Just three of 'em, I reckon. Unless they met up with others, but I doubt that. Don't like leavin' the horses behind, but we'll risk it for now. Let's work in a little ways to see what we can and come back for the horses later. Questions?"

Lee wore a dazzled expression when he said, "You jokin' again? Matt, I'll be honest. We could turn around right now. No problem with me. We chased 'em out of our area. Good enough for me. We're done."

Matt slid quietly to the ground and met Lee with a scowl that said turning back would never be the case. He motioned for Lee to dismount and get ready for the stalk. They finished loading their haversacks with ammo and checked the readiness of their weapons. Satisfied with their preparedness, Matt led the horses to a couple of elm trees further back from the hill and hidden from the trail. He tied them up and made them secure as possible.

Lee came up close as Matt whispered more instructions, "Let's keep the same formation. You hang back a little and we'll follow the trail to the top of the hill. If they cut to the side or anything unusual, we'll head back for the horses. We won't git too far from 'em. Those bucks are up there just a little ways. I can feel it."

Matt led the way to the crest of the hill, pausing to examine the low land before them. Pecan trees dominated the scene, spaced at irregular intervals, with branches drooping low from the weight of mature nuts. Fallen branches, jagged with broken tips, formed dams of limbs entangled with climbing vines of mustang grapes. Poison ivy grew mixed in the chaotic clutter, tinged with red fall leaves that radiated warning signs to keep away. Matt peered intently through this scene of wild growth, trying to find signs of his quarry. His senses were keenly alert to the hidden dangers that might be lurking in the woods.

Observing no sign of the Indians diverting off the trail, he led Lee down the hill and across the next section of the pony trail. They reached a point at the base of another slight rise where the woods closed in and crowded the path with impenetrable growth. Matt was breathing deeply when he motioned for Lee to come up even with him.

"Enough of this," he let out with a long breath. "They're right up yonder. I got that feelin'. Let's ease up to the crown of this hill. Take it slow. You head a little to the left of the trail. I'll take right. Stay even with me and don't git out of sight. You'll know when it's time to shoot. Questions?"

Lee's face paled with anxiety. He swallowed hard but nodded in agreement with the plan.

"When we git to the top, take a look around. If we see 'em, let's work up close as possible for our shot. Watch for my hand signs. Remember, there should just be three."

Matt took a few more deep breaths. Things were about to get interesting and he wanted time for Lee to compose himself. But it was no use. He was trembling when Matt reassured him, "You'll do just fine."

Lee made off to the left of the trail in a low crouch with his carbine in his right hand, fending off the brush slapping at his legs. Matt saw Lee well on his way before he carefully approached the hill directly before him. He veered to his right in order to space out his position from Lee, keeping an eye on him and moving forward an even amount. They both eased up to just below the brow of the hill.

Matt found an area relatively free of brush to his right that would give him a clear view of the backside of the hill. He removed his hat and lowered his large frame down to belly-crawl the last few feet. Reaching the crest of the hill, he tried to confirm that Lee was doing the same thing.

He was disappointed to realize Lee was no longer within sight.

"That's not good," he complained to himself.

Lee had been about forty yards away when Matt last saw him but was now out of sight. Matt had wanted to stay in view of each other for mutual support within rifle range. Several large trees shielded his view of Lee, and there was little he could do about it now with the top of the hill just inches away.

Deciding to risk it, Matt used his elbows for support and pushed his way to the brim for a quick glance on the other side. The soil was damp and pungent. The stench of decay filled his nostrils as the woods below came into focus. Scanning the area to the right and working slowly back to the left, he determined there was no obvious sign of Indians. The brush cover was heavy in front of the area Lee was supposed to be covering but seemed clear of danger from Matt's far-right perspective.

Returning his focus to survey the cluttered woods directly in front of him, Matt made out a slight movement through an opening in the underbrush. The motion resembled a deer feeding behind a cluster of bee-brush. It was hard to make out, but the color was right and the height was right. It looked like a deer with its head down feeding, but Matt reasoned deer would have scattered at the passing of Indians. It could be a man, but the height was not tall enough. No horses were visible from his viewpoint, despite the unmistakable whinny heard earlier. All he detected was slight movement of a buckskin color, partially hidden behind a screen of leafless gray brambles. Was it a deer, some other animal, or an Indian? Indecision set in, and he hesitated while pondering the next move to take. He wondered, what was Lee seeing?

The twang of bowstring releasing an arrow met Matt's ear without warning. Lee's howl of anguish shocked Matt from his uncertainty. The leaves were rustling from the direction Lee had taken, providing evidence of a contorted movement out of Matt's vision. He jumped to his feet and swung his Henry to his shoulder, ready for action.

Stepping around a knot of undergrowth that hid his brother from view, Matt caught an indistinct motion at the base of a massive pecan surrounded by fallen limbs. It was an Indian! The warrior slid behind the trunk for only a moment before emerging at the opposite side with a newly notched arrow. He quickly let the shaft fly at Lee, who was struggling to regain his balance and growling like a bear. The arrow flew within inches of Lee with an angry buzz before burying its point into a tree with a thud that reverberated through the woods.

Startled by the sudden and pressing assault, Lee fell backwards against the rough bark of a pecan tree. The solid trunk steadied him and he brought his Spencer to his waist to face the threat that had appeared from nowhere. As Matt raised his rifle for a shot, he noticed that the first arrow had pierced Lee and was protruding out his left side. The arrow presented an ugly and unnatural sight quivering out the back of his shirt. Before Matt could acquire a good bead, the warrior moved out from behind his cover one more step.

He already had a third arrow notched and aimed for another shot when the loud roar of Lee's Spencer exploded through the woods. The brave's arms flew upward with the impact of the bullet tearing into his chest and ripping out his back in a spray of tissue infused with blood. His bow dropped harmlessly to the ground as he staggered backwards over a log. He collapsed across the log with a vacant stare fixed towards the sky as his eyes clouded over in death. His legs convulsed, pushing at the leaves beneath his moccasins in a final struggle to hold on to the life he had known.

Matt looked on in apprehension at this sudden turn of events. His surprise was brief before he returned his attention to the original source of his uncertainty. Standing fully erect at the site of the unidentified movement was a buckskin-clad Comanche warrior. The brave was bewildered by the spectacle of his companion blown backwards through a plume of blood. He also saw Lee leaning against the tree, holding the deadly carbine that had killed his raiding brother. Scanning to the other side, his black eyes locked onto Matt in a mutual recognition of the bitter blood flowing with racial hatred of one another. And now, both of them were within striking range of their eternal enemy.

Matt saw the Indian for what he was in his primitive condition: a black-eyed barbarian with long greasy hair adorned by an eagle feather. A savage that was capable of senseless and wicked acts of violent murder. This Indian and his brothers were similar to a pack of wolves that decimated their prey in a frenzied attack satisfied only by the blood of their victims. Matt's contempt for what stood before him flowed through his veins and built in a rage-seeking vengeance. Swinging the Henry to his shoulder, he broke the stare-down with the Comanche, who now realized his peril. Startled at the danger he was in, he made a quick break for the heavy timber behind him.

Matt's first shot hit low and to the rear of his fleeing target. Branches blew apart in a spray of debris that pelted the legs of the frantic brave. Ejecting the spent case, Matt fed another round into the chamber while continuing to follow his target darting through the dense web of underbrush. The crafty brave dodged left and then right, weaving among small openings with the agility of a cat, never presenting a clear shot. Matt kept him lined up within his sights, but could see the shot opportunities were quickly evaporating in the dense growth.

One last clearing was directly ahead of the path the Indian followed. Matt prepared for the shot, holding high due to the increasing range. He fired the round in haste when the warrior ran into the small opening. The bullet buzzed on its way but missed the target and ricocheted off a limb near the Indian's head. The Comanche desperately dove for cover. Matt saw him regain his footing to scamper behind a screen of profuse foliage, where he vanished from sight.

Matt dashed off to his left, stumbling through the woodland rubble until he gained the open path of the trail. Using the clear trail to close the gap to his escaping target, he'd made up a small part of the distance separating them when the rumble of hooves became unmistakable. Busting out of the woods in a fine example of Indian horsemanship, rode the brave, bent low over his appaloosa mount, hugging close to the horse's neck and slipping to the opposite side to avoid any shots fired his way. Two more ponies, free of riders, followed closely, just as intent on escape as their leader riding like the wind.

When he hit the openness of the trail, the Comanche snuck a peek back at Matt to verify his adversary's position. His hair flew in the breeze as he coaxed his pony to top speed with a shower of mud flying from its hooves.

Matt stopped in his tracks to take aim, despite the increased distance to his departing target. He let go with several shots in rapid succession. He knew they would fall ineffective, but he could not resist the urge to inflict damage every chance he got. Cussing the short range of his Henry, Matt lowered the barrel to catch a last glimpse in the distant woods as Indian and horse faded into the folds of wilderness.

Frustration bore heavy on Matt as he realized the opportunity for success had just disappeared with the last blur of Indian vanishing in flight up the Colorado River. He stood for a moment, silently gazing into the pecan bottom, thinking of the one that just escaped, and the original one wounded but not found.

Full of regret, Matt decided to head back to Lee to determine the severity of the arrow wound. The potential for bad news was very real. A sick, nervous sensation spread through his body with the consideration that Lee could be in serious trouble out here in these wild lands with no help close at hand. Matt began to cuss under his breath as he trotted back to where he could see Lee resting against the tree but still holding his rifle.

Stepping alongside his brother, Matt could see Lee's rapid breathing and the loss of color in his face. The arrow dangled out of the soft flesh of his waist, buried in his skin up to the feathers. The bloody iron tip protruded well beyond the back of his torn shirt, and the pressure of the shaft was tormenting Lee. Blood flowed freely from the jagged cut of flesh around the exit wound, where the chokecherry shaft quivered from his rapid breathing. Lee looked up at his older brother with an uncertain expression filled with pain and searching for reassurance.

Matt leaned his gun against the tree trunk before he put a comforting hand on Lee's shoulder and calmly asked, "How you doing, Bud?"

Lee gasped for air, "Been better. Burns a little."

Matt stepped around Lee for a closer inspection of the damage and was happy to pronounce, "I don't think it hit your vitals. It's not too far into your side. Bleeding a little though"

Lee responded with a composed voice that surprised him, "No, it don't feel deep, but it sure feels tight and hot. Don't like it none. Damn!"

Matt shook his head at the predicament.

"Lee, I'm going to have to cut your shirt loose a little and pull the arrow on through. Gonna hurt a bit more."

"Yep, I figured so. Go on and git 'er done."

Matt pulled out his knife and sliced open the shirt to free up the arrow front and rear. He grabbed the arrow by its protruding shaft and got into a position to use leverage.

"Hold on now. I'll try to git it out with one pull."

Matt clamped down on the thin shaft with a firm grip and gave a downward pull, removing the arrow in one motion that produced a shrill curse from Lee, "Hot damn! Crap! Burns like hell now!"

Lee turned a shade lighter as the pain hit him hard. Taking a few deep breaths, he regained his composure, leaned back stiffly, and looked up at the passing clouds. He shut his eyes in an attempt to block out the blazing pain. Matt removed his bandana and put it in Lee's hand.

"Here, put this on your backside and hold it tight. That's where it's bleeding most. You done all right. Hard part is over, but now we got to plug up the holes with somethin' better. I'll go back for the horses. You sit tight."

Lee didn't argue while he found a place to sit on the downed trunk of a pecan.

"You stay alert while I'm gone. We still got one or two unaccounted for. One probably ain't good no more, but you never know. He is an Indian."

Lee absentmindedly jacked another round into his carbine and laid his pistol next to him on a stump for easy access. He sat staring at the dead Indian slumped awkwardly over the log just forty feet away.

"Matt, that sure was a close call. Could be me laid out like him." Shaking his head, Lee explained, "I saw him just in time to jump to the side or else he'd of drilled me straight to the gut. I had stood up 'cause I couldn't see nothin' through all the brush. And that's when he took his shot. Barely saw him in time. He must of been waitin' on us. I'm damn lucky is all. Whew!"

He gingerly laid back and stretched out on the log, catching his breath and holding the bandana snug to his waist.

"Lee, you sit on back up and pay attention while I go git the horses."

Lee waited a moment and groaned while he rose up, glancing around as if Indians were behind every tree. A worried look spread across his face when he asked, "You think some others are hidin' out there?"

"You never know for sure, but at least one is missin'. Three horses just left with the one that got away. Two bucks are still missin' if you count the one I shot this morning. Just stay alert. Keep the bandana pressed tight against your side. That'll slow the bleeding until I git a bandage on it."

Lee let out a sigh. "Don't be long. Throat's dry as hell."

FOUR

Matt rushed back to the trail and disappeared into the woods, leaving Lee to bear the weight of loneliness in an unforgiving land. Lee kept his head on a slow pivot, searching for trouble in the now placid bottoms. There was no movement or sound. Silence penetrated deep into his sagging spirit, feeding the melancholy mood settling within his soul. He had taken a life. Unlike Matt, this was a new experience for him that brought no satisfaction. A dismal state of mind seemed the perfect complement to the burning heat he felt pulsing from the arrow wound.

Fighting the urge to give into self-pity, Lee stood awkwardly to scan the woods behind him, finding everything in order. All of the woodland creatures were in hiding after the eruption of gunfire. He would like to join them, safe and secure from the Indian danger running rampant in their midst. The potential for another attack from an unseen foe kept him on edge until he finally heard the clomping of several horses approaching on the trail.

Matt reined up with a last-second stop, spraying dirt just short of the log where Lee rested. He swung his leg over the saddle and slid to the ground in one fluid movement while yanking his canteen from the saddle horn. There was no wasted motion. Tilting the canteen back, he gave Lee a long cool drink. Returning to his own bag, he threw open the flap and removed some cotton cloth. Lee grimaced as Matt hurriedly applied the bandage and roughly tied it in place with strips of worn-out shirts.

"Matt, you sure don't have much of a nurse's touch."

"Sorry there's a shortage out here. I'll have to do, or you can do it yourself."

"I'll take it. Thanks. Been thinkin' though."

"That will git you in trouble."

"Seems I'm in trouble enough. So I'll ask anyways."

"Fire away."

"How come you missed? You shot four times."

Matt finished his nurse work and heatedly threw the unused material back in the pouch. Turning back to Lee, he let his frustration out in a voice full of irritation, "I've had a sorry day with my shootin'. That buck was beyond this rifle's range. The first two shots I had to hurry and hold way over just to git 'em close. Plus, he was on the move both shots. They were close, but that ain't good enough, is it?"

Lee sat silently, waiting for further explanation.

"The last two were just parting gifts."

"Just askin'. You usually don't miss."

"How 'bout you, stud? One shot. One kill. And from the waist at that!"

"He didn't leave me no option. That first arrow scared the hell outta me. Didn't want another one. Didn't think he would miss twice neither. So I had to shoot right now. The waist shot is all I had time for. Just luck is all."

"No, it weren't luck. Was awful fine shootin' is what it was. Takes a steady nerve to pull that shot off." Matt paused and turned his head to view the sprawled-out body of the Comanche now attracting blowflies to the fresh blood. "Look at him staring up at the sky. All bled out. Won't be causing no more harm. Damn good shootin' is what I say. You done all right. You deserve credit. How 'bout some trophies?"

Matt made his way over to the dead body and slipped the bear-claw necklace off to take back to Lee. He also gathered up the bow and the remaining arrows and quiver. He left behind a badly abused knife worn next to a blood-soaked medicine bag.

Lee sat and watched while Matt secured the booty to Lee's saddle and explained the next chore to tackle, "We got one more thing to do. I want to go down to where the other buck was when I first saw him. He was doing somethin' down there and I got an idea what it was. You up to ridin'?"

Lee glanced up at Matt as if he was joking.

Matt understood. He had been there before. He said, "Walkin' it is."

Matt gave Lee a hand up and slipped the Colt back into his holster. He offered Lee an arm for support, but his brother pulled away from the assistance. Lee grabbed his carbine and hobbled away from the log, taking a few tentative steps to test his ability to move about. Satisfied with the results, he said, "You know, it don't hurt too bad. Reckon I can walk some if I have to."

Admiring Lee's spunk, Matt said, "That's good, 'cause we got a bit more work before the day's over. See the bee-brush down there about a hundred yards and to the right of the trail? That's where we're headin'."

Matt took the lead on foot again with the reins of both horses in hand. As the line of bee-brush came nearer, he passed the horses off to Lee with a motion for him to hang back. Matt eased up to the brushline, gun at the ready, pausing to sort out signs of danger. Finding none, he slowly made his way around the corner of the island of brush and stopped in his tracks. With his eyes locked to the ground, he motioned for Lee to come forward.

Lee came up to where Matt stood and laid eyes on the reason for the long, troubling day. "I'll be damned," he said. "He's the one from this mornin'."

Matt towered six feet over the Comanche stretched out on the ground, drained of energy and no longer posing danger. Blood stained his shirtless body and his chest heaved with the effort of breathing. His breath came in shallow gasps gurgling with pink blood. Beads of sweat flowed over his dirt-smeared skin, draining the last fluids of life back to the soil. With a pained effort, he partially opened his black eyes, now covered in a dull look of incomprehension.

His tone matter-of-fact, Matt said, "He ain't so tough no more. Startled me pretty damn good this morning, showin' up uninvited in the doorway. Looks like the trail took it all outta him. And now his help has done up and run off."

Lee held his canteen to his lips for another long draw, finding satisfaction in the wet coolness that refreshed his depleted body. Wearily brushing his sleeve across his lips, he observed, "What a difference, me and him. I got life, and his is meltin' away."

Matt remained silent at the comment but stepped forward and used the rifle barrel to tap the Comanche on his leg. The feeble warrior produced a rasping groan as he attempted to change position. He was too weak for body movement, but his head turned up to search for his tormenter. He struggled to crack open one eye. Finding the cold steel gaze of Matt scowling down at him, he managed to open both eyes fully. He returned Matt's gaze and the deep hatred and animosity he felt towards the white man lit a faint glow in his coal-black eyes. Unable to control his weakened body, the proud warrior lay prone with no chance to rise to his own defense.

Matt backed up a step, with his hand resting on the grip of the Colt carried on his right hip. He quietly worked over the options in his mind. Far off, high in the crowns of pecan trees, the crows resumed their loud calls up and down the dank river bottoms. Matt backed up a few more steps, lost in his thoughts and unaware of Lee or the surroundings.

Lee broke the silence with a question. "What's next, Matt?"

He didn't answer or acknowledge hearing Lee's voice. Lee repeated the question in a voice too forceful for Matt to ignore.

Snapping out of his reverie, Matt shot back, "What do ya think?"

"Hell, I don't know. You're the expert."

"We don't have many options."

"Seems to me we got a lot of 'em."

"Really? Well, first off, we gotta git you back for some good nursin' before blood poisoning gits you. That kinda ties our hands on options, wouldn't you think?"

"Well, yeah. I guess."

"That hole in your side don't feel good, does it? Think what it will feel like tomorrow. You need some proper treatment on it soon as possible."

"I reckon you're right. But what about him and the one that headed out?"

"The one that got away is a little tricky. I'd love to go after him and finish this business." Matt paused while he reflected on the Indian that had escaped. "But it ain't gonna happen. I gotta git you back since you ain't fit for no more pursuit. Are you?"

Lee didn't answer but kept his eyes on the ground, where their prisoner occasionally groaned in delirium. His eyes were now closed, oblivious to the discussion of his fate.

Matt continued, "I never could catch that buck no how. He's got two fresh mounts to rotate to whenever he wants. Damn shame, 'cause I sure would like to snuff his lamp." Matt turned and spat into the brush. "Which leaves us with this useless pile. Well, his days are over."

Matt pulled his Colt out and was in the process of raising it to take aim when Lee said, "Hey! Wait a minute here! He ain't going nowhere. What you gonna do?"

"Finish him off and send a message."

"A message? To who?"

"To that other buck. He may decide to loop back for his brother here."

"Hold on a second, Matt. This man ain't going nowhere."

Lee grimaced as a hot flash of pain scorched his side and spread out across his body.

"You're right, and I aim to see to that for sure. If the other buck comes back, he can see what to expect from us if he's caught snoopin' 'round our cabins again. And he may damn well come back. Maybe even tonight. Maybe even with help."

Lee took a moment to let this hard fact of life soak in. With his head hanging and in a voice full of resignation, he mumbled, "Burying 'em is out of the question?"

"Bury 'em? Hell, they're the same as animals in my mind. Let the wolves have at 'em."

Without another word, Lee turned from Matt and led the horses away, fighting the pain that burned like a hot iron held against his side. He ambled back up the trail thinking of home and the comfortable bed he would miss tonight. Ahead, he would pass the Indian he had killed. After that, a long pounding ride back to the cabin. Lee confided out loud to the horses, "I got no stomach for this."

Matt let Lee get out of sight before raising his pistol to take a bead on the closed eye of the Comanche struggling to hold onto life. Looking down the hard edge of the sights, Matt suffered a flashback of the arrow-riddled body of his son, scalped and covered in blackened blood. Five arrows had remained embedded in his youthful body that had turned a sickening ashen color, devoid of the eager buoyant spirit that had been his special gift. The smile that had always lifted those around him replaced with a stiff grimace reflecting the shocking pain of a brutal, premature death. This was the memory Matt carried with him at all times. It replayed in his mind over and over until it drove him mad with grief and guilt. Matt lowered the pistol to shake out the disturbing imagery that relentlessly haunted him.

Pausing to take a deep breath, he abruptly took aim again and pulled the trigger without hesitation. The report raced through the woods and bounced back in an echo off the riverside bluffs. The Comanche's face collapsed inward as the back of his head exploded in a shower of gore mixed with brain tissue, dirt, and leaves. A quiver spread down his body to his legs twitching with the last of his stored energy dissipating in futility. Silence settled on the woods as the echo of the shot faded away.

"Nothin' to it," Matt muttered to the dead Comanche, "rot in hell, you sorry bastard."

Lee was resting against a stump beside the trail when Matt caught up to him. He snapped his instructions, "Lee, we got less than an hour before dark. We got to put some distance from here in order to camp a little safer. You'll have to mount up. Hurt or not."

Lee accepted Matt's help up onto the saddle while he fought to hide the blinding pain starting to take hold. He shifted in the saddle, searching for a comfortable position but found it was useless. He resigned himself to endure the ride.

Matt wasted no time securing the weapons in the scabbard before mounting Whiskey. Stretching in the stirrups, he barked orders to Lee, "You head on out and I'll follow so I can keep an eye on you. I got an idea where we can hole up off the trail back in some woods. We'll be hidden from that buck that may want to pay us a visit. It'll be a cold camp, but we can be home tomorrow. Let's head it on out."

<<<<< • >>>>>

Resting on the horizon, the sun was slowly sinking on another day, basking the hillsides in a golden glow that radiated the strength of celestial power. To their back, and unseen by Matt or Lee, the hills fell away in fold after fold of valleys to the final ridgeline standing in dark silhouette along the flaming horizon. The vast wilderness of hills separated the Comanche from the encroaching homesteads that eroded the ancient relationship of man versus nature.

Owls began to hoot in the descending dusk, calling out their intentions to begin hunting their unsuspecting prey. From a hidden perch, a sudden whoosh of feathers sliced through the air, followed by powerful talons grasping a rabbit with an unyielding force. A painful screech reverberated through the woods as the cottontail briefly fought the inevitable death coming his way. The darkening woodlands began to stir with the ceaseless struggle to survive.

Far out in the wilderness, on the rim of an isolated canyon, a pack of

wolves set up their evening chorus of howls performed in a ritual that satisfied their predatory instincts. Tonight, from the depths of the same canyon,
immersed in complete blackness, the howls of the wolves mixed with the
baneful wail of a forlorn Comanche as he cried out into the uncaring black
heavens.

FIVE

The night passed slowly for Matt, one eerie noise after another. Off in the darkness a distant limb cracked and tumbled to the ground with a thud that echoed through the stillness. The deep thump of the rotten wood brought back the unpleasant memory of fellow soldiers falling from their horses, dead, from a Union bullet. Their limp bodies smacked the ground with a sickening heaviness, offering no resistance to their fate of death on unfamiliar soil. Departed and heaven bound in the split second after a slug found its mark, the gray-clad soldiers lay scattered across the battlefield as lifeless as the decayed limb he heard fall in the woods. Matt felt a keen awareness of an old but familiar sensation of hopelessness creeping through the back of his mind. Fighting his emotions, he remained alert, fearful of threats creeping in the murkiness of the nighttime woods.

The cold camp didn't offer the warm glow of a fire to fend off the curious and unwanted night prowlers of this world, nor the spiritual wanderers from beyond. Shadows took on peculiar shapes that mysteriously transformed appearance in subtle movements when viewed through the web of tangled branches surrounding his bedroll. With intense concentration, Matt remained awake, unraveling the real danger present in the wilderness from the imagined hazards that crawled through his doubt-plagued conscious.

The never-forgotten images of departed comrades combined with the current gloom of the woods gave Matt a real sense of their nearby spiritual presence, yet they remained untouchable. Their long-lost voices whispered softly in his mind. Or was it treetop leaves ruffled by a lightly blowing breeze? These spirits, set free in violence, remained with Matt at all times. They manifested during the calm times of night, when sleep proved as elusive to him as peace of mind.

Hours before daybreak, the thick brush surrounding camp hid the approach of wolves quietly traversing the woods in search of an easy meal. Matt heard their panting in the darkened brush as they circled the cold camp uncomfortably close. He felt their eyes piercing through the night. His skin prickled with awareness of his exposure. The wolves surely smelled the fresh blood soaking Lee's bandage. Matt cradled the Henry close for readiness if it was needed while Lee struggled to sleep, completely unaware of the menace surrounding their insecure camp. Tense moments crawled by for Matt while the prowling pack sized up the camp for opportunity. Ghostly forms moved stealthily at the perimeter of his vision.

A large gray figure stopped circling and sat on his haunches, studying the camp with cold calculation. The horses stomped the ground, snorting with annoyance. Matt rested the rifle on his knee, pointed in the direction of the sitting wolf. A standoff ensued that tested his patience. The wolf could wait all night, but Matt tired of the interruption in his attempt to sleep. Impulsively, he broke the tension in the air and growled an angry challenge to the alpha wolf. A couple of alarmed woofs echoed through the woods as the wary wolves decided nothing in the camp was worth risking the unusual confrontation presented to them. The pack gradually melted into the blackness for easier hunting elsewhere.

The trill of various night birds rang out all night long at random intervals until Matt suspected the sole reason for their disturbance was to prevent rest in his camp. Herons burst out long hoarse squawks, transmitting their annoyance at the roaming of a bobcat in the creek bed they roosted above. Whippoorwills called to each other with a lonesome and longing lament punctuated with the equally lonely sound of silence between each croon. Screech owls called out hauntingly with a quavering shriek that reverberated down from the treetops. The night woods literally breathed with the clamor of the ongoing effort to survive.

At one point shortly before dawn, a wail of unearthly proportions spilled across the camp, emitted from a tortured spirit deep in the throes of anguish. These unidentifiable wails of torment energized the woods with the possibility of extraordinary suffering. Matt wrapped his blanket tight around his shoulders and drew his knees up to his chest while taking in a deep breath of the cool night air. He felt crowded and alone at the same time with no option to relax. Flesh and blood or apparition, danger was ever present in the hills, and at times, hard to identify.

Matt began to stir with the first signs of the faint orange glow of sunrise lifting the prevailing gloom of darkness. Eager to move after enduring such a tortuous night, he stretched out his aching muscles and tossed aside the wool blanket he had used in the big war. He could make out Lee's prone figure at the base of an elm tree. He was not showing any signs of movement. It had been a long night for Lee too, but now he appeared to be resting in a deep sleep.

Matt gazed across the small opening in the dense woods they had picked for a safe campsite. He saw no signs of danger, though he could not shake the sense of peril that the long night reinforced with such strange unidentified noises.

"Things are not right out here," he mumbled. "Not that they ever are."

Satisfied there was no immediate cause for concern, he rolled his scratchy wool blanket up and stood to stretch away the remaining kinks. Grunting with the effort, he twisted his torso back and forth and pumped his arms to get blood flowing through his numb body. Leaves crunched under his boots as he waddled over to Lee. He nudged his sleeping brother with a gentle kick.

"Time to rise."

Lee opened one eye and looked up at Matt through a fog of incredulity. "Umm, huh," was all he could manage in response.

Impatiently, Matt kicked Lee's leg a little harder.

"Come on, Lee. Git up. Been a damn long night and I'm ready to git the hell out of here."

Matt jerked his bag off the ground for some hardtack to start the morning. He tossed a large piece of jerky down to Lee for a little breakfast in bed. That was nursing, Matt's style. Lee took his time to wake, rubbing his eyes before weakly munching on the jerky.

Matt got busy getting the horses ready for the trail after he finished up the hardtack. Rubbing his buckskin on the muzzle, he offered a soothing thanks to him for being such a dependable companion. Whiskey tweaked his ears as if understanding Matt's appreciation. Taking some of the sparse oats,

Matt gave Whiskey an early morning treat to get his day started right before he turned his attention to Lee's mare.

The horses saddled up, Matt was on edge to get an early start, but Lee had failed to break the hold his bedroll had on him. Matt strolled over to Lee and reproached him, "Lee, even the horses are ready to git a move on. Sorry, there ain't no coffee, but it's time to move."

"I'm sorry too. I'm movin' a little slow this mornin'. Sure could use a hot shot of joe."

"How's the side?"

"Tender as hell."

"Come on now. Git up and let me have a look."

Lee groaned as he stood up, taking his time to become fully erect. He lifted his shirt to let Matt check the damage. Matt gave the blood-soaked bandage a close inspection and stepped back, staring Lee in the eyes.

"The blood is dry. Seems to have quit bleedin'. You could use a clean bandage, but I know how you feel about my nursin' skills. Why don't we leave well enough alone? Let the women take care of it when we git back home."

"You'll git no argument out of me."

"Come on then. Let's git out of these woods. We can be home by dark. Will be a good hot meal tonight."

They led the horses out of the tangled woods on foot until Matt slowed at the approach of the trail they had followed yesterday. Their turnoff into the woods was plain to see, and Matt realized the loose Indian might have backtracked on them. He might be waiting in ambush.

"Here we go again," he thought out loud.

"Do what?" Lee asked.

"Nothin'. Just be ready for anything. Again. Just like yesterday. Anything can happen. Anytime."

Matt gave Lee a boost up onto the saddle of his mare before he mounted Whiskey. Then he fell in behind the mare to let Lee lead the way. This gave Matt a chance to keep an eye on his brother's condition and to adjust the pace as needed.

The eastern horizon was free of the fog from the morning before and was on fire with a crimson hue melting into the midnight blue of an expansive sky. Despite the beauty of a fall sunrise, Matt felt the tension of a new day's challenge tighten up in his chest. It was out there, hiding somewhere, waiting. Danger, injury, or possibly death was lurking. As sure as the coming sunrise, disaster would occur at its own time and choosing. They had no choice except to ride out on the trail and meet the challenge head-on. He knew there was no room out here for the timid. He prayed for the good Lord to be with them.

The pace was far slower than the headlong pursuit of the day before. With the tenderness of his wound, Lee could not take the punishment of a rapid ride. The long day would test him to his limit with the pounding gait on horseback. Lee grimaced and bore the pain with no complaining, which impressed Matt since he remembered all too well the experience of travel when wounded.

They took occasional breaks where Lee would stretch out on the ground, having discovered that made the most comfortable resting position. Matt let Lee doze for a short time when they stopped at Copperhead Springs to refill their canteens with the clear, cold water. Matt too was feeling the fatigue of no sleep, combined with constant travel, but he actually found a perverse satisfaction from the uncertainty and excitement encountered when on the trail. The chase invigorated him like nothing else he currently experienced in his life. Ranch work had become tedious with its monotony and repetition. The ranch formation was finished, and now it just required the everyday upkeep that provided little challenge to him.

Matt's past life out in the open and exposed to wartime dangers had left him with a sense of adventure that no longer seemed to be satisfied. The early years on the ranch were all-encompassing, but the commitment had worn old. The work continued with day-to-day regularity of little variety, except for these Indian scares or an occasional predator hunt. These exceptional occasions brought Matt a stimulated sense of life and rekindled the missing spirit that had led him to avoid town for a life on the edge of raw wilderness. Out here, where nobody staked a claim on him, he was his own man. The sense of freedom while in the woods was like fine liquor intoxicating his soul with a deep sense of contentment.

They left the shaded springs refreshed from the cool, rejuvenating waters they'd downed with greed. As they made their way up and over the extensive range of hills, the day wore on into late afternoon and the Ellis homestead came into view once again. Lee was in need of another break by that time of the day. Matt suggested another stop for rest and the opportunity to drop in and check on the welfare of the Ellis family. Lee was more than ready to accept the offer. They reined to a stop on the ridge overlooking the ranch below where Matt helped Lee off the horse. He gently eased him down to lie back in a soft patch of grass and took the extra effort to prop Lee's head on a rolled-up blanket.

Matt cautioned Lee, "You look like a good target, lying there like a sleepin' pig. I'd pay attention if I were you. Don't doze off. Be a shame to git this close to home and have you scalped while I'm just down the hill. I'd have a hard time explaining that one."

Lee gave Matt a go-to-hell look and shot back, "Just don't take too long with Mary and I'll be all right."

Matt tied up Midnight with enough slack for a little grazing. He ignored Lee's stinging comment about Mary. Mounting up, he gave the country a slow, thorough sweep and determined all was clear. He cut Whiskey sharply to head down the steep trail, spurring him hard enough to spray Lee with a few loose rocks.

Lee had been partially correct in his comment about Mary. Matt's civic duty was to keep his neighbors informed about the latest happenings, but that duty was not what made his pulse quicken. Next to trail life, nothing fired up his passion more than being near a fine-looking woman. Mary fit the description perfectly and it had been a while since he had been close enough to her for an exchange of words.

The absence of close contact had been by his design. He didn't need frustration setting in to fester like a sore without a suitable cure. Matt considered this an occasion to test his resolve while at the same time passing on critical information to a family down on their luck. Working down the steep, rocky path, he scanned ahead but could see no activity in the corral or yard. Chickens pecked around the bare ground outside their pens while the stock buried their noses in freshly strewn hay. Smoke was curling up from the chimney, indicating that meal preparations were under way, with all the women most likely inside tending to their individual duties.

Whiskey trotted into the empty yard and Matt dismounted, took the reins, and looped them around a fence rail. Turning to head to the cabin door, he was shocked to see Mary rounding the corner with a basket of corn in her left hand and a gun in her right.

She too was surprised. "I thought I heard a horse ride up. Didn't think it sounded Indian, but I didn't expect it would be you either."

Matt didn't reply at first. He just stood there, taking her all in. She was the picture of femininity in her sky-blue dress hugging tight on her slight waist, accenting her curved hips and full bust line. Her long blonde hair looked angelic, pulled back and held in place by a matching blue bow. Her dress was pinned up to stay off the dusty soil. Bare calves, smooth and slender, stretched down to colorfully beaded moccasins, handmade during the past winter months. Her eyes, as blue as the clearest topaz, searched Matt's face for the answer to his silence. His muted response lasted long enough to develop an awkwardness floating in the evening air.

Matt, rendered speechless by her unexpected appearance, began to laugh gently at the sight of the holster strapped below her waist. The manly leather garment was loaded with extra shells held in loops for the length of the belt, giving Mary a contrasting accessory to her very feminine dress. Returning the pistol to her holster, she put her hand on her hip and frowned.

"What's so funny?" she asked.

Matt remained silent while he continued to look her over in appreciation.

"Are you being rude, or did you lose your ability to talk?"

Matt snapped out of his reverie and answered, "No, I can still talk. Just a little surprised by your appearance. Thought you were all inside."

"Well, not everybody is inside. I was making my evening rounds."

"I can see that now. I just stopped by to see how it is around here."

He regained his composure enough to remove his hat in respect, and then it was Mary who started to giggle. Matt felt an unfamiliar feeling of embarrassment settle on him while his face turned warm with color.

He asked, "Now, what's so funny with you?"

Mary looked him up and down with a grin that put him back at ease. He found it strange how she possessed a manner that made him feel like a colt again.

"You can put your hat back on. Looks like mice have nested in your hair."

Matt hastily put the hat back in place where it rightfully belonged. Never made sense to him anyways, pulling a hat off just to greet a woman. Who started that custom? It had to be someone from back east or up north, where customs made little sense to a Southern man.

Remembering his sense of purpose, he said, "You can pull that holster off while we are appraising looks. It hardly compliments your fine-looking dress. But I'm glad to see you aren't letting your guard down. Had any trouble?"

"No. Not at all. Everything seems fine."

The question got her to thinking and she noticed Lee was not present. Glancing up the hill, she saw Lee's horse, but he was not visible. A look of anxiety swept over her face. In a panicked voice, she cried out, "Where's Lee? Did something happen?"

Matt read her body language and the concern in her voice. He calmly reassured her, "Lee's okay. He's a little hurt, but I think he'll be fine with good nursin'. Gotta git him home by dark, though."

"What happened? Do I need to go tend him?"

"He would probably like that, but he'll hold 'til we git home. He met an arrow, but I think he'll be all right. He's just stretched out on the ground to ease the pain a little. Been a long day for him."

She looked at Matt once again, probing his eyes with concern and care. The questions within her gaze prodded Matt to provide more details.

"We caught up with the red devils out in the pecan bottoms where the Comanche trail drops off to join up with the river. Brush is thick in there and a buck got the drop on Lee. He took the first arrow, but Lee was a little too quick for a second one. Shot the Comanch dead from his waist. He done real good, but he took a little punishment in return."

He left out the more gruesome facts. She had heard enough. More details would upset her. He continued on to cut off any further questions, "How's Frank?"

Mary was lost in her thoughts about Lee before Matt's question began to catch on. She gradually replied, "Oh, he is better. Sitting on the edge of the bed for longer spells. Still does not want to talk much or hear loud noises. He let me open the shutters today. So light is not bothering him as bad. But he has a ways to go before he is back to normal. Maybe next time he will stay in the saddle."

"That's good to hear, Mary. We all been concerned."

A moment of silence passed as they held each other in an attentive gaze. The late afternoon light fell on her face with a golden glow as lovely as Matt could imagine. Her natural beauty shone as if highlighted from within by God. A slight breeze lifted loose strands of her hair, playfully tossing them about. She brought a delicate hand up to remove the stray hair and tucked it back in place next to her bow. Matt soaked up the uniqueness of the situation.

His pulse began to quicken with the natural attraction he felt for her. She always produced the same intoxicating distress in him. He questioned why he allowed this to happen. Keeping a distance from such a potent attraction had always been the best path for him to follow. It was a mistake to check on her, but here he was. A feeling of captivation crept over him. She made him weak with a desire almost impossible to resist. Watching her through the silence, he sensed her needs were similar in nature, and he spoke up to break the lustful thoughts taking over his emotions.

"How are the girls?"

She seemed shocked as the question broke the spell they were both under. Stumbling for an answer she hesitated, "Oh. Oh...they're doing fine." Regaining her composure, she added, "They have doubled up on the chores with Frank in bed. It has been hard on them. But they keep the complaining to a minimum."

Matt cleared his throat and said, "Now that I'm back, I can send Travis to help out."

He felt more at ease talking about matters he understood. She exerted a strong influence on his thinking process. He had to be careful not to indulge in dreams of fantasy.

"Oh, that's all right for now. I'll get by. I think the hardest time is behind us."

"We'll stay in touch, just in case."

"That's good." She smiled as she said, "You are always welcome to come by. And by the way, the Johnston's dropped in early this morning. They were a little upset at your haste to take after the Indians. Said they would have liked in on the action."

"They would have slowed us down. Had no time to posse up."

She paused before putting the next question to him.

"Did you get them all?"

Matt glanced away as he spoke, "No, Mary. We left a loose end. One is still unaccounted for."

Mary took on a distant look full of turmoil. This news carried dangerous implications in her mind.

"Sorry to disappoint you, Mary, but there are plenty of 'em to go around besides the one that got loose. We probably scared him back to his kin, but twenty more could take his place tonight. Right now, for that matter, and right here as we speak. Don't mean to scare you none, but you gotta be on the lookout. I'll feel more relaxed once Frank is up and about. No disrespect intended. You appear well ready to take care of yourself with that pistol strapped on and all."

She cringed with a nervous laugh.

"If it looks good, I'll just wear it to the next dance."

"Have to go into Austin for a proper dance."

Another faraway expression returned as she thought of Austin. Shopping close at hand. People always about. Indian danger far off in the hills. Most attractive to her right now would be the occasional break from cooking. Eating out at a restaurant. What a treat that would be!

"Sorry to intrude on your thoughts, Mary, but Austin ain't all it might seem. Plenty of trouble in town. Renegades come in the white variety too."

Matt had read her mind about Austin. She wondered if he had also read her sinful thoughts that a married woman should not have. She blushed at the prospect and hoped he didn't notice the color on her cheeks, but she knew he did. His piercing eyes missed nothing and conveyed his understanding of her temperament.

He offered a comment to diffuse her embarrassment, "Come Thanksgiving, we can all gather 'round for some fiddle music."

"That would be nice," she said with a wan smile.

He began to feel uncomfortable about the length of conversation with a woman capable of arousing such conflicting emotions within him.

"Mary, I've got to git back up to Lee. Glad to see all's well. Keep your guard up, and give Frank and the girls hello from me."

Matt placed his boot in the stirrup and effortlessly swung into the saddle. He gave Mary a last lingering gaze. Their eyes met for a moment. Touching the brim of his hat, he nodded goodbye. Mary stood silent as she watched him trail up the hillside and shrink in the distance. His dark figure had reached the peak of the ridge when her daughter Sarah called out for help with finishing the evening meal. Mary released her pent-up emotions with a deep sigh and turned away from the scene on the ridge. Her duties inside the cabin now replaced her wishful thoughts of escape.

Reaching the top of the ridge, Matt found Lee in the same position he had left him in. Looking down on his brother, he said, "Come on, Lee. Let's git up. We about got it licked."

While Matt dismounted, Lee moaned with the pain and effort to reach a sitting position. Matt grabbed Lee under the arms and helped him stand upright. Lee wobbled on his feet before Matt steadied him enough to saddle up one more time. The long day had extracted a toll on Lee that left his face a pale shade of gray. He wore the listless expression of a man at his limits. His shoulders sagged and he sat in the saddle with a pronounced slump, leaning over the pommel. The reins hung loose in his grip while he hung his head low, gazing down at Matt. A fog clouded his eyes and Matt began to worry that this last stretch of trail would take Lee under.

"Come on, brother. Hang on a little longer. I'll take the lead and Midnight will follow. You just sit tight and hang on. We'll be home soon enough and will git you doctored up proper."

Lee mumbled a garbled response as if he were drunk. Matt patted Lee on the thigh and mounted Whiskey to guide him back home on the well-worn trail. An hour passed before they reached the hill that overlooked their homestead. The sun was set well below the horizon, with a faint glow of yellow-orange barely tinting the western skyline. Lee had continued to slump since leaving the Ellis ranch, and now he used his last store of energy to remain in the saddle on the steep slope. Loose rocks rolled ahead of Midnight with a clatter. Lee floundered in the saddle with her rocking efforts to maintain secure footing.

Reaching the bottom of the hill, Lee could not maintain the posture to sit upright any longer. Ignoring the sharp pain in his side, he slumped to the neck of his horse and wrapped his arms around her to keep from tumbling to the ground. Matt pulled alongside Midnight to steady Lee as he faded from control. They rode into the dimly lit yard outside the cabin, thoroughly fatigued.

This was the view that greeted Cora when she stepped out of the cabin with a tub full of dishwater. Her eyes flew open wide as she quickly surmised the situation. She tossed the water to the side and hollered, "Travis! Outside. Pronto!"

The rest of the kids followed him like dogs on a rabbit. Cora snapped at them to stay on the porch. The last to make it to the door was Becky, drying her hands on a cloth towel. Her husband was obviously in trouble and she pulled her skirt up as she ran past Cora to be at his side. She gave Matt a stern look of reprimand as she ran to Lee's side. Travis came alongside her, and with their combined help, they eased Lee from the saddle.

During the process, Becky reached around Lee's waist and found the bandage soaked with blood that stained her hands with a sticky fresh film. Lee fell to his knees and gasped for relief from his discomfort. A belching wave of nausea cleared remnants of the meager rations consumed during the day's demanding ride. He collapsed to his hands to brace himself from falling into the soiled dirt. Travis helped Lee stagger to his feet after he finished several agonizing rounds of retching. Becky got on the other side of Lee and helped brace him for the short walk to the cabin. Cora ran ahead of them to get a bed ready and start preparations for treatment.

Matt stood back, amazed at the efficiency he was witnessing. With hardly a spoken word, the entire family had moved into action to get Lee secured in the cabin. Life in these hills made you either a quick learner, or dead. He listened in as Lee explained his injury to Cora while she slowly looked over the blood-soaked bandage. Becky began to heat up some water and organize the medical supplies needed to treat the wound. The kids kept their distance from the women but didn't miss a detail in the care administered to Lee. They stood off to the side, transfixed as the ugliness of his wound was exposed.

Satisfied with the progress, Matt wandered into the yard where darkness prevailed. Taking a few minutes for his eyes to readjust to the lack of light, he lit up a cigar to celebrate a safe return from a mostly successful course of action. A long pull from the glowing cigar filled his lungs with a satisfying taste of contentment. He cherished the freedom of the hill country and would never hesitate to fight for his right to pursue life as he saw fit. Smoke billowed from his lungs and hung in a cloud that gradually floated away in the still night air.

He unsaddled the horses after his leisurely smoke. Once in the corral, he provided them with a generous helping of fresh feed as a reward for their exceptional performance. The heavy gate clunked as he closed it. Matt secured the gate against possible intruders with heavy chain and lock. Leaning against a fence rail, he surveyed the surrounding woods for movement. Nothing stirred. Gazing upward, he discovered the heavens filled with brilliant points of blue starlight sprinkled across the pitch-black night sky. He stood spellbound by the beauty.

The homestead appeared serene for the moment, with the stock securely bedded down and the serenity of the hills broken only by the mournful howls of coyotes in the darkened uplands. This was the time he enjoyed most. The peace that fell over the land after sunset wrapped a blanket of contentment over his shoulders when the day's work had been successful. The feeling was a temporary sensation, but it surpassed the warmth generated by the best whiskey he had ever consumed.

He was sore to the bone, but the pursuit had been necessary. Lee was home safe, where he could get better care. The Ellis family was currently secure. Apparently, no other neighbors reported bad Indian news. It was a good feeling, getting back home safely.

He breathed deeply the humid river air and exhaled the stress of the dangerous gamble taken. Regaining his strength from his moment of repose, he played over the situation that would now require his attention. He realized what had been in the back of his mind, tugging at his conscience. That Indian was not done. He was out there, still roaming. He would be biding his time until it was in his favor. He would strike again. Matt knew it. It was only a matter of time. Who found who first? Matt was dead tired and felt as if he had ridden into a wall, head on, at full speed. He decided time would tell and tonight was not the time. A hot supper would be good, followed by some deep sleep. It had been several nights since he'd enjoyed a good sleep, but first he knew he had to endure the buzz of voices in that small confining cabin.

SIX

The next morning Matt rose well before the others began to stir. He quietly slipped into clean clothes, careful not to wake the kids. He wanted a little quiet before the racket they'd create disturbed the peace. In the dark, he stepped lightly across the uneven wooden planks, creaking as he made his way to the door. He resented the noisy wood flooring Cora had insisted he install. Despite his subtle movement, she shifted in the bed and he knew she would be up shortly.

He eased the door open and peeked outside at the dim gray start of the day. Taking no chances, he went back for the Henry before stepping out onto the porch. The coolness of the morning air invigorated him. It was nice to be out of the stale air inside the cabin. He reached his arms up and stretched out the stiffness of long, hard days in the saddle. Shuffling to the edge of the porch, he checked on the stock, scanned the yard, and found all to be in order. He stepped down off the porch and roamed to the backside of the cabin. A raccoon startled by his presence slipped into the brush beneath the massive pecan above the creek. Matt was satisfied with the security of his place after seeing the coon going about his normal morning routine.

Content for the time being, he returned to the porch and grabbed a seat in an old beat-up rocker that groaned with his weight. Cora had persevered in bringing the rocker along with them years ago, when they first put down roots on the banks of the Colorado. There was not much room to bring the chair back then, but he remained glad she had convinced him to tote it along. Easing back into the creaking chair, he relaxed and let the brisk air soak in.

Songbirds were starting their early serenade. A mockingbird led the chorus in a variety of melodies that floated pleasantly in the still morning air. Crows began their coarse calls, echoing through the woods down on the river bottom. The intelligent birds made good sentinels that Matt had heeded in the past when danger was imminent. Midway up the hillside, a white-tail doe and her yearling cautiously fed along the edge of the oaks. Soaring above all of the early activity was a red-tailed hawk on the hunt. Catching the thermals, he floated high in the air above Tucker's Ridge before gliding over the treetops and disappearing from view.

Matt sat deep in the rocker to enjoy the peacefulness and solitude the early morning hours offered. He cradled the Henry in his lap for security but felt the morning was safe from harm. Danger was out there in the woods, but his senses were alert and no warnings pricked his intuition.

Inside he heard Cora at her usual routine of coffee making. She made a strong brew guaranteed to light you up with zest. There was very little she had not mastered out here where self-sufficiency was a requirement. The hot fried venison and potatoes she had prepared last night had restored his depleted energy, and he got to drift off to sleep in the comfort of his own bed with a full stomach. She had accented the fried food with hot cornbread dripping with butter that little Catherine had churned. His nine-year-old daughter was far along in learning skills from her mom with no complaining at the hard work Cora demanded. She knew her mom would not abide complaining.

Cora eased out the door with two steaming cups of her black brew and carefully handed a cup to Matt. He clasped his hands around the warm cup and blew gently across the top to dissipate the heat. Breathing in the rich aroma brought a slight smile to his face. This early-morning ritual of the first cup of coffee was satisfying here on the porch or out in the open woods around a pulsing campfire. It was nice to get back to this particular routine after several days of cold grub and no coffee. Cora took a seat on the large pecan stump that served as a chair. She too surveyed the yard for any sign of trouble before speaking to Matt. She wasted no time getting to what was on her mind.

Turning to face him, she blurted, "You didn't have much to say last night."

"Good mornin', Cora."

"Why so quiet?" she asked.

"Said good mornin'."

"That's not what I mean."

"Beautiful mornin'. Birds singing. And it was quiet, until a moment ago."

He felt the first pangs of aggravation.

Cora sat staring up at the hill, trying to ignore Matt's comments.

He continued to scan the far ridge where the deer had fed out of sight under the oak trees. He knew the deer were feeding on the abundant acorns scattered across the hillside. Not finding the deer, he searched the sky for another hawk that was sure to appear at any time. This area was a prime location for all kinds of wildlife. Living close to the land fulfilled some internal need for Matt. He never grew tired of new sightings of wildlife or riding across seldom-seen lands. A second hawk soaring above him seemed more important than last night's events.

Cora sighed and went inside to return with the coffee pot for the refills she was sure Matt would request. He always drank three cups or more before he headed out to his chores. Returning, she topped off his cup before she sat back down on the stump, her back supported by the rough-hewn cabin logs. She wrapped a small scrap of burlap around the pot to keep the heat in.

"Maybe a little coffee will loosen your tongue," Cora said.

"It usually helps," Matt said in between sips of the black coffee brewed thick enough to cut with a knife. Brewed just the way he liked it.

"Well then, why so quiet last night?"

"Wasn't quiet. Lee told you all you need to know. I didn't hear him leave any details out."

He finally saw another hawk swoop low over the hilltop. The sight of the early morning hunt pleased Matt. He respected and identified with the hawks' ability to scratch out a living despite the difficult challenge.

He asked Cora, "How's he doing?"

"He was sleeping fine. Becky is right by him. She will not let him want for anything. I'll recheck his dressing when he gets up. You leave him be for a while. That ride you put him through took it out of him. He's not you, you know."

Matt continued sipping on his coffee, ignoring her comments.

"Matt, you worry me with these romps you go off on. One day you may not come back. Lee barely made it back this time. What if you are next and not so lucky?"

Cora had a point. He understood that his fortune could turn in a split second, but somehow he always made it out of tight situations. He held a strong belief that the future would turn out the same. Lost in thoughts about past adventures, he found the image of Mary crossing his mind. She would be the sweetest adventure imaginable. He felt a strong current carrying him into unchartered waters, full of perils. Shaking those forbidden thoughts from his mind, he heard Cora droning on about her concerns and worries.

"Give it a break, woman. It's too early for this kind of talk. I came home. I always do. Now leave it alone."

"I just need to talk."

"Hell, it's all we ever do. Ain't nothin' else between us anymore. You're wearin' me out before the sun's hardly up."

Cora's spirit slumped a little after the scolding. Matt could not help the harsh tone of his voice and he was right. She knew he was. There was no physical contact between them anymore. It was her fault. She controlled that aspect of their relationship. But she didn't know how to recapture the desire. And there was the loss of Josh. She felt overwhelmed with so many difficulties to contend with. Life was drowning her in troubles and she knew the next topic of discussion would make it even worse.

"Matt, there's something else."

Matt turned and glared at her. His eyes cut like a knife. He recognized the tone in her voice and knew it didn't bode good news.

"Didn't want to tell you last night. There was enough going on to deal with." She hesitated. This news would really anger him. "We had a visitor yesterday afternoon. A Colonel Ames. Least he called himself a colonel. He wasn't in uniform, but he displayed that military arrogance. Looked at me like I was dirt to be swept away. Short on manners, he was."

Matt didn't like the sound of this. Disrespect or insolence to any of his family members was something he never tolerated. In fact, it could get you dead. His well-known temper was starting to percolate, fueled by the potent caffeine. He faced Cora with all of his attention. His gaze sharpened to a razor's edge. The peaceful morning spell was shattered.

"He had a couple of men with him I didn't recognize. They really gave our place a once-over but didn't say a thing. Looked like a couple of thieves.

Mister Ames did all the talking. Said they were touring the settlements outside
Austin. Just inspecting and gathering information. Didn't say what for. But
you and I know what for. The look in his eye said it all. He liked what he
saw."

She twisted her fingers in a tight knot that cracked her knuckles.

"That's when David came out with the scattergun. He stood right beside
me with the gun. Matt, I didn't like what I saw. Ames's helpers, if that's what
you want to call them. They came alive when David came out. They looked
like killers to me. Meaner than hell. Just hunting for a reason."

Matt knew it was coming. This day was inevitable. Rumors had been
spreading like wildfire. Now his place was in the path of flames. Gazing at
the ground, he felt the stirrings of a sick feeling. This news ruined what he
had hoped would be an uneventful day. Cora remained silent while he took
time to digest her story.

"Go on, finish up," he spat curtly.

"I stepped between David and the men. David didn't like it. Mister
Ames told me there was no cause for alarm. They meant no trouble and
would be on their way. David settled down a little at that point, but Matt,
they could have shot him! Right here in our own yard. Those men looked
eager to do it. He is only fourteen and does not have enough sense for situations such as this. He thinks he needs to be you. With you and Lee gone, he
thinks he's the man around here. He thinks he could handle it. You have to
talk to him. He worries me."

Matt was stewing on the unfortunate luck of missing the encounter. At
least his oldest son David displayed a little spunk. His combative spirit took
away some of the burn of insult, and his heart seemed to be in the right place.
David would turn out all right with more training and a few more years to
mature.

Cora, wound tight at this juncture, finished her story with the words
tumbling out, "That's not all. Before they left, Ames inquired on directions
to the Ellis place. At this point, I knew what they were up to and I acted
stupid. Said I didn't know the way. This offended the colonel and he got
testy with me. Told me it didn't matter to him. Said he could find his way to
the Ellis place and back to ours just as well. And then he looked around and
complimented me on the nice place we had. He said, *had*. Emphasized had.
Matt, I'm just sick. You know what this means?"

"Yeah, I do. It means I got to do some more things you're not goin' to like."

Matt rocked in his chair while he worked some options through his mind. He posed an obvious question to Cora in a stern tone that demanded attention. "Where was Travis when this happened? I left him in charge."

"He went down to the river with Luke to round up the cows. He wasn't gone an hour. I told them to bring the cows in closer."

Matt thought it over and refrained from criticism. Travis was his nephew and he'd gladly accepted the responsibility to finish his upbringing. Matt's brother Karson, had run Travis off with no intention of taking him back. There was no doubt Travis could be a test to be around. The boy possessed a strong will and didn't always do as directed. But he reacted better to Matt's leadership than that of his father. Matt had put him to good use and Travis would be ready to strike out on his own in a year or two. Matt's son Luke stuck to Travis like a cocklebur and it made sense they did the chores together.

Matt watched Cora and saw her face strained with worry. The times had begun to show on her complexion, with lines spreading out from her large brown eyes. Her auburn hair was now streaked with gray, earned from too much ranch work mixed with difficult child rearing. The birth of their last and fifth child, Josh, nearly cost Cora her life from excessive bleeding. Only the constant attention and application of hill country remedies by Granny Johnston had pulled her through. Cora had slowly regained her health after that close call, and she decided five children would have to do. In Matt's eyes, Cora remained an attractive woman, although her youthful vitality had evolved into a grim stubbornness to see her large workload completed on time and done well. The requirements of the day's chores left her with little energy to attend to any extras that Matt looked forward to at night.

He remembered the early years of their relationship with fondness and he felt a genuine love for this woman beside him, caught up in a state of anxiety. She was dressed in faded clothes lacking color and patched at the worn areas. The endless list of tasks required her dress to be functional first and attractive last. Her hair hung loose below her shoulders, sagging from the weight of worry over the visit by Colonel Ames. Her son's impulsive behavior also bothered her. David was showing signs of being like his father.

Shortly, she would stand up tall, pull her hair back into a practical bun, and straighten her shoulders up before heading inside to prepare breakfast for the family. She would meet this day with determination to persevere as she had countless times before. Any man would be proud to call Cora his wife, and Matt was no exception. She was dependable and a good partner to help run his spread. He felt the sting of guilt run through his conscience.

He slowly rose from the rocker and peered down at Cora, still reclining on the stump. She looked away, slumped in her seat, feeling the pressure of the struggle to get by. Matt felt a devoted sympathy for her concerns. It was his job to maintain their tenuous hold on their homestead. A burning sensation flared through his nerves. He hoped he was up to the task yet again.

"We'll do all right, Cora. You done good while I was gone. Lee done good with that Comanch. We been through worse times. What is bad can git better."

Cora sighed, "Matt, we don't have enough money to pay taxes."

He knew that all too well and didn't argue. Instead, he offered, "I'll go let the chickens out and take care of the horses. You just go do what you need to and don't worry. I'll think of somethin'."

He bounced off the porch and headed to the chicken coop, glad to be moving. The coffee had done its job and he was eager to tackle the chores of the day. He opened up the coop and the poultry scattered across the yard, scratching for something to eat. The kids could spread grain for them later, along with their other chores. He could hear the young ones waking and hollering at each other in the cabin. While brushing down Whiskey, he noticed smoke coming from the chimney. Breakfast was under way. Travis came out on the porch half dressed and yawning. The cool air didn't bother him and he trotted out to Matt on his bare feet.

"Uncle Matt, must of been some real excitement to hunt down them Comanche. Did Lee really shoot one from the hip? Boy! I wish I'd been there. I been missin' all the action. Wasn't even 'round when them Yankee scum showed up. When am I gittin' in on the fun?"

Matt held his hand up to slow Travis down a little.

"Ease up a bit. You're only seventeen. Your time will come, and you may find out it ain't what it seems. Lee got lucky. Another inch or two to the side and he would still be out there waiting on help — or death, whichever come first. Now does that sound like fun?"

Travis took a breath and shook his head. "No, it don't sound too good. But hangin' 'round here can git a little borin'."

"That be true. I suffer from that bug more than I like to admit."

"Where were you last night after Lee was brought in? I only saw you eat and turn in. I got a lotta questions."

Matt gave him a harsh glance to let him know it was too early for a lot of talk. Looking at Travis, Matt saw a young man full of vigor and a yearning for life, eager to be out on his own. A burning itch to prove he was a capable hand motivated Travis to tackle any job allotted to him. Matt could sense Travis was ready for the next step in managing frontier life.

"Tell you what, Travis. While I wrap up my chores out here, you go git yourself ready. After breakfast, you and me will head over to the Ellis place. You're gittin' loaned out to Frank for extra protection 'til the Indian question is settled. Grab the shotgun and extra cartridges, along with whatever else you need. You'll be gone for a few days to a week, maybe."

Travis gave Matt a quick nod and made his way back to the cabin with a light step. Matt knew the chance to be depended on would bolster the boy's confidence. He also knew Travis would use his time to get to know the oldest Ellis daughter, Sarah. It was an opportunity for Travis to grow in maturity with the extra responsibility of helping needy neighbors. The possibility for courting would be a side benefit for the boy. One that would require the diligent oversight of an adult.

Breakfast in the cabin overflowed with eggs and bacon fried up hot and served with pan-toasted bread dripping with fresh churned butter. The aroma of another pot of strong brewed coffee filled the cabin. Matt enjoyed the fact that home cooking was a sharp contrast to the meager food he endured out on the trail. The men and boys finished eating while the women hung back and kept plates and cups filled. Lee managed to get some food down while reclining in bed. Becky tended to him like he was a little lost calf. In Matt's mind, Lee deserved the extra attention after the ordeal of the last forty-eight hours.

With breakfast over, Matt wasted no time in mounting Whiskey, who pranced impatiently. Travis rushed to join up with Matt after hasty goodbyes shouted back to the family. Luke looked on with envy at the departure, but he knew his place and kept quiet.

Back on the well-used trail, Matt felt his body loosen up with the easy rolling pace in the cool morning air. Travis fell in behind Whiskey and remained silent while lost in his own personal thoughts. The upcoming chance to prove his abilities created a nervous tension and butterflies in his stomach he could not ignore.

Matt also rode quietly, mired in turmoil about his lack of hard currency. He needed money to solve the new financial dilemma and it was hard to come by. He realized this deficiency of dollars left his place wide open for seizure and exploitation by ruthless men who didn't deserve any benefits resulting from years of his hard labor.

Right or wrong didn't matter. Matt recognized the circumstance as a weakness that predatory men could and would seek out to capitalize upon. Pouncing on a soft spot was something he understood. He had taken advantage of his share of opportunities offered because of his enemy's weakness or oversight. The difference was that he fought against sworn enemies, not struggling neighbors. Everything he valued was at risk until the overdue tax bills were marked paid. Matt felt like he was in the dirt, on his back, his belly exposed to a cat's sharp claws, helpless to stop the coming assault.

The ride passed quickly while he mulled over his problems, and in a short time, they were clattering down the ridge above the Ellis place. As the horses entered the yard, the chickens scattered out of the way in a rising volume of irritated clucking. Hearing the ruckus, Mary emerged on the porch with her two youngest daughters in tow. Matt noticed she didn't have her Colt strapped to her hip this morning. The lapse in judgment could have been a mistake on her part, but he thought it better not to mention the lax security in front of the young ones.

Touching the brim of his hat, he said, "Mornin' ladies."

She seemed pleased by the unexpected guests, "Morning, Matt, Travis. What brings you back so soon?"

"Just dropping off a little extra help is all. Feel a little better with another man around y'all while there's Indians about. Least until Frank is up and movin' better."

Mary thought on it for a moment and nodded in agreement.

"Sure won't do any harm. Frank will appreciate another man around. Go ahead and unload your gear, Travis. Girls will get your stuff squared away in the cabin. Sarah is inside tending Frank."

Travis dropped out of the saddle, stirring up a bloom of powder under his boots. He puffed out his chest with being referred to as a man and the warm welcome Mary offered. He quickly untied his bags and allowed the younger girls to carry them off into the house. His survey of the place lingered on the open door, hoping to catch a glimpse of Sarah. Unsuccessful, he turned and led his palomino to the corral, where he disappeared inside the small barn to tend to its needs.

"Mary, he can stay on as long as he is needed. Or you can send him home when you feel it's best."

"Thanks, Matt. Means a lot to us. Not leaving you shorthanded, is it?"

Matt remained in the saddle, intent on avoiding the conflicting emotions generated when he was near this woman.

"No, we got plenty of help. David can handle most everything when I'm gone. Lee seems to be doing all right."

He made eye contact with her and immediately felt a smoldering sensation start to grow in his chest. She held his look, and in her sultry blue eyes, he saw her passionate attraction towards him. Matt fought his own feelings of lust, fueled by the craving that glowed in her tempting expression. Wild visions of uninhibited lovemaking took flight through his imagination. His gaze narrowed at the intensity of his need to have Mary. He was already losing control. This was not the time or place to take her. She stood silently watching him, fully aware of his inner turmoil.

Easing Whiskey a step closer, Matt peered straight down at her. His hard gray eyes bored into her, letting her know she could be his.

She eased back a step and averted her eyes. Her mind raced with confusion. Her heart beat like a cornered fawn. This man stirred emotions long left neglected. She yearned to surrender to him. She needed to feel the heat again. She needed it now. When she looked back at Matt, her natural beauty could not conceal the ache of her frustration.

Matt recognized her conflict. It was the same he was experiencing. This situation did neither of them any good. He hesitated as he decided to break the spell. Gathering his resolve, he shut out the thoughts of fantasy and returned his attention to current matters.

He said, "Mary, I got some bad news."

Hearing his own voice speak of the business of the day felt as if he had fallen off a cliff and landed with a thud.

The effect on Mary was instant. Dejection spread across her soft face. She assumed the appearance of a woman who had received more than her share of bad news.

Matt said, "Seems like a Yankee with money is making the rounds out here in our hills. His kind has already picked the town apart. Now they are out here lookin' for more plunder. Three of 'em came by my place. Gave it a once-over."

Mary shook her head as if she already knew the story.

"So that's who those men were this morning. Not too long after sunup, I saw three men on horseback up on the ridge giving our place a once-over. They just sat there looking down here while I did my early chores. Never waved and never came down. I didn't get a good feeling about them. Now I know why. My intuition usually works fairly well."

Matt stood in the stirrups, feeling a sudden need for action. The leather creaked as he stretched out his leg muscles. He tried to ease the tension knotting up in his back. He rolled his head side to side until his neck cracked from the release of coiled-up pressure. He eased back down in the saddle.

Mary's shoulders sagged at the weight of more unwanted news. She was a delicate lady caught in a world full of unrelenting troubles.

"Mary, I'm sorry they come by and bothered you. Problem is they got the law on their side. I don't know your finances, but if you're like the rest of us, y'all got a little behind on taxes. They aim to separate you from your place and me from mine. All because of a few lousy dollars. Hear they have done it in town. Put good families out on the streets. Sent 'em packing. Nice and legal."

She frowned as her gaze dropped to the ground.

"Matt, we don't have hardly a dime to our name. It will be hard to scrape up any money, with Frank hurt and not working. Those men sat up on that ridge for maybe fifteen minutes this morning. Could be they didn't like what they saw, since they never rode down."

Matt's face turned as hard as stone. His voice was sharp and full of resentment as he said, "Mary, that type of man never sees a thing he don't want. We all got trouble ain't goin' away. They will be back. Sorry to be blunt, but those are the facts."

Mary came over to the side of Whiskey facing away from the cabin and tenderly touched Matt's thigh. She had noticed his restlessness and took that as a sign he was heading out. In a soft pleading voice, she implored, "Matt, you leave those men alone. Stay out of trouble."

She continued to touch his thigh and began gently brushing her hand along his inner leg. Matt felt his arousal growing again, confusing his judgment. At a loss for words, he leaned forward, and in a husky voice said the first thing that popped into his mind, "Mary? Has Frank been laid up a little too long for you?"

She purred, "Just letting you know how I feel."

He felt his attraction intensify with her reply. She was ready.

Her hand rested high on Matt's thigh as she looked away. In a brooding voice she said, "I've seen enough of hard times. Age caught up to Frank long ago. He doesn't pay me any mind."

She was lost in thought for a moment as she absentmindedly stroked his leg. Remembering her intentions, she turned her lustful blue eyes back to Matt. He had not attempted to remove her hand. She noticed his heightened state of interest. Appreciating Matt's nearness, she cooed, "Besides, we've both known about this for a while now."

The sound of her voice, so close, so seductive, created a roaring sensation that boiled his senses. Matt felt dangerously close to capitulation. Summoning his willpower, he said, "That's right, Mary. We have. But this time is different. I'm close to taking you up on it."

"I dream of giving in to what we want. How long can we deny what's building stronger every time we see each other?"

Matt sat up erect in the saddle. From above, Mary appeared submissive and desirous of seduction. Her eyes softened with a longing reserved for the bedroom. She possessed an unfulfilled passion and wore the facade of a woman long denied satisfaction. He had often dreamed of this moment, but the timing was wrong. Matt hesitated with the words, but the message spilled out with an edge sharpened by frustration. "Mary, I guess I'll do what I must. Always have, always will."

She frowned, not hearing what she preferred. Her need for him burned hot. She removed her hand from his leg with a long tender brush. His leg trembled at her touch. That was the response she sought. She intended for him to remember her many charms. She could satisfy his desires whenever he wanted. He needed only to make an arrangement and find a place.

They held each other in a look that mirrored a carnal hunger tempting them with forbidden pleasures. She knew it was of no use and took a step back to put distance between her and such a strong attraction climaxing at an inopportune moment.

Matt recognized the wisdom of her movement. He straightened even higher in the saddle. He resembled a man with an iron rod for a backbone.

"Mary, I've got to git a move on. This ain't doin' neither of us any good."

She held his gaze, pouting.

He glanced toward the barn, nodding in its direction as he explained, "Before I head out, let me remind you to keep an eye out on Travis. He will do as he is told, but he is very fond of Sarah. They don't need any time alone."

His statement finally broke the spell. She had not seriously considered the possibilities, but now it dawned on her that her motherly duties would resume when Matt left. Responsibility was always waiting. With a tinge of anger in her voice, she confidently declared, "There won't be any romps in the hay! Sarah knows better."

They held each other in another long visual embrace. Matt shook his head in disappointment.

"Mary, I wish things were different."

Sadness permeated her voice when she said, "I do too."

He tipped his hat to her before he reined up on Whiskey and headed to the corrals where Travis had vanished to tend his horse. He quickly pulled alongside Travis, emerging from the barn. Matt leaned over and spoke in a low voice meant for just the two of them, "You be nothin' but help around here. You understand? Stay mindful of the Indians."

Travis stopped in his tracks. His mouth hung open in a surprised gape. His uncle seemed agitated.

Matt hesitated and finished his instructions in a voice that left no room for doubt, "Keep your pants pulled up around Sarah, or else Mary might do you a favor and shoot it off."

Travis was speechless, with no chance to reply as Matt spurred away towards the ridgeline. His advice to Travis was a bitter pill to swallow. He could not hide from the fact that *he* was the one contemplating going where he had no right to consider. He needed distance and he needed it quick.

SEVEN

Matt pushed Whiskey hard to the ridgetop and found where the three trespassers had milled around. This was where they discussed their plans to take what was not rightfully theirs. He easily followed their trail heading off to the northeast. Whiskey followed his command and readily maintained a steady canter with minimal effort to close the distance to Colonel Ames and his men. An hour later, he was following the well-worn trail that connected the heads of several draws above Lime Creek. The sun had begun to warm the air as Matt's mood continued to fester.

This situation followed a pattern that made an appearance ever so often in his life. Events were steadily moving beyond his choosing. Events were piling up, out of control. Unstable conditions would eventually force his hand to take actions with uncertain outcomes. Matt felt adrift on a flooded stream carrying him down to a tumbling set of rapids. He faced the prospect of a disorienting ride and a complete loss of direction. His mind swirled in a whirlpool of options. Slowing the pace, he reined Whiskey to a stop overlooking a winding creek far below the hills fading into a violet haze on the horizon. He wanted time to think.

The thermals rising from the canyon below carried the distinctive smell of cedar rolling over the ridgetop. Whiskey snorted, drawing in deep breaths of fresh hill country air while Matt collected his thoughts. Overtaking the three riders would be a dangerous proposition. In his current state of aggravation there was sure to be a hostile confrontation leading to a shooting. There would be several deaths or more. Maybe *his* death. The odds were against him. Three to one. Two hired guns and one ex-military officer. No doubt, the men were all capable hands. He was in the mood to fight, but the odds were too long.

He surveyed the expansive landscape before him, marveling at the remote, rugged beauty of the hills with their well-watered valleys he felt privileged to call home. The stream below ran clear, clean, and cool over the white limestone bed with frequent waterfalls. The gurgling water whispered a peaceful message that relaxed a man if he was inclined to listen. The hills rose away from the streambed in a steep ascent of rock ledges hidden behind a thick growth of cedar, broken occasionally by stands of live oaks. All appeared quiet for as far as the eye could see. No other horsemen could be seen for miles around the rock-strewn ridge where Matt had stopped. Wildlife had taken to their midday beds and not even a buzzard was evident.

Matt slapped the weathered pommel on his saddle. Damn the carpetbaggers. Damn the Indians raiding across the frontier. They ruined the peace this wild land offered. If a man let his guard down for one minute, the vermin would rob, steal, and murder any unsuspecting settler who offered opportunity to them. The hills tumbled away in hushed beauty, indifferent to his plight and hid incredible danger in their folds.

His mood grew darker as he recalled the memory of finding his son mutilated by Indians and tossed to the side in death like a worthless object. The red men responsible for the tragedy had escaped unpunished. That depressing fact would always be an unpleasant reminder of his ineffectiveness to protect the life of his innocent son.

He considered the possibility of the trail ahead hiding the same Indians off in the thick brush that bordered the path. Alone, he might be easy to overcome. But at least the fight could be waged without the fear of murder charges trumped up by some faraway sheriff. No doubt, the future was coming at him, and coming fast, ready or not.

Matt grabbed his canteen and tilted it to his lips for a cool draw of spring water. The liquid spilled from the corners of his mouth and beaded up in his dark beard, glowing amber in the sunlight. He wiped the water off with his dust-covered sleeve as he admired the creek flowing far below his ridgetop heights. While returning the canteen to his saddlebag, he heard the muffled boom of a rifle.

The first report sounded hollow, due to the distance. Two more shots followed in rapid succession. Whiskey turned his ears in the direction of the firing. Matt patted his horse, whispering, "It's okay, boy. Nothin' goin' on here. Not yet."

A few moments passed. The echo of the large-caliber rifle faded off into the distance. Matt sat motionless and waited for further developments. Shortly, another rumble wafted through the stillness of the morning. A final shot, fainter than the others, finished the unexpected sound of the distant firing.

Matt pondered the meaning of the shooting and concluded the shots probably came from one gun, except for the last, dimmer shot. That blast sounded different, but the shooter may have simply turned in a different direction when the shot went off. All the gunfire sounded as if it came from a large-caliber rifle. It didn't sound like a battle, and the direction the shots came from gave one clue. They definitely came from the direction of the Johnston place.

The trail split a quarter mile beyond the hill where Matt sat on Whiskey. One of the forks angled to the right towards the Johnston homestead. He placed his bet that the three culprits he was following had taken the branch leading toward the Johnston cabin.

He eased Whiskey down off the hill and was not surprised when the fresh sign of the three riders bore off to the right. He slid the Henry from his scabbard and rested it in the crook of his left arm. Riding slow enough to be on the lookout, he continued to follow the fresh sign as it led the way through meadows of thick blue grama grass waving gently in the slight breeze. Matt stopped behind a thick copse of live oaks that provided excellent cover with large limbs drooping to the ground.

Concealed, he scanned the Johnston place from a safe distance. The cabin appeared small at this range, and no commotion was in progress near the dwelling. The riders he had been following were nowhere in sight. It seemed as if all was in order at the cabin. At this distance, it was hard for him to tell, but it looked like old man Johnston was sitting on his front porch in the shadows. Matt decided on a closer inspection and slowly eased Whiskey towards the run-down cabin. Closing a quarter of the distance, he noticed that the fresh sign he'd been following had disappeared into the brush off to the side. Continuing until he got within shouting distance, he let go with a yell from deep in his belly, "Safe to enter?"

Old man Johnston had been watching the approaching rider and already knew it was Matt. He answered the question in the rough voice and irritable demeanor he was known for. "If'n permission was denied, this old Henry would've delivered your answer 'fore ya got a chance to ask. Don't be testin' me this mornin' with nonsense questions. Git your butt in here and set a spell. We got lots to talk about!"

Matt didn't like the sound of the greeting, but around the old man, a person got used to hearing things that burned the ears. He rode Whiskey up to the water trough and slid off to the bare soil of the yard. Before he could secure his horse, a pack of lean-boned hounds representing the Johnstons' pride and joy surrounded him. They didn't wag tails in greeting, just inspected, got his scent, and wandered back to scattered pockets of shade. A better collection of hunting dogs didn't exist in the hills west of Austin.

Finishing up with Whiskey, Matt turned to see Johnston sitting with his feet propped up on a battered wooden crate. He wore his usual dour expression. His impressive bulk was reclining in a beaten, splintered old chair with his battle-scarred Henry propped at his side, ready for action. The worn rifle was one of two Matt brought home from the blue and gray war. He had made a gift of this second rifle to the long-time favorite neighbor slouching before him. Matt saw a few spent casings spread out on the warped and rotting wooden planks that made an excuse for a deck under the covered porch.

The Johnston cabin was the first built this far west of Austin many years ago, and time had seasoned his entire collection of ranch buildings with the effects of harsh weather. Old man "Bull" Johnston resembled his hacienda in color and texture. His hair tumbled in unruly gray locks down to his shoulders, matched by an equally disheveled beard. His face bore the evidence of too much time spent in the unforgiving extremes of heat, cold, wind, and rain. The skin opened to exposure had darkened to resemble the complexion of the Comanche he carried an eternal hatred for. Wrinkles cracked with aging as they radiated in webs from the corners of his eyes. But those eyes still shone with the fierceness of the reckless days of his youth. It was those eyes, full of a fiery spirit, that caught Matt's gaze. Bull waved him up onto the porch to take a seat.

"You wouldn't shoot a man to deliver an answer, would you?" Matt said.

He stopped short of the steps and faced the old man to wait for a reply to his question. He meant to test the old man's orneriness.

"Depends on your business. Shoot varmints on sight. Two-legged or four. Makes me no difference."

"Do I look like a varmint?"

Bull gave him a thorough inspection and turned his head to spit a long stream of dark tobacco juice off the porch.

"Hell, you're one of the worst kind. A two-legged fox. Smart and cunnin'. Always calculatin'." Pausing, he added, "Hard to trust a young fox like you. You git in the chicken house and no hen is safe."

Damn, Matt thought. The son of a bitch knows how to get in a man's mind. What was it with him?

Bull noticed Matt's face change expression and realized he had hit a nerve. Hit a nerve and Matt had yet to take a seat! Just the way to keep it interesting.

"Ain't no hens 'round here to tempt you," Bull said. "Sorry to disappoint ya 'bout that. But I know you. This ain't no social call. Come on and pull up a seat. I've had a pretty interestin' mornin'."

Matt reluctantly stepped up on the porch and it cracked loudly in protest of his weight, causing him to worry about the old planks snapping into pieces. He grabbed a chair held together with wire and slid it away from Johnston to situate it so he could look out over the fields in front of the cabin. The fields contrasted with the dilapidated homestead in that they were a lush green and abundant with oats saved for the cold, lean months just around the corner. That was the time of year when the stock would need it most. The cedar rail fences outlining the enclosures were in need of repair but sufficed in their primary function to keep the stock out. Matt finished his survey of the chores that needed tending to, and he took a seat, satisfied that his own place didn't seem too bad at all in comparison. A charcoal-colored coon dog ambled over and plopped down at Matt's feet with a sigh.

"What's to talk about, Bull?"

"We can start with your lack of neighborly manners when there's a hunt on."

"Figured you might start there. Wasn't much I could do at the time."

Bull spat another thick stream of chew out into the yard. Brown spittle dripped into his beard as he said, "I can think of a few things could've been done different."

"Yeah, you always could think of a few things."

Matt didn't mean any disrespect to the old man because, truth be known, he held him in high esteem. Fact was that all the men living in the hills held the patriarch in high regard. In his day, he was a hell of a scrapper, and a man known to do the right thing regardless of the outcome. He was a man you wanted on your side, despite his rough manner.

Bull casually rocked, patiently waiting for a better explanation.

Matt continued, "I didn't have time to posse up. I wanted those bucks bad. Running these hills to gather up men would have cost time I didn't have. Plain and simple."

"Figured you'd say that. You're as bad as one of my hounds on the trail. Ain't no pullin' you up, once ya got the scent."

Bull remained silent for the next few minutes while Matt filled him in on the details of tracking down the Comanche. After hearing the story, Bull shook his head at the thought of Lee holding his own under pressure.

"Got one from the hip! Hell, Lee is becomin' a full-blown fighter. I'll be damned. Never thought the time would come when your little brother would outshoot you."

"Leave me be about that. It don't matter the one I shot at had distance on me. I'll never live down missin' the red bastard or just wingin' the first one."

Bull offered a chew, but Matt declined. He never acquired the habit of chewing and didn't understand the taste some men developed for the to-bacco. A fine cigar was more to his liking, especially when combined with smooth whiskey right at dusk around a crackling campfire.

"Speaking of missin'. Did you do a little missin' today? I heard the shots, but I don't see no results."

Bull's eyes narrowed at Matt's verbal jab.

"I don't miss, 'less I aim to!"

Now it was Matt's turn to wait.

Bull thought a moment longer before finishing his statement.

"That is just fact. Today I aimed to miss. But I got what I aimed at."

"What the hell does that mean?" Matt laughed.

Bull joined with a soft chuckle. "Means 'xactly what I said. I aimed to scare away some vermin, and I got the job done."

"Was there three of 'em?"

"Sure was. Three thievin' skunks! I heard tale they was out makin' the rounds. Knew who they was right off. Don't take brilliance to make out their kind. Actually, they were worth killin', but now's not the time. Yankee devils! I didn't want 'em 'round my place, or gittin' my dandruff up this beautiful mornin'. So, I jest commenced with a little target practice. They just happened to be a little too close to my chosen target."

Matt nodded his head in agreement. He knew exactly what Bull meant.

Raising an eyebrow, Bull glared directly at Matt and said, "Which I hit, by the way." He waved his arm to point at a blackened stump out in the field. "Hit it ever' time. Damn fine shootin', if I say so myself. Sure stopped them thieves in their tracks. They must've seen 'nough of my place at that point. Turned and headed out through the woods. Pretty damn quick too! A couple more target shots and I had my mornin' back to myself. Never had to leave my seat."

Matt frowned. "Ain't gonna work. They'll be back."

"My tactics will be different next time. Next time, could be, they'll be the targets. Won't miss then neither."

Bull was getting a little heat up. His eyes blazed with a flame from within, full of color. "Won't nobody take my place 'less I give it to 'em. I got four boys that'll give hell to anybody who tries to take what ain't theirs. And Matt, I'm here to tell ya, we won't play fair. If I decide on stayin', those men will be dead 'fore they know we're even 'round. At that point, come what may, the future can take care of its own damn self. Bastards. I despise 'em."

Matt thought it would be a good time to turn down the boil a little bit. "Where are the boys?"

Old man Johnston readily took the bait to discuss one of his favorite subjects. "The three youngest ones are out trailin' a cat. Picked up trail yesterday evenin', late. Must've stayed on a hot one. They ain't back yet. Wish my old bones could keep up; I'd be with 'em right now. As it is, I'll just ride this old chair."

He shifted his considerable weight around and rubbed the head of a bluetick hound leaning up against his chair. "Nate's inside fillin' his belly. Just got back from Austin this mornin'. Got some news that may interest you."

The blue put his head in Bull's lap, enjoying the attention coming his way. Bull let his comment hang in the air until Matt inquired, "What will interest me?"

Bull looked up from the hound with envy in his eyes.

"Ranger work."

Matt let the idea bounce around a moment.

"What do you mean? I haven't done Ranger work in near seven years."

"Ranger work. Pure and simple. Work you done seven years ago ain't changed much."

"Indian work or outlaw work?"

"Injun work. Been a lot of raids up and down the line, from north of here down to San Antone. They been a little too active to ignore anymore. Nate says them Comanche just killed a family of five over on the San Gabriel. Just one report of many. They're like fleas on a dog. Nate's goin' to scout for the boys."

Matt ran the possibilities through his mind. It was a tempting idea that might solve a problem or two. He was worried his restless yearning was likely to get the best of him if he stayed around the homestead any longer. No money in Ranger work though. Lack of pay was always an issue when considering Ranger work.

"So, Nate's goin' to scout?"

"Appears so. Hard to beat his skills. He learned all he knows from trailin' after them dogs. Times I think his nose is better than theirs."

"Who's in charge of the company Nate signed on with?"

"Cap'n Harris."

Matt knew of the captain. He came from a well-moneyed family in Austin that was big in business interests. With his elevated status, the man never wanted for anything. He never struggled to put food on the table like ordinary men did every day. He also spent time advancing his education beyond the average citizen's ability. Matt could not relate to a man of his position, but he couldn't think of a reason to hold it against the captain. Despite the prominent social position Harris held, Matt admired him for his military service in the Confederacy's losing efforts. He'd also led a few Ranger expeditions and had performed satisfactorily, according to the stories that circulated. Matt had served with far worse men. He didn't see a problem and voiced his opinion, "He's a good man."

Bull pushed the hound away and grabbed a jug sitting next to his chair. He offered Matt a pull, knowing he would decline. Bull shook his head at the denial and upended the jug for a long, deep pull of top-grade moonshine brewed by the master. A brew with a distinct flavor from secret ingredients blended to perfection over the years by trial and error. Bull was proud of his liquid creation. He savored the warmth that spread immediately across his chest and soothed the pain in his joints that was his constant companion. A blush of color ran across his cheeks as the liquor worked its desired effects. A devilish grin broke out under his gray beard that alerted Matt to possible shenanigans.

"Oh, he is a good man, and one you might like to know."

"Is that a fact?"

"Certainly is."

"Well, tell me how it is."

Bull took another, deeper pull. He set the jug down and let Matt hang for a moment in suspense.

"They need horses."

"Do tell?"

"Sure do."

"How many?"

"More than you got."

Matt thought it over but remained unconvinced.

"That could be good news, if it plays out right. Sure ain't givin' no horse flesh away from civic pride."

"Well, it gits better."

"How's that?"

Bull paused again for suspense. Let Matt wonder a little bit longer. News like this needed doling out a piece at a time. Worked for all it was worth. He grabbed the jug again and took an even longer pull that caused him to shake his head in order to dissipate the burn sinking down his throat. He puffed out his cheeks and let his breath escape between puckered lips in a big whoosh.

"Damn, this stuff is good! Sure you don't want some?"

"I'll pass, but thanks."

"Man, you're missin' out on some good shine. But yeah, it gits better."

"I'm listening."

"Nate says they want you."

"Do tell?"

"Want you to be second in command, Nate says. Cap'n Harris thinks you're the man for the job."

Matt mulled this unexpected news over in his mind. Ranger work. Be hell to pay at home. Cora would tear him a new one. That was for sure. No doubt about it, she would give him hell.

"Gits better," Bull goaded.

"Bullshit, Bull. I'm not so sure it's that great as it is. Sure, I could use the money the horses would bring. That is, if he is in a frame of mind not to cheat me on price. But I hate trips into Austin. I'd just as soon take a whippin' as take a trip into town. I like it just fine away from them town people. Kind of like you in that regard."

"There's the best part, you jackass. This whole deal done been dropped right in your lap. And you can thank Nate for his service!"

Matt stood up to pace while Bull had his fun poking at him. Hell, the man took his dear sweet time getting to the meat of the matter.

Bull chuckled while watching Matt twitch like a caged cat thinking of the possibilities. Thing is, you give a man news like this a little at a time. Put it out slow as possible, just for the entertainment value. Entertainment was a rare thing out in these hills, and Bull held the news in front of Matt's nose like a piece of fresh meat held above his hounds.

"Well, you goin' to thank Nate?"

"I don't know, Bull. I may never find out what's up at this rate!"

"Well, I reckon you'll find it worth the wait when them Rangers drop in on your place tomorrow for a little horse tradin'. Right on your own doorstep. That's hand delivered for sure. Right at your door."

"No jokin'?"

"Nooo jokin'. And it might git better still."

Matt stopped pacing. Bull paused a moment longer before delivering the dealmaker.

"They got cash."

Matt shook his head.

"They never have cash!"

"Do this time."

Matt seemed dumbfounded at the news.

Grinning, Bull drawled, "Cash for horses. Cash for man flesh too. Seems the gov'nor lost some kinfolk in one of them raids. Made the thing personal for him. That bein' the case, money been found for this project. But they're in a hurry. He wants the Rangers out in the field for justice, right now. Blood for blood was how he put it."

Matt searched Bull's eyes for treachery. He was known for some tall tales, but his eyes were glowing, and not with deceit. More of a shine, like a man bearing gifts. Matt sat down in the creaking old chair, lost in thought. The new information bounced around in his head before settling into an order that made sense to him. He began to see how this turn of events could hold off the money pressure closing in on all sides.

"This might mean a lot to me." Thinking awhile longer, he wondered aloud, "So, Nate is sure of the help needed, and the cash to pay? Not some far-off promise to pay?"

"Ask him yourself. We can go inside to grab a bite to eat. The old lady has plenty, and that's where he will be."

"Sounds good. But let me ask you a personal question along these same lines. What are you goin' to do about the visitors you had this mornin'?"

Bull let out a disgruntled laugh.

"Matt, I hardly have a dolla' to my name. I barter for my goods. Money don't mean a damn thing to me. That's why I live out here. I don't need their way of livin'. I always figured I take care of my own. I don't need them, and they don't need me. Only the good Lord above knows what the gov'ment men do with the money we send 'em. I sure don't. I suppose most of it goes in them crooked bastards' pockets. That right there is enough to stop me from sendin' any. I hardly paid a dime to 'em the whole time I been out here in these hills. So I'm in a hard spot. The little Nate brings in for scoutin' won't take care of what they'll be expectin'."

Bull took on a faraway look where he saw everything in the future at once, but nothing made sense in the here and now. Matt took note of the old man's expression and felt a pang of regret for the unfortunate position his good neighbor had to deal with.

"No sir, Matt. Change is a comin'. Cain't be stopped. And I hear the train bearin' down on me. Reckon when it's all said and done, there'll be a fight for my place. I know I cain't win. Trouble is, I cain't just turn it over to 'em either. Blood or surrender. Don't have a good choice."

He paused to spit another stream of tobacco out onto the growing wet spot in the dirt.

"Had some good times out here with my woman and raisin' the boys she gave me. Got grandkids. Weathered some tough times too. But we all did it together. Nothin' lasts forever, and one way or another, I suspect my days 'round here are 'bout gone."

Matt scowled at the predicament his long-time neighbor found himself snared in. Bull was probably correct in his assessment. The name of this game was money and the power contained therein. Carpetbaggers roaming the ravaged Southern cities could, and did, exercise control over those citizens without the means to resist. Ruthless and without compassion, the Northerners descended on Southern soil like a plague of locusts looking to devour anything of value. Texas was not as bad as other states, but a few of those scoundrels now operated in Austin. The South lost the big war, and her good men were currently losing the battle for their property, their dignity, and their souls.

The forces prying families from their dreams were overwhelming in strength and expanding beyond control. Bull was right. What could a man do? Fighting the law was a futile battle. A sheriff serving eviction papers was only doing his job. Gun the law down, and his deputies would return with more guns to finish the removal. Death in the act of defending your property would be the likely outcome. Hanging from a tree to pay for your defensive actions was a distinct possibility. Losing and death intertwined in this scenario. The alternative was to ride away and let the life you built up go peacefully. The loss would be a man's pride. For a man like Johnston, the loss of self-esteem was a condition harder to contemplate than death.

Bull read Matt's thoughts and spoke up to reveal his feelings.

"Matt, you been a good neighbor. You and Cora are fine folks with a fine family. I don't know how this'll work out, but like I said, my time is at hand. I won't lay down for no son of a bitch. The boys will do what I ask of 'em. I'll do what I gotta. You been a good compadre, and me and Granny are gonna miss you and Cora."

Matt shot back with raw emotion, "Nothin' has happened yet!"

Bull stood up to grab Matt firmly by the shoulder, squeezing him with a hand the size of a bear paw.

"Matt, you'll do fine. I got faith in ya. But now, let's go inside and git some food in our bellies. Don't let the situation stand in the way of a good meal. We got lots more to talk about over some mighty fine grub."

EIGHT

Matt awoke several hours before dawn in the darkened interior of the cabin. Murmurs of deep breathing resonated off the walls. Instantly, he was alert. His thoughts raced across the events of the past few days, remembering there was plenty to prepare for, and danger adrift in the hills surrounding his ranch. Shaking the cobwebs of sleep away, he sat on the edge of the bed and quickly put on the clothes left hanging from a peg at the bedside. He left his boots off to avoid waking the others and fumbled in the poor light to locate his holster. Finding the Colt pistol, he slung it over his shoulder. Silently, he made his way through the cabin to the front door, where the damp morning air seeped in between the cracks. He slowly slid the door latch open and pushed the heavy planked door aside to reveal a wall of pitch-black gloom.

Fresh, moist, invigorating air rolled across his face, stimulating his senses after a night spent enclosed in the cabin. Another morning would begin with a dense fog hanging low on the ground. Gently swirling mists cloaked the outbuildings and the surrounding woods in mystery. The musky aroma of soggy earth and decaying leaves floated onto the porch, mixed with a pungent odor from the stock droppings in the nearby corral. A steady drip of water rolled off the roof and plopped in dark puddles that soaked into the hard-packed soil of the yard. Matt pulled the door shut behind him and stood inert, at full attention. He allowed his eyes to adjust to the absence of light.

An ominous presence seemed to linger in the dense fog hovering in the woods. He sensed a hollow emptiness permeating the moist air between the trees and the yard. The steady plop of water dripping from the roof punctuated the stillness outside the cabin. Matt stood close to the door to blend into the murky cabin shadows under the porch cover. He became invisible, full of caution, and coiled up tight with apprehension. He didn't see a threat, but he felt dread creeping into his bones, fluttering anxiously in his stomach. A quiver of anticipation flowed through his nerves, carrying a premonition of approaching catastrophe. Danger was out there. Invisible, but real. Undetected, but waiting. Fear and uncertainty flowed with power through his blood.

Easing down into the chair, he scooted it back against the cabin wall and contemplated the dismal environment surrounding his ranch. Not much was discernible in the moisture-laden atmosphere. Matt knew his yard well, but a stealthy approach to within arrow range was possible in these conditions. He removed the Colt from the holster and laid it on top of the blanket he pulled across his lap. A sense of peril would not leave his thoughts as he tried to relax and let his eyes adjust to the dim conditions.

He sat motionless, slumped in the chair, while he pondered the impending problems he faced. He needed to formulate solutions to the difficulties of dealing with people. Taxmen wanted money he didn't have. Yankees wanted property they had no right to claim. The Indians on the prowl created the simplest problem he faced. They just wanted to kill him. They were easy to understand and easy to counteract. He had only to kill them first, with no confusing laws to make sense of and no messy follow-up by the sheriff, who would want explanations for his actions. Survival of the fittest suited him fine. People were crazy with all the self-imposed entanglements of right or wrong.

He mused to himself in the quiet solitude, "I would've made a good Indian."

At that precise moment, a bobcat cut loose with a snarl blasting through the calm woods in an intensity that seemed to originate from everywhere at once. The sudden force of the cry rang out of the blackness like a banshee on a demonic quest. Matt felt the hair on his neck tingle with shock. The cat was close.

A short pause occurred before another cat engaged the first in an all-out battle for dominance. High-pitched snarling rose and fell in shifting crescendos, intertwined with low growls that resonated with anger. The battle for survival carried the cats tumbling into the thickly woven underbrush. Muted sounds of limbs cracking from their brawl moved deeper into the woods. The fury rose to a climatic pitch until, suddenly, the clamor of conflict abruptly ceased. It was as if the bobcats never existed. The clash for dominance was resolved in a short moment. Silence once again settled throughout the dark woods. Nothing came easy, and the meager bounty of the hills made for a difficult living by man and beast alike.

Matt judged the cats were within forty yards of the porch where he sat in reflection. The brief fight between the cats fed the same animal instincts building up within him. His skin prickled with anticipation. He was eager to start preparing for the hunt. His pulse beat faster with the thrill of such a close encounter between cats battling for domination. It was a situation similar to the plight of people but not cloaked in moral considerations.

Cora meekly emerged a few minutes later, wrapped in her handmade quilt. She moved to her usual position beside Matt, sitting without speaking. Matt kept his tongue and continued to consider the coming day. Cora reached over and placed her hand upon his. Matt didn't respond to her touch.

"Matt, I didn't sleep well last night."

Matt remained indifferent while sitting beside her, absorbed in his thoughts.

"How about you? You sleep?"

Wearily, he answered, "Not much. Too much goin' on."

Cora observed, "Sure is the devil's weather out there." She paused before adding, "Spooky."

"Yeah, it is. A lot of bad stuff can hide in this mess. This reminds me of the other night. That Comanch sure took advantage of the cover this sort of weather provides. Unlucky for him, I was waitin'."

"Do you think there will come a time when we won't have to worry about Indians?"

"Oh, sooner or later. They already been pushed way beyond what they consider theirs. Like all of us, they got their time marked. The need for more land will never let up. They may have their camp set up a long ways from here, but it don't matter. Eventually the settlers will be plowin' or ranchin' wherever the Indians are. Just a matter of time."

"What about our land? We're getting pushed too. When does that stop?"

Matt didn't like the line of questions and he shifted in his seat.

"Cora, I've got no idea when it stops. Most likely, it won't. That's the harsh truth."

Turning her way, he looked at her in the dim light emerging through the fog. She seemed lost. Worried.

His voice was hard. "That's why I got to do what I got to do. I've got to keep the wolves at bay. They're always circlin'. Times, I can hear 'em howlin' at our door. Some day they're goin' to have us for lunch unless I stop 'em. We talked about this last night."

"I just don't like it. Bothers me that we can't find some other answer. You'll be gone awhile. I know it for sure, and the risk is high."

"Not as high as the risk of doin' nothin'. I will fight losin' our place anyway I can."

"I know you will. It's just that you always want to do this sort of thing."

"Hell, Cora. Does that make it bad?"

Cora thought it over. "No, it doesn't. Not necessarily. But the results could be bad."

"That's a risk I'll take if Captain Harris says the right things. If he offers the right amount."

Cora felt a chill run through her body. Stimulated by her worse fears, she shivered enough that Matt noticed. Removing her hand from his, she tucked her arms tight against her chest. She felt captured in a current as strong as the Colorado after a hard rain. Powerless, she'd drift where future events took her. Not much different than driftwood in a flood, she thought. The tax dilemma, combined with the morning chill, bore in on her sense of comfort. She stood and began to pace in order to generate some warmth. Looking down at Matt, she felt remorse for their relationship.

"Matt, I'm sorry for getting upset last night. I don't want you gone. You joining the Rangers makes me feel like we are flirting with disaster again."

Matt stared straight out into the gloom of a dismal morning.

"I know you're doing what's best for us," she sighed.

Matt didn't reply.

Cora opened the door to go inside and stopped one last time. "I'll support your decision and tend to the kids while you're gone."

Matt turned and faced Cora. The shadows hid the details of his expression.

"Cora, it's going to be a long day today. I'm sitting out here until full light to keep an eye out. After breakfast, I'll be busy all day gittin' things in shape. I need you to git the trail food ready. You know the routine."

"That will be fine," Cora blandly responded. "I'll do all I can." She hesitated before she added, "When you get back, we need a trip into Austin. Just the two of us. I need some dress material. A meal I don't have to fix. Some time alone. Just the two of us."

Matt got out of the chair, stretched, and made his way to the edge of the porch. Looking out into the dim murkiness of a thick fog continued to distract him. His only reply was, "We'll see."

<<<<< • >>>>>

The fog lifted midmorning to reveal a ranch buzzing with activity. Matt put his two teenage sons to work grooming horses to show their best when the time came to present them for sale. David and Luke eagerly accepted the chores and put forth a good effort with brush and comb. Matt's small supply of horse stock began to shape up nicely as the day wore on until lunchtime neared. At fourteen years of age, David ran the job. Luke was a year younger and accepted his lower-ranked duties without complaint. They knew Matt would not tolerate bickering, and the importance of the upcoming arrival of Rangers was not lost on them. Growing up in the isolated hill country brought them to an early state of maturity. They recognized the necessity of their role in the successful operation of the ranch.

Lee spent a few minutes with the boys, supervising them until the tenderness of his wound drove him back inside to rest. He made sure the boys attended to Midnight with an extra ration of oats before he left. His horse needed the extra feed to help restore her strength lost in bringing him home safely from the pursuit of the Comanche. Lee felt an unusual bond with his mount after sharing the dangers of the trail with her. She got him home safely and he owed her a debt of gratitude.

Cora performed her duties inside the cabin with her usual efficiency, assisted by Lee's new wife, Becky. The two women carried on the chores of meal preparation in muted conversation, each preoccupied by private thoughts about the upcoming changes. Both were full of apprehension about their shared future. Cora tended to a large boiling pot full of cubed beef that she combined with chunks of potato, carrots, onion, and corn. Added to this simmering pot was her collection of herbs, mixed with carefully selected spices that seasoned the meal to the satisfaction of all who sampled her cooking creations. The strong aroma of the upcoming meal spilled out of the cabin windows and floated across the yard, tempting those outside with fragrant reminders of her special skills. It was Cora's custom to send Matt off with a pleasant memory of home life. She knew how to motivate an expedited return to their cabin on the banks of the Colorado. A home she helped build into a comfortable retreat from the howling wilderness that surrounded their family.

Becky busied herself with baking fresh bread. She set the loaves on the dining table fashioned out of live oak planks worn smooth and darkened from a decade of use. She also prepared an apple pie she spiced with a liberal coating of sugar and cinnamon caramelized on the checkerboard crust. The desert was sure to please the men. While Becky put the finishing touches on her baked goods, Matt's two young daughters, Catherine and Susan, packed his bags with jerked meat, pecans, and pemmican. They added parched corn to the bag, along with a special treat of canned peaches. Cora knew that an unexpected discovery of the sweet peaches would brighten a future moment for Matt. It would serve as a reminder of her thoughtfulness, despite her lack of support for his plans.

Cora rattled the wrought iron dinner bell with authority to summon the scattered members of her family. The metallic clanging she produced may have been overkill, but it pleased her with the immediate response she knew it would bring. Chores dropped immediately, and shouts filled the air as the family members made haste to the cabin for lunch. Matt emerged from the backside of the corral shed, wiping his hands and following the two boys already at a trot towards the door.

A lively session of conversation started after the family gathered around the table and Cora finished the blessing over their meal. She fought the dark mood that bubbled just beneath the surface and savored this time spent to-gether, unsure of the upcoming Ranger visit. Matt sat at the head of the table, mostly silent, as he listened to the banter between Lee and the younger children.

Becky sat next to Lee and if bothered by Matt's possible departure, it never showed. She was content now that Lee was by her side with no chance of leaving anytime soon. Her confidence that the future was secure shone on her smooth, milky complexion, not worn with the strains of time.

Cora, a little older and wiser, kept her troubled feelings bottled up. Her once youthful face now bore evidence of the stress of frontier living. At family times such as these, the memory of the loss of their youngest son, Josh, was ever present in her mind. By all rights, he should be here sharing these moments. The reality was that Indians delivered one of life's hardest lessons in an unexpected rush of brutality. Josh, dead and arrow-riddled, still haunted her, and forever would until her own death relieved her from constant mourning.

The meal was finished and the endless chores resumed, with Becky and the girls assisting in the cleanup. Cora was passing by the kitchen window with a pot to clean when she caught a glimpse of horsemen approaching the cabin yard. A double column of men bounced in the saddle at a rapid gait, led by a rider sitting rigid and tall. He sat atop an oversized paint blessed with striking colors of black and white. Cora found the horse beautiful to behold with its pitch-black shoulders matching the hindquarters crisply divided by brilliant white withers and flank. The horse led the way into the yard. He pranced with head held high and eyes that blazed with intelligence under the control of a self-confident Ranger mounted firmly in the saddle.

The other riders followed behind their leader and scattered into different positions around the yard, kicking up clods of dirt when they reined up to dismount. The captain on the paint remained mounted, barking orders to his men while pivoting in the saddle to observe their performance. His rigid bearing accented the all-business appearance he radiated in black pants and vest, matched by a sharply creased black hat casting a dark shadow over his face. His manner of dress created an air of mysterious power that attracted the womanly side of Cora. She felt movement in her desires long suppressed.

Becky came to the window and stood beside Cora, observing the arrival of the famed Texas Rangers. She raised her eyebrows at the sight of the heavily armed men primed with self-assurance and full of testosterone. The atmosphere around them reeked of the abundant energy contained in their bodies. These men were yearning for action. Becky embarrassed herself, blushing with the effect of so much raw masculinity on display. She was unaccustomed to such scenes and commented softly to Cora, "That's a sight to see."

"A sight I'd rather not see. Seen too much of it in the past."

"What a tough-looking bunch," Becky spoke in awe. "I wouldn't want to mess with them."

She twisted the towel in her hand absentmindedly while her innocent eyes grew wide at the sight of the men dismounting. A low murmur grew among the Rangers as they attended to the work of checking their gear and watering the horses.

Cora remained quiet, struggling to keep her emotions in control. These men were well prepared for hostilities, as evidenced by the collection of rifles in the scabbards and bulky pistols strapped to their waist. Most of the men had large knives at the ready, worn on the belt opposite the pistol. A couple of them carried an additional scattergun in their scabbard for close-in fighting. Cora detected the cockiness the men possessed. They believed they were up to the challenges that lay ahead of them. She didn't share their belief. Far too many times in the past she had witnessed the results of an expedition such as this one that came home with empty saddles. The heavy feeling in her chest threatened to grind her into the floor.

A few of the younger riders removed tobacco from their pouches and calmly rolled a smoke with seemingly no concern in life at all. To them, this was an adventure full of intrigue. The tribulations of the trail would be woven into a grandiose tale when they were safely back at home. Life to them didn't get better than this. Out in the wild lands up against all nature had to offer while pursuing a dangerous and crafty adversary.

The polished leader of the cavalrymen dismounted in a stiff, arrogant style, full of the power of command. He strutted in the yard like a rooster on display. Matt wandered up and greeted him with a long, firm handshake.

Cora grimaced in annoyance of the senior officer who would probably whisk her husband away on a peril-filled mission. Becky, not missing any details of the activities in the yard, commented to Cora, "Matt seems to know that man."

Cora answered in a voice that betrayed her true feelings of despair, "That's Captain Harris. He will be in charge, according to Matt. He has been around for a long time. Led a few other expeditions against the Indians. Some not so lucky." Her chest heaved with an expansive sigh.

In her state of excitement, Becky didn't notice Cora's uneasiness. She continued to pepper Cora with questions as the younger girls crept in to peek around them at the men gathering outside. Cora recognized only a few of the older men while she took note of the overall youthfulness of the bunch.

Robert Brown was one of the older men hanging back a short distance from Matt and the captain while they engaged in conversation. He was dressed in faded gray pants below a white cotton shirt, torn at the elbow and worn under a brown leather vest that was frayed along the edges. Pushed back on his head rested a sweat-stained hat that accented the air of a man unconcerned about his surroundings. His posture was relaxed. He was comfortable from the experience a man his age possessed. His friendship with Matt went back as far as Cora could remember. He was a man she trusted.

The younger men resembled colts — frisky, tense, and full of adrenaline. Out west of Matt's place was untamed territory, savage and uninhabited land where the real hunt would begin. They were eager for the chase to start in earnest and knew they were on the border of the real jump-off to pursue the Indians.

Becky observed the intensity level among the men and remarked to Cora, "Seems to be a high level of spirit on display out there. I believe I'll stay indoors."

Cora gazed at Becky's young, shapely figure and nodded her head in agreement. There once was a time when she too attracted attention from careless young men, but those days were long gone.

Becky continued to gawk in wonderment at the power the men exuded. Her sheltered background didn't prepare her for aspects of hill country living that included the gathering of men intent upon violence. Her scrutiny drifted to the rear of the assembled horses and took notice of one distinct individual hanging off to the side, alone under the shade of a gnarled oak tree.

His skin set him apart from the other riders. He appeared to be as bronzed as a Comanche warrior, but his manner of dress identified him as Mexican. His hat was large, round, and tan-colored. It drooped at the sides and hung low at the back, unlike the standard hat worn by the other Rangers. His buckskin shirt matched his leather pants, decorated with loose fringe down the outer edge. A serape, faded in once bright colors, draped over his shoulders. A huge Bowie knife encased in a blue beaded sheath hung from his concho-laden belt. He leaned against the massive oak tree, obviously at ease, separated contentedly from the other men. The knife rested on his left hip for the entire world to see. Becky found her attention drawn to the lethal appearance its size suggested.

"That man under the oak looks out of place," she said to Cora.

Cora found him and instantly recognized his identity.

"He's not out of place. If there's a killing to be done, he'll be nearby. That's Antonio Blanco. He is a half-breed. Part Tonkawa from his mom and part Mexican from his dad. Or so I've been told. Comanche killed his parents a while back, when he was a lot younger. He holds a fierce hatred for them now. He is a mystery to me, and I would steer clear of him. Never trusted him."

At that instant, Antonio shifted his attention and caught the women staring at him. Becky made eye contact for a moment before she instinctively shied and ducked quickly into the shadow of the room. Cora stood her ground, allowing her gaze to meet his coal-black eyes, as cold as a snake sizing up a mouse. Their stare locked in an embrace that provoked Antonio to stand erect, separating from the oak without removing his focus from Cora. It was as if he felt challenged. Cora held his stare until she tired of the uselessness it represented, and then turned to see Becky plastered against the wall, out of sight.

"He gives me a bad feeling!" Becky said.

"Your imagination is running away with you, kid," Cora replied.

"I don't think so! He seemed to undress me with his eyes. I got that bad feeling that he's no good."

"Any man can undress you. That's just what they do. They are like dogs. Always ready to hump. Don't worry, he won't be here long."

Becky listened to Cora's advice but didn't seem consoled with her wisdom. Her face wrinkled up, thinking of the man not far away, consumed with basic animal instincts.

Cora turned back to find Antonio still in place, watching her. A slow grin spread across his face when their gaze locked again. He casually rested his hand on the heavy knife at his side and turned his back to her, slowly disappearing into the woods.

Cora watched him until he faded behind the underbrush. Satisfied that he was gone, she turned her attention to the other end of the yard. Matt was leaving the corrals with Captain Harris after looking over the stock. They were setting a fast pace to the cabin, engaged in animated conversation. Stopping midway in the yard, away from the hearing range of the other men, they continued their conversation in low tones. Matt was giving the other men a closer examination until he seemed distracted. He glanced toward the oak tree where Antonio had been isolated.

Cora noticed Matt's expression change when his eyes focused on the area near the tree. She turned back to the oak and was surprised to find Antonio had returned to his former position, resting against the tree, watching Matt converse with the captain. Matt gave Antonio a long, hard stare and nodded towards him while still talking to the captain. It was apparent to Cora that the discussion between the two men had taken on a subdued tenor. Continuing the conversation for a few more minutes, Matt looked Antonio's way one more time before extending his hand to shake on a deal with the leader of the Rangers.

Cora felt her heart slump at the sight of their handshake. The deal was done. Matt would soon be riding away. A sense of depression swept over her in a cool flush that penetrated her heart. She turned to hug Becky, who was still hanging back, out of sight. Cora fought hard to control her overwhelming urge to cry, knowing that Matt would not tolerate tears at a time like this. Becky's presence gave her strength to control her emotions. They needed to prepare for a proper goodbye in front of the assembled men.

Cora heard the heavy clunk of Matt's boots stomping onto the porch before the door cracked open. The intense masculine dominance that had been building in the yard spilled into the cabin when Matt entered. An aura of purpose surrounded him in a way that affected people's reactions towards him. Cora's facial features communicated the distress she felt, despite her best efforts to control her inner turmoil. Matt was disappointed when he saw her discomfort, but he didn't have the patience to deal with her problems while the men waited outside.

"Cora, it's time for me to go."

There it was. The news she had been dreading, delivered. She felt hollow inside, drained of strength. She felt herself drifting. The old feelings of uncertainty at his departure reemerged from the past. Her thoughts clouded like the reoccurrence of a dreadful nightmare. Grabbing Becky around the waist for support, she read the look on his face she'd seen many times before. He was all business and the steel tone of his voice let her know the time for subservience had arrived.

He said, "Come on outside. We've got things to talk over with Lee."

Eyeing Becky standing beside Cora, he quickly summed up the situation. He didn't hesitate to put her in her place. "Becky, you'd best stay inside with the girls until these Rangers ride on."

He spun on his heels and headed back out the door to Lee, who rested in the chair under the shade of the porch cover.

"Lee, it will be up to you for the next month or so. Could take us longer, but I doubt we'll be back any sooner."

Lee continued to watch Captain Harris and the other Rangers organize the extra horses and rearrange the gear to accommodate faster riding. Cursing and shouts filled the air as the eager men went about their tasks. Lee nodded his head in acknowledgement of his role.

Matt continued, "You seem up to it to me. Healing real fast, seeing as how you got youth on your side."

"Yeah, I got youth, but more important, I got luck on my side. Which is no substitute for age. You got plenty of that." He grinned and added, "But I reckon I can hold the place down while you're gone."

"Smart ass. You see to it nothin' bad happens 'round here and one day you may be lucky enough to reach my ripe age."

Cora gently brushed against Matt and took her place close by his side. He was her security. Without him, her world would fall apart, and she sensed a strong premonition about this expedition. Matt was pushing his luck once again. He didn't back down, regardless of the danger. That quality was at once his strength and his weakness. He would force the issue when the time came. He always operated on the edge, and she knew that any man had a numbered set of chances in life, regardless of his abilities. Her worry possessed an intensity impossible to ignore. She desperately needed him for rearing the children and providing for the family's subsistence. Her desperation bordered on anger. Death seemed a shadow that forever followed him.

He tightened up at her touch and pulled away to put a firm, comforting hand on her shoulder. She always needed reassuring. At times, he resented her weakness. He would never be happy about her insecurities, but he understood her dependence on him. The only method he knew to console her was to assume the role of a man. It was his job to perform the necessary work and this expedition was required for many valid reasons. She didn't approve of his involvement with the Rangers, but the job benefited the family in the long haul. The bottom line was that she would have to get over her objections. He always did what he felt was best, and this decision was no different than any other occasion in his mind. The fact that he enjoyed the experience out on the trail was beside the point.

"Cora, you and Lee have to watch the place real close. Harris said the Indians are on a rampage all up and down the hills. No reason they can't still be anywheres from here to Austin. Keep the kids in close to the house for now. Word is the Comanche took a couple of kids captive and headed out west with 'em. We're after the kids, although it's a tall order to git 'em back."

Cora's face turned ashen. Her system was overloaded with unsettling news.

"Do we know the family?"

"It's the Havens family from over on Walnut Creek. Damn Indians are gittin' brave, comin' in that close to town. Killed the older brother and made off with the two younger ones while they were out tendin' cows. That's why Harris is in a hurry. The trail is still fresh."

Cora sat next to Lee, fighting the bile welling up in her throat. She was sickened at the thought of what the children were enduring. Lee put an arm around her and offered his own brand of encouragement to Matt.

"Kill as many as ya can. It'll leave fewer to breed."

"Oh, I intend to do just that. My patience is worn."

Cora spoke up, "What about Travis? He's over at the Ellis place alone!"

"He'll have to be the man he wants to be. I don't have time to tend him. We're headed the opposite way to strike the trail Nate figures the Comanch to be on. Cap is in a hurry. Travis knows what to do."

Matt pushed the door open and stepped inside to embrace his daughters. He knelt down, pulled them both into his arms in a tight hug and breathed in their sweet smell of innocence. His mind raced at the thought of their small, frail bodies in the control of savages. In a gruff voice, he admonished them to stick close to their mom or Lee. They meekly assured him of their good intentions to follow his demands. Taking a long last look, he stood and patted them on their heads before stepping into the yard, where his boys now waited. He repeated the instructions to them and they nodded their heads in understanding. He gave each of them a one-arm hug so as not to embarrass them in front of the waiting Rangers.

By this time, the captain had ordered the men to mount up, and Matt rushed his final instructions to Lee. "You be thinkin' of ways to increase our horse stock. Harris said the cavalry and the Rangers are goin' to need more in the future. Could be the cash crop we need to weather the hard times."

Matt declined a show of affection to Cora. Instead, he placed both hands on her shoulders and took the moment to look in her eyes with his cool gray stare. She stood immobile, searching for assurance in his mannerisms. He remained confident, despite their serious troubles, and she tried to feed off of his strength. Where she felt fear, he exuded optimism. But the hard look in his eyes didn't remove her doubts. She knew he could end up returning home draped across the back of a horse, like the other dead Rangers she had witnessed in the past. She was powerless. This was the man she'd married.

"Cora, you quit your worrying," he said. "It's enough to drive a man crazy. Look at it this way. It's actually a blessing. This comes at a time when we need it most. In more ways than you know. I'll come back and we'll have more than enough money to weather the winter. And pay the taxes. It'll end up bein' for the overall good."

With those final words, he jerked his bags off the porch and snatched his Henry from Lee. They watched as Matt secured his gear to Whiskey before mounting up in one fluid movement, as supple as a cat. Taking the reins into his hands, he moved Whiskey into position next to Captain Harris. With Matt established as his second in command, Harris raised his gloved hand and waved the men to move out.

A clatter of hooves and horse snorting resonated with the departure of a dozen men on the trail that led to the river crossing upstream of the homestead. Matt sat easily in the saddle and once more made his way off into the hazards of the wilderness with a slight nod directed to Cora and a wave of his hat to the family.

Cora watched the procession of Rangers until they disappeared in the pecan bottoms. A strange passive mood fell upon the yard. No conversation passed between Lee and herself. The girls remained silent after Becky ushered them outside to witness the sight of the men fading into the distance. Catherine and Susan surrounded Cora at each side, wrapping their arms around their mother for mutual comfort. Lee took Becky under his arm for support, leaning lightly upon her as the boys stood off to the side in stoic silence, lost in their personal thoughts. The pall of loss hung heavy over the small gathering of family. The final sight of Matt riding off became a memory locked forever in their minds.

Cora shooed the others back into the house, with Becky leading them inside. She found it impossible to refrain from speaking her mind. With prying ears out of range, she confided to Lee, "You know what, Lee? Sometimes, I don't believe Matt. Not at all. Not much good has happened out here this year and it's not likely to."

NINE

After crossing the Colorado, Matt felt a sense of release from the grips of tension coiled inside him. The river gurgling softly at his back created a barrier between his former problems and the newly defined sense of purpose that united all the men. He ducked low in the saddle to avoid the mustang grape vines that crowded the faint game trail. After clearing the thick growth along the riverbank, Whiskey's easy canter put some distance between the Rangers focused on honorable goals and the contemptible schemes of land thieves from Austin. The exhilaration of taking part in a rescue brought a man alive in an awareness that heightened all of his senses. Colors became brighter. Sounds registered more acutely. Odors took on a degree of scent as if freshly discovered. Matt craved the stimulation this hunt was sure to provide.

The column of Rangers fell into an easy pace over the open hills rolling away from the river bottom. They followed a well-worn game trail through tall grasses that required little concentration. Matt allowed his thoughts to roll back to Mary and the smoldering passion he felt for her touch. The two of them were perilously close to surrender and needed only a spark to ignite their mutual attraction. Once lit, the flames of an illicit affair would burn out of control, consuming those too near the heat. His decision to flee before temptation got the best of him prevented what surely would have been a disastrous turn of events that would tear lives apart.

Mary had made it clear she also longed for the return of the passion missing from her life. They shared a fascination for each other rising out of the cold ashes of separate marriages grown stagnate. He considered marriage to be an institution designed to strangle the life out of the desire for one's mate. It seemed to be a natural evolution other married couples he knew suffered from. Familiarity bred contempt. The necessity of making a living crowded out the time needed to nurture a close relationship. Kids demanded attention. Chores came first. The effort it took to maintain a marriage became more trouble than the pleasure it produced. Alienation from one's spouse seemed a common occurrence in frontier life.

Mary was an exceptional woman who turned the head of any man fortunate enough to be in her presence. Matt found it a pleasant distraction to contemplate her seductive appearance while out on the trail. The knowledge that she could be his for the taking produced a euphoric effect on his mood. He entertained the fantasy of conquest. It had been a long time since his last lover before he married Cora, but time didn't erase his memory of the exhilaration secured in the arms of a new woman. Appealing images of Mary succumbing to his advances played across his imagination. His chest swelled with the notion that he was still the young lion prowling for love he had once been.

His unchecked daydream met a wall of frustration at the reality of the circumstance. To give in to their obvious attraction would undoubtedly be a gift of intense short-term pleasure. A searing blaze fueled by the highest physical ecstasy possible between a man and a willing woman. And that would be that. Once initiated, the affair would suspend good judgment. A quest for satisfaction would displace anything or anyone standing in the way. The ensuing trap would spring with an abrupt clamp, inflicting profound and long-lasting pain. Kids, relationships, and property sacrificed in a force as destructive as a Comanche raid. Families ripped apart.

It had been all he could do to turn away from the carnal pleasures Mary offered. Cora was distant to him. Their last time spent alone was beyond memory. His needs ignored at home, this mission in the hills was a good escape from his quandary. Unanswered was the question nagging at him out here on the trail. Upon return home, could he continue to resist the allure of Mary? And did he want to? Or did he care anymore? The crossing of the Colorado put the issue behind him for later consideration.

While these thoughts ran through his mind, Matt had grown silent long enough that Harris noticed.

"Matt, have you something to say?"

Matt kept his focus straight ahead, watching Antonio disappear over a ridge to the right of the trail. Nate had already roamed far beyond the column's line of sight. He was intent on looking for sign to prove his value over the competition Antonio provided.

"No sir. Just thinking."

"Well, if you have something to add to our current endeavor, please feel free to comment. I value your opinion and will rely upon your advice when required."

"Captain, my thoughts are generally strong on opinion. Some tend to be offended by my bluntness."

"The same has been said of me. That is the price you pay when in command. Those offended by the bluntness of truth must be ignored. Unless, of course, they are of a higher rank. In that case, the situation does present a bit of a problem."

Matt nodded his head in understanding. He'd dealt with many officers above his rank as sergeant in the Confederacy. Quite a few of them didn't have a clue how to lead effectively.

Harris continued, "But, let me assure you. In the current action, I want your help on an equal basis. The return of the Havens children will be our primary focus, although my optimism on the reality of the situation is not very high. Second in purpose will be the destruction of as many Comanche as possible. On that matter, I am highly optimistic that our ability to travel quickly will lead to success. Those extra mounts should afford us the mobility to compete with the Indian ponies. I believe the Comanche will be surprised at our tenacity on their trail. With two good scouts, we will strike their main trail and stick to it. Once delivered into fighting range, our boys will get the job done."

"I appreciate the confidence, Captain. That's half the battle. There is no room for indecision out here. The Comanche can smell it, and they'll steal your options from you."

Harris looked Matt over in appreciation of the man he rode with. Matt maintained a rugged appearance formed by years in the weather and numerous battles on the frontier. His broad shoulders rose and fell with the gait of the horse that matched him in the appearance of power bottled up, aching to be unleashed. Whiskey's well-defined muscles rippled with exertion beneath

Matt's loose riding style. Man and horse were a matched pair that Harris admired for the dependability and strength they represented.

Matt also admired Harris, but for a different set of reasons. Harris might be a bit of a dandy with his sharp manner of dress, but he was also a man's man. He was proud and full of self-confidence. He possessed an intellect superior to most of the men striving to live in these wide-ranging hills beyond the security of town. A career in politics was on the horizon, and the captain planned to use his abilities to fight the injustice abounding inside Austin's political arena. Matt held a sincere admiration for a man capable of riding beside him into harm's way, beyond any hope for help, and then returning to civilization to take on an ever-increasing supply of scoundrels. Harris was a capable man in many different ways than Matt.

They continued to ride side by side in an easy lope that ate the distance up without undue fatigue on their mounts. Ahead of them, the sun was sinking below the horizon, burning a brilliant orange with a sharp, distinct edge in the clear western sky. A golden radiance bathed the waist-high grasslands at the top of a ridge, where they pulled up to scan the violet-crowned hills. The ridges melted into the remote expanse in crests that lost distinction as their distance increased. Matt pulled his hat down to shade his eyes as he surveyed the terrain ahead of them for any sign of movement. Harris held his hand up to halt the command in place.

Matt continued to peer into the hills rolling away from them, thinking. He was unsure of the exact role Harris intended for him. Every officer had different opinions on the correct balance of decision-making protocol. He was uneasy about one detail of the command and he wanted to reach an understanding before the mission continued.

He asked Harris, "Permission to speak freely, sir?"

Harris seemed a little surprised by Matt's formal question.

"Permission is granted at all times." He rose in his saddle, stretched, and settled back down. Looking at Matt, he continued, "I do not want any hesitation in communication to impede what needs to be done. Conditions that warrant doubt are to be discussed between us if possible. Of course, final decisions, by necessity have to reside with me."

Matt liked what he heard.

"Sounds fine with me. Operated the same way at times in the big war. It seemed to produce good results as long as the men were of the right mind."

"Great then! We have an understanding."

Matt hesitated before he said, "Captain, I do have one concern that needs further discussion."

"Speak your mind."

"Antonio Blanco."

Harris nodded at the anticipated subject.

"Glad you brought him up. I understand he has a questionable reputation that makes some men uncomfortable."

"He is a quick-tempered man. Unafraid to act on his emotions."

Harris displayed an intense interest in the topic. "That is also one of his strengths," he said. "Especially when engaged with the enemy. Are you talking about the campfire incident?"

"Yes, sir."

"I have heard of this event for years. I am curious. What is your point of view?"

Matt turned pensive. He remembered the event as if it had just occurred. "Well, I saw the entire episode unfold. The quickness of his knife would have to be seen to be believed."

"Was he not taunted?"

"Yes sir, he most certainly was. The soldier was drunk and way out of line. I would not defend the soldier's actions. If a man plays with a snake, he deserves to git bitten. What I'm sayin' is Antonio spilled the man's guts out onto the ground. One quick slash with his knife. Like I said, it would have to be seen to be believed. It ruined a productive expedition and destroyed morale among the men. The soldier took a while to die. The sight of his insides fallin' out on the ground will be one I'll never forgit. We didn't accomplish anything else on that trip. We were all glad to git home."

"I have heard a lot of different tales about this incident and I appreciate yours as the truth. Destroying morale is a disaster I will not allow to happen. These men are handpicked. Not a one is a drunk or a man known to bully others. I will allow Antonio is a quiet sort. Hard to comprehend. He carries an intimidating presence. On the positive side, he is a tracker second to none. He is as stealthy as an Apache and an expert with his bow, as well as his knife. Those attributes provide us with a surreptitious offensive weapon. He can also rustle us up fresh meat without firing a shot. That alone could be the difference between success and failure. He is as much an Indian as our foe.

He understands their culture and intentions better than any white man. In my opinion, his skills outweigh any social deficiency he possesses."

Matt thought over the captain's position and agreed with his analysis. "Your points are well made."

"Any problems with him can be dealt with at your discretion." He paused and looked at Matt. "Any further concerns?"

Matt could not think of any other potential problems. Harris saw the situation clearly. He seemed to be a leader to take decisive, positive action. Satisfied for now, Matt said, "That clears up my main doubts."

Harris motioned for the other men to join them on the ridge. They gathered behind Matt within hearing distance and listened to the captain explain his plans for the evening.

"We are going to push on until a little after dark. Nate knows of a nice little spring up the trail that is well sheltered. Small fires for coffee will be all right. Lush grass for our beds and feed for the horses. Should be a comfortable night. Might be the last one for a while."

Turning to Matt, he smiled and added, "Pays to have two good scouts. What one doesn't know, the other one will."

The small band of Rangers fell into a column clattering off the rock-strewn ridge, riding single file, following an ancient trail used by the native people for decades. A somber gray shadow of dusk covered the hillside they descended with muted color that slowly blended the details of woods and meadow into obscure features.

The diffused light of day's end ushered in the start of the hunt by the feral predators scattered throughout the desolate lands of the vast hill country. A horned owl perched deep within the recesses of a splintered hackberry hooted three times to announce his stirring hunger. Cougars emerged on distant ridgelines, stretching their muscles, stiff from afternoon slumber. They coolly surveyed the clearings beneath them, where deer timidly browsed in an ever-vigilant state of awareness.

The whitetails' large brown eyes scanned the woodland edge for menace, and their sensitive nostrils worked to detect the odor of encroaching danger. Their ears turned backwards to detect threats from their blind side. Tails flicked as they nervously browsed under the dense canopy of oaks. The whitetails developed a keen sense of alarm and bolted in a flash at any slight disturbance of their environment.

The challenge to the cats was great, but an equally keen sense of patience allowed them to wait for that rare moment of opportunity to arrive. When the time came, the muscular cats pounced on the unsuspecting deer and seized them by the throat. No amount of struggle could deliver escape from their strong grasp. Death descended and the blood of the vulnerable slowly ebbed into the soil. The land showed neither concern nor remorse.

TEN

Black Owl possessed the patience of a cougar. From careful and extended observation, he learned the skills of all the predators, ranging from the rolling hills to the high plains that his tribe of Penateka Comanche called home. Each predator practiced a particular style that offered a valuable lesson to a young warrior learning to take his place in the society of The People. He watched mountain lions remain frozen for any length of time necessary to accomplish their task of concealment until the correct moment for ambush arrived. Stealth served the cats well, and he learned valuable lessons from countless time spent in observation of their successful stalks.

He sat motionless behind the thick screen of underbrush, viewing all that was important on the Ellis ranch spread before him. He watched the activities around the white man's strange dwelling, confident of their ignorance of his presence. Concealment was his strategy. Patience was his ally.

He thought back to his youth, when he spent hour after hour learning from his grandfather the variety of skills practiced by the animals he admired most. The great black bears of the hills used their brute strength to provide a living. They dug out rotten tree trunks to dine on fat, juicy grubs. Foraging far and wide, they subsisted on any easy meal they could find. Welcomed into their diet were berries, bulbs, and a small rodent occasionally discovered when digging for roots. Finding a decaying buffalo meant a feast they would preside over for days, guarding with a vengeance against interlopers. From the bear, he learned to make use of whatever was available. Grandfather made the point that an empty stomach dictated compromise on taste. Wisdom he fully understood from frequent hunger.

Black Owl had learned cooperation in the hunt from tactics used by the wolf packs that stalked the roaming herds of buffalo. Wolves used coordinated pack efforts to pressure their intended prey into a mistake or wear them down through relentless pursuit. Each individual performed a key role to bring the selected quarry to the ground. Black Owl considered the wolf hunt a wondrous event to watch and recollected a pack that singled out a shaggy old bull at the edge of the cross-oak timberlands. They had nipped and bit at the old bull's hindquarters to separate him from the security of the herd, which stampeded away from the menace of the prowling pack. The wolves worried the aged beast constantly until it stumbled across a prairie dog hole and fell in a dusty cloud of confusion.

The bull had staggered to his feet with the black alpha male clinging to his hind leg. Blood poured from the fresh gash across his hindquarter. Rolling his eyes in panic, he lurched around in a tight circle only to find more wolves covering every possibility of escape. Shaking his mighty head in defiance, he slung spittle across the enclosing pack.

In Black Owl's memory, the savageness of the final attack was a thing of beauty, admirable and worthy of copying. The emboldened wolves, sensing victory, had come at the defenseless beast from all angles, snarling and ripping with vicious sharp fangs. Overwhelmed and bleeding out, the old bull disappeared under the onslaught of the pack leaping upon him when he tumbled to the ground. Disemboweled, he succumbed to their combined strength, and the pack gorged on exposed intestines while the old bull gasped for his last breath. The power of domination over another living creature continued to inspire Black Owl to this very moment.

While he crouched in the brush, patiently waiting for a mistake by the pale-skinned intruders, he found time for reflection on the recent disaster that had befallen his small band of warriors. Unlike the wolves exercising sound tactics, his group of three had split up, despite his counsel that it was unwise to do so. Walks Alone led the raid at the time, and he suffered from a weakness for the food found in the wickiup white men maintained separate from their large wooden tipi. The food definitely filled a need and was flavored with an unusual but good taste.

Black Owl remembered counseling that the risk was far too great on that fog-shrouded night. There was not time to do the proper scouting, but

Walks Alone ignored the peril the raid was sure to present. He insisted on performing the task alone. It was his raiding party, and as leader, he made the decisions. He sought the main glory to carry back to the village. As his name suggested, he disappeared down the hill alone and left Bear Claw to wait with Black Owl on the desolate ridgetop huddled together, where they discussed the other options.

The option that seemed to provide the greatest glory was the intended raid on the place where only women dwelt. The three of them had scouted the area and found no sign of white men present. The women were outside in the open on a regular basis, offering strong temptations for easy plunder and the potential satisfaction of glory. Opportunity to rape was foremost on their minds for the pleasure they received from the act and the humiliation the women would forever bear. In this way, they also achieved a higher level of degradation over the lives of the white men that occupied the land that was formerly theirs. Visions of women bound and powerless submitting to their sexual dominance created an urgency for Walks Alone to be quick. They warned him to return as fast as possible from his ill-advised raid for food.

Bear Claw was in the middle of explaining his anticipation of the stalk on the women when they had heard a gunshot explode in the stillness of the night. The coming cascade of bad medicine started at the moment Walks Alone received the severe wound from the white man hiding like a snake. The men with hairy faces had followed them relentlessly all day and never allowed them the time needed to escape. The inability to travel fast with one of their party so severely wounded had severe consequences for all three of them. Walks Alone's weak power continued to haunt them, and Bear Claw had died trying to protect him from the advancing white men. They had not conducted themselves as wolves on the hunt, resulting in lost lives and the pall of disgrace to bring back to The People.

Black Owl recalled his flight from the white man with the rapidly firing weapon that sent angry hornets buzzing past his head from such a long range. Exploding bark near him provided evidence of the fury and power the hornets possessed. He had been forced to abandon his dying brothers, Bear Claw and Walks Alone. The shame he felt was deep. Disgrace prevented him from a rendezvous with one of the widely scattered bands conducting their own raids across the thinly settled lands of the hill country.

It was hard to understand, but the pale eyes failed to follow him out into the wild uplands above the river. After a long, dejected night alone, he had decided to adopt the methods of the cougar. Using stealth, he easily back-tracked and shadowed the men returning to their dwellings. He dared not tangle with their shooting sticks again but verified their return to the scene of Walks Alone's ambush. He decided not to linger near that area of potent bad medicine.

Instead, he sat here in the woods patiently waiting for a favorable moment at the place where only women dwelt. To make matters difficult and oppor-tunities fewer, he discovered men now to be present at the place where wom-en dwelt. One, a younger man, carried a shooting stick. The other, older man, presented himself one time for a short walk where his weakness was easy to identify. He moved slowly with uneasiness. This man was vulnerable and offered an advantage for a warrior with patience to exploit. The young one with the weapon was potentially dangerous and to be avoided if possible.

The women no longer presented an easy target. The oldest female with hair the color of autumn grass always carried a hand weapon that had more range than an arrow and spoke loudly with deadliness. He was disappointed in the lost chance for conquest over the frail white women, but revenge and the honor of a scalp were higher achievements to bring back to the village.

Waiting undetected in the woods, he saw all the strange activities the white men engaged in, and he knew the time would eventually arrive to launch a surprise attack and restore his lost pride. He had to practice the pa-tience of a cougar. He identified his intended quarry and considered the risks involved to increase his odds for success. Stealth, combined with patience, was required for his victory. The spirits that he prayed to would deliver the right moment for him to reclaim his honor. Of this, he was certain.

The sun set slowly below the sharp-edged horizon to usher in the twilight. Pale gray light illuminated the final moments of the cool fall evening. Small wrens hopped about the tangle of branches, searching for their last meal. They dislodged small fragments of bark that fell upon Black Owl's immobile form, crouched comfortably against an old hackberry tree. Leaves rustled softly as cardinals scratched through the litter of the forest floor, seeking one last meal before darkness clamped down to end the day. One dull-colored female fed aggressively within inches of his feet, completely unaware of his presence, confirming that he had melded into the concealment of the brush. He willed his body to merge into the clutter of limbs and become one with his surroundings, both in the spiritual and physical sense. The only movement came from his dark eyes as he scanned the cabin and corrals, praying for deliverance of an encounter with the weak white man before darkness fully descended.

A burst of conversation punctuated by laughter erupted from inside the wooden tipi walls. He delighted in the settlers' ignorance of his presence, safely secreted inside their territory. A smile spread across his coal-black face, painted to aid in his concealment and to represent the dour mood residing in his heart. He knew if the pale men were to see him, the sight of his face transformed in such a wicked manner would instill fear in their souls before he sent them to the spirit world. Their succumbing to horror would give him a memorable sight that he could tell and retell around the campfire long after the satisfaction of spilling their blood had passed. His smile quickly faded, replaced by the grim determination to carry out his murderous deed. His bow lay within easy reach on his lap, and a deadly bone-handled knife was secure in its buffalo-hide sheath strapped to his side. Time was an ally for one with the patience of a cat.

The sun had sunk below the horizon for ten minutes when he saw the door swing open. The slow older man with dark hair emerged. His family followed behind him onto the porch, engaged in conversation Black Owl could not hear. He did see the elder man pointing to the yard and then to the corral shed near the position where he waited beneath the hackberry. After a few minutes of discussion, the woman with long golden hair that ignited his lust ducked back inside with the two youngest girls.

That left the oldest of the girls with the two men outside. Black Owl felt anticipation rise with the hope a mistake would happen that he could use to his advantage. He watched as the weakened man stepped off the porch and made hand motions sweeping at the odd birds in front of the cabin. The colorful birds did not fly but shuffled in front of him. Slowly, but deliberately, the three of them walked behind the strange birds and coaxed them toward an enclosure made of materials similar to the white man's tipi. Black Owl took notice of the details.

He noticed the younger of the two men was too young to have warrior experience that he should fear. His face was still rounded, with no hair or hard lines that older white warriors acquired. This confirmed his inexperience in Black Owl's mind. Hair on the face was a strange custom these intruders were fond of and The People found disdainful. Comanche women thought it laughable that men would grow hair in such unusual places. This particular youth also seemed distracted by the young girl beside him. They kept up a laughing conversation as they followed behind the ambling, dark-haired man. The boy, carelessly, was not paying attention to his surroundings.

She too was distracted and didn't notice any details beyond the birds at her feet and her obviously interested male companion. Slowly, the three of them made their way closer to his concealed position, unaware of their state of peril. He began to entertain thoughts about the young squaw. She resembled the older squaw that went back inside, although less endowed in mature feminine qualities. But her movements swayed her hips in a way suggesting she was a squaw capable of satisfying a brave's unquenchable thirst for dominance. She was a young trophy any Comanche warrior would be proud to boast of taking. He prayed to the spirits for a sweeping victory over the two males to allow time to enjoy her attributes. A full conquest over these pale intruders would help eliminate the shame of needlessly losing his two brothers. With every step closer, his anticipation took on a fevered pitch, testing his endurance. He readied his bow in slow, undetectable movements.

Black Owl watched the older white man lead the two young ones in his direction, seemingly content in his simple task of herding the clucking birds. What kind of man was this paleface that only appeared at odd times, and only for a moment? This male displayed no warrior traits and deserved the fate that awaited him. All three arriving at once presented complications. Putting an arrow into one would be no problem, except the other two would scatter and make the following kills more difficult. Killing all three would probably not be possible and would surely be a high risk not worth taking, considering his solitude deep in dangerous lands. Having his way with the young squaw appeared unlikely, although he strongly desired the chance to force her to his will. He also had to remember that noise could bring the longhaired squaw with her hand weapon that could bite from a distance. She was a danger beyond his control, and he could not act until the odds were in his favor.

On they came, at a sluggish, torturous pace, until they finally reached the strange wooden enclosure with wire strung across the front. Here they all paused while the two younger ones coaxed the birds inside the shelter. He had observed this custom before at other locations of settlement and admired the cunningness of white men to secure their live food source from predators in such a manner. The white men deserved to be feared for their intelligence and the use of their powerful magic to make war. The sticks that roared with thunder struck many times over when compared to his short-range arrows. He vowed to acquire a weapon such as the one carried by the young man. Perhaps he could obtain that very weapon if the spirits were willing.

After watching the whites for close to two days, this was as close as he had been to them. He was close enough he could smell their peculiar odor, which resembled the pungency of burned wood dampened with moisture. His pulse quickened at his proximity to the men. Their threat was genuine, and he struggled to maintain a calm demeanor so near to impending death. He could hear the conversation in their strange tongue but understood none of its meaning. It was at this time that the spirits delivered a gift to him as the two youths turned and started walking back to their cabin. They held hands and were lost in their youthful dreams.

His selected prey was finally within reach, separated and alone in his vulnerability, unconscious of the danger lurking out of sight. Focused on the dark-haired paleface, Black Owl noticed the large white streak in the man's hair on his right scalp. This unusual marking would make a good source of conversation when hanging from his lodge pole. The odd man continued past the birds now secured in their pen and drifted along the cedar-railed fence that led to the back of the corral. He was heading towards two scrawny cows feeding at the far end. The area that was closest to Black Owl.

Black Owl prepared for the turning of his medicine. The spirits were guiding this moment in time to deliver answers to his pleadings. The disappointment of not collecting the squaw dissipated with this chance to spill blood from his mortal enemy. The man paused at the fence, lost in a dreamy faraway look directed out beyond the backside of the corral. He leaned against the top railing and turned his back to Black Owl, less than thirty feet away, crouched motionless in the mottled patterns of brush and limbs covered in murky shadows.

Black Owl seized this moment of the white man's inattention to bring his bow gently into position while at the same time quietly notching an arrow. Stealthily, he rose on stiff limbs to draw the arrow back fully to achieve maximum power. He steadied his aim through a gap in the brush as he acquired his target. At that precise moment, an owl cut loose with a long melancholic call that echoed hauntingly through the woods. His guiding spirit had spoken! The paleface turned slightly to his right to search for the owl's location hidden high in the treetops in the closing dusk.

Sighting down the arrow, Black Owl saw the unexpected movement of the paleface and released the arrow on its way. Its feathered shaft flew on a straight path with the speed and accuracy of a diving falcon. Clearing the entanglement of brush, the arrow closed the distance to its target in a blur of lethal speed.

Frank never had a chance to find the owl as he turned and exposed his side. A dreadful thump sounded with the impact of the arrow as it drove between his ribs, through both of his lungs, and partially exited out his left rib cage. The momentum of the iron-tipped shaft knocked him off balance and sent him stumbling into the fence.

He grabbed the upper rail for support and inadvertently drove the extended arrow tip into the bark of the rail as he wobbled unsteadily on his feet. Pain seared his body with scorching white heat that blinded his vision. His eyes rolled backwards in wild astonishment. He wanted to scream out in agony, but his punctured lungs were absent of air as they began to fill with blood. His left arm caught a hold on the top fence rail. The exposed arrow point dug into the wood and peeled back dried bark until it broke free. It slipped below the railing, releasing the pressure on the shaft. He too slid roughly down between the middle and bottom rail. A pink froth gurgled between his lips, spilled onto his neck, and ran down onto his chest hair, collecting in a wet mat. Gasping at the pain, he came to rest forced against the knotted bottom rail with his left arm caught at an unnatural angle extended above his shoulders.

Slumping in his weakened, powerless condition, his sight came back to him, along with the realization he was a dead man. He looked at the arrow's feathers soaked in blood flowing freely down the finely crafted chokecherry shaft. Frank summoned his remaining energy and raised his eyes in time to view the Comanche approaching him in a smug, stalking saunter.

Looking into the impassive black eyes, he saw no compassion, only a cold, distant gaze of angry vengeance. Frank made out the movements as the black-faced devil reached for his knife and took a knee beside him. Struggling, with his world growing darker, Frank felt the Indian grab his hair in his hands and then violently jerk his head backwards.

The knife blade flashed in front of his eyes, followed by the feel of the steel blade slicing a cut around his scalp to the back of his neck. Blood flowed over his eyes. His vision blurred in a warm descending curtain of red oblivion. He heard his scalp pop loudly when a vicious jerk yanked it free to expose his bare skull. A final and intolerable rush of pain overwhelmed his failing senses. Frank collapsed into darkness. He bent at the waist and fell face first into the rock-littered dirt. His eyes remained open and fixed, staring without comprehension into the mysterious void of death.

Black Owl held the scalp high above his head, admiring the hard-earned prize dripping blood down his forearm. A sense of triumph swelled in his chest as he broke his stoic silence with a deep guttural war cry. Startled doves flushed in flight as dark silhouettes across the faint orange glow on the horizon. The exultation he felt could no longer be contained. He let out another shrill cry of victory while shaking the loose hair he clutched in his fist. He glanced toward the house to see the boy and girl looking on, frozen in silent shock. The girl cupped her hand over her mouth and commenced with a long wail of anguish.

The door of the cabin flew open behind them. Black Owl could see the startled expression on the older, light-haired squaw. Her radiant beauty was replaced with the shock of abject horror as her shouts of panic shook the young white man from inaction.

Black Owl saw him raise his shooting stick and point it in his direction. He quickly dashed into the brush to put obstacles between him and the young white brave. A thunderous report exploded as the boy let his long stick snarl. A second boom quickly followed the first. Fragments of branches shattered around him. But Black Owl escaped injury as he ducked and weaved behind the tangled screen of brush. As fleet as a deer, he was behind the trunks of massive trees and deep into the protection of the dusky woods, leaving no trace of the direction of his escape.

Darkness was falling quickly, but he knew the way back to his pony, securely tethered far back in the extensive woodland. His heart pounded with pride at his redemptive murder and well-planned escape. The white boy would never be able to locate him. Black Owl would be miles away from any other white men when dawn broke. The scalp with the white streak would be proof that the deaths of Walks Alone and Bear Claw stood avenged. Most importantly, his personal status would be restored and secure among the elders and fellow tribesmen when he returned to their camp high on the grass-covered plains.

ELEVEN

Matt rolled over onto his back and rubbed his eyes clear of the fog of sleep. He pulled his old blanket up snug against his neck, tucking it tight between his shoulders and the saddle he used as a pillow. Overnight, the air had cooled and settled to the ground, crisp, with a sharp bite to it. Heavy dew accumulated along with the cooler air, making him appreciate the added protection of his rain slicker spread over his bedroll.

Looking up into the expansive blanket of stars above him, an old feeling of insignificance welled up inside with the staggering scope of the heavens stretching from horizon to horizon. Blue pinpoints of lustrous starlight danced in a twinkling display of immense beauty that he suffered to understand. At this time of year, he made out the shape of the Orion constellation with his long sword trailing behind as he marched across the fall sky. Matt marked Orion's path each time he awoke all night long, which was often. Orion was nearing the western horizon and Matt knew the advanced position of the constellation signaled the start of a new day, with no clouds or thick fog to contend with. The camp would soon begin to stir.

He made out the presence of other men in camp from the low snoring mixed in with the sound of tossing and turning. A camp full of men scattered across the ground made a surprising amount of racket. He knew that Hunter and J.B. were out of sight while they did guard duty. The picket line of horses occasionally stomped the ground when they shifted their weight. Low nickering verified the stock was content. All was normal in the camp and the sounds reassured Matt as he slowly began to shake out the cobwebs of poor sleep.

Robert Brown had sacked out next to Matt the night before and he noticed Matt's movements.

He asked Matt, "Sleep well?"

"Hell no. Never do out here on this hard-ass ground."

"Me neither. I'm not like those young bucks. I lost count of how many rocks been pokin' me all night. Don't know where they come from. They weren't there right at first."

"You're just too sensitive."

Robert snorted, "Gittin' too old for lyin' on the ground. Miss my bed."

"Sure is early in the trip to be complainin'."

"Not complainin'. Just statin' facts. Ground ain't gittin' no softer, the older I git."

Matt stretched out his legs to acquire some circulation in the tight muscles. Too much trailside camping had the same effect on him, although he tried to never admit it to anyone.

"Facts are, we got a lot more of this comin' up and not as comfortable as this area."

"Sure do," Robert responded while suppressing a yawn.

"Speaking of beddin' down, did you happen to see where Antonio bunked down at?"

"Nope. Didn't pay it no mind."

"I did. He bunked down over next to the horses. He crawled up into the thickest clump of brush he could find and cleared out an area to bed down. You'd never see him if you didn't know he was there. I've never seen a man do that before."

"Some might say he ain't all man," Robert said. "Seems a little strange, but you reckon maybe he's just smarter than us?"

Matt sat up and faced Robert to reply, "I never thought of him as smart. Least ways not people smart. Animal smart, hell yeah. Smart as a fox."

Robert shared his opinion, "Out here it takes both kinds. He certainly is people smart when it comes to Indians. More than me, and I could use a little of his animal instincts too."

"You're probably right. I shouldn't sell him short. Strange as I find him, he does have the tools."

"Yes, he does."

Matt made out the dim profile of Tom moving about on the opposite side of camp. Soon he would have a small fire going to brew coffee while he fried up some bacon for a quick breakfast. He was the designated cook with proven abilities to put together passable meals in the trying conditions they were sure to encounter. The men understood that hot meals could be few and far between. Tom's skills this first morning out guaranteed that his companions appreciated his presence.

Robert spoke in a low tone meant to be in confidence, "Matt, what do you think our chances are to bring those kids back?"

Matt thought it over and didn't like the answer, but there it was. Facts are facts and his voice reflected the truth. "Fair to none. Closer to none. Them Comanch aren't goin' to let us have 'em back. Sorry as it is. They'd just as soon kill them kids first. Just to keep 'em from us. Usually the best chance to git a hostage back is to wait and trade for 'em somewhere down the road. Comanche like to git paid for their captives. Comancheros sometimes can git 'em back for us up on the high plains. Trouble is, by then, they're ruined. "

"I think you got it pegged." Robert shook his head, letting out a long sigh. "Won't please the powers back in Austin if we come home empty-handed. That's the only reason we're out here. Those kids are related to the governor. He pulled the strings to git the money for our outfit. Didn't trust the regular cavalry or foot soldiers to do the job. Can't blame him on that. Their performance has been pretty dismal here of late. And he looked the other way, considerin' a few of us served the South. Some of them boys in office don't like it that independent-minded men will be organized under Harris."

"So, they are worried our small band is goin' to turn on 'em?" Matt chuckled.

"Guess so. Those boys in Austin don't have a real backbone. Man to man is too much for most of 'em. They like hidin' behind the law and the big shield it gives 'em."

"They ought to come out here to deal with some real problems. Deal with the Comanche. Deal with men like Antonio. And some of my neighbors that would love to give them a piece of their mind and a stick up aside the head to boot."

"Won't ever happen with their kind. They will not leave the comforts of city life."

Tom had the fire stoked up and the bacon sizzling in the grease. A battered and blackened coffee pot sat over the glowing coals, sending the stimulating aroma drifting over the men crawling out of restless sleep. Captain Harris was up, completely dressed and ready for action. He made his way through the darkened camp and knelt beside Matt.

He inquired, "You men ready for the day?"

Matt and Robert grumbled their affirmative answer as they threw their blankets to the side.

"I figured as much. Is this temperature not invigorating? There is nothing like a cool fall morning to make a man ready for a day in the saddle. This will probably be the last hot breakfast for a while. Soon as it is light enough, we will head out. It will be a slow pace at first. At least until the direction of the trail is firmly established. There is a difference of opinion between the scouts on the correct headings. Nate thinks the trail will head due west. Antonio, northwest. They are leaving early and we will rendezvous with them near the Pedernales crossing sometime around midday. As soon as we get their intelligence and determine a definite direction to pursue, we will pick up the pace. I intend to never relent until the Comanche are overtaken and defeated, and the kids are safely delivered into our hands."

Matt spoke up at this point, full of doubt. "Captain, we were just talkin' about this bein' one hard task that's been laid out for us. Those kids are in a precarious position. Comanche aren't known for compassion."

Harris reflected on Matt's observation. Mulling it over, he frowned in response before he said, "That may be the case. But we have to remain positive and seize any opportunity for success in our mission. The sooner we have the Comanche in sight, the less chance they have to inflict any further terror on those children. As it stands, the Comanche control the situation. The sooner we reach them, the sooner we can correct the problem. "

He paused a little longer this time. His expression turned blank, as if disturbed by abstract thoughts. An awkward silence replaced the discussion. Matt gave Robert a puzzled glance as they both wondered what the captain had on his mind.

Harris suddenly snapped back into form and stood abruptly. Clearing his throat, he said, "With God's help, the children will survive their ordeal. Prayer is advisable, if you are of such a mind. Please excuse me, gentlemen.

I have to attend to the pickets."

He turned to march off to relieve the guards in his typical military precision. He wasted no motion in his movement or his analysis. His thought process mirrored the preciseness with which he strived to conduct his affairs.

Robert confided to Matt as he watched the captain fade into the morning darkness. "He'll make a helluva politician."

"Think so?"

"Without a doubt. He is always calculatin'. Told me he plans to run for office as soon as it's possible. This little expedition is a chance for some positive news articles about his abilities."

Matt's cheeks puffed under his eyes as his nose scrunched up. He appeared as if he smelled a skunk.

"I didn't think he operated that way."

"He does now. He's tired of the poor treatment us Texans have been gittin' at the hands of a few of the Yanks and other men of low character. Plans on gittin' elected to have at 'em in the capitol. He's an able man. Seems to have good intentions. If he wants to use this chance for political gain, it's for good reason."

"Might be so, but I hope he's not blinded to the reality of life out here. He may have been in town too long. These hills got their own ways. Indians got their own ways too. That's my worries."

"That's why he wanted you, Matt. He knows where he is weak. We done talked it all over in town. I came in for some supplies and he stopped me right as I passed his office. Picked me right on the spot. Said he needed my experience. Then he told me was he wanted you next. Told me he would git you too. He's an able man. I have faith in him."

Matt finished rolling up his bedroll and organizing his gear. Other men around the camp were engaged in the same activities. A few were returning from their early morning routine carried on outside the camp shrouded in the predawn darkness. The treeline above the men cut a jagged black edge across the sky filled with the cold blue diamond sparkle of starlight. Matt was enjoying the presence of the men under the raw beauty of the night sky when a bright meteorite plummeted across his field of view in a downward streak of dazzling brilliance. The accelerating velocity of the falling star caused it to break apart into two diverging but equally brilliant paths shimmering with silver sparkles that faded to black as quickly as they appeared.

Matt gasped at the sight of such an unusual occurrence.

"Robert! Did you see that?"

"Sure did! Quite a sight!"

"Never seen one split up before."

"Me neither. Heard tell of it, but never seen it."

A pensive mood struck Matt as he thought on the marvel of natural occurrences and man's inability to understand the forces surrounding him. He felt insignificant staring into the vastness of the night sky.

"Makes you wonder, don't it?" Matt said. "Sometimes I think the most important sign comes from above. Yes, I'll follow the Cap, and I'll do what needs doing. But I'll keep my faith in the good Lord above who supplies us with so many mysteries. And down here I'll put my trust in my Henry. It manages to solve many of my problems."

"Amen to that," Robert agreed.

Matt hoisted his saddle off the ground to move nearer to the inviting fire and fresh coffee. Robert followed his lead. Close companionship with like-minded Rangers would get the day started right.

The men shared a generous portion of sizzling bacon served up with hardtack, washed down by a steaming cup of coffee strong enough to bring life back to a dead man. Camp spirits ran high as the men mounted up after the hot breakfast. They were ready to ride as the sun began to peek over the horizon.

<<<<< • >>>>>

Nate and Antonio preceded the movement of the main camp to begin their individual search for fresh sign. Each scout believed in his own abilities, but both formed different opinions on the likely direction of the kidnapping Indians. They split apart to go their own way shortly after leaving the comfortable camp. Nate followed his hunch and headed west to a trail he had confidence in. Antonio took a route to the northwest that was a more direct path to where the Pedernales flowed between steep limestone cliffs.

Behind the scouts, the Rangers moved at an unhurried pace further into the little-known and harsh lands of the deeply carved Pedernales drainage. Haste was unnecessary until the scouts confirmed the route of the Indian raiders. Matt naturally assumed his place at the head of the column beside the captain. Charles Mossberg followed close behind them on his chestnut mare in his role as corporal and third in command. He was a competent and able-bodied frontiersman experienced in fighting Indians since his arrival from Kentucky fifteen years before. Behind him, the other men trailed out loosely, with the packhorses bringing up the rear of the column. The care of the extra stock was in the hands of Sam Anderson. He was a stoutly built man possessed of a playful, joking manner that belied his fighting abilities. He was the best horse wrangler and barroom brawler that Matt knew of.

The column crested the top of a high ridge a few miles from camp when Captain Harris signaled a halt. Matt stood in his stirrups, surveying the hills and valleys rolling into the distance and looking for signs of Indians. Harris pulled out his monocular to employ it in his search for a clue to lead the way. The land lay still and unyielding of information. The enormity of the territory suppressed any optimism of success in overtaking Indians born and raised to prosper in such an inhospitable environment. A lonely chorus of howls drifted across the hilltop, answered faintly by a single howl from miles away.

Harris said, "You hear that coyote?"

Matt cleared his throat and spit into a thick bed of cactus. "Not coyotes, Cap."

Harris sat silent, listening for more howls. The hills remained deadly silent.

"Wolves?"

"Yep. More lonesome soundin' than coyotes. A little deeper howl. They mean business."

"Been a while since I heard a wolf."

"Oh, you've been hearin' wolves. But they been the two-legged kind. They talk the same language as you, but they're a hell of a lot more danger-ous than these out here."

"Can't argue there. Some men in Austin will look you right in the eyes. Shake your hand to take your measure. And then knife you in the back if they smell weakness or opportunity."

Matt sat back down in the saddle, nodding his head in agreement with the facts of town life. Since the end of the war, life in Austin revolved around what the corrupt leaders dictated.

"Out here, Captain, danger don't walk up, shake your hand, ask how do you do? Out here, bad news smacks you unexpected up aside the head. Grabs your throat. Chokes the life out of ya. All the while lookin' you in the eye just to let you know it owns you. There ain't a damn thing you can do about it. Just like them wolves out there. Once they got you, you best wish for it to end soon. That's just the way it is."

He spat another load on the cactus and turned back to the captain to judge his reaction.

Harris was staring at Matt with a stern expression on his face.

"I have not forgotten the realities of Indian fighting."

"Didn't say you did."

"Are you doubting I am up to the task?"

"Captain, I ain't doubtin' nobody. But the truth of the matter is, I won't know if I'm up to the task myself until the time arrives. Too many variables in Indians. They got their own rules, and them rules sure don't match ours. I've seen stuff would shake up any man."

"Matt, try not to be so bleak."

"Just tellin' it how it is."

"Perhaps so, but I prefer to stay on the positive side with action over doubt."

"Only way to operate, Captain."

"Good then. Glad we are in agreement."

Matt eyed Harris. The shadow of Matt's hat concealed his cold assessing gaze taking the captain's measure.

Harris rotated in his saddle, a little exasperated with Matt. He checked on the men behind him. They were not in hearing distance of the unusual verbal exchange.

Satisfied with the column's position, he asked Matt, "You see anything of interest out there besides a couple of wolves howling?"

"No, sir. Not a thing."

Matt scanned the cut-up landscape one more time and said, "I'm afraid we won't see Indians 'til they're ready for us to see 'em. That's always the worry about trailin' the Comanch."

"That's why we have Antonio and Nate."

"True. If we git on a good trail, we might can force the issue on them bastards."

"Let's not waste more time here. We will head toward the rendezvous point above the Pedernales. Hopefully, one of the scouts will have hard sign to follow."

He turned to face his command and bellowed in an authoritarian voice, "Move it out!

TWELVE

Bull sat tall in his saddle, casting a long shadow on the ridge over-looking the Ellis place. He hesitated on the high spot, staring down at the cabin while soaking up the warmth of the morning sun on his back. The heat penetrated his sore old muscles, momentarily helping him forget the consequence of too many years spent in the unforgiving Texas hill country. His youngest son, Jake, tagged along to assist him in checking on his neighbors' welfare. Bull made it a habit to ride the circle of ranches bordering his place on a regular basis to keep up on the news and offer assistance if so requested. It was a custom he'd developed to help ward off boredom.

Something about the appearance of the ranch below troubled him. There was nothing he could put a finger on, just a bad feeling rising in his gut. Something below them was out of sorts. He knew Frank was still recovering from the fall that had delivered a hard blow to his head. But Bull felt a strong hunch in his gut that something more than a head injury was amiss down at the Ellis place.

"You thinkin' what I'm thinkin'?"

"What's that, Pa?" Jake answered.

"Somethin's wrong down there. Don't seem to be no activity. No chickens about. No smoke from the chimney. Place seems dead. Don't feel right."

Jake took notice that his father was right. He removed his Sharps carbine from its scabbard and peered up and down the valley. He turned in the saddle and verified the rear was clear. They were both vulnerable out in the open if trouble was near.

"You may be right. Somethin' seems different. But then again, them cows are still in the corral. Could be a good sign. Horses back behind them trees. Probably wouldn't be there if Injuns had their way."

"Maybe so, but I hope they ain't seen bad times."

Bull thought of Mary and the passion she ignited in any man half alive. She also had the older daughter who was following in her footsteps. Damn Injun would be glad to get his hands on them and do a lot of harm. The thought of what he might find made Bull's blood run cold. Comanche were known for their brutal way of working women over, and he'd seen the results more than once. He remembered the women he'd seen that survived a Comanche encounter. Their lives were a living nightmare after the savages mutilated them and scarred their former beauty. The terror the women lived through found permanent residence in their tortured souls that never healed. They would be better off dead, but the Comanche preferred to leave survivors at times. It was a special way to torment the white men.

Bull readied the beat-up Henry that he carried when on horseback. He worked his dapple gray off the lip of the ridge, down the well-used rocky trail.

Jake gave his father time to separate and put distance between them before he followed down the trail. He kept a sharp lookout for trouble potentially lurking in the nearby grove of woods. Reaching the bottom of the hill with no sign of danger, he pulled up alongside Bull.

"Jake, it's too quiet down here. Somethin' ain't right. I'm afraid they all dead. Hopefully, they just hidin' out somewheres else."

Jake nodded his head in agreement and said, "Let's git within hollerin' distance of the house."

Approaching the house, they shied away from the treeline that sheltered a heavy growth of underbrush. There was no sense getting close to places of concealment.

Bull halted his horse in the open yard and hailed in his deep voice, "Hello in the house!"

The front door burst open with a slam. Travis led the way out in a rush with Sarah on his heels. He ran up to Bull and started babbling too rapidly to make any sense to the old man.

Mary stepped out onto the porch with Becky and Carol clinging to her waist. She wore the strain of grief on her face. Sarah was no help explaining as the tears flooded her eyes and she choked up in deep convulsive sobs.

Bull put his rifle back in the scabbard and swung his leg over the saddle. His boots hit the ground hard and he let out a groan as his bones protested the hasty dismount. He grabbed Travis by the shoulder with a firm hand.

"Boy, slow down. I cain't hardly understand a word you're sayin'."

Travis inhaled an extended breath to compose himself.

"Mister Johnston, I did what he said to do. I was told to go back. I did what he said to do. I went back. I didn't know!"

"Didn't know what, boy?"

Travis appeared sick to Bull. His eyes bulged with excitement. He was struggling to control his rapid breathing. No words came from his mouth. He looked gut shot.

Johnston repeated, "Didn't know what, boy?"

Jake had dismounted. He thoroughly scanned the area surrounding the yard before he made his way up to the porch, trailing his horse. He cradled his rifle in his arms at the ready.

Travis managed to stutter, "I ... I didn't know he. He ... was in the woods. I didn't see him."

The last words fell quietly from his lips as he relived the events in his mind, head turned away in shame.

"Who was in the woods?"

Travis snapped back to face Bull with fire in his eyes.

He shouted his answer with anger, "Indian! No good, damn Indian."

Sarah cried harder at the mention of the Indian. Bull pulled her close to him in a strong embrace. Her tears rolled down her cheek in torrents and he felt their wet warmth spread across his skin.

"So you seen a Injun in the woods. Y'all seem fine to me. 'Cept." He paused, scanning them all. "Frank. Where's Frank at?"

Sarah bawled like a lost lamb. She was drowning in her grief.

Bull noticed the tears streaming down Mary's cheeks. The girls buried their faces in their mother's dress.

Travis's face transformed into a countenance full of spite and hatred. The muscles in his arms hardened. He clenched his fists.

"The Indian killed him!" He spit it out with vile bitterness. "He's gone. The no good bastard shot him with an arrow. He never stood no chance."

Bull realized his worst fears were true.

Travis cried with rage and frustration, "I'm gonna kill ever last damn Indian I see from here on out."

He screamed his last words at Bull. "I'll kill 'em all, every one of 'em! I tell you, I will!"

His face contorted in the pain of guilt. He looked past Bull to the end of the corrals, wanting a chance to bring Frank back.

Bull understood the guilt the boy suffered. There was little he could do to assuage the damage done to Travis. The entire family needed attention and it was hard to determine where to begin. He saw Jake was up on the porch standing next to Mary. She was sitting in a rocker with her arms wrapped around her daughters, sobbing.

Bull felt the sadness creep in upon him. Crying females everywhere and little he could do to remedy the loss. He felt helpless to repair the raw, grieving wounds this family now suffered. That was something they had to do on their own, with the help of time. He remembered plenty of frontier families that never recovered and never healed.

It was essential to know more, and he asked Travis, "What happened to the Injun?"

"I shot at him." Travis replayed the event once more in his mind. Dejected, with his head hanging low, he mumbled, "I missed."

"There was only one?"

"All I saw."

"Which way'd he head out?"

"In the woods is all I know. He was out at the end of the corral. Almost dark when he shot Frank."

Bull glanced in the direction Travis pointed. He marked it as an area that needed studying after tending to the dire necessities now facing them.

He told Sarah, "Come on darlin'. Let's go see your ma."

They turned in unison and he tenderly escorted her up the porch steps where Mary sat, watching them. She had regained control of her emotions and stood to embrace Sarah.

Looking over Sarah's shoulder, Mary said, "Bull, I am so glad you came. We need help bad."

"Mary, I'm just sorry I wasn't here sooner. I come too late."

She turned to him and he embraced her in a gentle hug conveying his sympathy for her loss. She held his embrace longer than he anticipated. He felt the circumstance was weighing her down with a burden crushing her will to go on. She finally pulled away from him, her expression full of bewilderment.

"Sweet Mary, I'm so sorry 'bout Frank."

Her head slumped and she gasped, "What am I to do? We are lost without him. What will all of this come to mean?"

Bull already knew the answer to the precarious situation she found herself in, but this was not the time to discuss her alternatives. From past experiences, he knew how the future would most likely play out. Silence was his best option at this time.

She began weeping again and fell against his chest for support. He felt her fragile body heaving against him in mournful sobs while the two younger daughters stood and wrapped their arms around their mother. Sarah sat in a chair with Travis dropping a comforting arm across her shoulders. Jake remained to the side of them all, unsure what to do in the presence of so much anguish. They all stayed in one spot for what seemed like an eternity to Bull.

Eventually, the need for contact passed and Mary found a chair to take a seat. Gathering her wits, she instructed the girls to tend to the Johnstons' mounts. The girls seemed eager to do something constructive that took them away from the grief of the house. Without hesitation, the three of them grabbed the horses' reins and led them to a watering trough. They gathered oats and hand fed them. Travis remained behind in order to hear the adults' decisions but went to the edge of the porch to keep a close eye on the girls. The shotgun was in his hands when he decided it was best to follow them out into the yard.

With the porch cleared of young ears, Bull said, "Mary, I hate to bring it up, but where's Frank?"

She heard the question that seemed to come from someone far away. She took a moment to form a response but eventually said, "We brought him inside. I could not stand the thought of leaving him outside all night. He's inside. Covered up."

Bull peeked inside the partially open cabin door. Frank was lying rigid on the floor. His boots stuck out from under the old blanket Mary had placed over him. A pool of dried blood gathered around the edge of the blanket near his head. Bull glanced back outside at Mary, who was watching him.

He held his hat in his hand when he approached her and asked in a low voice full of sympathy, "Mary, do you have any preferences on what to do next?"

She looked at Bull with eyes aged in years since he had last seen her. Her hauntingly beautiful blue eyes were now recessed in their sockets, bloodshot red. Wrinkles creased across her once smooth complexion. He realized in that moment, she would never be the same woman again. Her vitality seemed to pool and drain between the cracks in the porch, right before his very eyes.

"They scalped him! Why did they have to do that? Why Bull, why? That will never leave my mind. I'll never forget the sight of him!"

Anger boiled inside Bull. He hated the damn Indians.

In a defeated and crumbling voice, she said, "We are ruined. Can't do it alone. Can't pay taxes. I'm alone with three kids to raise."

She brushed past Bull and wandered into the yard, haunted by her memories. She stood alone, gazing up to the ridgetop where the well-used trail started its descent to her formerly secure home. She was numb with grief and confusion. Her back turned to her home and the recent life her family used to share. She was gone from a world she no longer understood and could never return to.

THIRTEEN

The column of Rangers moved north by northwest across the broken hill country terrain at a moderate pace. They were careful not to push ahead of the scouting effort in front of their advancement. A faint trail led them over the highlands, lush in waving fields of grass that reached the bellies of their horses. Bee Creek dissected the rolling hills, and the men gladly stopped along its banks to water the horses and refill their canteens. The creek flowed crystal clear across a limestone bed littered with bulky chalk-covered boulders that broke the shallow current into separate thin streams. Several men dipped their hands into the cool water to drink directly from the creek. They used a refreshing splash to remove the trail dust that covered their faces. The horses lapped at the water greedily.

After the brief watering, the column ascended through the thick bee-brush lining the creek to resume a steady march over the higher land that afforded better views. From the trail that followed the undulating ridgeline, they could see thirty miles away to the dim violet horizon blending as one with the sky full of a dusty blue haze.

The sun was nearing its zenith when the Pedernales River breaks started taking shape with sheer gray cliffs jutting upwards just below the horizon. Matt was contemplating the upcoming river crossing when he saw a rider approaching the column off to his right. He notified the captain of the rider and Harris slowed the men down to a halt.

"I believe that's Antonio coming our way," Matt said.

Harris stood in the stirrups for a better view.

"You are correct. I hope he bears good news."

Antonio rode up, relaxed and at ease on his coal-black pony. He bowed his back, absorbing the punishment of the trail with no ill effects. Every rocking, jarring motion passed through his body back into the horse in a fluid movement, uniting them in purpose. Matt marveled at the unusual combination of man and horse blending together until they seemed as one.

The half-breed pulled his pony up to the captain close enough that their horses' muzzles came in contact. Antonio spoke to them in his mixed tongue.

"I knows the dirección."

Harris puffed out his chest with the news.

"Excellent! What do you have?"

"Followed the trail long ways. Pony tracks the same in Austin. Dirección, the rock."

"The rock?" Captain Harris was confused.

Matt understood Antonio and said, "He's talkin' about the big granite mountain northwest of here. It's an area full of huge granite domes."

Harris nodded his head and replied, "Oh yes, I remember hearing about the area. It is supposed to be an area of important spiritual significance to the Comanche. They seek visions and perform spiritual dances there. I also have been told they sacrifice lives there, but I'm not sure if it's myth or fact."

"I'm not sure about the sacrifice part, but I wouldn't put it past 'em. I do know they believe the largest rock in the area is the home of spirits. The Comanche are in awe of the power comin' from the rock."

"Superstitious devils." Harris seemed amused at the primitive concept.

"Fact is, they may not be wrong. I've heard firsthand reports from white men 'bout the rock groaning with unusual noise. Don't happen often, but when it does, the sound seems to spill out of its guts. They said the noise they heard was like nothin' in the real world. Imagine a beast in your wildest nightmare, growlin' his most horrible growl. That's the rock when it's in the mood for the spirits to speak."

"That talk is nonsense!"

Matt let his gaze fall to the ground.

"Well, I've not heard it. Neither have you Cap, but that don't mean it ain't so."

"True enough, but I do not believe in fables or tall tales. Indians are prone to superstitious beliefs, and I can imagine their fears getting the best of them. But white men? What say you, Antonio?"

Antonio turned his focus to Harris with the cold black eyes of a reptile hiding his intentions. He gave nothing away. The large brim of his hat deepened his brown complexion in dark shadow. His tobacco-stained teeth shown as he smiled.

He said, "Sí. Mucho spirit. They real. Un día. You see. You regret doubts, no? You regret you no ready. Who know, you see today?"

Harris wore a blank look.

Antonio shrugged his shoulders and said, "Maybe tonight, eh?" A slight chuckle escaped under his breath as he eyed the man he considered inexperienced about life's mysteries.

Captain Harris listened, at a loss for words. An uncomfortable silence fell across the three of them. Antonio grinned like he knew things they did not.

Matt made a comment to relieve the tension. "Captain, this talk don't make no matter. We ain't here to convert the heathen or change opinions. It don't matter if spirits are real or how many there are. Antonio, how fresh is the sign them Comanch left behind?"

"Muy fresh. No pushin' hard. Possible, no afraid."

Harris was indignant at Antonio's taunting replies. His voice betrayed his patience wearing thin as he growled, "If that is the case, we can oblige them. They will regret not hurrying. We can catch them before they do more harm to the children. Perhaps it's time to shove off."

Matt shook his head in disagreement.

"Cap, let's wait for Nate and his report. He may have valuable information. We'll catch them Comanch in due time. He should be along directly. He's generally punctual."

Harris thought it over for a moment and agreed. He called for a temporary break. The men didn't hesitate to dismount and take advantage of the free time. Water flushed down the dry jerky they chewed on. A few rolled a fresh smoke while seated on the massive trunk of a live oak that had toppled to the ground long ago. Horses grazed contentedly on the ample grass available far away from the gluttonous stock of the settlements. The men appreciated the unexpected break in the pursuit after the long hours in the saddle. Sam offered a lively anecdote that created a flicker of laughter among the men within hearing distance of his off-color remarks.

Matt and Harris, separated from the men, missed the entertaining story-telling Sam was known for. He frequently kept the men amused with tall tales full of rough frontier humor.

The shared responsibility of command kept Matt alienated from some of the camaraderie shared by the younger men while on the trail. He took turns scanning the countryside with the monocular Harris brought with him, intent to find any bit of knowledge to help their cause. Time spent enjoying the company of the men was secondary to leading them to a satisfactory conclusion of their mission. Antonio retreated down the hill in the direction he had trailed in from. He now reclined in rest on a barren spot of soil, using a smooth rock as a pillow. Matt returned the glass to Harris and retrieved a chunk of pemmican from his bag before taking a seat on a nearby charred stump.

Chewing on the tasty pemmican prepared by Cora gave Matt time to think on the situation at hand. He felt confident about Antonio's report. The reclusive half-breed exhibited a strange set of habits, but he possessed intangible abilities. Matt understood that the scout was more Indian than the rest of them. He firmly believed this fact allowed Antonio to better divine the ways of the redskins they were after. Antonio presented a surly confidence that he knew the most likely direction the Comanche would follow. The more Matt considered the problem, the more comfortable he became about heeding the advice the scout offered. He soon grew restless to take up the trail but resisted the powerful urge to take action without all the intelligence required for a proper decision. They still needed Nate's report to avoid heading off in the wrong direction.

Harris started to pace with his own nervous energy. Matt immediately noticed his impatience and tested the captain with an offer.

"We can go ahead and leave now. Let Nate catch up. Our sign would be easy for him to follow."

Harris stopped in his tracks to think over the suggestion.

He said, "No, let's give him a few more minutes. You were right, he may have good information."

"He may indeed. But I been thinkin'. Antonio's report will be hard to beat."

Harris didn't reply as he went back to glassing the extensive area spread out before the small collection of Rangers. With his sight restricted to the narrow field of view the glass offered, he missed the approaching rider ascending from a draw to the west. Matt saw the lone horseman galloping their way and at a distance made him out to be Nate.

"Captain, here comes Nate."

Returning his looking glass to its case, Harris sneered, "About time. I was ready to ride on. This waiting game was getting the best of me. I hope he has something to make the wait worthwhile."

Nate spurred his horse and swiftly closed the distance. He reined to a stop with his mount prancing sideways, quivering with excess enthusiasm. Nate mimicked his horse with a vitality he could not contain.

"Sorry I'm late, but I've got some great news. Found all kinds of sign. Be easy to follow."

Harris responded in his most official officer's tone. "Apology accepted. Carry on with your report."

"Followed a trail that headed a little west from here until another group of ponies joined up with 'em from the southwest. Make it out to be three or four of 'em joined up with the group we been trailin'. Trail will be easy to follow. I suggest we make haste and git on their ass."

Harris turned with a raised eyebrow and questioned Matt, "We have a bit of a dilemma. What do you think?"

Matt ran the options through his head. At other times, this second trail would have been a good thing. In this circumstance, the second option only muddied the water. The hostage kids depended on correct analysis about the direction to proceed. Trouble might brew between the scouts over the decision he felt the most confident in. This turning point could rest on his intuition honed from years of experience.

"Captain, we best take the trail Antonio scouted. No offense to you, Nate. You done a good job. But Antonio seemed mighty sure of them Comanches' intentions."

Nate didn't hesitate to raise his voice in objection. "Cap, I got good sign and plenty of it. Cain't be ignored! Several bands joined together. I'm sure of it! We cain't let 'em git away."

Harris was hesitant about his decision. The success or failure of the mission rode with ascertaining the correct direction to follow. The final decision was his alone to make. He motioned for Matt to accompany him as he moved away from the men. All of the other men were now standing to watch the conversation between the scout and their leaders. Their meals and canteens sat ignored as they waited for a verdict to end the uncertainty.

Making it to the lip of a nearby ledge, Harris stopped and faced away from the men.

"Matt, I am inclined to go with Nate. His confidence is contagious. He offers a hot trail full of more Indians."

"Yes, he does. But is it the one the kids are on? Best think on it."

"Antonio says he knows where they are headed. To this rock full of spirits! How would he know? What does he base this belief on? Why couldn't the children be on the trail Nate scouted? Antonio has no proof!"

"No, he doesn't, except he says the pony tracks are the same as the ones from Austin. Nate don't have positive proof either. The fact that Indians joined up from a different direction don't mean squat to us. We just want the kids, not more Indians to fight. I go with Antonio."

The stress of the situation bore down on Harris. He studied the rocks at his feet. He took a deep breath, held it, and then puffed his cheeks out as he exhaled with an indecisive sigh. The wrong decision could doom the entire mission. He stammered with indecision. "Blanco! You! You get up here."

Antonio slowly rose to his feet and pushed his hat back on his head. In his unhurried, deliberate way, he made the climb up to where Harris stood with Matt.

"Antonio, how are you so certain the kids are with the group you identified?"

"Pony tracks tell."

"You can be so sure just from the tracks? You can read them that well?"

"Sí. Tracks from Austin."

Harris removed his hat to wipe the sweat from his brow. He held the hat in his hand and gazed up to the clear blue sky. Buzzards circled high above him, black shapes gliding on the imperceptible rising currents of warm air. They rose and fell with the thermals in irregular, shifting formations. From their heights, they carried on an endless search for subsistence, creating patterns high in the sky that meandered in their hunt for the life that death delivered. He watched the hypnotizing flight for a moment before replacing his hat and facing Matt.

"Pony tracks from the raid near Austin do not guarantee the children are still on those ponies. Nate has found stronger sign. We have two options. One, we split up and follow both trails. Two, we all follow Nate's trail."

Matt could smell the uncertainty emanating from the captain. He detected the battle Harris dealt with in exercising his power to decide. Two young lives hung in the balance.

Matt could not remain silent. "Captain, we have a third choice, but first things first. We can't split up, in my opinion. That would leave us too thin, operating in a country full of who knows how many Indians."

He let Harris think on it a little before finishing his take on the situation. "Antonio knows these Indians and how they operate. He's certain his trail holds the group with the kids, and he knows where they're headed. We can increase our pace of pursuit if we know where they're going. Captain, we got to risk it. He has the best sign. We have to go with Antonio."

Harris didn't seem convinced. The consternation on his face was evident.

Matt didn't speak while the captain continued thinking the situation over. Seeing the futility of time wasting, Matt offered a compromise to Harris. "I'll take the blame if I'm wrong."

Harris stood rigid, gaze locked in a steel glare on Matt as he spoke. His eyes were full of intensity as Matt's opinion rebutted his analysis. He bit on his bottom lip after Matt finished his statement. Silently, he contemplated the options once again as he looked down at his dust-covered boots. Taking a moment to run the angles, he made his final decision.

"Mount up men! We are heading out. Antonio, lead the way!"

The men scrambled to get ready and gathered up the loose gear, busily securing things for the anticipated pace of the pursuit. Good-natured bantering punctuated their activity now that they were to pursue a definite course of action.

Nate remained seated on his horse with a look of shock overtaking him. He muttered to nobody in particular. "I'll be damned. We're goin' to follow that damned half-breed and leave good sign unchecked. I'm a son of a bitch. I cain't believe it!"

The men rapidly formed up in column. Harris moved them out to follow behind Antonio, despite Nate's complaints. Still grumbling under his breath, Nate fell in alongside the formation, determined not to breathe dust after his advice fell on deaf ears. A hurried pace evolved as Harris pushed the riders. The caution and restraint used up to this point in the pursuit disappeared.

They were free to ride as fast as the trail dictated. A sense of urgency drove them to close the distance, now that they possessed a clear direction laid out by their enigmatic scout. Matt bore in on the tail of Antonio's pony, pushing him to maintain the momentum, now that a degree of optimism carried the men's thoughts. Sweat began to lather the horses' sides in the exertion they expended.

<<<<< • >>>>>

Miles of the faint trail receded in the expanse behind the hard-riding column before Antonio slowed to a stop at the edge of a bluff overlooking the Pedernales crossing. Matt rode up beside him and together they viewed the deep canyon the river had cut through the pale gray bluffs of limestone. Irregular-shaped boulders the size of small cabins littered the banks of the river and made passage difficult, except at this narrow location. Glistening like a string of aquamarine pearls, the water collected in pools along the canyon bottom between massive cypress trees cloaked in burnt orange leaves. A trail showing signs of recent use descended to their left in a natural break of the bluffs outlining the gorge like ancient walls of a fortress.

Captain Harris joined them and after a quick survey of the area determined there was no sign of Indians present. But he wanted verification. He ordered Nate to the front to accompany Antonio down the trail to scout for hidden trouble at the crossing. This was the spot where the men would be the most vulnerable. A scowl formed on Nate's face, but he held his tongue in check and followed Antonio, who was already disappearing around the first switchback.

The two scouts cautiously approached the shallow river crossing, with Nate holding back while Antonio took the lead. They scanned the brush on both sides of the river thoroughly. Nate eased up to Antonio's position after assessing the situation to his satisfaction. A moment's pause and Antonio splashed across to the opposite shore while Nate turned his observation to the wooded bluffs above the crossing. Antonio hesitated at the riverbank before urging his pony up onto the dirt shoulder above the shallow riffles at the crossing. Nate quickly joined him and they both scrambled into the brush, hiding them from the view of the men watching above with keen interest. A few minutes passed before Nate reemerged at the crossing to give the all-clear signal. Harris waved the men to follow and they began their descent to the sound of loose rocks clattering down the trail.

Nate waited until Harris reached the riverbank and he held his hand up to stop him. He said, "Captain, why don't you wait here while me and the Mexican go check out them bluff tops. You never know, they could be waitin' somewhere up there to jump us."

"Good idea, Nate. We will take the opportunity to water the horses. Who knows where the next good water will be."

Nate reined around and spurred his horse up the trail to join Antonio, where he scouted out of sight. The men spread out to water their thirsty mounts eager to muzzle the cool water flowing shallow over the rounded river rocks.

"He seems to have overcome his disappointments," Harris remarked to Matt.

"Can't be sure, but I think he's man enough to overcome most setbacks. No room for friction out here. With your permission, I'll scout ahead a little myself."

Harris touched the brim of his hat.

"Be my guest. Keep an eye out."

Matt spurred Whiskey up over the bank. The two scouts carried out their duties ahead of him in an efficient manner until they verified the absence of ambush. Matt held back to let them do their jobs until the top of the bluffs came into view. From a clear area above a sharp drop-off, Antonio gave the signal to bring the men up the trail. He then wheeled his pony around and kept his head down, searching for clues, leaving Nate alone with Matt. Nate watched him ride away, unable to hide his feelings of disgust over the situation.

Matt said, "Don't let it git to you too much, Nate."

"Hell Matt, I ain't never had to share duty before. People call on me to scout sign, and they always go with what I say. It's what I do. Ain't used to bein' second-guessed."

"Well, it's the captain's show. And Antonio has some qualities that are hard to define. He understands the Comanch better than any of us."

"Could be, but I don't gotta like it. Do I?"

"No, you don't."

"Was some damned good trail back there. Dad would've loved to track a trail that fresh! I hope y'all are right 'bout this. There'll be hell to pay if we're wastin' our time out chasin' a dead end."

"You're right 'bout that Nate. And I don't doubt your convictions. You saw what you saw. We didn't. But choices have to be made and we'll have to live with the results. Good or bad. Hopefully, we made the right decision. Time will tell."

"I guess you're right. Time will tell a lot of things, come soon."

He had a worried frown on his face that Matt knew had nothing to do with wounded pride.

"What's on your mind, son?"

Nate shook his head in resignation.

"This here will probably be my last ride in these parts."

"How's that?" Matt asked, although he suspected he already knew the answer.

Nate was slow to respond. "I don't like to talk 'bout it, but we're in a jam at home. Pa done said we most likely will be movin' out come spring. Says the land 'round here don't interest him much no more. Says he has a fancy to see California. Or maybe Colorado. Anywhere it ain't so settled."

"Don't look settled out here where we're at, does it?"

"No, but it's still Texas, and Texas ain't treatin' us so well here lately. He wants all us kids to pull up stakes and go with him and Ma when he decides. We all got no choice. If we stay, there'll be a killin' or two. Law will be all over us, and we cain't fight all of 'em. We got no money. Really ain't got no choice."

His gaze wandered over the distant hills that faded away into a smoky haze. A heavy cloud of regret darkened his face.

"When I'm done out here with this little chore, I most likely gotta head back to make ready to pull up roots."

"Damn sorry to hear bad news, Nate. Maybe it don't gotta be."

Matt knew it was a distinct possibility he could lose the company of his best neighbors, but he held out hope for a different ending.

"Appreciate that, Matt. But you're not as sorry as me. You know what worries me most right now is the old man will lose patience and kill one of the bastards trying to steal our land. I asked him not to pull the trigger, but you know how ornery he can git."

Matt didn't respond, but he did know how Bull could be. He was a true Texan who had made a good life out of these inhospitable hills. No Yankee or thieving scum deserved to rob decent, honest folks of their life's blood. These interlopers moved among the original settlers like a disease spreading sickness, infecting all that made contact with them. The injustice of the situation ate at Matt and produced an angst that festered in his gut and made him anxious for vengeance.

As he steamed at the thought of his neighbors' plight, he heard the rapid approach of the column cresting the ridge. Harris burst out of the brush upon Nate and Matt, full of energy and pomp.

"The crossing slowed us down a little, but let's catch up with Antonio. This trail is fresh!"

Nate glared at Harris with a flash of irritation in his eyes. He harshly spurred his horse to action, leading the way to the trail Antonio had long since disappeared down. Harris chose to ignore the display that Nate put on and urged his responsive paint to lunge after the departing scout. Matt fell in behind the captain, and the rest of the men were swift to fall into line. Sam brought up the rear, with the packhorses under his able control.

FOURTEEN

Mile after mile of hard rocky trail led the small band of Rangers deeper into the wilderness, further from the comforts of home and loved ones. Matt once again gave thanks for the easy gait Whiskey possessed. Some of the other mounts were beating the men into submission with their hammering pace taking its toll on them. Whiskey's superb conditioning and ease of riding gave Matt the edge over the lesser-mounted men, but he worried about the effect of the grueling ride on them as fighters. Would the men be able to perform if conflict broke out unexpectedly?

This gathering of men was untested and the mettle of these individuals collected together as a fighting group remained uncertain in his mind. He had witnessed tragedy from men thrown together, fatigued and unproven in their role as a unit in combat. Those past disasters occurred during the rough times of blue versus gray. His current challenge was to see to the successful performance of these untried men under pressure against the barbaric tactics of Indians. If they were to overtake the far-ranging Comanche, it was sure to be in a state of fatigue. But this was a risk they would have to accept.

Countless brush-choked ravines alternated with barren hills receding behind them as the day wore thin. Blessed with a pleasant fall day, the men also enjoyed a comfortable breeze that helped them avoid the punishment of heat straight from hell, like a typical Texas summer day. The autumn sun painted the landscape in radiant light as it sank near the western horizon. Matt admired the qualities of the warm glow reflecting off the passing wild country. If not for the grim circumstances, this trip could be enjoyable. He entertained the fantasy of a time in the future when he could hunt and camp in this area with his companions unconcerned about the presence of marauding Indians.

Less than an hour of daylight remained when Matt first made out the top of a huge sycamore rising out of the confluence of two shallow draws. The dead tree stood alone, devoid of leaves, extending bone-white limbs skyward like the hand of a skeleton stretching out of the gully, searching for salvation from the heavens. Approaching nearer to the tree, Matt could see the fire-blackened trunk protruding out of the rock-filled ravine the tree had taken root in. At the base of the trunk, he detected Antonio, dismounted and peering intently at the ground. Nate stood next to Antonio and glanced up to see the approaching Rangers. He quickly mounted his high-spirited dun and spurred away from the dead sycamore. He appeared to be in a terrible hurry to close the distance and headed straight for Matt.

Nate reached the column in a heightened state of agitation and ordered the men to stop while the dun pranced beneath him. Harris obliged Nate and held his hand up to call the men to a halt.

"What is the meaning of this?" he demanded of Nate.

Nate watched Matt as he answered the captain. "Bad sight under the tree up yonder. Just wanted to warn you beforehand."

Matt could see the revulsion on Nate's face and asked him sternly, "What is it, Nate?"

Nate shook his head. Looking away from Matt, he said, "It ain't good."

Fearing the worse, Matt growled, "What ain't good?"

Summoning his courage and ignoring the other men, Nate turned to meet Matt's intense stare. He spoke directly to him, "Don't go up there, Matt. Stay here and let us take care of it."

Matt started Whiskey forward, but Nate blocked his path with a sudden movement.

"Matt! I'm tellin' ya! Don't go up there. You don't need to see what's up there!"

Matt wheeled Whiskey aggressively, bumping chests with Nate's horse in a loud thump. The dun neighed deeply and reared up, throwing Nate off balance, forcing him to grapple for control. Matt seized the opening and thundered past Nate on his floundering mount.

Regaining control, Nate snapped at Harris, "He don't need to see what's up there!"

Antonio moved to block Matt's view when he reined Whiskey to a stop in a shower of rocks. But he was unable to prevent Matt from getting another full dose of the reality of Indian culture. The scene shocked Matt's senses like a direct strike of lighting. Behind Antonio, Matt made out the naked body of the Havens boy, covered in lacerations darkened with dried blood and crawling with flies. His body was a ghostly white, robbed of his child-hood spirit. His thin, narrow shoulders reminded Matt of the boy's lack of power. He never stood a chance against his heartless captors. Tossed aside like a worthless object, he now laid contorted and stiff on the hard ground beneath the ancient sycamore, far from his family. His innocent life had ended in extreme cruelty at the hands of a renegade band of savage men that placed no value on life, save their own.

Matt felt the familiar rage building inside his chest. His vision narrowed and voices became muffled as if he had dropped into a hole in the ground. He vaulted from the saddle and stood looking down at the pitiful sight of a young life wasted. His mind played on the images of terror the powerless child must have endured. A rising flood of anger flushed his face as emotion overcame his senses. Images of his arrow-riddled son reemerged as fresh as if the Comanche had murdered him just this morning.

He picked up a large fallen limb and swung it in a powerful arc against the charred skin of the sycamore trunk. An explosion of bark flew away from the vicious impact. Fragments of wood rattled out into the surrounding brush. Left holding the jagged remnants of the limb in his hand, numb with reverberations from the swing, he bellowed, "Sorry bastards! Damn them all to hell!"

The men were stunned at the fury that had overtaken Matt and turned him into a spectacle of seething hatred. He stalked beyond the lonesome sycamore, his back to the men as he stared out into the western sky, lost in an overwhelming frustration mingled with the grinding presence of fresh grief.

Nobody uttered a word. There was nothing left to say. They all under-stood Matt's sentiments. Harris dismounted and slowly made his way over to Matt and placed a comforting hand on his shoulder. Matt remained oblivi-ous to comforting, lost in his personal remorse, alienated from all men.

Nate whispered to Robert, "I tried to warn him. He didn't have to see it. I knew his feelings would be raw. I tried to stop him."

Robert's voice was full of sad regret, "You did your best, Nate. Nobody's ever stopped him from doin' what he wants. Some part of him needs to be reminded of his loss, I guess. Keeps his anger fueled. He wants things back that will never be, and he don't want to forgit it."

Nate watched as Harris attempted to console Matt. It was no use. Matt stalked away to stand with his back to the men, alone.

Sliding out of the saddle, Robert said under his breath, "Looks like we got a burial to do."

The men gathered around the pitiful sight and Sam produced a shovel to dig a shallow grave in the thin, rocky soil. Robert tenderly wrapped the boy in an old wool blanket while the grave was prepared. Nate assisted Sam in lowering the boy to a shallow and isolated resting place, absent his family's love. The rest of the men collected large rocks to pile over the low-mounded soil in a manner that protected the body from prowling wolves. Robert retrieved his bible to read Psalm 23 over the grave of eight-year-old Gary Havens. Matt remained detached from the depressing ceremony on the far side of the sycamore, burning in his private hell. The rest of the men gathered around the gravesite and concluded their brief service with a recital in unison of The Lord's Prayer. Matt stepped out from behind the tree to join them in time for the last few lines.

After the final amen, he abruptly mounted Whiskey and declared, "There's still some light left! Now, let's go git the little girl and punish the red devils that done this!"

FIFTEEN

Bull sat outside on the porch along with Mary in her rocker, silent beside him. He was hard pressed to remember the last time a day seemed so long. Attempting to restore order to the day after the shock of finding Frank lying dead in the cabin extracted a heavy toll. He guided Mary in as gentle a fashion as possible to make the fateful decisions now facing her. They both reached an agreement that Frank needed burial as soon as possible. He was loaded into the wagon and hauled down to the creek bottom, where the black soil was deep and loose. Mary chose a site beneath a huge pecan that Frank was fond of. He had spent many hours beneath the tree in happier times hunting, or just harvesting the abundant fall crop of nuts.

Travis joined Jake in digging the grave to a suitable depth. The hard work covered them both in rich black dirt that stuck to their sweat-stained bodies. When the depth of the grave reached their chests, the soil became hardened with large rocks, impeding their progress. Bull deemed the depth of the hole appropriate and the men assisted Mary to wrap Frank for burial in the best quilt the family owned.

Mary gathered her daughters under her arms while Bull said a few words of heartfelt prayer over his neighbor's body. The stillness of the creek bottom crept over the small gathering after Bull concluded the brief ceremony. It was as if the woods were silently listening.

Using a web of ropes, the men gently lowered Frank down into his dark, damp, eternal resting place. His daughters started a mournful wail as the first shovel of dirt fell with a muffled thump into the black cavity of the grave. The brutal finality of their father's death became too heavy a burden for their youthful innocence to bear. Mary gathered the kids up and ushered them away from the torment of watching their father's burial.

Bull joined her back at the wagon, where he immediately noticed the dramatic change in her demeanor. Her tears were gone. She transformed into a rock, her jaw locked in grim determination. Soft blue eyes became as cold as winter ice. Her mind, caught up in turmoil, hardened the very moment he climbed up onto the seat beside her.

<<<<< • >>>>>

Now they sat on the porch in the last waning hour of the day. Mary had spoken little during the return to the cabin. She invited him out onto the porch to talk in confidence away from the children. Travis sat with the girls huddled together inside the cabin. They were devastated and lost in confusion with the first death of a close loved one. Travis was offering them the best comfort he was capable of and doing an adequate job, considering the burden of guilt weighing him down. Jake was patrolling the area behind the cabin on horseback.

Out on the porch, Mary broke the silence with a plea for Bull to accompany her on a short walk. Bull grabbed his rifle and followed her off the porch, stepping into the dusty yard. She wandered ahead of him while he pondered what thoughts were troubling her the most as she ambled along.

She stopped at the chicken coop and glared out into the woods. Anger flared across her face. She then looked down towards the far end of the corral, where Frank had fallen to the arrow.

She asked Bull, "Do you mind?"

"No Mary. Do what you need."

She continued on along the fence rails until she got to the bloodstained spot that marked Frank's last struggles. Bull kept his eyes on the woods that closed in on them near the corral. He never trusted the Indians and there was no reason the Comanche might not be lurking in the tangled mass of tree and brush. Jake had thoroughly scouted the area and found no sign to follow. In Bull's mind, the lack of sign meant the Comanche that murdered Frank was a skilled warrior. A foe requiring respect for the damage he was capable of inflicting. Leaning against the fence, Bull faced the woods, just in case.

Mary gazed out into the corral at her poor collection of cows.

"Bull, I appreciate what you and Jake have done for us today."

He looked down at the blackened bloodstain on the ground. Frank had been alive at this time yesterday. It was a depressing thing to contemplate. The damn Indians had a way that made you hate them.

"Wouldn't have it any other way," he answered.

"I needed to come out here, one last time. Won't ever see him again. This spot is as close as I'll ever get to him being alive."

Bull didn't know what to say. He had felt the sting of loss many times in his life and understood her grief. It was a hard thing for him to do, but he realized it was best to remain silent.

She placed her clasped hands on top of the fence post and rested her cheek on them, gazing back towards the cabin.

"The girls are going to miss him something awful. Life without their dad will be so hard for them."

She fought down her emotions, just stating the facts. Her voice was somber and she was using Bull as a sounding board.

Bull just listened. Sometimes all a person needed was a friend to lend an ear.

"You know, Bull. Seems most times I was displeased with Frank."

She paused, thinking.

"I guess most women feel that way about their men at some point or another. I feel ashamed now. But the truth is I never wanted to come out to these hills. It's just too damned hard to make a living out here. All of this," she waved her arms above the fence rail, "it was his dream, not mine. I just went along. We fought over it, but that was so long ago. It's hard to remember those early times and what we went through. He had his heart set on it. Said he wanted to be his own man. I didn't want this life, but I came to understand how much it meant to him. So, I gave in. It meant everything to him."

Bull nodded in agreement. He had been there. His wife felt the same way when they had come out here so many years ago. They were the first to settle this far out. Times had been very hard, stuffed full of wild events, but she had settled in and didn't regret a day now. Something told him a woman like Mary didn't feel the same way. There was too much city in her.

"Now he's gone. He isn't coming back. Gonna take some getting use to. Going to be very lonely, here on out."

She stepped in closer and hugged the fence post.

"We're done out here." The words came out heavy. She looked wistfully out across the land to the hillside on the far side of the corral, now deep in shadow. Tears rolled down her cheek.

"Bull, I can't make it out here alone. Frank took care of things. I'll need a man to run the place, now that he's gone. A good man would be the only way I could stay here at the ranch. But if I got the man I want, it would cause a breakup among our neighbors. I can't let that happen, and if I stay, it will happen."

She let her comment have time to sink in. Bull was not exactly sure what she was alluding to, but he had a good enough idea of the underlying subject to agree with her.

"We all seen 'nough problems already, Mary. No need to add to other people's troubles."

"Humph! That does it then. This place can go to dust, for all I care. Let the taxman have it. I don't have the money unless I sell everything I own. Even that wouldn't be enough to please them, so what is the point? Frank is gone and I'm beat. I don't want it anymore."

She grew morose while she thought it over. Her eyes settled on the horizon, where the sun had already disappeared, setting the sky on fire in a deep red glow that she used to enjoy. Today, her state of mind clouded with mourning prevented appreciation. She was lost in another world, the world of the unknown and the uncaring. Her soft complexion blushed in the last warm light of the day. She presented a picture of vulnerability that tugged at Bull's heart.

"Bull, I don't see any way around it. I've got to move back to Austin. I've got kin there. I can find a way to make a living. Teach, or work at the hotel. I can find a way. I have to. It really is my only option. I can sell the stock and some of the other things I don't need anymore. That's where you come in."

"Mary, I will help any way I can. My son can fetch our wagon from home, and between yours and mine, we can haul most all of your necessities. We can drive your stock to Austin. I'll see you git a fair price. What little we git should give you a nest egg to tide you over while you figure things out."

"Thanks, Bull. You are a good friend. The kids won't like it none. This place is all they've ever known."

"They can git used to it. They may like bein' 'round other young uns all the time."

Mary gave Bull a hug and said, "Let's go back in the cabin and I'll break it to the kids tomorrow morning. They've had enough today. If we are lucky, maybe we can leave by tomorrow evening."

SIXTEEN

Harris led the Rangers at a punishing pace until well beyond the last of the good light. A forlorn demeanor permeated the ranks after the hasty burial of the young boy. A child's life lost to violence was hard to comprehend, even for men accustomed to the harsh realities of frontier life. Matt had not uttered two words on the forced ride.

Harris surmised that putting distance between them and the troubling discovery of the Havens boy was the best medicine for the men. Positive action to boost morale was required, in his opinion. Every mile closer to the Indians put them closer to retribution.

Antonio was so sure of the trail they were following that he required only an occasional confirmation of the route. All the sign suggested the Comanche were still bound for the mystical rock surrounded by legends. Harris ordered him to follow the obvious trail until pitch-black darkness made travel impossible and forced him to call for a halt. The men immediately got busy securing their camp located alongside a clear running stream that meandered through bulky blocks of pink granite. Sam, along with Hunter, kept a watchful eye on the fatigued horses turned out to graze the lush grass along the creek.

Some of the other men haggled with each other about swapping out their tired mounts for fresher rides come morning. They tended to their gear and pre-arranged it for quick departure when the time came. All the while, a coarse vein of conversation passed back and forth between the young Rangers.

Matt attended to Whiskey off to the side of the other men. He took his time caring for the horse. Together, they would face the challenges of the upcoming day, and he wanted his companion in the best condition possible. After tethering Whiskey to the picket line, he realized his depleted energy required some rest of his own.

Wandering a short way in the dark, he found a likely spot and dropped on his haunches against a lichen-covered boulder located above camp. A cool drink of water spiked with a healthy shot of whiskey helped him unwind the knots of tension building in his lower back muscles. The extended activity of the last few days was taking its toll.

Harris felt there was no danger of Indians in the vicinity and he allowed Tom to build a small fire for coffee, accompanied by pinto beans. Harris believed the men deserved a comfortable camp with a hot meal, due to the long pounding pace of the day, topped off with the unsettling discovery of the Havens boy. Soon, the men were reclining around the warm pulsating flames of the fire, exchanging tales in a low murmur of voices accented by an occasional subdued laugh.

Robert found Matt beyond the glow of the firelight and inquired, "Is that seat reserved?"

"No, help yourself and pull up a rock. Nothin' but the best in this joint."

Robert tossed his bedroll down and spread it out by kicking it flat with his boots. His joints creaked and cracked as he slowly reclined on the ground blanket.

"Your old bones sound like they got grit in 'em."

Robert grumbled, "Hell, they got gravel in 'em after a day like today. This kinda trail ride brings out the old in you."

"Hate to tell you, but the old is in there, trail or not."

Robert, now seated and spread out comfortably, eyed Matt from a close position.

"I can go sit with Antonio if you're of a mind to insult me."

Matt replied, "Ain't insult. Just fact."

"Well, remember, you're not too far behind."

"Oh, there ain't no doubt about it. No argument here on that point. It's just that I ain't old enough to be cantankerous, like some around here."

"Aw, shut up," Robert admonished Matt as he placed his hands behind his head. He leaned back while peering up at the sky starting to fill with stars. "Man, does this ever feel good! Can't wait for Tom's beans."

Matt followed Robert's lead and stretched his legs out, using a saddlebag for a pillow. He gazed up at the clear night sky sprinkled liberally with pinpoints of flickering blue light. The moon was yet to rise and the black velvet darkness pulsated with stars that appeared to breathe with life. Matt pondered the mysterious vastness of the heavens that always humbled him when he attempted to understand his role in life.

"Ever wonder what's out there?"

Robert laughed softly. "God only knows." Thinking it over, he mused, "Let's put it in perspective from our point of view. There ain't no Indians out there."

"How do you know? Might be more of them up there than down here."

"Can't imagine a higher power allowing them up there."

Matt argued, "He allows 'em down here."

Robert saw the futility of continuing with this line of logic. He deemed it wise to remain silent.

Matt was not willing to give up the conversation.

"Why do you reckon we got to deal with Indians down here? I can't understand them."

Robert realized there was no avoiding the subject. Matt was determined. He took the bait and said, "Man is imperfect. We all do it to each other. Hell Matt, we just fought a war with our blue brothers to the north."

"At least they're civilized."

"Wasn't a civilized war, if you're asking me."

"Most of them blue-bellies didn't wage war on children."

Robert could not argue with the truth of Matt's statement. "Plenty of kids died as a result of their actions," he countered.

"But they didn't do it one on one. Face to face against a harmless child."

Matt was calm as he spoke. Too calm, Robert thought. He appeared to be under the influence of a drug, and not at all the man full of fire that everybody knew.

He asked Matt, "You all right?"

Matt did not hesitate. His voice grew belligerent.

"No I ain't. I seen the last kid I ever want to see dead on account of Indians. I aim to kill every damn Indian that gives me half a chance from this point on. Time has come to even the score."

The changed tone in Matt's voice concerned Robert. He recognized that the hardening of Matt's attitude meant quite a few red men would lose their lives in the near future. Matt never talked just to hear his own voice. He would back it up, with deadly consequences.

They'd both fell silent, lost in their thoughts when Tom announced the coffee was ready. Men scrambled to fill their cups and wash down the dry sausage passed around while the beans boiled. Dark silhouettes moved about the yellow flickering flames of the campfire. Low conversations floated on the cooling night air.

Captain Harris found the pair reclining on their blankets and joined them with two steaming cups of the potent coffee. He extended one cup to Matt.

"Sorry Robert, I only brought one extra cup."

Robert waved him off with thanks. "I'll git mine when the beans are ready."

"What do you gentlemen think? Not a bad spot for camp."

"No, sir," Matt said. "It is fine enough. Be a little better if we was out huntin' deer instead of Comanch. Someday I intend to return to these parts and have a proper hunt for a few trophies. Just have to remove them red vermin first."

Matt gently blew away the vapor curling up from his cup after he finished his observation.

Robert took an interest and said, "Add my name to the party list. This here is mighty fine country. I'd like to trail through these parts again."

"Sounds like a plan to me," Harris said. Contemplating the novelty of the idea, he added, "Until then, we have a lot of work to do. How are you men holding up?"

"I'm doin' fine," Matt lied.

Robert nodded in agreement.

"Good to hear it. The miles were brutal. That I will grant you, but Antonio says we are catching up. And that is what concerns me. The Comanche do not seem to be making much effort to stay out of reach. Do they know something we do not? Or, are they sucking us in on purpose?"

Matt and Robert sat quietly thinking over the captain's observation.

Harris continued, "Usually when they raid, they head out with no chance of us overtaking them. Antonio said at this pace we could be on them by this time tomorrow. Or the next morning at the latest. He remains certain the Indians will be at the rock."

Matt oozed confidence when he replied, "Captain, I think them Comanch don't think we can catch 'em. They done been spoiled by the sloppy work of the regular cavalry boys these last few years. Them yahoos never could catch, much less punish, the war parties that been raidin' down here. It's been a while since them Comanch had to deal with us Rangers. I think them redskins done got lazy. Maybe just overconfident. Or both. Don't really matter which. We catch 'em and they will be reminded us Texans don't fight like those regular cavalry boys."

Harris gave Matt's comments some thought and nodded his head in agreement. "I believe you may have a good point," he said. "It has been a time since I've heard of any raids followed up with any punishment to speak of."

"Hell no, there ain't been! That's my point. It's been way too damn long since a Texas Ranger taught a lesson to them Comanche. That's why they're raidin' all over the damn place! They done got used to things bein' easy, although me and Lee taught a couple of 'em a lesson that put an end to their days."

Matt managed to smirk at his memory of retribution.

"Well, we got a chance to teach them a lesson soon," Harris said. "But it will take some more hard miles of trailing. How is your ride holding up?"

"Whiskey will do whatever I ask."

"How about yours, Robert?"

"She's doin' fine."

"Some of the other mounts are wearing thin already. Glad we have your stock for backup. I believe it will pay dividends tomorrow. We should be able to stay together with no stragglers." Harris turned to face the camp. "Well boys, rest up. We have a lot of action coming up."

He started to make his way to the fire when Matt stopped him.

"Captain, I want the little girl back."

Harris jerked to a stop, caught off guard by Matt's tone of voice.

"We all do, Matt. We all do."

"Killin' Indians is secondary to gittin' the girl back," Matt insisted. "Won't mean nothin' if we don't git her back. Git her back, and then we kill all them bastards we can. But she comes first."

"I'm in agreement, Matt. We will do what it takes."

Disturbed, the captain strolled to the fire, where he was lost to Matt's view in the mixture of men milling about the simmering pot of beans.

Matt downed his coffee in silence, brooding over the loss of the boy. Robert reclined beside him and they both remained quiet as the night wore on, until Tom warned the men to get ready for grub. Together, they made their way to the boiling pot and filled their plates to the brim with pinto beans spiced with slabs of bacon that Tom threw in to sweeten the meal.

Returning to their spots, they dug into their hot plates of beans, soaking up the brown broth with hard tack. Topping the meal off with hot coffee helped ease the toils of the day. A warm sense of contentment settled over the mood of the weary men.

Matt stretched out in a reclining position to take in the entertainment of the night sky streaked with an occasional meteorite. Robert broke into a sad ballad sung with feeling while sharing the expansive view with Matt. His voice was mellow, profound, and full of sorrow. He fashioned a melancholy tale of a relationship gone sour just before the untimely death of a lover. The lyrics of the song tapped into the depths of depression brought on by missed opportunities of reconciliation. The message spoke directly to Matt's troubled state of mind. He became spellbound under the influence of Robert's rich voice spinning an unexpected tale of love and loss out here in the heartless, black wilderness.

Matt wasted no time on sentiment when Robert finished his song.

"Why're you out here, Robert?"

Robert was shocked at the obtrusive question. He finally realized it was just Matt's direct manner and he meant no offense by it.

"Good question."

"I thought it was or I wouldn't of asked it."

"Git to the point, don't you?"

"Don't waste anybody's time that way."

"You want the truth?"

"I ain't much on beatin' around the bush. The truth will do."

Robert ran the reasons through his mind until he realized there was no one reason.

"I'm out here for a lot of reasons."

"Just give me one to git it started."

Robert crunched his lip up into his nose thinking it over.

"I suppose the main reason is I had to git outta the house. The walls were closin' in on me."

"I'm familiar with the feeling. Some would say I got a problem with it."

"So I've heard. When the walls start to close in, it's because a man's got an itch he better scratch. You always have been one that needs the action, the adventure. Me, I just miss my wife. With her gone, I can only take so much of stayin' in the house."

Matt contemplated what life must be like for Robert. Living alone, children all moved out. He asked, "How long she been gone now?"

"She died two years ago, this past September. It sure ain't been the same since. Never will be. It's hard to admit, but life don't mean as much anymore. Oh, I see the kids once and again, but Peggy was the glue that held us all together. She made it all special. Without her ..."

A pained look overcame him. He looked away from Matt before continuing, "Without her, I found out nothin' means that much anymore. Gits mighty lonesome and I miss her as much as ever. Yeah, the walls do close in. Harris came to me, and the chance to git away seemed pretty damn good."

Matt was chewing on a blade of grass and Robert could tell he was pondering the comments he'd made. Matt's face appeared ghostlike in the dim starlight. His dark beard covered his mouth as he worked the grass back and forth between his lips. His eyes focused high in the sky, searching, sad and reflective in the poor light.

"You know what, Robert? I don't know what happens when people die. Can't seem to understand it, hard as I try. It's like a mystery we're not supposed to figure out. I can't help but try, but the meaning always slips away like sand through my hands."

Robert didn't know what to say. This was a side of Matt he had never seen. Matt was troubled and Robert knew only one answer.

"Faith, Matt. Gotta have faith."

Matt laughed softly. "Humph. Faith is hard to hold onto. Kind of like that sand, ain't it?"

"Comes from inside, is all I can tell you. It sustains me when times are tough and I start feelin' low."

"Hard to hold onto faith when there's young uns being killed by animals that I judge ain't fit to be livin'."

Robert offered his opinion again. "Faith comes from within, Matt. Gift from the Lord. You gotta allow it a place to take root."

"I'll be findin' my kind of faith soon enough. Right at the end of my rifle sights."

Robert saw the subject was futile.

"Can't kill all them Indians by yourself, Matt."

"No, I can't. Goin' to need your help, partner." He started to rise and added with a grunt, "Appreciate the company, but it's time for me to do a little guard duty. You git some shut-eye and I'll be sure to keep them Comanch off you."

Matt stood, stretching out his stiff muscles tightened with the inactivity. The air was cooling and affecting his leg. He rubbed the sore muscles to warm up his circulation. After limbering up, he gave Robert a nod and disappeared into the darkness to relieve Lloyd from guard duty.

Matt found Lloyd placed as sentinel just beyond the end of the picket line. He was using an elm tree as a leaning post, his back to the camp. Matt let out a low whistle to warn Lloyd he was approaching. Lloyd remained planted in his boots, showing no sign of hearing Matt's whistle. Matt stopped and watched him from a distance. The man was armed and dangerous. Visibility was poor in the dark. Matt didn't intend to become another victim shot by a guard with a case of nerves. He put the trunk of a tree between him and the rifle Lloyd cradled in his arms. He whistled a little louder and hailed him by name.

Lloyd jumped when it dawned on him that he had company. Somebody had snuck up undetected. His confidence dropped a notch lower.

"Who the hell is it?" Lloyd barked nervously.

"It's me. Matt."

"You scared the crap out of me!"

Matt sidled up next to the elm tree.

"Jumpy, are you?"

"Been hearing a lot of noises out there," Lloyd answered.

"Don't worry about the ones you hear. It's the ones ya don't hear that'll git you."

"That don't make much sense, but a lot of what happens out here doesn't."

The creek gurgled soft as a newborn calf nursing below the small rise they were standing on. Bullfrogs croaked hoarsely from their hidden spots under the lush vegetation clogging the banks of the stream. Crickets joined in the serenade of frogs and insects to create a crescendo of natural harmony suddenly joined from the distant hills by the howl of a lonesome coyote.

"It is a noisy night out here, ain't it?" Matt said.

Lloyd calmed a bit and said, "Can't hear anything but critters all around. If an Indian wanted to, he could walk right up and tap me on my shoulder. I wouldn't hear him 'til he said, 'You're dead.'"

"He wouldn't have manners 'nough to let you know he was around. His message would be delivered on the tip of an arrow. He'd talk to you maybe while he lifted your scalp. Course, you'd have a problem hearin' at that point."

"You're not helping things one bit."

Matt grinned and said, "You're not ready to git back in camp?"

"You offering?"

"Best you'll git."

Matt made out the beginning of a smile in the diffused light.

"I'd be a fool not take you up on it. I haven't slept worth two cents since we hit the trail."

"None of us do for the first couple a days. Then a man gits used to it. This your first Ranger outing?"

Lloyd hesitated. The answer was embarrassing, but he said, "First of any kind of outing, unless hunting coons overnight counts."

"Those count. But huntin' Indians is a tad different."

Lloyd's answer confirmed the doubts Matt held about his experience. Lloyd appeared too young and soft for a fighting man.

"What brings you out with us?"

Lloyd kicked at the ground to avoid Matt's piercing eyes.

"Captain thought I could use the experience."

Matt stiffened his stance. He peered intently past Lloyd, out into the jumble of trees that formed a black wall in the night, hiding the unknown. Danger in countless forms roamed beyond the camp. Nighttime woods were unforgiving, full of peril that tested the most prepared man. An unprepared man had no chance out here where death existed in many treacherous forms. The image of the Havens boy flashed across Matt's mind. He felt a strong premonition of more deaths coursing through him beside the disturbing memory of the unnecessary loss of a young life. Lloyd was a prime candidate for an encounter he had never prepared for.

Matt turned and faced Lloyd.

"And the captain insisted?"

Lloyd paused before replying, "Insisted? Yeah, I guess you could say so. He thought it might help on the campaign."

"The campaign?"

"Yes, I'm going to help him run for office come next election. I'll be his manager. You know, help him with the paperwork and speeches. I've got a good education. He thinks my experience out here will help with the votes."

Matt chuckled, but not in humor.

"We aren't winnin' any votes so far. One child is already dead. The other is most likely lost. We got our work cut out for us before you can start countin' votes." He sucked in a deep breath and let out a long sigh before he asked, "How old are you?"

Lloyd puffed out his chest in protest.

"What's that got to do with it? I told you, I'm educated. I'm capable!"

"Slow down there. It's just a question. I was young once too."

Lloyd looked at the ground.

"I'm twenty-two."

"What a great age. I envy you. Got the whole world ahead of you. You'll do fine out here if ya understand your limitations. Problem is, out here, the first lesson on limitations can be your last. So take it easy and stay within what you're capable of. With luck, you'll do fine. Hold back and learn the lessons one at a time. Don't git in no hurry. That's my recommendations."

Lloyd calmed with the passing of wisdom and concern that Matt conveyed. He wasn't condescending.

"I appreciate the advice. It is intimidating out here, considering what I've already seen today."

"Bad as it was today, it ain't nothin' compared to what can be. Son, it can git real ugly." Matt stared off into the woods, searching for the nearly imperceptible movement of evil. "You look out into them woods yonder. You look for what any normal man can see. Problem is, you hardly ever see 'em. They might be there, but you won't see 'em at all. Ya got to learn how to feel their presence. Crazy as it sounds, that's the truth. There's a side to Indian fightin' takes time to git used to. No offense to you, you just haven't had time."

"No, probably not. Makes book learning seem easy."

"For you, maybe. Not me. Book learning bored the hell outta me. I'll take the lessons I've learned out here any day."

The moon began to crawl above the horizon in a glow the color of campfire embers. Matt caught sight of the first sliver of orange peeking over the hilltops. He welcomed the arrival of the soft illumination soon to cover the land.

"Here comes our streetlamp. The moon will make it easier to see any critters sneakin' up. You done your part. Time for a bite to eat and then some sack time. Git on back to camp. I've got this covered."

"Thanks, Sarge. Bed and some food do sound good."

"Make the most of it. Tomorrow will be more of the same as today."

Matt listened as Lloyd crunched back to camp and the natural hum of life continued unabated along the sandy creek bottom. Overhead, Matt could make out the darting silhouettes of bats in the diffused moonlight filtering through the treetops. They would appear only for a moment as a fleeting silhouette and then disappear in their irregular flight path, seeking out insects on the wing. At times, two or three were visible performing their acrobatics in unison. He ducked involuntarily when a dark shape plunged to within a foot of his face before abruptly peeling off. After such a close call, he decided to retreat to the elm where Lloyd had staked his post.

With his back against the tree, he ran his eyes over the woods spreading up and over the hills that rose above the creek. He listened intently for any unusual sounds, such as brush rustling or a branch snapping while he remained completely motionless, blending into the bark of the elm to become part of its appearance. Time slowed to a crawl, lacking importance. He enjoyed guard duty and observing the feel of the land.

The moon, several widths above the eastern hills, cast its subtle glow across his field of view, creating harsh shadows that stretched out from the overhanging trees. The enchanting effect of light and shadow in the creek bottom did nothing to stop his mind from wandering over the problems of home life that stuck to him like a coyote on a rabbit. Despite the distance, problems loomed in his life as large as ever out here in the land of the red man. The difficulties of home constantly bore down with heavy pressure on his shoulders. The weight never relented.

He understood that Cora would stand by his decisions come hell or high water. If they were to lose the ranch, she would adapt and make do wherever they landed. She had proven her toughness during the lean years, when they'd started their homestead on the banks of the Colorado. She readily played an equal role with him in building the place up out of a howling wilderness with hardly a complaint. Continuing on through difficult childbirth, the obstacles of living without basic necessities required double the effort on her part. Her responsibilities continued to multiply with every child born, until they had five energetic children to contend with.

Then the war started, and with it, the call of duty had become too strong for him to resist. In his mind, the North had no right to dictate to men in the South what they could or could not do. The powers from the North failed to understand the independent streak of Southern men. The issues could be damned, his fighting side was piqued, and he'd left the ranch to Cora and Lee. She'd managed without his presence for four long years. Lee had filled in on the chores she couldn't manage and saved them all from an unwanted move back into Austin. The ranch squeaked by in his absence, and he owed her a debt for the troubles she overcame without his assistance. That debt included acknowledging her long-ignored preference to live nearer to other people.

Indian danger seemed to pale in comparison to taxes and the thieves that fed on the liens used in Austin courts to remove people from their lands. It was only a matter of time before the Indians would be forced beyond reach of the settlements. However, the greed of men in power was another subject that grew more formidable every day. Problems of corruption in government would take an impressive defense beyond the capabilities of his neighbors, and most likely, beyond his.

Men like Harris had to band together to fight the opposition in political battles that would take years to play out. Meanwhile, the unscrupulous men in Austin would manipulate the laws to their advantage. He could support the few honest politicians he knew of, but he was not one of the politically powerful. He was much too blunt to play the political game. He knew heartache was sure to prevail among the frontiersman he called neighbors.

The only escape he contemplated from the hardscrabble life he lived was his unquenched thirst for Mary. The attraction they felt for each other was burning with an intensity they'd both subdued for a long time. Her touch had inflamed desires that were constantly at play in the back of his mind. Standing alone on guard, he floated back to the warm sensation of her hand upon his thigh. At another time and place, he would have thrown caution to the wind and suffered the consequences of giving in to her allure. She reenergized the excitement he had known as a young man, and he felt the years of toil and the effects of time fall away at her simple touch. The memory of her long blonde hair falling across her shoulders evoked thoughts of pleasure that excluded the other difficulties crowding his mind. Scene after scene of lovemaking occupied his time as the night slowly passed. He relaxed against the tree, lost in the distraction of ecstatic fantasy.

The night grew peaceful as the moon rose higher in the sky above him. The insects and frogs went into hiding. Coyotes prowled in silence. Matt enjoyed the woods now wrapped in a deceptive tranquility, accented by the soft moonlight that suited his amorous thoughts. He could make out the haphazard placement of granite boulders spread across the hillside above the camp. The water in the creek glowed silver in the muted moonlight, gurgling from pool to pool. Deep shadows of darkness painted the fields in quilts of black below the trees and alongside the boulders in stark contrast to the moon's delicate glow.

Below the hummock he stood on, a dead pecan tree extended bare weathered branches out across the moonlit sky in a contorted black silhouette. Hidden within a crook between the branches, a great horned owl cut loose with a reverberating hoot that shattered the stillness of the night air. The deep call echoed through the woods and sent a chill down Matt's spine. He recoiled in surprise at the first call and spun to locate the owl as more calls tumbled out. The bird's large eyes, illuminated by the moon, gave its position away as he swiveled his huge head to glare down directly at Matt in a scowl of disdain. Its last hoot blasted directly at Matt, as if the owl possessed personal animosity towards him.

After its final call, the owl spread its wings and pushed off the branch in an effortless glide above Matt that carried it out into the field where it disappeared below the waist-high grass. A panicked shriek erupted from the owl's sudden swoop on an unsuspecting rabbit. The high-pitched squeal mixed with the rustling of grass and gravel as the lopsided struggle came to a hasty conclusion. A life was lost, and silence returned to the area as if nothing of importance had occurred.

Matt's heart raced with the unusually close encounter he had never experienced before. In his distant recollection, he remembered the Indian lore of an owl calling out your name. According to the old Indian tale, if an owl called your name, it held great significance. The Indians considered the owl to hold wisdom concerning the direction of the spiritual travels of men. From their perch high above the mortal man, owls could portend future events. For one to hear an owl call his name, the future was sure to hold bad times. To hear your name called meant one thing alone: your death was imminent. Matt was confident he had just heard his name called, loud and clear.

SEVENTEEN

Matt rolled over to his side to turn away from the grating rasp of men snoring. A sweet scent of crushed grass rose from under the scratchy wool blanket he rearranged around his shoulders. The temperature had dropped steadily all night, until the cooler air seeped under the blanket, creating a chill that added to his discomfort. His ground blanket provided little padding, as the grass under it compressed from the endless tossing he endured after Robert relieved him from guard duty. Peace of mind proved elusive as the long night wore on. He grew increasingly impatient waiting for dawn. He craved action. He felt his pent-up energy building and his legs twitched involuntarily. He forced himself to remain still for the meager benefit his uneasy rest provided.

Thoughts of the Havens boy plagued his mind in distressing repetition. Failure to rescue the boy seared the disturbing images of Indian brutality into his memory. He realized that he bore no personal responsibility for the failure, yet the tragedy of the boy's death did not allow him any consolation. The challenge to right the wrongs of life was a personal responsibility he felt obligated to achieve, although reality frequently stood in his way.

His memory wandered back to the Civil War, when he'd considered the Yankees his sworn enemy and fought them harder than any man did. The many horrors he had witnessed on the battlefield came back into focus with a ruthless vengeance. Shots fired in anger years ago still reverberated in his conscious. Sights of blood, gore, and disfigured men screaming in agony mired his mind in thoughts of a past he was powerless to change.

A pall of smoke had floated over the fields after the intense action of battle and its haze covered the site with the bitter stench of gunpowder. From this fog of combat, he remembered his brothers in gray emerging with men captured from the Yankee forces. A palpable smell of fear had emanated from these prisoners as they'd passed on their way to the rear of the lines to endure the inhumane treatment they knew was coming. He'd witnessed many acts of cruelty against the men who wore blue, now captives and denied the ability to defend themselves. The Southern men now in control were no different than the soldiers of prior armies. War reduced most every man to a low level of savageness.

As much as he loathed the Union soldier, he'd never condoned malicious handling of them. If a Confederate soldier didn't cease the cruel management of a captured enemy combatant, he'd meet the wrath of the Sarge. Matt had not hesitated to club a fellow soldier senseless if his demands for humane treatment of prisoners went ignored.

His reputation spread throughout the ranks, until his orders carried the stigma of immediate punishment if not obeyed, both on and off the field of battle. A stern look from him sent men scurrying to fulfill his demands. His control of the soldiers who served under him was absolute, and his effectiveness with them had caused promotions to pass him over. The officers above him needed his services on the line too much to offer a step up in rank. It had suited him fine to stay out of the politics practiced by officers always seeking an advantage to serve their personal interest.

Restlessly rolling over onto his back, Matt placed his hands behind his head for an additional cushion. These old war memories were his constant nemesis but did nothing to help him understand the unquenchable blood thirst of the Comanche. He felt impotent in his ability to stop their marauding raids from inflicting harm that lasted long after they returned to their remote haunts on the prairie. The sting of failure to rescue the innocent young Havens boy pierced his heart with remorse and guilt. The same feelings of guilt beguiled him now as when his son Josh fell to a fast-moving band of Comanche raiders. The cunning Indians had taken advantage of a moment of inattention on his part to wreak everlasting havoc in his life.

Matt didn't dignify the Indians with warrior status. To him, they were simply savages hell-bent on wanton destruction. They didn't deserve distinction as warriors. The newspapermen back in the eastern cities who defended the red man should venture out here to see their barbaric deeds first hand before editorializing about Indian mistreatment. Most of the men in power could go to hell with their ignorance. "Educated" men possessed very little real knowledge of the reality of the life lived by those they wished to rule over. In Matt's mind, men's abuse of power was rampant and always would be.

At this most unusual time, he started making connections that usually proved evasive. Revelations often came to him unexpectedly in the dead quiet moments of night. The loss of Josh and the memory of his color-drained body bristling with arrows haunted Matt like no other death he had ever encountered. The memory of his son's ghastly appearance was raw and buried deep, never discussed with Cora or other family members. Some things hurt too much to deal with, and so it was with the death of his son. Despite Matt's hardened frontiersman attitude, Josh's death was unfathomable and created an ache beyond his ability to repair.

It was an insight to lie here under the night sky, linking his son's death with the detachment of his relationship with Cora. He now recognized their drift apart had started at that point in time. She no longer desired him. Most likely, she blamed him for the tragic loss of Josh. Perhaps that was why he no longer strived to please her. Guilt worked in devious ways. He didn't know for sure why they drifted apart and still didn't know without a doubt. The only fact he was sure of was their detachment from each other had started with Josh's death, and the heartbreaking event was beyond discussion. With a startling clarity, he realized the time for a painful conversation with Cora was long overdue.

Springing up into a sitting position, Matt tossed the blanket off to the side. A jolt of cool fresh air washed over his skin. He immediately got to his feet before the cold could penetrate to his bones. Wasting no time, he threw on his range coat and grabbed his Henry before hustling past the smoldering campfire. Stepping around the slumbering men, he approached the picket line in the faint light of the moon, now sinking low in the western sky. He was plainly visible to the guards in the moon's silver glow and felt comfortable enough to make his way down to the creek just below the horses.

Reaching the bank, he knelt down and scooped up a handful of the fresh cold water. He splashed it across his face repeatedly until his beard was soaked and dripping onto his shirt. The brisk washing invigorated his senses.

He used his bandana to dry his face and beard while surveying the meadow across the creek. There was no movement in the field to concern him.

Stimulated, he was ready to hit the trail, despite the early hour. Stepping back up to the picket line, he stopped to check on Whiskey before reentering the campsite. Near the fire, he found the captain sitting up in his bedroll, rubbing his eyes, lost somewhere in the void between alertness and slumber.

Yawning, Harris mumbled, "What are you doing up so early?"

"Ain't too early, Cap. Couldn't sleep no ways."

"Who can out here? What time is it, you suppose?"

"The sun is over an hour before risin'. But we got moon and it will do the job if you're ready to start."

Harris flared his eyes trying to think. He said, "The men got enough rest?"

"Don't matter, we got trail to make. Git 'em roused. A cold breakfast is what I suggest."

"Sounds fine to me. Wanted to head out a little early anyway. I'll go bring in Hunter. He's on the east post. You go bring in Robert."

Matt spun on his heels and crunched across the coarse granite gravel that surrounded the campfire. Confidence was in his stride. His spirits were lifted. Identifying a problem was half the battle, and now he had something imperative to discuss with Cora when he returned home. Most importantly, the Havens girl could be within their reach with an early start. Delivering the youngster home to her parents would be a godsend for all involved. This day was new to mold and put to good use. The fresh opportunity for positive developments elated him.

Before he could reach Robert, the weight of the situation displaced his optimism. The challenge the men faced was enormous. Countless obstacles remained before a happy family reunion could become even a remote possibility. The Havens boy would never be coming home. His parents would be devastated at their additional loss. Cora might remain cold as ice. It was foolish to let high hopes carry him away. A lot of hard work remained before thoughts of a successful return home should enter the picture.

He paused when the elm tree used as a sentry post loomed up in shadow. The moon hung behind the upper branches of the tree, outlined in darkness across the muted silver glow of the sky. Robert was visible off to the side of the trunk, and Matt hailed him with a sharp whistle.

He casually turned to acknowledge Matt and waved him on.

Robert spoke in his slow drawl, "Little early, ain't it?"

"Not to me, it's not. We got work to do today and need all the time we can steal. With luck, them Comanch will be in range by day's end."

"I'm with you."

Matt thought back to his unusual encounter with the owl and asked, "See anything?"

"Yeah I did. An hour ago. Somethin' on the other side of the creek. Was low and long. Probably a cat on the prowl. Couldn't be sure. Just got a glimpse of him."

"No owls in the area?"

"Nope, didn't see no owls. A couple a deer over near where the cat was at. Coyotes yelpin'. That's about it."

Matt decided to forget about the encounter with the owl. It was just an old Indian tale that meant nothing. What the hell did he care about Indian myths?

Robert cradled his rifle in his right arm as they started back to camp. On the way back, they saw Antonio emerge from a thick cluster of brush.

Robert laughed, "Don't he remind you of a rabbit holed up in a briar patch?"

Matt agreed but remained silent. Antonio had some strange habits compared to a white man, but those differences didn't make him wrong. He began to open his mind to the fact that Antonio could teach them all a few lessons. A man was never too old to learn, or he was a fool to think so.

They reached camp, where Harris had the men roused and moving about, making preparations for departure. The captain met them at the edge of camp, fully charged with adrenaline for the challenges the day was sure to provide.

"Have you given any thought to the day and the proper way to pursue?" Harris inquired.

Matt scoffed, "Hell, it's about all I did last night. Wasn't no sleep to be had. Just laid there and thought about things all night long."

"Well, let's have your thoughts."

Harris turned to Charles, motioning for the corporal to join in the discussion. Nate saw the gathering and slipped up beside Matt to listen in.

Matt said, "Captain, I think speed is the answer, like we talked about.

From what I've gathered, Antonio is the only one of us that knows exactly where this rock is. That true, Nate? Have you ever been there?"

Nate shrugged his shoulders.

"Nah, I've never been there. Been pretty close, I suppose, up where Sandy Creek meets the Colorado. But I never put my eyes on it. None of the other men has been there, so far as I know."

"That's what I thought. So, Cap, I recommend Antonio continue to lead the way out front alone. He works best without interference. Then I'd have Nate and one of the other men follow behind Antonio a distance back. Maybe take Mark with him. And then we follow them two, as far back as possible without losin' sight of 'em. That'll keep most of us far enough back to let Antonio do his work. Also leaves us close enough to offer support if the Comanch surprise the point men and attack."

Nodding his head, Harris agreed with Matt.

Matt continued, "I say we should start right now. Make our time with the moonlight. I think we risk it all and try to close on 'em today."

Harris agreed with the plan with no further discussion and shouted out, "Mark! Get ready. You are joining Nate out on second point behind Antonio. The rest of you, gather around."

Young and frontier experienced beyond his age, Mark came alive at the mention of his name. Blessed with a boundless energy accented by his flaming red hair, his freckled face beamed at the opportunity to ride at the front. He let out a whoop of excitement.

The men assembled in a circle around Harris, where he crisply delivered instructions for the upcoming forced ride. "Cold breakfast. No coffee. Move out in twenty. Dismissed."

Antonio waited until the men were ready before leading the way out of camp, splashing across the shallow creek. He headed upstream in a bouncing gait on his small pony, serape flapping in the breeze. Nate and Mark fell in behind Antonio at the distance suggested by the orders. Matt and Harris led the rest of the column closely behind the point men in order to stay within sight in the faint moonlit conditions. Sam followed them all with the pack train under his steady control.

Once again, Matt fell into the easy cadence that separated Whiskey from the other mounts. He thought over the dangers of the bold move the column was undertaking. They could stumble into an unknown camp of

Indians and all hell would break loose in a complete loss of control. But it was a risk they had to take. He placed his faith in Antonio's experience to prevent that from happening, but it was still a distinct possibility. The Havens girl would be in grave danger should they unknowingly run into the Comanche. Then again, her only hope rested in a quick rescue resulting from such a daring advancement of the Rangers. The Indians could disappear on the plains if given the time, and Matt felt it was now or never to prevent their escape to the immense grasslands of the prairie.

The men scoured away many miles before the eastern sky began to blaze with the sun reflecting orange off the high, wispy cloud cover. Matt didn't allow a halt, for fear of losing track of Antonio on a hot trail. Matt's tenacity only added to his well-known reputation for having an iron butt. They all suffered hours of chilled riding before Antonio finally paused at a stream snaking along the base of an oak-covered hill.

The narrow stream where Antonio watered his pony drew the attention of all the winded horses. The men let their thirsty stock spread out along the water to drink their fill. While the mounts drank, the men roamed the creek bank to generate circulation in their cold, stiff legs.

Matt listened as Antonio explained that once past the hill above them, they would be in sight of a canyon that cut through an extremely rugged range of hills. The creek flowing inside the gorge went by the name Sandy Creek for a good reason. The creek bottom was covered in deep sand and difficult to travel, but its course would eventually lead the men to the rock. He also explained that the canyon was very narrow and a perilous route under tall cliffs, but offered the most direct line to reach the enchanted rock. The route through the pass saved half a day of travel time. Matt suggested to Harris that they climb the hill to have a look at the gorge.

Harris followed Matt, climbing on foot to the peak of the steep incline. They carefully avoided sky lining their bodies once they neared the top of the hill. Taking advantage of the tree cover, they found a spot clear of debris and sprawled out flat on the ground. Harris produced his monocular and gave the area near the canyon's mouth a thorough glassing. He saw nothing of interest.

He offered the instrument to Matt, who scanned the rough hills spreading across the horizon as far as the eye could see. He ended his inspection with his focus on the gash cut through the imposing range of hills.

"The canyon looks intimidating."

"Yes it does," Harris agreed.

"Good spot for an ambush."

Harris recoiled at the prospect.

"You're right. Perhaps the extra time to avoid it would be prudent. We can't risk a disaster."

"Avoid somethin' we don't even know exists? My dad always said, 'Can't never did nothin'.' I figure it's a chance we have to take. If only for the sake of the girl."

"We could ride into a trap and lose lives."

"Or we could save valuable time and rescue one. That's what we're here for."

Harris put the glass back up to his eye, buying time to think while he viewed the same area again. Matt felt a simmering of impatience with the time wasted in useless glassing. Feeling the tension mounting in Matt close beside him, Harris shoved the glass back in the leather case.

He asked Matt, "If we were to pass through the canyon, what is your plan?"

"I don't know. We figure that out when we git there. I seen enough here. Let's git back down and git the men movin'."

Harris snuck one last peek at the ravine before he led the way down, slipping and sliding on the loose gravel.

The column quickly organized and trailed around the foot of the hill to head for the gorge, using the lower lands for concealment. Antonio displayed a superb understanding of topography and used every natural feature available to conceal movement from the distant hills, where hidden eyes could be watching. Matt's appreciation of Antonio's skill grew with every good decision the man made.

In short time, the entrance to the canyon loomed before the advancing column. Antonio waited for the men to pull even with him in the protection of a dry gully overhung with a dense grove of mesquite trees. Matt hopped off Whiskey to scramble up the dirt bank for a better view of the gorge.

His concern deepened at the sight of the narrow cliffs rising abruptly from the wooded creek banks covered in shadow. The rust-tinted bluffs shot straight up a hundred feet to brush-covered slopes that offered plenty of cover for ambush. The creek bottom filled the valley floor thirty yards wide with deep sand and a thin sheen of water meandering in the center of the bed. A few islands of flimsy brush popped up in scattered groves that offered little protection for the men, should an ambush occur. Along the eroded banks above the creek, a mixture of oak and elm trees provided numerous areas of concealment for the Comanche. If the Indians knew of their presence, this was the perfect place for a trap. Matt could visualize an ambush and almost smell the putrid odor of death.

"Captain, I don't like what I see at all. Come up here and take a look."

Harris huffed up beside Matt in a belly-crawl. It didn't take him long to concur with Matt's assessment.

"I agree with you. It looks like the perfect place to trap us. What do you recommend?"

Matt shook his head, realizing that proper scouting would waste a lot of valuable time they didn't have. Without the search for Comanche in the canyon, the men would be at grave risk. But his overwhelming concern was time, and the Havens girl was never out of his thoughts.

"Hell Captain, it takes a while to scout out a canyon like this one. There's a good chance the Comanche are in there somewhere. But you'll never see 'em 'til it's too late. They'd probably kill a scout or two before they even got a chance to report back to us. I would hate to lose Nate or Antonio on some fool mission."

He paused to think on the problem. It didn't take long before he made a decision.

"Takes too long to do a proper military scout. So here's what I think. Comanch may be in there. They may be in there in large numbers. But I know they can't shoot worth a crap and have little gumption when faced with repeatin' rifles and revolvers."

He turned and questioned Antonio, "How long is the damn canyon?"

Antonio grinned. He knew what Matt was thinking.

"No mucho. Una milla."

Matt inhaled a deep breath. He looked back at the gorge once more and let out a long sigh between parched lips coated in dust. Harris waited for Matt to finish his analysis.

Matt said, "That's quite a ways to be exposed."

He peered into the shadowed canyon walls, trying to detect the hidden dangers, hesitating to think over the options. In his experience, the best course of action was bold, unexpected movements that surprised the enemy and embroiled them in confusion. In his mind's eye, he saw the upcoming action unfold. The captain could agree or not, but he was sure of his sense of battle and confident in the plan now taking shape in his mind.

He spoke lowly to Harris, "Here's what I suggest. I'll lead out, and the men need to space out thirty or so yards apart, behind me. Put the packhorses and Sam in the middle of the column. Locate the best shots at the front and bringin' up the rear. We head into the canyon full out. If they attack, I'm bettin' they can't hit us from where they'll be hidin'. If they pounce on us hard, we all ride to the shootin'. Things may happen fast, but the plan is simple and one the men can follow if it heats up."

Harris wore a frown as the plan spilled out.

"Damn risky, Matt."

"Yes it is. Haven't been in a battle yet that wasn't all about risk. But I believe we can handle it. If we can't handle it here, we probably won't be able to handle it wherever we are. To me, it's now or possibly never."

"What if they hit us hard and we're all spread out?"

"They won't be able to hit all of us at once if we're spread out. But if they do, we'll be close enough together for mutual support."

"They could hit us all along our line at once."

"Captain, I don't believe that's their way of fightin'. They only risk exposure when the odds are way in their favor. But if they do, then we gotta improvise. The men can handle it. I'm confident in 'em."

Harris still hesitated. Another command decision had arrived, and he wasn't sure of the proper course of action. He favored a slow, methodical reconnaissance of the canyon to determine the hazards. Waffling in indecision, he noticed Antonio grinning up at him. What was the scout thinking that made him wear such a smug grin? He felt the half-breed's black eyes boring into him, taking a measure of his manhood and his ability to command. The uneducated scout wore an air of superiority that indicated he possessed better knowledge of the situation than the "gringos."

The pressure of indecision built until Harris sensed a breaking point boiling to the surface. He had to decide, right or wrong.

"Matt, I don't have a better idea. Let's go with yours and be on with it. Take the lead, like you said."

Without hesitation, Matt scrambled down the hill in a tumble of loose stones clattering ahead of him. Harris slid in the tracks behind Matt and curtly snapped out orders when he reached the men.

"Antonio, you help Sam with the horses. Your damn bow will do little good if there are bullets flying. Nate, you help Sam too. Hunter and J.B. will bring up the rear. I'll be just ahead of the horses in the middle. Matt will pick the men he needs up front. The others fall in where needed."

Matt was impatient to move into action. He pointed at Charles Mossberg and asked, "You're a decent shot, right?"

The corporal wore the cocky smirk he was known for when he answered, "Well, hell yeah!"

"Good then. Fall in behind me, along with Mark."

Mark slapped his hands together in a loud crack. This day was delivering plenty of good news. He craved to be involved in action and he figured riding at the front upped his chances.

Matt continued with his instructions, "Everybody double-check your weapons. Git your ammo handy. Keep thirty yards spacing. We move fast through the canyon. If shootin' starts, ride to the sound. Be ready to improvise if the situation dictates. And be ready to pour it to 'em hard!"

EIGHTEEN

Exploding from a grove of oaks, the men swiftly crossed an open field of bluestem. They cut a wake through the lush grass as the riders spread apart the distance ordered. Reaching the entrance to the gorge, Matt cut away from a dense grove of trees that flanked the Rangers on the left bank. He galloped to the creek bank and without hesitation leapt Whiskey off the edge down into the sandy bed. Whiskey stumbled, sagging in the knees as the loose sand sucked at his momentum. Matt lost his balance and struggled to stay in the saddle. Wavering, he deftly shifted his weight at the last possible second to save himself from an embarrassing tumble into the creek.

The coarse gravel in the streambed crunched loudly as they charged upstream under the towering bluffs. Matt strained to detect movement along the brush-covered banks. There were plenty of locations for ambush, but nothing stirred. Thus far, the plan was sound.

The tarnished, rust-colored walls of the bluffs rose high above Matt as he entered the shade of the gap. The cliffs resembled the gaping jaws of an angry bear in Matt's overly stimulated imagination. He turned in the saddle to see the men maintaining good spacing and control throughout the entire column. The deception of such an easy entry worried him. He thought of the possibilities the narrow canyon presented for ambush as they penetrated its course. It was a situation he'd been in many times in the past, but the feeling of vulnerability remained sharp.

He maneuvered Whiskey past the slow rivulets into the center of the creek, where the main channel of water ran deeper. Whiskey labored to maintain the momentum Matt desired. The wet sand sucked and pulled at each step Whiskey took. No firm footing existed anywhere in the creek bottom, and the line of Rangers dropped off their initial pace. The slower tempo made the men easier targets, but all of the horses continued to labor to their limits.

Above the rocky edges of the overhanging bluffs, the slopes rose away in steep slants covered in trees and shrubs that offered good firing positions. Matt didn't worry about bows, but if the Comanche owned rifles, the men were now within range. Discounting the chance of attack from above, he focused his attention on the woodlands encroaching along the banks of the stream. The dense growth of trees presented a much closer point to launch an attack. These areas where the open creek passage hugged in close to the hardwoods worried him the most.

He chose to keep the men to the middle of the creek, where the thin brush whipped against his wet pants. Whiskey slowed up considerably as larger rocks became more frequent and hampered his footing. Behind him, the men spread out in a line too far away to see J.B. or Hunter bringing up the rear. The packhorses appeared to be in control behind the captain, although some of the gear had worked loose and gyrated wildly during the rough ride.

After rounding a few more bends, Matt got his first sight of the exit from the tight ravine. He felt a wave of relief that the end of the passage was in sight. The column had ridden through a risky gauntlet. They were all fortunate no ambush had materialized from the many places offering concealment. Matt drew in a deep breath of air, full of the resinous scent of cedar carried on the stiff breeze.

Up ahead, a profuse grove of cedar crowded a bend in the creek. Its deep green foliage offered yet another opportunistic place for Indians to hide. He worried that the men were still in danger of ambush.

Whiskey slowed to a trot by the time they began to round the bend, as did all of the other mounts, exhausted by the forced run in deep sand. Matt was wary of the narrowing creek passage, overgrown with the abundant cedar. Rounding a dogleg turn in the bend, he was shocked to see the creek blocked by a massive cottonwood wedged in tight from bank to bank. The tree trunk was huge and limbs protruded at every angle, resting in the position the last flood had left it stranded. It was too large to jump, and the banks around it were plugged with an impenetrable mixture of cedar and cat's claw brush.

There was no sign of a clear exit.

The men began to crowd in close to each other as Matt sought a way out of their predicament. This blockage was now the most likely scene of ambush. He felt the stirrings of desperation as the men bunched up in confusion. Should the Indians be hiding behind the trees, a catastrophe could suddenly envelop them as they milled about in such confined quarters.

With a sense of urgency, he scanned the bank on both sides for an exit, or worse yet, an Indian. Soon the packhorses joined the cluster of riders. Matt began to hear shouts erupting from the men engaged in controlling their mounts.

Mossberg screamed at Matt to be heard above the increasing tumult, "What the hell do we do now?"

Matt tightened up with tension. The cedar crowded out the left bank completely, and he expected a salvo of arrows at any time. He turned Whiskey to face downstream and saw where a game trail led up the opposite bank to a small opening in the thick bee-brush.

Harris rode up to Matt and shouted, "This is turning into a hell of a mess!"

"Yes sir, it is. See that trail over yonder. Let's make for it and hope the Comanch aren't in them woods. If they are, it'll be a little close for comfort."

Pulling his revolver from his holster, he hollered at the men to follow him and make ready for close action. He spurred Whiskey to the bank, praying no arrow would meet him on the way. The old trail broke down the bank at an angle facing downstream, full of loose dirt crushed into fine silt from the frequent use of buffalo in the area. Clutching the Colt in his right hand, Matt approached the trail carefully, while scanning the woods for hidden Comanche. He knew that the first sign of Indians would probably be an arrow whizzing in flight, zeroed in on his chest. Reaching the foot of the bank, he paused to reconsider the unknown dangers secreted within the woods.

The men were watching him. This plan had been his idea. Comanche were fierce fighters. Nobody in their right mind sought a close encounter with them. Impulsively, he spurred Whiskey up the trail, brushing aside the web of small branches clogging the trail. He disappeared from view in the packed growth of brush before Mossberg could follow his lead.

Matt led the men deeper into the brushy maze on horseback, frequently ducking low-hanging limbs. His pace was slow as he methodically worked through the woods, anticipating the sound of a Comanche war cry and the release of an arrow at any second. His pulse spiked when a covey of small birds took flight with a rush of beating wings scraping noisily against the tightly woven limbs in the bee-brush. He motioned for Mossberg to fall back a little when the brush thickened enough to force him to dismount Whiskey.

The Comanche could be anywhere. They could be on him in a split second with their blood-curdling war whoops. The rotten odor of death hung like a cloud in the compact tunnel the trail wound through. His nostrils burned with the caustic stench of decay. Somewhere in the brush, a carcass of some sort of beast — or man — lay in an advanced state of decomposition.

He began to bleed from a cut across his cheek. The stream of blood mixed with sweat to drain into the corner of his mouth. He spat the salty mixture onto a cactus and wiped his bloody cheek with a dirty sleeve. Whiskey wrestled to break past tight clusters of limbs entangled with thorny vines. Behind him, Matt heard men cursing the situation and horses snorting in frustration. Traversing this game trail was more unnerving than the ride up the open bottom of the ravine.

Finally, Matt saw the brush thin out to reveal several trails feeding through a meadow. The paths merged into the main trail the men currently followed. He breathed a deep sigh of relief to step into the open field and escape the claustrophobic tunnel of brush. He moved to the side with Whiskey to make room for the men to join him in the open.

Out in the meadow, a grove of live oaks stood alone as an island of green surrounded by the burnt orange fall grasses swaying in the brisk breeze. Matt removed his hat to let the breeze dry his sweat-soaked hair. Beneath the oaks, he made out a small band of buffalo rising from their beds and warily looking his way. As more men emerged, the buffalo sensed danger and started to flee in their slow, lumbering way, kicking up a cloud of dust in the wind. Their large rumps were just visible when Antonio caught sight of the last few running off. He cursed strongly in his odd tongue about the fine meal he saw escaping.

Harris was the last to arrive, leading his horse up to Matt. Shaking his head, he said, "By good fortune, no Indians were in that jungle. They could have cut us to pieces. No doubt about it."

Matt placed his hat back on his head and took out his bandana to apply pressure to the fresh cut on his cheek. Looking at the captain, he mused,

"That's the risk ya take out here. Ain't none of us guaranteed tomorrow. Or today's sunset, for that matter."

"All the same, I don't fancy looking death in the eye. That was a nerve-racking ride. I'm calling for a rest. I think we have earned it. Let's make for those oaks."

The men mounted up for the short ride to the oaks, where they turned their horses out to graze on the plentiful grass. Canteens full of cool water relieved the dehydrated thirst of men stressed by the threatening ride through the canyon. A ride already passed into history in a joking manner among the men. The good-natured banter about their perilous route accented the pleasure of trail food passed among them. They were glad to celebrate the good fortune they shared. They knew it had been a stroke of luck that no Comanche were waiting in ambush.

Robert ambled up to Matt with a generous portion of pecans in his haversack and a tasty chew of smoked sausage in his mouth. Matt munched contentedly on Cora's pemmican. The tasty treat satisfied his sweet tooth, with her liberal addition of berries making it an exceptional recipe. He held out a chunk to Robert that he gladly accepted.

Robert savored the sweet morsel in genuine appreciation. He smacked his lips while he addressed Matt, "That ride got my blood to pumpin'. I expected the red bastards at any time. Especially in the real thick stuff. Woo-wee! You got nerve to take the lead through all that cat's claw. They could've been in there anywhere."

Matt dabbed at the cut oozing a thin trickle of blood.

"Maybe it's not nerve I got. Maybe I got less sense than most. Thought I saw several Comanch in there. My mind played a few tricks on me."

"Yeah, me too. Almost shot a stump. Looked like Buffalo Hump sittin' off to the side."

Robert laughed at the imagined warrior that popped into his head.

Matt turned serious.

"You ever seen Hump for real?"

"Only in my nightmares, but that stump looked like what I reckon him to be."

"Funny you should mention him. We trailed him once about ten years ago. Always wanted to nail that sorry old bastard."

"He done a lot of killin', from what I heard."

"Yes he has. Saw it firsthand. We trailed him up to the headwaters of the Guadalupe but lost him in the cut-ups. It's some rough country up there. They split up and went off in every direction. All we managed was to surprise a couple of 'em in their camp early one mornin'. They had three white scalps amongst them, but we made 'em pay the highest price possible for their murderin' ways. 'Twas the best we could do on that ride. Hump got away. I ain't never got close to him again. He's still out there raisin' hell."

"Someday we'll think back on this trip the same way. Hopefully, with better results."

Matt looked back at the thick woods where the trail entered the maze. A scowl formed when he said, "Some of us will. Some, maybe not."

Robert didn't hesitate. "I plan on bein' one that will,"

Smiling, Matt said, "Well, Robert, that's always my plan too."

Matt finished the pemmican and checked Whiskey over to verify none of his gear was loose or missing. Happy with the readiness of his rig, he asked Harris if he was ready to make trail.

Harris responded with a command for the men to mount up. Within minutes, the column re-formed to head out of the oaks, with Antonio back in the point position. Nate and Mark followed out at the proper distance behind Antonio. They maneuvered beside the creek for several miles as it wound upstream away from the narrow canyon.

The undulating hills grew progressively in size as the day wore into late afternoon. The character of the land became more rugged as they approached an imposing range of high hills littered across the slopes with chunks of granite boulders. The weather-beaten boulders appeared as if randomly dropped from the sky. Gullies began to slash through the coarse soil, steep and eroded, bare of vegetation, exposing loose gravel and treacherous footing for the horses. Antonio led the men into this higher range of hills, using the saddles between the peaks to avoid detection and skirting the gullies that could trap the Rangers.

The column began to string out as yet another saddle strewn with loose granite debris rose in front of them. The men, along with their mounts, were beginning to feel the exhaustion of a long day with little nourishment or water. Maintaining cohesion along the line was becoming difficult. Matt felt weak and lightheaded in the saddle as he struggled to remain in sight of Nate. He knew that all of the men were in desperate need of a break after their endless pursuit over harsh ground.

Rounding a dense cluster of oaks, Matt glanced up to see Antonio off his pony near the crest of the pass they were slowly ascending. Nate and Mark had just joined him and were dropping like whipped pups out of their saddles. Matt felt tremendous relief to pull alongside Antonio and slide off of Whiskey to firm ground. He bent over and grabbed his boots to stretch out stiff back muscles that tormented him in pain. Reaching for the sky, he arched backwards to work the stiffness the other way. He noticed that Antonio wore a smile, watching him perform his antics. He assumed the scout enjoyed the sight of an older man feeling his age.

Harris reached the spot next to Matt and dropped off his mount while nodding towards Antonio, who still wore a satisfied expression.

He asked the scout, "What's the meaning of this stop?"

Antonio pointed to the brow of the hill that was hiding the sun and said, "The rock."

Matt became excited and forgot about the physical pain he was suffering. He said, "About damn time. Cap, bring the glass. He means we can finally see the damn rock."

Harris grabbed the glass and followed Matt, already rushing to the brim of the hill. Matt slowed as he neared the top and removed his hat to finish his approach in a crouch. He fought his way through clotted brush until he found a small clearing at the top of the hill. He crawled forward to find a spot where the countryside opened up to his view. He could hear Harris cursing behind him as the thorn-filled brush blocked his progress.

Matt sucked in his breath at the stunning sight before him. There it was, sitting in command of the smaller hills nearby. The rock. It spread out along the horizon in a massive, naked, dirty pink dome of granite. The immense size dominated the surrounding landscape and surpassed Matt's preconceived notion of its appearance. The granite dome rose high out of the ground to rein supreme above similar, but smaller, formations falling away to the west and towards him to the east. It lay silent, just standing there. Its bulk radiated power and dominion that needed no clarification. The hand of God's creation manifested itself in the magnitude of command the rock held over its environment. Massive block-shaped boulders lay scattered in abundance around its base. These boulders spread away from the prominence held by the main granite dome and disappeared into the solid cover of hardwoods that surrounded all of the immediate rock formations.

A flight of buzzards was circling a sharp drop-off at the side of the eminence nearest Matt's observation point. The vertical cliffs below the vultures darkened in shadow as the sun dipped near the scalloped western horizon. The buzzards soared on the evening thermals rising off the bluffs and then swooped down low to the trees above the drop-offs, searching for a suitable perch to spend the night on. A few of the scavengers landed along the edge of the cliffs, where they held an unassailable view of the woodlands below. Matt began to appreciate the legends permeating the area, and the awe Indians held for the rock.

Antonio eventually came alongside Matt, opposite Harris, who busied himself with observing the rock through his monocular. The scout grinned at Matt, obviously proud of his accomplishment.

"Muy grande, no?"

"Yes it is. More than I imagined. Comanche out there?"

Antonio raised his eyebrows and smirked as he answered, "Muy probable."

"We need to make sure. There's no room for error after the effort we made to reach this point. Cap, you see anything with those eagle eyes?"

Harris continued to work the scene before him. He kept the glass pressed to his eye when he said, "Nothing yet, but that doesn't surprise me. Those Comanche are not going to be on top of these rocks saying, 'Here we are.' They will be camping somewhere secluded."

He put the glass down and confided to Matt, "I will say, these rocks are a geological wonder. They are a damn impressive collection that needs studying. No telling what they hide. Perhaps mineral wealth. Meantime, they present us with a dilemma. Where do you think those Indians would hole up?"

"Hell if I know. Could be anywhere out there, far as I know. Your guess would be as good as mine."

Harris passed his monocular to Matt and rubbed his temples, trying to massage the fatigue away. He took a swig from his canteen and mumbled to Matt, "I didn't see anything to give us a clue."

While Matt peered through the glass, Harris looked down the slope behind them and saw his men taking care of the horses. They were also passing around their food for a quick cold supper. Separated from the others was Nate. He was coming up the slope at a quick pace. Reaching Matt and Harris, he worked his way into a spot to peek over the top. His eyes widened when the granite dome came into view.

"Wow! What I've heard is true. That's a helluva sight! Those mountains are some big sons of bitches. They could hold a whole tribe of Comanche. For that matter, they could hold some of them spirits too."

Antonio said, "Es true."

Matt had his eyes glued to the monocular. He said, "True or not, I don't see a damn thing! Spirit or Comanch, they're all hidin' right now. Only thing out there I can make out is a lotta rough terrain. We need to know where they're at."

He grumbled under his breath with frustration and handed the monocular back to Harris.

Harris continued to rub his temple. He was tired, hungry, and thirsty. His voice seemed full of sand when he said, "This is a problem. You have any suggestions, Matt?"

Matt was pulling on his beard, thinking.

"Yes, I do. We got two damn good scouts. After moonrise, send 'em out to determine if the Comanch are out there. And, if so, where are they campin'?"

He was staring directly at Nate when he spoke. A frown spread across Nate's face. The implications of Matt's idea did not please him.

Matt took the measure of Nate's disapproval.

"Speak your mind, Nate. You got a better idea?"

Nate glared at Matt. A sneer rose from the corner of his lips when he said, "No, I don't. But pokin' 'round in the dark in an area I don't know. Indians about. Well. Whew! That's rough duty. If them mountains out there don't spook you, then you're not right."

Harris quipped, "That's what you're getting paid for."

Matt let the comment slide but didn't take his gaze off of Nate.

Directing his next question to the scout sprawled out beside him, Matt asked, "How about you, Antonio? You ready to search them hills?"

"Sí, señor. Am ready."

Nate shook his head in wonder. He snapped, "Damn half-breed. Like I said, he ain't normal. Hell, yeah! He lives for that kind of crap. He's half animal."

Harris puffed up his chest and spoke curtly as an officer in command, "Are you declining an order?"

"I ain't heard an order yet. I just hear a discussion. I'll speak my damn mind if I want. It'll be my ass on the line out there. I'll reserve my right to bitch if I want!"

Harris growled in rising indignation, "I'm warning you. Do not get insubordinate with me. You are under my command and will do as ordered."

Nate stared directly at Harris with eyes closing down to resemble the cold slits of a rattler about to strike. His voice was cold and slow, "Ain't nobody got control over me. Don't try to pull that bullshit. It won't work."

Harris slowly moved his right hand down to the revolver on his hip. His eyes never left Nate.

Nate hissed, "Captain, you pull that gun out and I'll shove it up your ass!"

Matt reached over and put a firm grip on Harris's arm. He sent a message impossible for the captain to ignore.

"Captain, why don't you and Antonio go on down and work out some details. Give me a minute here with Nate."

Commander and scout were engaged in a fierce scowl, and neither displayed signs of backing down. The captain's hand remained on the pistol.

Nate, still coiled up tight, was ready to unleash for a quick blow. He glared at the captain, full of contempt for authority.

Neither man flinched. There appeared to be no honorable exit, short of conflict. Tension floated on the breeze that rustled the leaves above them.

Matt removed his hand from Harris. The men were free to do as they chose. Time slowed to a crawl as neither man backed down.

Matt broke the silence in a calm voice, "Captain, we got other fish to fry."

Harris hesitated. He didn't seem convinced. Slowly, he began to withdraw his hand from his revolver. He continued to glare at Nate. Never looking away, he motioned to Antonio with his head to follow him as he slid wordlessly off the crest of the hill. Matt waited until the two of them descended beyond hearing range.

"Nate, you picked a bad time to make a stand."

"I don't pick the time. The time picks me. His kind are a burr under my saddle. What's he so damn touchy for?"

"That's the Cap. He sees things different than you or I. But you were on the edge with me too. It don't do no good to git cocky with the boss, no matter who he happens to be."

"You serious?" Nate shook his head in bemusement as he continued, "Hell, I guess I ain't been 'round folks enough. Just speakin' my mind 'bout them woods after dark. That moon won't offer much light. Man would be a fool not to be leery of them mountains with Comanch hidin' out there. Antonio, well, he don't count. He ain't right."

He gazed out over the majestic dome of granite as the sun slipped below the pewter-stained slopes. A sense of dread laced his comment, "Hell, look at them rocks, Matt. Don't they give you the spooks?"

Matt stared out at the exposed granite. He had to admit there was a quality to their appearance evoking the supernatural. The assortment of peculiar formations spoke of ancient times passed over the eons without the presence of civilized man. They produced a mysterious influence not felt in the hills nearer to Austin. A peculiar power existed here in these rocks that he was unfamiliar with in his countless miles of trail from Texas to Virginia. He felt humbled in proximity to the great bulk of rock rising hundreds of feet above the surrounding woods. It took no leap of imagination to picture hordes of tormented spirits residing under the veneer of rock slabs scattered along the steep slopes.

He shook his head to break the spell.

"Don't let your imagination run away with you, Nate. Them are just rocks, like all the others you ever seen. Little bigger is all."

"That may be. But the Injuns are real 'nough."

"So you'll go scout?"

"Never said I wouldn't. Captain jumped the gun, is all. May not like it, but I'll scout out this side of the rock. Least I can see some of it now. That will help when it gits dark. Antonio can take the north side if he wants. We're close 'nough, I can start out soon as the moon comes up and be back 'fore too long. That is, if the Comanch don't scalp me."

"Sounds like a plan to me."

"It'll do. But Matt, keep that pompous ass away from me. I know my business. I do things my own way. He can go to hell as far as I'm concerned."

Matt nodded his head in understanding. But, my God, he thought; people were a pain in the ass.

NINETEEN

Matt rested his head on his saddle while lying against the hard ground and listened to the wind whisper through the treetops swaying against the starlight. A few leaves broke loose from the limbs above him and fluttered down invisible in the darkness to brush across his face. The moon remained hidden beyond the black ridgeline to the east. He thought of Nate and Antonio out in the somber night, silently stalking through the desolate terrain. They would need the eyes of a cat to pierce the murkiness where death stalked its victims in the dense woods.

Most likely, the two scouts were waiting on the moon to rise before they made their way deep into the mysterious areas tucked between the huge granite formations. He figured they would use the open creek bottom to close the distance to the main rock where they would separately wait on the appearance of the moon. Once there was sufficient light, they would probe the canyons most likely to contain the suspected Comanche campground. The Indians could be anywhere in the woods, but Antonio was aware of their favorite campsite, and he had decided to recon the side of the mountain most likely to hide them.

That decision suited Nate just fine. He had become reconciled to Antonio's proven worth on this mission, even taking a last bit of advice from the hardened scout before they both set out in different directions. Nate steered clear of Harris after receiving the final instructions from Matt. He was actually relieved to be away from the Ranger camp and to let Matt do the communicating with Harris, who approved of the idea of Nate investigating the south side of the rock.

The scouting plan fit well into Antonio's belief that the Comanche would be located on the north side of the largest dome. He wanted the challenge of finding them, without any distractions to interfere with his concentration. Nate was fine with the final plan since he also believed that he worked better alone.

Matt relaxed by himself in the dark solitude, enjoying a break from dealing with abrasive personalities. He sipped from his canteen, thinking about the day's events and listening to Whiskey munching grass nearby.

The long ride had exhausted all the men, and the confrontation between Harris and Nate was a sure sign of their fatigue. All of the men required a rest if a showdown with the Comanche developed the next morning. Matt intended to get in as much sleep as possible, isolated off to the side. Harris had bedded down on the opposite side of camp, next to Mossberg. The position of the men around the camp pleased Matt. He was not sure what Harris thought of his intervention with Nate, and the time apart from each other would allow any differences of opinion a chance to simmer down.

He gazed up into the canopy of limbs swaying with the wind across the milky blue haze of starlight. Thoughts of home danced across his mind. How were the girls doing? Were the boys doing their part to keep the place straight? Did Lee still feel troubled by his wound, or was he moving about closer to normal?

He imagined Cora going about the chores in her usual resourceful manner and then lying awake at night twisted up in worry about him out in the God-forsaken wilderness. The woman was always a worrier. That was the female side of her. She worked hard and worried harder. Her mind seemed to focus on the chances of a negative outcome, thus making his time away from home a time of anguish for her. He never failed to make it back from his excursions, but each trip took a toll on her in immeasurable ways.

The shame of it was that he enjoyed the time apart, despite her complaints about his absence. Chewing on an unlit cigar, he peered into the endless heavens above him and wondered if his fascination with life on the trail would ever decline.

Once again, Mary began to creep across his mind, along with the lustful desires that ached within him when he thought of her soft curves. She was full of feminine charm. Out here in the wild lands, Mary was an abstract contemplation that filled his idle time with wonderful thoughts of sensual pleasure. She provided an agreeable distraction to the disturbing realities of life on the frontier complicated by Indians. Once at home, she became flesh and blood, real and tantalizing. She would be easy to seduce and difficult to refuse.

His mind rolled over the options to his dilemma. When it was all cut and dried, he knew when he returned to the ranch, the idea of seeing Mary on the sly would have to die. It was a fascinating proposition to think of, but too fraught with upheaval to act upon. He had to avoid her temptations at all costs. Being with her had no chance of remaining secret. The Ellis ranch was off limits once he returned home. It was that simple.

The sound of grumbling snapped him out of his reverie. Someone was approaching his bedroll, but in the dark, he couldn't make out who it was. He heard a stumble, followed by a growling curse he recognized.

"Who goes there?" He held back a laugh.

"Son of a bitch! Didn't see that root and 'bout planted my face. It's me, Robert."

"Well, quit stumbling around like a drunk and pull up a spot."

Robert threw his saddle on the dirt with a thump and spread out his blanket next to it. He groaned as he went about his bed preparations, sliding stiffly to the ground on the blanket.

"Oh boy, I hurt in places I didn't know I existed. Was a helluva long ride today."

"Yes, it was," Matt replied, "but look at it this way. It will be a short ride tomorrow if we find what we're lookin' for."

"What are the odds?"

"Damn good, is what I think."

"What makes you think so?"

"Hell, I can feel it in the air. Them rocks, they look like Indian territory. I can sense Comanch out there. Nate got mighty spooked by them hills. Even he feels somethin' different is up. I can understand it if Indians find spirits in those rocks. They are something unusual. Never seen nothing like 'em"

"So you think there's a good chance for shootin' tomorrow?"

"I would bet on it. If we play our cards right, I'm countin' on it."

"You sure do seem to be lookin' forward to it."

Matt pulled another drink from his canteen, letting Robert's statement speak for itself. Robert settled in with his hands folded over his chest. He watched the night sky in silence, broken by the hollow thumps of upper tree branches bumping together in the occasional strong gusts from the south. The clunks echoed through the woods to dissipate into the blackness, where feral beasts waited for better light to hunt by.

Matt thought of the wilderness surrounding the small gathering of Texans. He spoke in a relaxed drawl, "Tell you what I really do look forward to. Been givin' it some more thought."

"What's that?"

"Gittin' a few men together and comin' out here to hunt for a month or two. Got to do it sometime soon, before the settlers crowd this area out."

"Matt, you ever thought that maybe you should've been an Indian?"

The statement amused Matt. He chuckled, "Yeah, maybe so."

"You'd be a natural at it, the way you enjoy the woods."

Matt plucked a stem of grass next to him and pealed back the outer sheath to expose the sweet inner stem. Putting his cigar aside, he rolled the tender grass between his lips, savoring its cool sweetness. Contemplating Robert's observation, he smiled at the thought of being Indian.

"You might be on to somethin' there. Take a look at it. Start with, them Indians don't ever do anything but camp. I certainly like a comfortable camp. Much like this one here, 'cept I like it better with a big fire blazin' and a shot of whiskey to top off the day. Maybe even have a lit cigar I didn't have to worry about Indians smelling."

"If we was Indian, we would have a big fire," Robert added.

"Yes we would, with some nice buffalo steak sizzlin' instead of this jerky I'm gittin' a little tired of. Indians do eat well. And it's hard to beat fresh meat over a nice campfire."

"I'd take a camp steak any day over home cooked. Tastes better out here in the woods." Robert was warming to the idea of a hunt.

"Yep, and that's the other thing. Git tired of your camp, hell, let's load it up and move, boys! Git on over to that sweet little shady spot on the Llano River I know of. Git tired of that camp? Load her up and move again. Now, to me, that's the idea of freedom!"

"Yes, it would be. Wouldn't have to look at the same country all the time." Robert spoke with enthusiasm, "Do you reckon they fish any?"

"Hell if I know. Don't matter none. If you and me was Indian, we'd be fishin' Indians! Fish in the mornin' and hunt in the afternoon! Bring home the meat and tell the squaw to cook it right. That's what them bucks do. They do the huntin' and the women do the work. Now I ask you Robert, how do ya beat livin' that way?"

"Don't think ya can. Maybe the white man has it all wrong."

Matt said, "Yeah, maybe so, 'cept for one thing. We think they got it made, but somethin' tells me they don't, or else they wouldn't make war on the young uns."

The reality of hard facts cracked like a whip that shut their lighthearted exchange down cold. They both fell silent as their personal thoughts churned with the crushing sense of animosity felt towards the Comanche. They hunted the Comanche like the wolves they both knew they were.

Matt spoke next, his voice breaking from the raw memory of loss. "You know what else, Robert? The Comanche could be livin' in utopia out here. But that ain't the way it is. Them bastards are always at war with pretty much anybody that ain't Comanche. Ask Antonio what a Comanche will do to a Tonkawa, or to an Apache if given the chance. These Indians out here been fightin' each other for a long time before we came into these hills. It's been one tribe against another for as long as them mountains been around. And you know what else?"

"What's that, Matt?"

"Them Comanch are now up against a stronger tribe than they ever seen. They just don't git it yet. They are about to be defeated and pushed off this land, just like they done to their own red brothers. They don't show no respect to their red or their white neighbors, and payback time is drawin' near. The white tribe is goin' to punish their sorry red ass. Tomorrow will be another hard lesson for 'em to learn. Problem is, they're slow learners. And it's goin' to take more blood flowing before they understand."

Matt took a breath to slow his tirade. He blew the blade of grass to the side, picked up his cigar, and placed it in the corner of his mouth before he continued. "Well, I understand. I may not have a formal education like that youngster Lloyd, but my daddy didn't raise me to be a fool. Look 'round at our recent history. Mexicans tried to rule Texans. Didn't work out too well for them bean eaters. The good ole U.S. had to come down here and pop 'em again in forty-six. Then the South lost to the damn Yankees. Now a few of them blue-bellies are down here tryin' to rape our neighbors. Them corrupt blue bastards can all go to hell."

He paused while thinking about the visit at his ranch by Colonel Ames and his hired guns.

"Got no use for them sorry Yankees or the Comanche. Take them Comanche, they've always tried to run off their rival tribes. Hell, it's goin' on all the time. Everybody wants the same land. Don't matter the name of the tribe. Don't matter the color. Red, brown, or white. It's always about which tribe's the most powerful and the most inclined to use their power to dominate. It's always been that way and it ain't never going to change. Never. This land will always be a hard land to rule."

"Matt." Robert hesitated, "You ever think of runnin' for office?"

"Hah, you're too damn funny. I'd rather shoot most politicians than debate 'em."

"You knew Harris is goin' to run?"

"So I heard."

"What do you think, now that you've worked with him?"

"I don't. But I suppose he'd be better than most of the thievin' skunks in Austin right now."

"He may be at that, I agree." Robert lowered his voice, "What happened earlier up on the hill?"

"You mean with Nate?"

"Yes I do. I overheard Harris tell Mossberg he was going to arrest Nate for threatening an officer. Said Nate was insubordinate."

"Oh my God! The Cap is just ventin'. He ain't gonna arrest nobody."

"He sounded serious to me. What'd Nate do?"

"Oh, he got cocky all right. If he was in regular military, he'd be in deep trouble. But he ain't. He's a scout. Captain can't do nothin'."

"I heard him say that when we git back, he will personally arrest Nate. Told Mossberg to be on the watch for Nate. Said he can't be trusted. Mossberg don't know any different. He'll do as he's told."

"I'll be damned. Captain's got it all wrong. He don't understand these hill country boys." With a deep sigh, he told Robert, "Don't worry about it. I'll talk to Harris. He'll probably calm down after some action tomorrow. If not, he's makin' a big mistake. If ya mess with one Johnston, you mess with 'em all. And that's one hornet's nest best left alone."

Matt checked his rifle and placed it under the extra wool blanket he drew up over him. He rested his revolver under the opposite side and closed his eyes, giving in to his deep exhaustion.

"Best git some rest. We're both goin' to need it."

<<<<< • >>>>>

Matt drifted in a dreamlike state, not asleep and not completely awake. He wasn't aware of his surroundings and he floated in a surreal land where sounds echoed inside his head, cluttered in confusion, not making the proper connections. The rumble of Robert's snoring close by rang an alarm in the distant corners of Matt's conscience, ensnared in misinterpretation of sounds.

He garbled a warning, "Cora! The bear is charging!"

At that point, he bolted upright, sitting in a defensive mode. Adrenaline rushed through his slumbering mind to bring him fully awake, but he was not sure of his location. He blinked his eyes in bewilderment. The moon cast a dim blush over the men gathered under a mosaic pattern of dark shadows beneath the trees filtering the soft light. Slowly, the realization of his location settled in when he saw someone moving at the edge of camp. He reached over to give Robert a solid shake that stopped his snoring.

Rubbing his hands across his face, Matt noticed a figure that was headed his direction. From the moon's location, he realized there were several more hours before the sun came up. Ready or not, the day was about to begin.

Nate hopped up to Matt, wild with excitement. He buzzed with enthusiasm when he said, "Matt, we found 'em! Or I should say, Antonio found 'em. I didn't see a damn thing. I scouted all along the south side of those mountains plumb to the ones furthest west. Didn't see a damn thing until Antonio scared the hell outta me! He just appeared outta nowhere, right next to me. Like a damn ghost! If he'd of been an Indian, I wouldn't be talkin' to you right now."

Matt said, "Slow down a bit. Where'd he find 'em?"

"Said he found the Comanch over in a canyon that exits to the north side. He's over there fillin' Harris in on the details. We can git to the canyon in no time. Antonio thinks there are more than twenty of 'em. They're all in one canyon. We got our work cut out for us."

Matt was completely awake now. Robert began to stir in time to make out most of what Nate had to say. Matt got up, energized, and relieved of fatigue.

"Take a break, Nate. You done good. Ought to be proud of your scoutin'. I reckon we'll move out shortly. Git what rest you can. I'll see what the Cap has in mind."

Matt weaved his way through the sleeping men to where Harris and Mossberg knelt discussing the situation with Antonio. The three of them were arranged in a tight circle. Antonio was drawing in the dirt, dimly lit by a small torch burning a dull yellow. He was explaining the layout of the terrain to Harris. Matt took position standing next to Antonio and closely watched the briefing over the scout's shoulder. The sharp odor rising off Antonio reminded Matt of the musky smell of Comanche he had been near. The excitement in Antonio's voice rose as he delivered the results of his work to Harris. The rest of the men in camp were now moving about, and a low murmur filled the air. They knew Antonio had found the Indian camp. Anticipation was rising.

Antonio finished his explanation and Harris moved off to the side. He motioned for Matt to accompany him so they could speak in confidence. They looked out on the creek far below them where it disappeared into the hills under the dim glow of the moon.

Harris said, "Our hard riding is about to pay off. The Comanche are in a canyon with only one good way out and I aim to seal that end with our men. Antonio says this canyon is a religious area for them where he figured they would be holed up. He was right. Hell of a scout! He didn't see the girl, but I feel strongly that she is there. Here is my idea. To keep from spooking the Comanche, we ride only partway to our destination. Set up an ambush on foot across the canyon mouth. This will be the blocking force, but I need some men to scale the rock to look down into the camp. These men will be able to see more of the camp, initiate the attack when needed, and possibly be responsible for the rescue of the Haven's girl. What do you think?"

Matt contemplated the diagram in the dirt and nodded his head in agreement. "Cap, it looks good to me. I see a few problems, but any movement like this will present unknowns. I like the plan. And I'd like to lead the men over the rock. If we can locate the girl from above, it may simplify our mission. Increase our chances to git her out."

"Good then. I suggest you take Nate. He has already been over the ground in that area and can guide you. Antonio says the climb is not too steep and there are boulders for your concealment above the camp. Take Tom to look after the horses while your men climb the rock. I'll take Sam for my stock."

"I'd like Robert and Mark for my other men."

Harris didn't hesitate. "You got it. Now let's get rounded up!"

The men were notified of the final roster and individually went about their preparations. Ammo was loaded into every available space on their person and haversacks bulged with extra bullets. The jingle of cartridges clinked throughout the camp as darkened shadows of men moved about. Canteens draped over shoulders sloshed with water while the men stuffed jerky and smoked sausage wherever it would fit. Tom and Sam separated the horses and readied them for travel, with gear cinched firmly in place to prevent rattling.

Preparations completed, the men mounted up behind their assigned leaders, with Matt at the front, riding into the bed of Sandy Creek. The water in the creek flowed in a cool silver luminance that reflected the moonlight off the surface of the pools. The sound of hooves on the coarse granite gravel made a surprising amount of racket in the still night atmosphere. Splashing water accompanied the dull crunch of the sand as the Rangers worked their way upstream. They were very visible from the highlands rising above the bank to their right. Matt became concerned about detection from a lookout or the inadvertent transfer of noise to the Indians on some mysterious breeze. He eyed the black, silhouetted ridgelines above the creek with suspicion, worried over the countless possibilities he could not control.

Concerned, Matt held up until the captain rode up beside him. Harris called for a halt. The column came to a stop, but a horse nickered at the change. Matt felt his hair stand on end with the extra noise.

Speaking in a low tone, Matt told Harris, "Can't risk a much closer approach. We sound like a herd of buffalo stampedin' down this creek. I'm goin' to ditch the horses first chance we git. Tom can seclude 'em up in the woods somewhere. This place puts the spook in me. I feel like them hills up there got eyes lookin' down on us. I don't want to risk too much, after gittin' this close."

Harris was in agreement with Matt and suggested, "There is a creek not too far up ahead where Antonio said my group of men will peel off. You can ditch the stock near there. At that point, my men will circle around to the backside of the rock to find the canyon mouth. With luck, we can trap them in the canyon. I want my horses a little closer to my position, in case they attempt a breakout and we have to pursue. You will not be in a position to chase them, but you can catch up later if the situation dictates. Antonio said they could exit your way but would have to leave their ponies behind because it is too rough and steep. So that option for them is probably ruled out."

The men proceeded up the faintly lit creek without any problems until Antonio signaled the time for the columns to part. Harris gave Matt his final instructions, "I'll get my men in blocking position well before dawn. When the light is right, commence shooting when you think it appropriate. I guarantee we will be ready when you are. If they do not flee, we will begin a pressure movement into the canyon. Hold your position or get the girl, but be aware, we may enter the camp if conditions dictate."

"Captain, I will git the girl first. She's our priority. Killin' Comanche is second. So be patient. I'll work out the details when I see the camp in good light."

"We will be patient. The commencement of killing is at your discretion, unless my hand is forced."

"Captain, you've done a good job. Let's finish it properly."

Harris handed the monocular to Matt. They shook hands before Harris reined his horse to the right and led his men up the draw in a cascade of gravel crumbling down the embankment. Matt watched until the last rider disappeared into the gloom of the woodland shadows.

TWENTY

Without waiting for instructions, Nate signaled for Matt to follow him further up the creek that meandered below the granite outcroppings on their right. They slowly proceeded past tall, ominous peaks positioned as sentinels guarding the approach to the largest mountain, occasionally seen standing pale in the distance. Heavy woods encroached on the banks of the creek until a towering mass of rock protruded ahead of them, above the black barrier of treetops. Even in the diffused light of the moon, this formation stood apart from the others with a multitude of rough cracks ripping up into the granite peak. Jagged drop-offs plummeted to where the woodland base merged into the creek bed. The rough upper heights reached into the night sky like a turkey's neck straining for a better view. Nate pulled up to wait for Matt and gazed up at the granite summit bare of vegetation.

When Matt rode alongside, Nate said, "Somethin' else, ain't it?"

"Yes it is," Matt dryly observed, "but I ain't here for sightseein'. What's on your mind?"

"I figure we go just beyond this here spectacle and ditch the horses. Earlier, I found a spot on a little flat up in the woods where we can hide 'em. It's near the foot of the main mountain."

Matt pointed with his chin. "Lead the way."

Nate led the men past the tall turkey peak and they soon gained a closer perspective of their destination. The immense rock broke into view from behind the thick tree cover on the banks of Sandy Creek. Bald slopes of the granite mountain plunged downward into the creek bed in front of them and also rose above the treetops off to their right, fading into distant darkness. The mountain's rounded bulk reflected the moon glow a charcoal gray and resembled an elephant lying prone, its trunk sucking water from the creek. The men rode in awe of the phenomenal site of natural wonder, growing larger as they followed Nate splashing through the shallow water.

Pausing to gain his bearings, Nate located a game path climbing over the creek bank choked with brush. It led towards the base of the imposing granite monolith. He motioned for the men to follow him up the narrow trail. Weaving through the brush, they came into a flat meadow encircled by stout oaks. A border of impenetrable brush outlined the edges of the opening. Nate rode to the middle of the small clearing and dismounted.

"This is as good as it gits to stash the horses."

Matt nodded in understanding and slid off Whiskey, his boots silently compressing the profuse grama grass. He removed his Henry and loaded his bags with extra ammo.

He addressed the men grimly, "Haul all the ammo ya can. Won't be any resupply runs. Full canteen. Some food. This job could take a while."

The men followed his orders without question. Tom went about securing the horses under low-hanging oak limbs, where they would be out of view when the day broke. In minutes, the men were ready and Nate motioned them to follow him out of the woods on foot.

Matt hung back to give Tom a last suggestion.

"Keep your eyes peeled. If you hear shootin', sit tight, but be ready for anything. We may need the horses in a hurry, but we'll try to do the job without 'em."

"Don't worry none 'bout these horses," Tom answered in his husky drawl. "They'll be here when you need 'em. Just be sure to bring the girl back. A few scalps wouldn't hurt none either."

Matt left Tom under the oaks and caught up to the men trailing behind Nate. He led them slithering through a tangle of thorny brush. The barbed scrub caught and tugged on their clothes, slowing them down and testing their patience in the poor light. Finally, the path opened up and gradually strayed upward to the broad base of the mountain, where a maze of boulders began to appear. Some of the boulders rose above the men the size of a room in a cabin, while others as bulky as several barns combined blocked their view. Nate skirted around the smaller rocks and sometimes threaded the men through crevasses that separated exceptionally large boulders. Emerging from behind a boulder, he came to a clear section of the slope. He remained hidden in shadow while he stared out onto the naked face of the main rock.

Hesitating before his first steps out of cover, Nate said, "Ain't no avoidin' this, Matt. A lot of our route will be in the open the higher we go. The canyon where they're at is out of sight, so I don't think they'll see us. And be careful on the wet rock. It's mighty slick from dewfall."

Hunched over, Nate shot across the open area and ducked into the closest brush he could locate, beneath a grove of shabby oaks barely clinging to life in the thin soil. One by one, the men joined him until they'd all gathered in a group under the sagging oak branches. They weaved through the brush to the far edge of the gnarled trees. Reaching the last of the oak branches, they came to another open area and once again repeated the crossing sequence.

Every movement led them higher in elevation until they could look down on the surrounding wild lands bathed in the blush of the moon. Above them, the immense flanks of granite extended far up into the night sky, hiding the eventual crest of the rock behind a succession of false summits. Occasionally, along the rough surface of the wet granite high above them, a flash of glistening radiance seemed to float along, suspended in the air and liberated from the surface. These unusual displays of iridescence caught Matt's eye and he pondered what they were as they flickered in a baffling flight across the face of the rock. He stopped Nate in the shadow of a huge boulder and asked him about the puzzling occurrence.

"You seen them little lights out yonder?"

The men all huddled next to Matt after he stopped Nate. They all heard his question and their interest held them in check. Nate stared at the top of the expansive area stretching above them, contemplating Matt's question.

"Yeah, I been seeing 'em."

"What are they?" Mark, the youngest in the group, seemed puzzled when he spoke.

Robert looked at the random display with a blank expression. Finally, he observed in a dry tone, "They seem to come and go as we move along. That's the damnedest thing."

The men grew silent and spellbound by the presence of a mystery none of them could explain.

"It's like they're followin' us." A faint worry infected Mark's voice.

Matt spat out, "Don't let your imagination git the best of ya."

Nate said, "Little spirits, I would guess. That's what Antonio told me they were on the way back to camp. He said the Indians are afraid to go up on the rock on moonlit nights like this."

"Hell, Nate, you ain't helpin' much. They ain't no damn spirits. There's some logical explanation for them sparkles." Matt balked at talk of the supernatural. "I ain't believin' no damn savage talk. Them Indians got their minds all messed up with such nonsense."

Nate shook his head. "Well, I don't know what they are. But it sure is a damn strange sight I ain't never seen before."

Mark's anxious voice didn't convey confidence in the conversation's direction. "Looks like whatever it is, is followin' us. All them lights seem to be well above us, least ways. Cain't do no harm to us from far away. Can they?"

Matt was growing impatient. He said, "Well, let 'em follow us. Whatever it is, it ain't spirits. I refuse to believe such stuff. It's just some kind of natural occurrence. And one that is holdin' us up. We can't pay it no mind. Let's git on to where we need to be."

He nodded toward the last stand of trees available to hide behind on the open slope. Glaring at Nate, he implored him to get a move on. Nate took another peek over his shoulder before crouching down and sprinting to the oaks clumped together in a small depression on the slope. The men all bunched up behind Nate under the oak limbs burdened with hairy gray clusters of Spanish moss. Nate looked up the bare slopes that ascended steeply until fading from view behind a long ridge.

"Gits interestin' from here on out. I didn't come this far up on my scout, but Antonio said we reach a spot lookin' down on the canyon the Comanche are camped in. He said there should be some flat slabs of rock we can hide behind well above their camp."

Matt said, "Don't see nothin' from here."

Nate pointed up the slope and said, "I reckon it's just a little further past that rise way over yonder."

Matt struggled to see beyond the rise Nate pointed towards. It was barely discernible in the pale light. He thought of the stealth needed for four men to move across the bare rock. Surprise was essential to their success.

"Nate, when we git to the top of the rise, we got to be careful the Indians don't bust us. When we git close, we really got to ease on in."

"Do the best I can."

"Then head it on out, and we'll keep following."

Ten minutes later, the men were crouched on the exposed flanks high up on the rock. Below them was the chasm, exactly as Antonio described it. It was heavily wooded, with huge boulders concentrated at the upper end. A small stream emerged from the jumble of granite to meander along the canyon floor. A few open areas in the bottom were visible from their high perch, but no Indians moved in sight.

On the other side of the ravine stood enormous granite outcroppings far more rugged than the boulders on their side. These cabin-sized boulders were perched on a much steeper slope than the one the men occupied. A few of the boulders had broken free in the past and tumbled down into the bottom of the canyon to take up final residence under an abundant growth of hardwood trees.

Peering up the gorge, Matt made out the steep and narrow southern exit strewn with a puzzle of irregular-shaped rocks up to the saddle connecting the two granite mountains. The constricted exit didn't seem to hold an appealing choice for Indians hard pressed by armed Rangers. To the north lay the canyon mouth, with a level gradient leading out of the valley. This area supported a dense tree growth that would screen most Indian movement from his present position.

Sizing up the circumstances, Matt began to doubt whether the captain had enough men for an effective seal of such a wide wooded area. His own position was too high on the rock to be of use. Scanning the location, he noticed a collection of flat slabs of rock below him that offered closer concealment to the canyon floor. The chunks of granite appeared to be in shooting distance of an Indian camp if they were in fact down in the bottoms. These had to be the rocks Antonio had mentioned.

Working his eyes over the landscape, Matt didn't detect another position he could put to good use. The absence of Indian sign worried him. His men had to be in the best location available before sunrise to increase their chance of success. Not positive of his next move, he detected a faint odor of smoke that provided a sure clue of a Comanche encampment below them. He made his decision.

"Men, let's slide on down to those slabs of rock below us. Them Comanche are down there for sure. I smell their smoke. We'll spread out among them slabs and hide until it gits light enough to see. Keep it real quiet. Remove your boots to keep the noise down. We can't take a chance they'll hear us."

Matt swung his ammo bags over his shoulder and clutched his boots and Henry in his hands as he descended in an awkward duck walk. He angled back and forth to maintain control on the steep, slippery incline. His knees popped with sharp bolts of pain protesting the awkward movement that inched him down to the protection of the rocks. Nate and Mark passed him by with no difficulty, slithering down the slope like a snake closing in on an easy meal. Matt cursed them in his mind for their youth and agility.

Reaching the nearest slab of granite, Matt reclined behind it, gasping to catch his breath. He heard Robert shuffling to a position just above him. Nate and Mark spread out below them as they all put their boots back on behind the large slabs of granite.

Matt remained silent, peering up at the moon as it slipped behind a slow-moving cloud, turning the naked rock face a darker shade of gray. Swiveling his head, he peeked over the angular block of stone to see the woods below losing distinction as the shadow of the cloud darkened them. A Comanche pony nickered from out of the murky woods nearer to the mouth of the canyon. Matt considered the possibility that the encampment of Comanche might not be in view from this vantage point.

Nate dispelled Matt's suspicions when he crawled up next to him and gleefully whispered, "I can smell 'em. We're damn close!"

"You can smell Indian?"

"Hell yeah! You cain't?"

"I smell smoke, but my nose ain't good 'nough to smell Indian."

"They smell like old grease."

"All right then, if you say so. Where do you think they're camped?"

"Some are right below us. Smell pretty strong. Others are off towards the mouth, behind them trees."

"I'll have to take your word for it." Taking a moment to consider his options, Matt said, "I guess we wait for the sun to come up. Maybe then, we can git an idea of their camp layout. Hopefully, locate the girl."

"Come on over by us. There's some brush you can hide behind and glass the bottoms."

"Sounds good." Frowning, Matt said, "Meanwhile, I hope they don't discover the captain."

Nate twitched his nose like a hound searching for scent.

"I think we're good here. The little bit of breeze we got is blowin' away from the Comanch. These slabs we're behind make for great firin' positions. We can cover the whole damn area. Them Injuns cain't touch us." He paused before adding, "Now, Cap is another story."

Matt watched as Nate eased back to his spot next to Mark. They had an hour or less to wait for better light to glass by. There was plenty of time for a wandering buck to stumble into Harris and his men and spoil all their hard riding. He strained his neck backwards to verify Robert's position and received a thumbs up that he was ready.

On the slope above Robert, a shaft of moonlight broke through the cloud cover. The moonbeam poured across the upper mountain, illuminating a glistening silver reflection in its path. Unable to define the wonder of what he witnessed, he marveled at another mystery the hill country presented. He chuckled softly, "Spirits, hell. They look like lightnin' bugs to me."

TWENTY-ONE

The eastern horizon glowed with the red-orange tint of the approaching sunrise reflected off the thin clouds gliding northward. False dawn awakened the songbirds down in the gorge, and their melody bounced off the granite slopes in ringing clarity. An early-rising canyon wren hopped from stone to stone until he plunged into the brush directly in front of Matt. The small brown bird went about his search for breakfast at a frantic pace, leaping from twig to twig among the tight cluster of branches hiding Matt. Perching on the outer limbs, the wren paused in his efforts to break out in a sharp, clear, warble of happiness that echoed across the open granite pitch high above the Indian encampment. His song loudly proclaimed, "Here I am. Look at me. There is nothing to fear on this fine morning." From the upper end of the canyon, another wren returned the trill greeting, initiating an ongoing exchange of cheerful notes between the two birds. They carried on in ignorance of the malevolent affairs of men.

Matt ignored the small bird hopping about and cautiously placed the monocular to his eye for the first detailed assessment of the canyon floor. He followed the course of the small stream running around the base of the larger boulders until it wandered into the middle of the flats under the trees. Working the glass along the edge of the shallow water, he made a discovery that quickened his pulse.

Spread out on a brown blanket, a dark-skinned Comanche was lost in deep slumber, unaware of his imminent danger. Moving the glass through the immediate vicinity, Matt made out the movement of another brave partially hidden behind the wide trunk of an oak. This buck was stretching out his legs, getting ready to rise from his bed. Matt focused on him until he sat up and rubbed the back of his neck. Long, greasy, black hair hung over his shoulders, unkempt from the night's sleep, tangled in braids that dead leaves clung to. His body was wiry but hardened with bronze-stained muscle. In a sleepy daze, the brave reclined against the oak, yawned, and then stretched out again beside the trunk. He snoozed unaware.

Matt whispered, "Psst. We got company down there."

Nate replied, "Yeah, I seen him movin'."

"Don't show yourself. Got to give it some time. Find the girl. See what else they got."

He continued to glass up and down the canyon floor, but all he could find was the two sleeping Comanche. Up in the tree canopy on the opposing canyon wall he heard a squirrel start chattering. Another Indian pony nickered from a location hidden deep within the trees. The world was waking up. Glassing above the trees where the squirrel fussed, he made out movement between two boulders perched high on the upper ridgeline. The fleeting motion was too quick to identify. It was the color of buckskin, whatever it was.

The Comanche snoozing near the oak stood up and peered into the area near the chattering squirrel. He never showed a sign of alarm, but sauntered over to the brave sleeping on the blanket and gruffly kicked him in the ribs. A harsh curse from the offended Comanche carried up to Matt. Briefly, the two of them exchanged heated words in the sharp dialect of their native tongue. The brave on the ground made a sudden movement for the legs of the tall, slim buck, but he missed. The mistake delighted the standing warrior enough that he delivered another kick to the ribs before he spun to escape to the other side of the creek. More cursing filled the air.

From out of the woods, a shout from another Comanche erupted with authority before he appeared on a direct stride toward the warriors at the creek side. This brave stood erect and proud. His movements were precise, crisp. In contrast to the other braves, his clothing and hair displayed vain attention to the details of personal grooming. His physique blistered with power. Matt trained his glasses on him as the Indian unleashed a torrent of cursing on the two that were clowning around. They both remained silent and respectfully subdued as he reprimanded them. Matt was able to study him while he stood stationary in the open, admonishing his fellow tribesman. His leather shirt hung loose on his body, with fringe hanging from the sleeves accented with a few blue beads dangling at the ends. A large knife with a deer bone handle resided on his hip, attached to a black leather strap around his waist. The leather in his garments was in a remarkably clean condition compared to the other warriors'.

Finished with the correction of the boisterous braves, he turned his other side to Matt's view before disappearing back into the woods. Matt cussed under his breath at the sight on his hip, opposite the knife. A white man's scalp dangled from the strap around the Indian's waist. Focusing on the scalp, he noticed it was dark hair, the length a white man would wear. Surprising Matt was the unusual patch of white that stood out from the darker hair.

Matt put the glasses down and muttered, "If I didn't know better, I would swear that was Frank's scalp. But there's no way. It couldn't be."

The sight of the scalp disturbed him. He had to suppress his urge to seek immediate retribution on the Comanche. Patience would be his ally. Matt thought of what he'd learned from his observations: there were three known Comanche, but in the woods, there was an unknown number. He was positive there were no Indians to his left, up in the head of the draw. The opposite canyon wall was too steep to camp in, so all the other braves would be to the right, down towards the mouth of the canyon, towards Harris. Whatever stirred up the squirrel had to be ignored as a deer, or maybe some other critter roaming about. Surely, it wasn't an Indian. The movement he had seen in the rocks was too brief to identify. He wondered if it was possible that Antonio was sneaking through the area above the camp. It would be just like Antonio to operate on his own, close to the enemy. No matter, what Matt needed to know was where the Havens girl was. Was she still alive? Any future action depended on her situation. Matt motioned to the men to remain hidden while they waited on further developments.

The squabble down in the camp was over and the original two braves stepped to the edge of some brush to relieve themselves, staring directly at Matt's location above them. He froze, praying that his men remained concealed. His stomach churned in expectation of discovery. A tart taste of acid rose in his throat. The Indians must not discover the men after all of their efforts to find the camp. Combat would come suddenly if they discovered the presence of white men. Control would be lost, along with the chance for rescue. The girl's future depended on their current location remaining secret.

The warriors leisurely finished their business while gazing up the rock slopes. It seemed forever to Matt, but finally they turned their backs without any indication of detecting his men. They hopped over the stream and took up sitting positions on their blankets, turned away from the Rangers hiding in ambush above them.

A familiar flush of relief relaxed his tensed-up muscles. Taking a deep breath, he recomposed himself. He thought of the Comanche wearing the scalp. The brave had disappeared back into the screen of trees. That was where he suspected other Indians were beginning to awaken. Action of some sort was rapidly approaching.

Matt squirmed behind the rock slabs and whispered to the men, "Be patient. They're surrounded and don't know it. They ain't leavin' here without a scrap of some kind. We got to figure out where the girl is first."

Nate added his thoughts, "They're in rifle range from right here. We can pop 'em whenever you say."

Robert listened quietly to the peaceful sounds of the fall morning with a look of resignation on his face. He didn't fear the conflict but knew death was waiting. Some good men would not see the sun set on this day. He rolled over to face heaven and closed his eyes, trying to put the morbid thoughts out of his mind.

Matt ignored the men while he continued to glass the two Comanche through the thin gap in the brush he hid behind. Immediately, he noticed one of them fiddling with a carbine. The presence of rifles in the camp changed the situation. The Rangers' advantage of range and firepower now became one notch closer to a state of balance with the Comanche. If the Indians also possessed repeaters, the balance would become closer still. If that were the situation, and he suspected it would be, his men would have to rely on their superior accuracy and position to regain the lost advantage.

<<<<< • >>>>>

Time seemed to crawl as the gray of false dawn gave way to bright beams of sunshine streaming through gaps in the low clouds that hugged the horizon. The early morning chill began to fade as the sun provided the promise of a warm day. A southern breeze kicked up as the morning sun increased in strength.

The wren returned to search the cracks in the rocks, accompanied by a mate in a relentless pursuit of food. They scurried about occasionally within an arm's reach of the immobile men. Matt figured the presence of the small birds added to the appearance of normal activity to help fool the Indians below them. A red-shouldered hawk rode the breeze up the canyon and over the cactus-strewn saddle, screeching as he glided effortlessly on the wind. Bird life was abundant and fully awake down in the canyon and their songs filled the air with crystal clear melodies.

Several different Comanche visited the upper end of camp, where Matt kept his eye on the original two sitting on their blankets, taking their time with an early morning meal. Matt noticed another rifle in their possession and that upped the ante, considering it was a repeating Spencer. Although he felt contempt for the tribe, he never lost sight of their danger as a fierce foe. Once engaged, the Comanche were ferocious fighters full of bravery. They were always ready to exploit any weakness with bold and unpredictable individual movements.

Matt contemplated the problems stacking up against the Rangers. At least seven warriors thus far had made their appearance known in the camp, and they possessed at least two known rifles between them. Time was working against his plans. The sun was climbing well above the horizon, and each passing moment increased the odds of the Indians discovering the threat surrounding them. The location of the girl was still unknown. Anticipation of armed conflict grated on any man's nerves and he knew the patience among the spread-out Rangers would be wearing thin as the morning advanced. His own patience was at the breaking point. He strongly craved pulling the trigger and starting the fight. His empty stomach continued to swell with acid while he tried to remain calm and choke it down.

Then he heard the crying.

It was unmistakable. A young girl was sobbing. The faint sound of her crying barely reached his ears, but he immediately knew the Havens girl was in the camp. Resentment built in his heart as the reality of her peril became clear. He dared not think of her treatment at the hands of the Comanche. It was then that the girl stumbled into view, roughly shoved by a young buck, who laughed at her loss of control. She fell to the coarse gravel and he yanked her back up by the hair, pushing her towards the upper end of camp.

The brave with the white man's scalp accompanied the younger buck. He never touched the girl. He seemed aloof and distant to her plight. She was grimy and her dress was slashed down the middle to reveal her bare back. Dried blood blackened her dress at the site of the rip. Long soiled hair hung over her shoulders in a twisted mess entangled with grass.

With her hair knotted up into his hand, the buck guided her to the two warriors sitting on their blankets and shoved her to the ground at their feet. Another council commenced among them until one of them got up to escort the girl out of sight behind some boulders. Matt realized the time for action had arrived and he motioned to the men to get ready.

"Nate, you and Robert will provide covering fire. Mark and I are headed down. We'll swing around and use the boulders up canyon for cover. You two keep 'em pinned down. Our ass depends on it. Once we git down there, I'll make a play for the girl. Wait for the right time to shoot. Questions?"

No questions came from the grim men.

Nate grinned at Matt and said, "Let's nail the bastards."

Matt slithered his way down the slab of rock to Mark and got in position for another glance at the camp. Robert and Nate removed their ammo and made it ready for quick access. When Matt put the glass to his eyes, he found the two Comanche tying the girl to a nearby elm. No other braves were in sight. The girl looked like a beaten dog with her hair ratted up and head hung low. Matt cased the glasses and gave the final signal for action.

They burst from behind the slabs of granite they were using for cover. Mark stuck tight to Matt's tail. Both of them scrambled at a steep angle towards the randomly scattered boulders at the head of the canyon. The hard granite surface made for slippery traction and they slid, on the verge of falling. Their boots scraped stones loose to roll clinking down the steep incline.

Behind them, they heard the first roar of Nate's rifle.

Matt continued to scamper down the slope but caught a glimpse over his shoulder of a Comanche falling backwards. The front of the Indian's chest burst open from the explosive contact of a slug fired from Nate's carbine. The powerful round passed through the Comanche to kick up a shower of gravel behind him.

His bronzed companion had just enough time to notice the other's misfortune before Robert fired a bullet that severed his spine. The second

Comanche pitched over onto his blanket and convulsed violently in the throes of death. The Havens girl let out a piercing scream, her face splattered with blood and two dead Indians stretched out on the ground less than ten feet away.

Distracted by the firing behind him, Matt slipped on the granite and pounded his thigh in a fall to the coarse surface. His pants ripped open, exposing bloody flesh gouged on the rough granite. Mark passed him and made the cover of a wagon-sized boulder at the bottom. He immediately swung his rifle up, searching for targets.

Matt had quickly checked his slide down the rock but came up running with a limp. Blood trickled down his badly scraped right leg. Ignoring the scorching pain, he stumbled beside Mark, who was intently searching the camp for targets.

The Haven's girl cowered behind a tree less than forty yards away. The problem was the area that separated them was mostly open, with only a few trees for cover. Beyond the girl, Matt saw movement headed their way.

He understood that the door of opportunity closed swiftly in battle and shouted at Mark, "Cover me. I'm goin' in!"

"Wait a second," Mark implored. "Slow down!"

The words bounced off Matt's back as he sprinted for the first large oak between them and the girl. Rifle fire boomed from Nate's higher position. He gave the Comanche reason to pause behind their dense cover of trees.

Mark looked over the sights on his Henry in a vain attempt to locate any suitable targets. All he saw was the fleeting movements of Comanche dashing between tree trunks and small boulders. He fired a few rounds in the direction of their probable locations to slow their advancement. His random shots, combined with the firing from above, echoed off the canyon walls. A constant rumble rolled through the bottoms in a confusing din that assaulted his senses.

Matt charged behind the oak and paused, out of breath. He anxiously peered around the edge of the trunk, searching for the girl. A bullet buzzed angrily past his head and ricocheted off a nearby boulder. The careening round screeched into the distance like a banshee.

Ignoring the near miss of the bullet, Matt saw a Comanche crawling closer to the girl. She was now hugging her knees to her chest in a vain attempt to escape the clamor and death enveloping her. She was terrified.

Matt confidently threw his rifle to his shoulder. He would eliminate the threat of the stalking Indian. Carefully drawing a bead, he gently squeezed the trigger and felt the familiar recoil against his shoulder. The shot was good. He knew it as soon as he pulled the trigger. The creeping warrior took the round straight into his head, which exploded like a pumpkin dropped from a roof. Matt's chest swelled. His confidence grew.

With the most pressing threat eliminated, he pushed off to scramble to the tree nearest the girl. He became agitated when he saw a bullet blow bark off the trunk inches from her head. The Comanche were aiming at her! She crunched up as small as the rope wrapped around her would allow. She was fragile and withdrawn in disbelief. Her life had become unbearably full of horror.

Matt heard the crack of Mark's rifle behind him. Comanche bullets buzzed to the left and right of the tree he was hiding behind. Above, he made out the reassuring reports of Nate and Robert providing crossfire to cover his movements.

Now was the time!

He sucked in a deep breath and broke for the girl in a wild dash. His boots churned up a shower of loose gravel as he sprinted across the open terrain. A bullet sizzled close by his head. His left ear filled with a crackling hiss at the near miss. He ducked and rolled in a reckless panic, tumbling at her feet just as another round splat against the tree next to them. Bullets ricocheted and whined through the air as both sides exchanged a fury of shots. A constant thunder echoed over the canyon bottoms.

Matt fumbled for his knife and yanked it from its sheath. He sliced at the rope that held her to the trunk. The girl trembled in fear, afraid to make eye contact.

"Git me out of here," she sobbed. "They've been mean!"

Matt's heart broke at her pitiful condition.

"I intend to, hon."

With a final desperate cut, the last of the bindings fell loose at her side.

Finally free, she fell into Matt's grasp to clutch the scant security he offered. His arms instinctively wrapped around her. That was when he saw a fierce-looking Comanche spring from behind a nearby boulder, wielding a knife in his hand.

The young warrior made a mad dash toward Matt. He was intent on counting coup while Matt was distracted with the girl. The warrior screamed a furious war whoop. He closed the distance between them in an instant.

In one fluid movement, Matt threw the girl to the side and rolled in the dirt to free up his right hand. She struck the ground hard, moaning with the unexpected impact.

The young buck misjudged his leap when Matt rolled. He swung the knife wildly in Matt's direction. The blade slashed a long gash in the back of Matt's shirt, narrowly missing flesh. Matt felt the tug of the knife cutting the cloth as he finished his roll.

Now turned, he saw the Comanche, already rising to start another lunge in his direction. From his prone position, Matt jerked his Colt free of the holster and intuitively squeezed the trigger.

Fire belched from the revolver in a deafening roar that sent the lethal round ripping into the astonished brave. The bullet struck him high in the right breast and spun him violently in the air. His knife clattered harmlessly to the gravel near the terrified girl. He tumbled out of control and collapsed to the ground with a thump. Blood spread across his bare chest as he struggled to his knees, leering at Matt with a black glare of defiance.

Without hesitation, Matt drew a bead on the center of the Indian's chest. He let the authority of his Colt explode a second time. The brave's black eyes flew open wide as the shock rampaged through his body, blowing out an exit hole of flesh, blood, and bone in a crimson mist. He pitched over backwards with his legs bent awkwardly beneath him, black eyes clouded over and devoid of life.

The Havens girl whimpered in paralyzing fear as the violence escalated all around her. She was shaking out of control. Frozen in place. Incapable of movement.

Shots continued to reverberate in the canyon and sporadic gunfire started to occur from the position of the men stationed with Harris. The battle was escalating. His time was running out. Matt returned the Colt to his holster.

Looking up the slope, Matt could see Robert calmly taking aim as a round from a Comanche blew apart a chunk of granite near his head. It was then that Matt realized some of the Indians might be decent marksman after all. Robert, unfazed by the near miss, continued to take deliberate aim before returning fire.

Another bullet buzzed near Matt's head. With time and luck running out, he scooped the girl up and began dashing back to Mark. Matt wrapped his left arm around her waist, surprised at her frailness and light weight. Gripping his Henry in his right hand, he began to weave toward Mark.

Up ahead, Mark was working the lever of his rifle in a steady motion. He swiveled the barrel back and forth, covering several warriors at once. It was no use; Matt could feel and hear angry hornets humming by him in his lumbering run, slowed by the girl who clung to him. His boots felt like they were full of wet sand. Each step seemed restrained as if in a bad dream. He could not pump his legs any faster. Mark didn't appear to be getting closer. The girl flailed in his grasp. He was losing the race to safety.

All of his senses rang alarms as Comanche rifles bellowed, sending hot lead his direction. He knew he would take a slug. The scream of self-preservation demanded he drop the girl to take cover. Resisting his strong survival urge, he continued to weave and duck in an effort to throw off the Comanche's accuracy. He weaved in vain right into a bullet that tore through his shirt and nicked a chunk of flesh off his waist. He felt the tug of the fabric and the hot sting of the scorching round. Warm blood immediately flowed from the wound and mixed with his free flowing sweat. A dark stain spread across the torn shirt.

A second slug blew through his hat and knocked it off to the side at an angle. He knew his time was up. The Comanche had his range. Desperation swept him. He had the girl so near safety only to fail at the last moment. Mark was so close, yet so far away. Matt's vision narrowed in his state of dismay.

TWENTY-TWO

The experienced warrior that had Matt in his sights paused to take a better rest against the tree he was firing from behind. Placing the forestock against the trunk for firm support, he drew a final bead on the white man's broad back. One more shot was all he needed to do the job. He had the range of the man carrying the captive girl. He desperately wanted the girl back. She was to be the source of future pleasure and possibly a rich trade with the Comancheros on the high plains when he tired of her. His hatred of the Texans drove him to kill them all or to rape their women at every chance he got. This sluggish white man provided a good target. The other whites shooting at his exposed brothers couldn't see him. He would take his time for the next killing shot. One last shot would be all he needed.

He positioned his sights squarely on the center of the man's broad back. He slowly began the final squeeze of the trigger. From his peripheral vision, he saw the streak of an object towards him. He recognized the whoosh of the arrow just as the shaft drove through his neck. The iron-tipped arrow severed his carotid artery and sliced open his throat. He staggered, falling backwards and gasped for air. He dropped his rifle to clutch at the blood pulsing in torrents out of his neck. Sinking to his knees, he managed to make out the source of the arrow.

It came from an odd-looking character on top of a boulder uphill from where he now kneeled in his own blood. He fought to remain conscious. Focusing through his pain, he saw an unusual round hat shading the face of the stranger. His enemy drew and notched another arrow. He wanted to flee, but there was no time. Another arrow was floating on the air straight at him. It flew with incredible speed he was unable to avoid. The arrow struck his chest like the kick of a horse. The hollow thump was the last sound he heard before the brightness of the sky tapered to a closing darkness. He collapsed into a lifeless heap of twisted limbs. Dead before the arrow shaft stopped quivering.

Antonio broke into a grin that signified satisfaction over his kill. He dropped off the backside of the boulder, undetected and in search of his next victim.

Matt finally stumbled into the safety of Mark's position, surprised that the close rounds never struck him down. He plopped in behind the rock and placed the girl out of harm's way. His chest heaved with the effort to breathe while he stretched out on his back. His hand slid down to the fresh wound at his waist. He felt the sticky blood soaking into his shirt. The burn was intense, but he was satisfied that the torn skin was external. The bullet had done no damage a bandage couldn't handle.

He looked over at the girl, who shook violently. She was in shock at the sudden turn of events and completely unsure what the new situation meant for her. Tears flowed through the dirt on her cheeks. A lull in the firing occurred between his men and the Indians, although the rumble of battle escalated in the direction of the men posted with Harris.

"Son of a bitch! I thought I was a dead man."

Mark said, "You damn near were. I couldn't cover all the heads I saw firin' your way. Nate and Robert stayed busy too. Too many targets. We got 'em real pissed off. More of 'em in there than I thought. How are ya?"

He let go with another round before Matt could answer.

"Doin' all right. Got a flesh wound on my side. Stings like hell, but I'll be all right. My hat is now ventilated." He examined the hole in the hat and felt his scalp, afraid some would be missing. "Several inches lower and it would've been lights out."

He noticed the girl watching him with bulging eyes full of fear. She hugged her knees up to her chest while lying on her side. Her large blue eyes watered over in a questioning gaze full of uncertainty.

"It's all right, hon. We aren't goin' to hurt you none. We're here to take you back home to your mom and dad."

The girl didn't say anything. Silently, she stared at him while shaking harder.

"You're goin' home, sweetheart. Them Indians ain't goin' to hurt you no more. Mom and Dad are waitin' for you. That's where we'll take you. I promise. Do you understand?"

She nodded her head, but fear gripped her too much for words. She unleashed an uncontrollable flow of tears. Matt thought about what she had seen and experienced the last few days. No child deserved her fate. She was forever changed. He put an arm around her to pull her up and hug her to his chest. He wanted her home, safe with her family. To him, this was personal.

"Mark, you're a young buck. How 'bout you run her up to Nate and Robert? Git her further away from these red devils. I can cover you better from down here."

Mark nodded his approval of the suggestion and asked, "Do you think she can run? Would go faster up the hill if she can."

"How about it, hon? Can you run up that hill with Mark here?"

She glanced up the hill and did not hesitate. "Yes."

"Mighty fine. Here's what you do. Mark, lead her to that rise behind us to put distance between you and them Indians. I'll cover. You hold her hand and don't let go, no matter what. Git her up there safe while we have a lull."

Matt methodically checked his weapons and reloaded. He placed a box of shells next to him and slipped a bandana over his wound. He grimaced at the burn of his ripped flesh. Rising above the protective rock, he got a good view of the camp. Several dead Indians sprawled out in front of him. Otherwise, there was no movement or sign of Comanche. The steady din of a fusillade indicated the men with Harris remained heavily engaged out of sight at the canyon's mouth.

He nodded to Mark to head it on out.

Mark grabbed the girl's hand and darted away from Matt in a low crouch. She strode along beside him, but the pace was slow due to the rough, rocky terrain. Immediately, a shot rang out and a bullet hummed in their direction, kicking up a spray of dirt near Mark's boot.

Matt sprang into action. He worked the Henry in the direction the firing came from, silencing the location. Other random gunfire burst in Mark's direction. The Indians were still active, but none of the firing had any conse-quence. Matt was relieved when Mark had led the girl out of the Comanche's sight. The plan was working well. With the girl secured, he was now free to kill Comanche.

Turning his attention to the task of killing Indians, Matt took stock of the situation. The Rangers effectively surrounded the Comanche, and he personally held control of the narrow box end, where they were least likely to escape. Mark would join Nate and Robert above him. With three rifles, they held their position strong enough to discourage any upward movements. That left the captain's men to hold their blocking position, or to move into the canyon and pressure the warriors. If the men did move his direction, a deadly storm of crossfire would envelop the Comanche. He decided to hold his position and see how the conflict developed. There was a good chance that scattered braves would flush his way.

Twenty minutes passed with only an occasional shot fired by Nate or Robert. The men above him had burrowed into the best defensive positions that hid them well. They were intent on staying put and delivering punishment. He did see Mark make it to the rocks with the little girl, much safer high up on the rock. She was secluded out of sight behind three well-armed men.

The Indians hunkered down during the lull in the fighting and did little moving. The Comanche were conserving their ammunition, and getting a better hold on their predicament.

Targets became hard to acquire, and that caused Matt to worry about plans the Comanche might be contemplating. He firmly believed in pressuring the enemy at all times. He believed in not allowing an opponent to have a reprieve. But alone, he was in no position to act on his preferred tactics. He would have to wait for the actions of Harris and his men to flush the braves out of hiding.

Minutes crawled by, each one passing longer than the last. He noticed there was almost no firing at all from the mouth of the canyon. Flies began to buzz around his bloodstained shirt, crawling under the torn cotton and becoming a constant nuisance he swatted at. With the sun climbing steadily, he also began to suffer from thirst. The day was unseasonably warm. The southern breeze loaded with moisture from the Gulf of Mexico raised the humidity until the air was thick, holding the rising temperature close and sticking against his skin. His canteen was up on the rock where Mark waved at him to verify each other's location and safety.

Licking his dry, cracked lips with his tongue did no good. His parched throat and cottonmouth craved water until it was an intolerable distraction. Scrounging in the gravel, he found a relatively smooth stone, brushed it off, and plopped it into his mouth to stimulate saliva. It wouldn't replace water but was better than nothing.

Peeking around the rock, Matt couldn't see any Indians. They were out there, but kept well hidden. The current stalemate would last all day if the Comanche desired. They were masters at waiting, unlike the white men. He knew the Comanche viewed the passage of time differently than white men. Time was for deliberating options to be used to their benefit. The Indians trained their entire lives to take advantage of the opportunities patience provided them. Knowing they were boxed in and taking heavy casualties motivated them to remain content in seclusion. They would let time turn to their benefit. If they held out until nightfall, it was possible for them to escape undetected one by one. On the other hand, they might mount their ponies to make a charge out of the canyon's mouth in a hail of gunfire. If Harris did nothing, the stalling would benefit the Comanche one way or another. Matt's strong urge was to get up and work his way into the camp to force the battle to a conclusion. He always favored action over sitting and waiting. Time and again, bold movements had won the day for him in past encounters with red men and white alike.

Rolling the stone around in his mouth, he mumbled, "What the hell is Cap doing?"

At that moment, Matt heard the eruption of rifle fire, followed by the screaming war whoops of Comanche hidden deep in the oaks. The distinct thud of bullets impacting solid objects mixed with the increasing thunder of an intense battle. He heard the rebel yell of one of the Rangers. All hell was breaking loose just beyond the treeline that screened the combatants from his view. The smell of blood was in the air.

From his position, he couldn't see a bit of the unfolding drama. The frustration was overwhelming. Shouts from both sides of the conflict elevated above the echoes of gunfire. A variety of weapons discharged in the tumult. Bullets tore through the woods as the two sides converged. He knew the results of the close fighting would end in sudden death on each side.

Up the hill, Matt saw his men standing tall and upright, straining to get a better view of the fighting concealed below them at the canyon's mouth. They stood out, unprotected by cover, but drew no attention from the

Comanche. The Indians were attempting a breakout!

A sudden rush of warriors meant the captain's men had their hands more than full. The successful containment of the Comanche was now in doubt. Matt instinctively knew the Rangers needed any help they could get, and he began to work his way deeper into the Indian encampment, using boulders and trees to cover his advance. Reaching the flaccid bodies of the first slain Comanche, he glanced up the rock to see all three of his men watching his progress. He pointed at them to get their attention and signaled with hand motions for them to remain where they were. If things went bad in the canyon, he wanted the girl well protected.

He crept up to the tree where he had rescued the girl. The young warrior that had rushed him with the knife stared into the sky, eyes crawling with flies. Here beside the tree, Matt paused to take stock of the situation. A few stray rounds hummed through the foliage ahead of him, trimming off leaves that drifted to the ground. Ricochets whined overhead, cutting random paths through the air. This position put him close enough to pick off retreating Comanche but far enough back to avoid most of the errant bullets.

It didn't take long to make out the backs of a few braves retreating before the onslaught of the Rangers with Harris. The Indians were backing up. They were focused on the white men applying steady pressure to their front, unaware of Matt's concealed location at their rear. One skinny warrior carried only a bow with a half-full quiver of arrows slung over his bare back. His bow did no good against the rifles firing against him. He was the first to retreat into Matt's range.

Matt pulled the Henry snug against his shoulder, pressed his finger gently against the trigger, and put the Comanche square in his sights. He slowly applied pressure on the trigger until it tripped smoothly. The rifle responded with a snarl expressing his wrath. The skinny brave never knew he was in danger until the round smacked against his back and slashed through his body. His bow flew violently from his grip. He tumbled heavily across a boulder and rolled limply to the dirt.

Another Comanche took notice of the effect of Matt's shot. In a panic, he hurried a poorly aimed shot from his battered rifle. The bullet buzzed harmlessly past Matt. With practiced precision, Matt levered a fresh round into the chamber of his Henry. In a fluid movement, he swung the rifle around to acquire the new target. The surprised brave now stared straight into the business end of the Henry held by the bearded white man. Before he had time to dodge, fire blew from the end of the Henry barrel. The .44 caliber slug thundered with all its energy to deliver death to another Comanche.

Matt ducked behind the tree for protection as the firing of Harris and his men intensified and came much closer. Bullets slammed into nearby trees with distinct thumps. Small branches dropped to the ground after ricocheting bullets clipped them free. Rangers screamed curses as they advanced. A constant volley roared throughout the canyon.

Comanche darted rearward in a desperate scramble away from the hail of lead raining down on them. They soon found their positions hard pressed against the steep slopes that rose above the canyon.

Matt didn't dare risk exposure to his fellow Rangers' fire on the canyon floor. He decided to hold his location until one of the other men recognized his position.

Minutes later, he made out the nearby commands of Harris directing the men to move forward. He was ordering them to continue pressing the remaining Comanche. Recognizing his opportunity to become involved in the action, Matt hollered at Harris as loud as he could to be heard above the clamor of rifle fire.

"It's Matt! I'm over here. Behind the tree!"

Surprised, Harris caught sight of him and eagerly ran up to the tree. He slapped Matt on the back with enthusiasm. Keeping his gaze to the front, he told Matt, "We've got them on the run! Been giving them a damn hard licking. There's dead Indians all through those woods!"

"Good work, Captain! We got the girl with the boys up on the rock. She's in decent shape and safer up there with them."

"Hell of a good job, Matt! Outstanding! The day has shaped up real well."

A fresh volley of fire erupted in the woods tight against the base of the opposing slopes. The men had the remaining Comanche cornered, with no way for them to escape. The deadly accuracy of the Rangers continued to extract the high price of blood from the beleaguered braves. Shouts of anger accompanied the rounds that pumped into the surrounded warriors. The remaining Comanche were still fighting with the desperation of a cornered bear. Bullets flew between both sides in rapid succession and prompted Matt and Harris to maneuver into better firing positions.

Reaching an open line of sight, Harris stopped and took quick aim at a temporarily exposed brave. Knowing the target presented a small window of opportunity, he fired in haste and hit a tree near the Comanche. The experienced brave was a chief trying to rally his remaining tribesmen. After the near miss, he recognized his state of peril in time to twist his body in a smooth motion for an expertly delivered round back at Harris. The well-aimed shot sped with a crackling sizzle towards Harris, squarely centered on his chest. Its deadly trajectory cut straight through the humid air until it encountered a small branch. The limb blew into scattered pieces and sent the bullet tumbling out of control through the woods.

Behind and off to the right of Harris, Matt turned his head at the sound of the rapid firing. In a split second of taking another step and turning to face the challenge, Matt met the errant bullet as it crashed into his forehead with a ferocious impact. He immediately stopped moving. Standing upright, he wavered momentarily before sinking to his knees. He swayed awkwardly with a vacant expression and collapsed across the rotting carcass of a tree trunk. His arms hung at his side, lifeless, as his face plowed unchecked into the leaves that littered the rough gravel of the canyon soil. His Henry clattered to the ground with the barrel digging into dirt. Blood poured from between his eyes, which stared absently without the ability to perceive the cool blue sky of a fall morning.

TWENTY-THREE

Harris fought off panic when he realized the danger his missed shot and open position placed him in. He saw the Indian that missed him rack in another round for a second attempt. With no time to hide, Harris held his breath and centered his sights on the older Comanche's chest. Harris saw the brave at the end of a sharply focused tunnel. That old familiar feeling of confidence indicated he was precisely on target. As he applied an even pressure on the trigger, he knew his second shot would hammer home before his rifle cracked. The warrior chief had made it halfway through his own trigger pull when the slug Harris sent his way slammed against his breast and drove through his heart. The warrior's beat-up Spencer jerked upward with the vicious impact of Harris's bullet. In a spasm, the brave's finger squeezed the trigger. But the round sliced harmlessly into the overhanging tree limbs.

Harris saw the splatter of blood on the Comanche's chest as he stumbled backwards and the rifle tumbled from his hands. Mouth gaping in shock, the experienced warrior fell to the ground, out of view. Other tribesman near the dead chief scrambled for cover as bullets sprayed around them in fierce splats against boulder and bark. Their fighting spirit failed them when they saw their trusted leader fall dead in the dirt. They ducked and dodged in a wild scramble to avoid bullets that seemed to arrive from every direction. A few Comanche wailed a mournful death song after they had retreated as far as the boulder-filled terrain allowed.

Forced into a dead end, the discouraged Comanche found their position against the bluff smothering them in a trap. They now faced the relentless pressure of the determined Rangers firing steadily from behind well-chosen cover. With only a few rifles left to return fire, they knew the battle was lost, but they intended to hold on for as long as possible against the hated white men. The desperate Comanche found that these Rangers fought with the tenacity of a wolf pack, like the Texans from years ago.

The men, under directions from Harris, continued to search for the most advanced positions to fire from as they tightened the stranglehold on the be-sieged Comanche. It didn't take long until the men's improved deployment held the Indians completely pinned down. This allowed Mossberg the oppor-tunity to achieve position at the exposed flank of the hunkered-down braves while they concentrated on the fire originating from their front. He found a boulder to the side of a large oak tree that offered great concealment and a nice clear line of sight behind the warriors now caught in a vise.

Waving back at Harris, Mossberg signaled for a constant covering fire to overwhelm the warriors before they had a chance to become aware of his presence. The Rangers responded with a hailstorm of lead pumping into the area. The Indians did not dare raise their head. With the Comanche cower-ing, it became an easy task for Mossberg to acquire a steady aim resting against the boulder.

He calmly dispatched the nearest warrior. The tremendous roar of the rifles firing in the valley echoed off the rock bluffs in a volume that masked the singular report of Mossberg's deadly aim. Working his way down the line, he fired at will until the last surviving brave collapsed dead beneath the granite boulders that loomed over his fallen brothers.

With the death of the last Comanche, Mossberg stood up shouting, "That's it boys! That was the last one down on this end. I think their done for!"

The men cautiously peered through the woods, unsure. They exchanged questioning glances. Gradually, a few began to stand up. Satisfied the danger was over; they finally let their guard down with eruptions of cheering. They gathered near Harris and slapped one another on the back with congratula-tions. Wide grins spread all around the men, now that the uncertainty of battle had passed.

Harris swelled with pride over their performance and boomed with joy, "Damn good job, men! Damn good!

All the men returned his acknowledgement as a euphoric mood swept over them. They made their way towards Mossberg and the last stand of the Indians with shouts of triumph. Harris and the men walked among their enemy, scattered about in contortions of violent death. Mossberg found one of his victims still gasping for breath and clutching his chest, which frothed with pink blood full of bubbles. The rumble of his revolver blasted throughout the hushed canyon as he sent another Comanche to his spirit world.

"That's the last one. Captain, your coverin' fire kept 'em pinned down good. Made my job easy. They never knew where I was at. Easy as shootin' pigs at the trough. Shot right on down their line without 'em ever knowin' it. Hot damn! It don't git better than this."

"Good work, Mossberg." Harris spread his arms wide. "Good work to all you men. This day will be talked about for a long time."

Antonio made his appearance at the top of a boulder, rising above the men just as Harris finished congratulating Mossberg. He let out a trembling war whoop as genuine as any the Comanche ever used. He raised his hand triumphantly in the air and shook two bloody scalps of long black Comanche hair. A wickedly wide grin puckered his cheeks beneath his reptilian eyes. He swept his cold gaze over the men spread beneath his granite perch. Cocking his head back, he let go with another tremulous howl of victory. His war whoops carried from the canyon floor up to Nate in a rolling echo of primitive rapture. Antonio completed his savage celebrations, pounding his chest with the gory scalps before hopping off the backside of the boulder to join the men.

As Antonio strutted up to the gathering, a slow realization began to dawn on Captain Harris. Caught up in the exhilarated mood of victory, he had failed to notice the absence of several men. Alarmed at the obvious oversight, he shouted to the men, "Where is Matt?"

Dumbfounded, the men looked at each other with blank expressions. No answers came. A surreal silence filled the air. Emptiness permeated the woods.

"He was behind me right before we made the last push. He said they got the girl. Where the hell is he now?"

Harris broke into a run towards the area where he'd last seen Matt. The men fell in behind their captain, not certain they wanted to know the answer to the question.

Their suspicions were confirmed when Harris suddenly stopped and shouted out in dismay, "NO!"

The men could see Matt sprawled out before Harris in a position similar to the dead Comanche they had just left behind. Blood poured beneath his head, collecting in a crimson pool, already congealing along the edges. His eyes were closed and caked with dirt. His body was contorted and motionless. Lifeless. Matt was dead!

Harris knelt beside Matt, his voice cracking with emotion, "Son of a bitch! This can't be. He was just behind me."

The other men gathered around as a solemn mood darkened their faces, replacing their recent jubilation. No words disturbed the eerily silent woods. All heads hung low with the unexpected tragedy. Matt possessed the most experience among them. This should not happen to a man of his background. The men were speechless at his misfortune. A cloud of depression dampened their mood at the sight of Matt crumpled at their feet, devoid of the power he'd once exuded.

Harris summoned his courage and reached down to pick up Matt's pale hand, searching his wrist for a pulse. Not detecting one, he gazed up sadly at the men. Several men turned and walked away. It was a sight they would just as soon forget. They had seen enough.

Shaking his head in disbelief, Harris lowered his ear to Matt's chest. He listened for a moment before jerking away with excitement.

He cried out, "He's still with us! It's weak, but he has a beat."

With optimism building, he looked closer at the wound on Matt's forehead flowing with blood. It didn't take long before Harris looked up at the men with hope replacing the concern in his eyes.

"Hell men. That's just one nasty rip across his head. The bullet did not enter! He's just knocked out cold. Head wounds always bleed badly. If we can get him to wake up, he may prove to be fine."

Harris stood and snapped orders with authority, "Get some bandages and salve to stop the bleeding. The horses need bringing in. The supplies we need are in the packs. Do not move him until then. He is in bad shape and head wounds require caution."

He stepped out from under the canopy of the trees to wave Nate and the others in. Returning to Matt, Harris found Mossberg already attending to him. He spoke gently, trying to revive him.

Matt remained unresponsive.

Harris commented in a dull voice full of grief, "Hard to believe he took a bullet."

"Captain, any of us could've took a bullet," Mossberg replied. "There was plenty of 'em in the air."

Harris stood silent, watching Mossberg do the best he could for Matt with the limited supplies. A frown soured Harris's expression when he said, "I just realized Lloyd is not here. Has anybody seen him?"

Mossberg placed a wet bandana across Matt's neck. He removed his hat and wiped his sweat-streaked brow with his shirtsleeve. What he had to say would not go over well.

"Sir, Lloyd didn't make it."

"What do you mean?" Harris asked incredulously.

"Over to the far right of our original line when them Comanch made their break for it ..." He hesitated to complete the explanation. "Well, sir, one of 'em got Lloyd."

Harris found a seat on an ancient log deteriorating into the soil. With a mournful sigh, he bent forward and looked at the dirt, asking in disbelief, "What happened?"

"He was on the far end when they made their break. Not a very protected area he was in. Things started happenin' fast. Them Indians come out of the woods hell bent on gittin' gone. We got most of 'em or at least got their horses. But there was a couple of 'em that made it through our fire, and they rode for the flats between Lloyd and that point of rocks off to our right. Was the only place for 'em to escape, and the one in the lead, well, he put on a helluva a show. He rode fast and low on his pony. Didn't nobody hit him with all the other targets 'round."

Mossberg paused in his explanation, reliving the tumult of the Indians breaking out of the line anchored on the right by Lloyd. "Hell Captain. That Injun was good. He drove an arrow through Lloyd and never slowed up a bit. He made it past us and two more followed him 'fore we bottled 'em back up."

Harris was silent for a moment, taking the news like a punch to his gut.

"Lloyd didn't make it." Speaking to the ground, he mumbled, "You're sure?"

"Yes sir. I checked on him. He was gone."

Harris slumped in his shoulders and gazed absently at his scuffed-up boots. His thoughts buried deep in guilt.

"Sir, the Injun that shot Lloyd was sportin' a white man's scalp on his belt. He knew his business. Lloyd was just in the wrong spot at the wrong time. Could've been anyone of us that got in that Injun's way."

"He was a good kid. I brought him out here. I am responsible."

"Sir, we done damn good, if you ask me. Sure, I'd like another shot at the ones that got away. We all would. But they're long gone by now. We bit 'em hard enough to make 'em think twice about comin' back 'round here. When it's all said and done, we gave 'em a helluva lickin', with minimal loss on our side."

Matt lay silent beside his comrades while they discussed the situation. Lloyd lay dead and alone out in the dry grass of the canyon's mouth. Mossberg held his tongue while Harris regained his composure from this series of setbacks. A sense of loss settled over the band of Rangers, now robbed of the thrill of victory.

Harris abruptly bounced to his feet, unwilling to surrender to the remorse he felt drowning his ability to lead the men. He strode to the stream, bent over, and cupped cool water in his palms. Returning to Matt, he knelt and let the fresh liquid drip onto Matt's cracked lips, with no perceptible effect. Matt remained unresponsive to the stimulation. Harris let the remaining water trickle through his fingers onto the ground.

"I don't know what else to do for him except pray and hope for the best after we bandage him up. Head wounds are funny things. They can heal quickly or slowly. There is not much telling how this one will go. Nothing else we can do for now."

By this time, Nate had arrived, trailed by Mark and Robert escorting the Havens girl. The sight of Matt collapsed on the ground produced a state of shock among them all. Robert held the young girl back from the bloody sight and insulated her from the sights and smells of the battleground as best he could. His fatherly abilities came forward to shelter her from the endless assault of her senses.

Nate's compulsive attitude swelled up inside him at the sight of his neighbor incapacitated and covered in blood.

"What the hell happened?" he barked.

"We don't know for sure," Mossberg said. "We found him this away after the shootin' stopped. Already sent for the packhorses to bring up bandages and medicine. He's breathin', but it don't look so good right now."

Nate bent over and placed his hand against Matt's neck.

"He feels hot as hell! Gimme the canteen."

Harris said, "I just tried to give him some water. He did not respond."

Nate ignored the captain's comment and worked on opening Matt's shirt. Taking the canteen from Mark, he poured water across Matt's bare chest and neck. Matt twitched at the cool splash of water against his skin. He groaned and mumbled incoherently. Nate repeated the dousing until the canteen emptied, but Matt remained impassive.

Impatiently, he slapped Matt hard on the arm, grimly urging, "Matt, you wake up. Don't you leave us."

Mossberg got out of Nate's way and eyed Harris with a questioning look. The captain shook his head no, as if to tell Mossberg not to intervene.

Nate grabbed Matt's arm and gently shook it. He raised his voice when Matt did not respond. "Matt! Git on back here. You wake up, you ain't goin' nowhere."

A crack formed in Matt's eyelid.

"Come on, Matt, we got the Comanch on the run!"

The whites of his eyes began to appear.

"That's right. You'll want to see 'em skedaddle. We scattered 'em good! Come on Matt, open up."

Finally, Matt's eyes opened partially to reveal the frantic and uncomprehending expression of a lost man. The unfamiliar aspect on his face alarmed the men, who were used to Matt's steel gaze coldly assessing them for indications of courage and strength.

Matt weakly mumbled, "Where am I?"

Nate answered, "You're out fightin' Comanche."

His eyes flew open as if frightened at the prospect of a fight. Wild fear danced behind his dilated pupils. His voice rose in a coarse, rasping pitch, uncertain of reality, "Where am I?"

"Out in the hills, Matt. This is Nate."

Nate's voice only increased Matt's terror. He felt the fear of a cornered animal with no options for escape. His body was unresponsive and disconnected from his rampaging thoughts.

"What happened? There's Comanch in them hills. We're surrounded!"

Nate took a steady position beside Matt and placed his hands on his shoulders in order to suppress any sudden movements. Matt was beyond hearing the facts.

"Where am I? What happened?"

"Matt, calm down. You're with friends."

"Cora! Where's Cora? Git the kids in the house! The bears!"

Nate held Matt firm as he began to squirm and tried to shift his head. The blood pooled over his eyes, ran down his cheeks, and dripped into the leaf-covered dirt. He drifted back into the confusion of unconsciousness, oblivious of reality and lost in a terrifying world of incoherent dreams.

TWENTY-FOUR

It was late morning when Tom brought in the last of the packhorses. A hot fall sun baked the rocks as the day wore on with the men occupied in securing the area. Harris put the men to work dragging the dead Comanche out of the canyon to dispose of them in a deep gully beyond the woods of their former camp. The Rangers made preparations to spend the evening near Matt, who drifted in and out of consciousness all afternoon. The delirium he suffered from continued unabated.

Harris decided at least one night in the old Comanche camp was called for to give Matt a chance to recover for the return ride home. He sent Antonio out to ride the area north of camp and scout for any additional sign of the Comanche. Mark accompanied Nate on a scout to the south of the rock that occupied the rest of the day.

Harris helped bring in Lloyd's body to a secluded location in the canyon where the soil was deep enough to provide a shallow grave. The men buried him in a solemn ceremony read over by Tom and collected rocks afterward for the customary grave covering. The men took the time to arrange the rocks in a natural-looking manner to hide the location of the burial site so Indians wouldn't discover it in the future.

The camp was in relatively good order and secured as well as could be expected this far into the wilderness. With a few pickets posted, the men felt reasonably protected in the heart of Comanche land. The earlier lesson of their harsh defeat would teach the Indians that the Texans meant business. Harris knew the Comanche would hesitate to return.

Antonio rode into camp with a fat whitetail strapped across his pony. Tom eagerly prepared a large fire to cook the fresh meat over. There was no reason to fear discovery. The Indians knew where they were. A leisurely meal of fresh venison shared around a cheery fire buoyed the lagging spirits as dusk began to descend.

Neither Nate nor Antonio found any fresh sign of Indians on their scouts, and this added to the relaxed atmosphere of the camp. Harris was sure the three Comanche that got away were making quick time in a straight route towards the open plains and the security of the vast grasslands. Antonio felt certain the Comanche would not stop until arriving at their village, most likely five or six days of hard riding away. He sat facing the coals of the fire and watching the deer roast slowly while explaining where the tribe's main village would most likely be located.

Tales of the day's exploits began to circulate among the men in grand style. A sense of achievement from their successful rescue of the girl displaced some of their negative feelings of loss. As twilight descended, an invigorating chill from a northern breeze washed down into the bottom of the canyon. The unusual warmth of the day quickly dissipated and the men gathered near to the comfort of the fire.

They milled lazily about the fire, eating hot venison while discussing the ferocious battle and the significance of their overwhelming success. After discussing the topic, they concluded a new era of punishment against the Indians had dawned with their victory. There was no doubt in their minds that the Comanche could be defeated and driven away from their settlements if the Rangers were allowed to remain organized. Although the loss of Lloyd would haunt their memories for a long time, they agreed the price could have been a lot higher. The deer Antonio provided was a fitting touch to their celebration of success against such a dangerous foe.

The Havens girl had regained her composure, surrounded by the comfort and security the men offered. She watched intently while the deer was cooked. Robert continued to dote on her and provided her with ample portions of succulent tenderloin. Her eyes lit up at the opportunity for fresh meat after days of paltry Indian food.

Mossberg alternated with Tom and Robert, keeping a close watch on Matt. Robert tied a bandage across Matt's head to stop the flow of blood. They managed to keep his fever down with frequent wet bathing during the exceptionally warm day. The bullet wound on Matt's waist, expertly treated by Tom, didn't present any current risk. A couple of rolled-out blankets made him a comfortable bed on the soft soil beside the creek. Water dribbled into his mouth provided the moisture Matt needed in the warm weather.

With night coming on, he rested fitfully. He remained incoherent and rambled on in rabid descriptions of subjects that confused the men. Concern for his well-being was foremost in his companions' thoughts as they constantly checked on his welfare. Tom placed a blanket over Matt as the evening air began to cool quickly.

Out in the mouth of the canyon a lonesome whippoorwill made a call full of sad longing that drifted through the trees to the men in camp. A melancholy mood once again descended on the men as night fell and ended the day not all of them had lived through. Conversation ground to a halt in the brooding atmosphere. The woods lost details in the deep shadows of dusk that provided cover for the nocturnal prowling of a mixture of cunning beasts. Coyotes followed the call of the lonesome whippoorwill with their nightly chorus of nervous yips rattling through the expansive land. They had started to assemble the pack together for the evening hunt to begin.

The proximity of the coyotes to the dead and discarded Comanche guaranteed easy hunting on this particular evening. A grisly feast was sure to occur — one that was best left unobserved under the blanket of blackness. The Rangers gave little thought or regard to their rough disposal of the braves. But Antonio understood the significance of the disrespect shown to the once-proud warriors. Word of the lack of respect would filter back to the tribes currently hunting out on the plains. It was easy for him to predict retribution carried out on innocent white lives in the near future. It was the Comanche way of life. Antonio sat quietly among the white men, aware of spiritual meanings the whites continually failed to perceive. The ignorance of their race never ceased to amaze him.

Lost in his personal thoughts, Antonio peacefully chewed on a chunk of backstrap when he heard the first muffled groan. It floated mysteriously through the darkness. He raised his head, listening intently. Following the first faint murmur, a deep, disembodied, guttural moan came from within the very bowels of the rock. The dissonance built faintly at first. And then a gravelly cry of anguish reverberated in a coarse rumble across the hushed canyon bottoms. The darkened woods seemed possessed by a force that cried out in suffering.

Just as suddenly as it had originated, the disturbance abruptly ceased. The groan didn't seem to have a direct origin but appeared to emerge from the entire bulk of the rock that hovered over the camp in its domineering presence. Antonio held the meat to his mouth but didn't take another bite. He listened with apprehension for the strange growling to continue. The men exchanged wide-eyed glances with each other in disbelief. They were too shocked to make a remark. The silence that replaced the rumbling noise was deafening in its own right.

Mark finally broke the tension, timidly asking, "What the hell was that?"

No answers were forthcoming from the perplexed men. They didn't want to believe what they all had distinctly heard. They continued to gape at one another with astonished expressions on their faces. Their arms dropped useless to their sides.

Harris arched his eyebrows and tried to make sense of what he didn't understand. He didn't believe what his ears told him. A racket like the one they all heard was not possible out here away from machines.

Only Antonio knew what the sound indicated, and he quivered with understanding where the others were ignorant.

Before the men regained their composure, a second menacing growl floated down through the trees. This created further trepidation in the camp. The grating cry permeated the woodlands. Wavering shadows in the trees seemed to pulsate with evil intention in their outstretched branches. The origin of the growl did not make itself known. The moaning floated on the breeze, carrying a sorrowful message of distress. The sad sense of remorse in the groaning grew with a coarseness that gradually increased in power and volume. Some of the men stood up, as if to flee, but uncertainty kept them anchored in place.

Reaching a high state of anxiety, Nate shouted, "What the hell?"

He scanned the woods with a wild blaze in his eyes, ready to bolt. His boots crunched on the coarse gravel as he pivoted in place, unsure of the right thing to do, or think.

Worried expressions spread among the men. Heads turned, searching for the source of their bewilderment. The resonance was everywhere at once but nowhere in particular. Another separate and melancholic dissonance blended with the original bellow that now tapered to a close. This new rumble seemed to come from a different location and displayed a different pitch, but it exercised the same influence on the men.

Despair traveled along with the hoarse grinding noise as it roamed the length of the canyon, descending on the men completely wrapped up in a state of stunned disbelief. Antonio threw the backstrap onto his blanket, ready to ride away.

Mark placed his hand on his pistol as if there were a target he could actually draw a bead on. The action gave him a false sense of security in the face of an unknown, invisible tormenter.

The mysterious rumbling became constant. Rising shifts in volume mixed in with a variety of rough reverberations that flowed across the Rangers collected together in a circle around the flickering fire.

Matt emerged from his unconsciousness at the height of the men's concern. He opened his eyes and finally recognized some of his surroundings. Tom was standing over him with a peculiar look on his face that was puzzling to Matt's already clouded thinking. Matt felt an enormous throbbing in his head accompanied by an awful moaning that echoed painfully in his ears. The rasping murmur didn't seem to come from the world he was familiar with. The strangeness of the noise was his last conscious impression before he slipped back into a state of delirium.

TWENTY-FIVE

Matt's soul floated weightlessly in a dreamlike state, disconnected from his body. He realized he didn't possess a body. He was a floating spirit, unseen by others but fully aware of the presence of people nearby. Or at least he was aware of their spiritual presence, which resembled their former bodies. Family members who'd already passed away wandered aimlessly around him, taking no notice of his existence. He seemed invisible to them and of no consequence to anybody. A feeling of worthlessness overwhelmed his sense of identity.

He saw his long-lost father calling out to his deceased uncle. They both became engaged in a conversation of words he did not understand. The two of them stood boot to boot encased in an electric blue haze that outlined their bodily presence in an aura humming with power. They were unconcerned by the energy that surrounded them. They walked away from him, engaged in a language that was not of this world. He remained tethered in place by unseen forces, watching as they faded into distant space. The blue energy surrounding them dissipated. They were gone and he didn't matter.

Other departed family members meandered into sight. Their voices cut like a knife with sharp clicks of their tongues. Unfamiliar language rattled near his invisibly tethered location. He distinctly heard each word, but he couldn't understand their meanings. Frustrated, he now recognized some of his currently living relatives mingling with the walking dead. In this state of being, the difference between alive and dead possessed no meaning to him, or apparently to them either. They took no notice of him while they all appeared to be aware of each other with clear communications between them presenting no problems of comprehension. He was isolated. He was not there with them.

Slowly, he noticed a change in their perception. It was as if they all received a signal at the same time. In unison, they all turned to face the arrival of a new, smaller individual. The group gathered before him parted to allow the passage of the unidentified newcomer.

He saw a young boy emerge from the group, and the sight of him produced a warm, comforting sensation of tranquility. The boy's soft, innocent, brown eyes looked at him, acknowledging his presence. Matt felt a hot flood of joy when he beheld his lost son for the first time since his burial. Josh now appeared whole, fresh, and full of the virtue that the Comanche arrows had stolen from him. A sincere sense of peace resided in his son. No words passed, but the connection between their souls was soothing and healing. They stared at each other for only a moment, but the unspoken meaning communicated between them went far beyond the power of words.

Josh knew of his father's feelings of guilt and the unbearable suffering and devastating emotions that crushed him at times. Josh knew Matt never escaped his deep regrets over his horrible death. It would have been avoidable if only Matt had exercised better control on his wandering son. Josh let Matt know he understood his father's inability to forget the tragedy. The event had actually been beyond their power to control. None of the past mattered now. Josh was at peace and he passed that knowledge on without speaking.

Everything was all right now. Josh never reached out to Matt physically, but he conveyed the understanding that peace should be with him. Matt had failed to understand the meaning all along. It was simple. The past was as it was ordained to be. Death could not be altered. Ever. But a person had to carry on through all the pain that death inflicted. Preordained and permanent.

With a final glimpse over his shoulder, Josh made his way into a room at the side, slowly fading from view before he entered. A joyful sense of peace filled the area he passed through. Matt wasn't sure what was real and what was not.

Matt's father and uncle reemerged, still bathed in a luminous blue light. They continued to ignore him as they glided without effort up above him into a pitch-black void of space. A sharp edge of remorse cut through Matt as the men receded into the blackness behind him. Pangs of dread swept over him in his isolation. Did they not realize he missed them? Why did they ignore him?

He now descended into a deep, dark, watery pool, empty of life. He was in another world, cut off from his previous existence. Completely alone now, he once again faced an unknown energy that hovered beyond his control. Everybody had vanished. A crushing weight of reality replaced the temporary utopia he'd felt when in the presence of Josh. Matt carried his burden alone, its load pressing in on him from all directions at once. No support existed. The force was unbearable.

A deafening roar suddenly filled the emptiness around him. Out of the blackness, a massive silver-tipped grizzly charged with his mouth curled open in a snarl that frothed with saliva dripping across his black lips. Crazed ebony eyes burned with intensity. Yellow stained teeth gleamed while snapping against each other in a distinctive chomp full of threat. The grizzly roared with an insatiable anger. Looming upright on two legs, he towered over Matt and stared straight through him with the heartless gaze of a predator searching for a victim. All of the great bear's instincts were honed over time to make him an efficient and savage killing machine. He tilted his immense head back and shook it from side to side while another tremendous growl reverberated through the core of Matt's consciousness.

At the end of the growl, the bear's eyes sparkled with recognition of a situation meant for exploitation. He dropped to all fours and hunched up his solidly muscled shoulders in preparation for an explosive charge. Chomping his jaws in ravenous anticipation, the beast reared back to erupt in a burst of speed toward the intended victim unseen by Matt. Splashing through the water, the beast sent up showers of sea-green liquid, glowing as if lit from within. Energy cracked in the air like lightning. The power unleashed by the bear's churning legs parted the luminous green water with ease. Ahead of the bear, Matt finally made out the faint transparent figure of its chosen prey.

The bear's quarry stood stationary on the far bank of the pool. Frozen in place, she seemed unafraid and actually appeared peaceful, despite knowing full well the brutal charge would crush her. Strangely transparent, she wasn't recognizable to Matt. She stood her ground, with her arms hanging loose at her sides in resignation to the inevitability of the attack.

The bear was within feet of her when she made eye contact with Matt.

There was no mistaking those eyes. All of the meaningful experience of their shared history connected with him, deep in his heart. Love and understanding passed between them. She didn't have to speak. They knew each other's thoughts well. She remained stoic as the great bear covered her in a mound of grizzled fur. The deafening roar of the bear's rage thundered in Matt's head. He wanted to run to her defense, but he stood mired in a heavy sucking sludge that pulled him down into the decomposing stench of death at the bottom of the pool.

She disappeared in a fury of ripping claws and teeth.

He screamed her name, "Cora!"

He was yelling, but no sound came out.

Frustrated, he tried in vain again, "Cora!"

It was useless. He didn't have a voice. He was mute and powerless. He was the only one who heard his screams. The bear's growling grew deep and guttural as he eagerly tore at his helpless prey.

<<<<< • >>>>>

The men huddled closer to each other as the grating rumble from the rock continued. The pitch rose and fell without a discernible rhythm. For a short period, there would be quiet, followed by another long and grinding noise of anguish that escalated in volume. The men suffered through the tormenting sound of grief that seemed to originate from the upper flanks of the rock, where a huge collection of boulders rested. As a group, they were a powerless gathering of mortals in a canyon bottom dwarfed by the overwhelming presence of the granite mountain. Each of them stood separate and alone in their attempt to comprehend the baffling phenomenon.

The mysterious moaning left Antonio awestruck and speechless with indecision. He knew of legends told around Comanche campfires. These tales mentioned the absolute certainty of spirits residing in the massive domed mountain. Confronting the legends in person made him doubt his courage. He didn't possess a weapon to do battle with disgruntled spirits. Fighting the urge to take flight, he stuck close to the men. Fear etched itself on his furrowed, weather-beaten face.

Harris seemed the least concerned of the men, and he commented in a dry, aloof voice, "This is some kind of evening, out here camping beneath restless spirits."

Mark didn't appreciate the captain's lack of concern. His resolve, full of apprehension, contrasted with the confidence of Harris. "Captain, what the hell is that? Ain't nobody answered me that question and I damn sure could use an answer."

A chorus of answers rang out from the restless men, not waiting for their leader's explanation.

"Damn spirits are pissed with us."

"Injun spirits, too!"

"Don't make no sense."

"I'm for gittin' the hell outta here!"

The opinions rolled off their tongues too fast for comprehension. Nate took the opportunity to explain what he knew after the men calmed down a bit.

"This is what I've heard tale of. These strange damn sounds are blamed on the spirits. Same as them funny lookin' lights that seemed to follow us this mornin' before the sun come up. The Comanche believe this rock is home to spirits. Right now I'd have to believe 'em."

Antonio mumbled, "Sí, spirits."

He fumbled for the scalps hanging off his belt and attempted to hand them to Nate, who jumped back at the offer.

"I don't want them damn things. Specially now!"

Antonio held the trophies up for others to take, and they all looked at him like he was crazy. When it became obvious nobody wanted his bloody scalps, he went to the base of a nearby boulder illuminated by the campfire. Scooping out a cavity, he placed the scalps under the rock and covered them securely with gravel. For good measure, he placed large rocks over the loose gravel. He quickly returned to the circle of men when a particularly wicked grumble commenced rising in volume, louder than the previous bellowing.

Growing impatient, Harris made a move toward an area above the men where the large boulders sat in a confusing jumble of irregular shapes and sizes. Crevasses snaked threateningly upward into the boulders. Hidden caves lay scattered and buried throughout the collection all the way up to a crown that rose out of sight in the dark night.

Stopping just within sight of the men, he shouted back to them, "I'd swear the noise is coming from this area right above me."

Nate did not dare to approach the captain but shouted out his agreement from a safe distance, "If I was a spirit, that's where I'd be. Looks like a good spot for the devil himself."

As if on cue, another loud grinding reverberation commenced that sent Harris scrambling back to the men shouting, "Son of a bitch! Don't piss 'em off."

Matt wriggled on his bedroll behind the men. With their attention focused on Harris's antics, they didn't take notice of him. Matt's chest heaved with the effort to speak. Rolling his head to find someone, he tried in vain to form words. His mouth opened with a low raspy sound, barely scratching out a grunt, unheard. He rolled over onto his side and fought the pain pounding in his head. His chest expanded with the effort to force out one word, "Cora."

Robert, standing to the rear of the men, heard him. He turned to see Matt awkwardly attempting to rise from his bed. Getting to his knees, he gazed around with a strained expression on his face and sputtered, "Cora ... run!"

Jumping to his side, Robert steadied Matt on his wobbly knees. Matt attempted to stand but lacked the strength or coordination to make it. Robert let him slowly collapse back to his blanket on the ground. Nate also took notice of Matt's condition. He stood ready to help Robert if needed. Robert eased a rolled-up blanket under Matt's head while he continued to ramble on about a bear mauling Cora.

Nate appeared puzzled. He asked, "What's he talkin' about?"

"Dreamin', I would imagine. Don't make sense what he's sayin'."

Robert splashed a little water on Matt's face to shake him out of his trance. The wild flame in Matt's eyes slowly faded, replaced with a dull recognition of the men kneeling beside him.

Robert said, "Ain't no bears, Matt."

Matt's voice had the scratch of sandpaper, "Bear got her. She's gone."

"Ain't so, Matt. You been dreamin'."

"Seen it. She's ... gone." His voice slurred in the depths of despondency.

"She's not gone. You been out cold for a bit. Here take a drink."

Matt slurped out of the canteen. Water spilled onto his chest as his eyes closed. He returned to his nightmares.

Nate patted Robert on the back and told him, "Well, that's a good sign."

"Yep. Glad to hear him talkin', crazy as it is. Thought we might lose him for sure. He still has a ways to go though."

A deep black night encased the small camp in an unsolved mystery as the rock finally ceased its mournful groaning. To ward off the presence of angry spirits, Antonio piled extra logs onto the fire. The dry wood crackled in the heat and spit glowing sparks out into the darkness. Yellow-orange flames shot up from the growing bonfire. An illumination of dancing shadows projected onto the gloomy woods surrounding the men. Friendly faces collected near the large fire and sought solace from the haunting sounds of the rock.

The more familiar rhythm of chirping crickets returned a sense of normalcy welcomed by the small band of Rangers. With nerves settled, the men began a vigorous discussion of the evening's mystifying events. The general agreement among most of them was a belief that the sounds were from displeased spirits that didn't appreciate the presence of the white men. They were guilty of murdering the departed spirits' red brothers. This was the home of the Comanche, and white men didn't belong here. The spirits were sending a warning to the unwanted interlopers. It was obvious; the Rangers needed to leave.

Harris held fast in his opinion that the enigmatic groaning came from a natural occurrence, but he couldn't convince the younger men differently. Antonio emphatically believed that angry spirits surrounded the camp, and he insisted he'd head home right now. Rangers could come along or not. He would not remain at a haunted location any longer than needed. Harris struggled to convince him to stay for the night. It went against Antonio's better judgment, but he finally agreed to postpone his start for home until first light.

Robert sat next to Matt during the deliberations and tended to his needs with an occasional drink of water and the reassurance of close companionship. He replaced the original blood-soaked bandage and applied a salve that helped soothe the pain and assisted in congealing the blood still oozing from the gash. As the night wore on, Matt began to recognize Robert more often and managed to thank him for the nursing he needed so badly.

TWENTY-SIX

Antonio tended the fire all night long with an acute awareness of his proximity to a supernatural world full of antagonized spirits. He kept the flames leaping and never closed his eyes, lest some evil demon descend upon him to deliver harm. The other Rangers around the fire gradually slipped off to sleep, one by one, until only the crackling of the flames broke the silence in the cool night air. Guard duty rotated once in the early hours of the morning while Antonio continued to hug the fire in the center of the camp. He never considered a remote bed in this hauntingly enchanted area. As the orange glow of morning rose across the eastern horizon, he threw a final log on the fire and readied his gear to hit the trail for home as soon as possible.

Harris noticed Antonio's impatience and roused the men from their slumber, issuing orders for an early departure. Most of the men threw off their blankets without hesitation. They were ready to be on the trail home and away from the granite rock disturbed with the menacing world of spirits. A crisp fall morning greeted the early risers and provided additional motivation for them to get on the move. The smell of fresh brewed coffee soon wafted through the canyon bottoms, courtesy of Tom.

Robert remained sitting next to Matt, continually checking on his condition as the camp started to bustle with activity. Matt slept soundly through the commotion of men banging their gear together in their haste to hit the trail. Gruff talk spiced the animated conversation as they went about taking care of their chores. All of them eventually wandered over and talked to Robert about Matt's condition. Their concern was unanimous and evident in their subdued questioning.

Bacon began to sizzle in the fire-blackened frying pan as Tom worked busily on a hot breakfast. Robert stood and stretched his arms above his head to loosen up his aching muscles. It had been a long, sleepless night. Harris finished tending to the duties of organizing the men and came over for a word with Robert.

He stopped at Matt's feet and inquired, "How is he doing?"

Robert stifled a yawn, "He's doin' better. Woke a few times during the night and wanted water. Didn't say much. He doesn't have a fever right now, but his head is goin' to ache somethin' fierce for a while. I believe he'll be fine with a little time."

Harris contemplated the meaning of Robert's comments. He wore a stern frown and grimaced as he spoke, "He will not be ready for travel today."

It was not a question but just a dry statement of fact from a man forced into unpleasant decisions.

Robert stared at Harris.

"Most likely not. What do ya have in mind?"

Harris kicked a rock off into the brush and watched it tumble into a pile of leaves.

"Hell, I don't like it, but I figured he would not be ready for travel. The trouble is, we have to move out this morning."

"What are you sayin'?"

"I need volunteers to stay behind with him."

Robert arched an eyebrow as he saw Nate approaching from behind the captain. The crunch of gravel alerted Harris and he turned to face the insubordinate scout. He was in no mood to listen to differing opinions.

Nate got right to the point and asked, "What's the plan this mornin'?"

Robert chimed in, hoping to temper the news of the captain's intentions.

"Cap is needing some volunteers, Nate."

Nate's voice possessed an icy edge, "That right? For what?"

Harris squared up to Nate. He knew the idea would not go over well.

"I need some men to stay behind with Matt while he recovers."

"Hmm. You movin' out? What's the rush? Matt ain't ready to ride."

"Thus the need for the volunteers to stay behind while I lead the men back home."

"Like I said, what's the rush?"

Harris bristled as his chest expanded.

"Nate, I owe you no explanation, but I will appease you just once this fine morning. We have had an excellent mission. Our goal has been accomplished. The girl is to be returned to her parents at once to ease their suffering. It is unfortunate that Matt will require time to mend, but such is the case. My other scout is leaving with or without us. I choose for our men to strike for home as soon as breakfast is complete. As for you, Nate, you are volunteering to stay behind with Matt."

"You're leavin' us behind? In the middle of Injun country!"

Harris fixed a firm stare on Nate. His hard piercing eyes scorched Nate with contempt. He said nothing as the silence deepened. Nate stood his ground, facing his adversary with clinched fists. Mutual dislike filled the empty void between them. Destructive energy craved to be unleashed. Nate took a menacing step towards Harris, who found his hand resting on his revolver once again.

Robert calmly stepped between the two antagonists but faced Nate.

"I volunteered to stay behind. I could use a day or two off myself."

He challenged Nate with the appearance of someone not willing to back down. He meant business. Keeping his firm stare on Nate, he said to Harris, "We just need some grub and a few spare horses for our gear. Maybe another volunteer to help us out."

Nate respected Robert's experience. He sighed when he realized another direct challenge to authority would only darken the current cloud of animosity hanging over him.

Seizing the moment, Harris didn't hesitate to take Robert up on his offer.

"I'm happy you understand, Robert. I'm sure I can find another man for the job. Perhaps Mark will volunteer. You men made a good team yesterday."

Harris gave Nate a final look of disgust as he turned to leave the men alone with Matt. Before the captain got out of hearing range, Nate spat out his opinion with cutting words, "He's lettin' Antonio force him out too early."

Harris paused in between steps when he heard the words. But he decided it would be better to let it drop so he could focus on the more important details. Dealing with Nate could wait. He continued on his way back to the other men preparing for departure.

Robert cautioned Nate, "He's doin' what a leader does. Makin' the hard decisions. Don't do no good to doubt the man in charge. It's mostly a thankless job he does. A job I wouldn't want. Matt could take days to recover. Harris can't hold up the entire mission on account of one man. Matt would understand."

"Matt would, but I don't. I got no use for Harris or his kind." He let go with a morning wad of phlegm, splattering at the base of an oak. "Who needs a bastard like him anyway?"

"Nate, there is always a bastard like him around. That is just the way of things. Like it or not, when people gather together, somebody is goin' to take charge. Most of the times, it's a bastard. Sometimes you git lucky and it ain't. But I've noticed them kind of leaders usually don't last too long. Especially out here."

"Maybe so, but that's what makes headin' out of Texas sound pretty good. Pa has been talkin' about it, here of late."

"Well, it looks like the captain will soon be out of our hair. We'll do as we choose when Matt heals up. Meanwhile, why don't you grab some grub and coffee? Things will seem a little better with your belly stoked up."

Nate picked up a stone and tossed it hard into the shallow stream, cursing under his breath before heading over to the fire. The camp was active with preparations for departure creating a buzz of energy running through the men. The Havens girl sat next to the fire, where Tom tended to her while also finishing up the cooking. He made sure she was the first to get a bite to eat and didn't want for anything that he could take care of. She relaxed with the careful attention he doled out to her. Robert saw Harris talking to Mark at the far edge of camp and the nodding head told him the agreement to stay behind would play out.

Matt opened his eyes enough at that moment to see the early morning activity. "What happened?" he mumbled to Robert. "I'm feelin' a little foggy."

"We got the girl. You got no reason to worry."

A slight smile cracked on Matt's face before he closed his eyes and once again drifted back to sleep.

It didn't take the men long to wolf down the hot breakfast. Then they announced their readiness for the trail with boisterous shouts of excitement. Harris made sure plenty of provisions were left behind for the four men who would be on their own after the departure of the rest of the Rangers. Four strong horses were tethered for backup at the base of the boulder where Antonio buried the scalps. With all the arrangements completed, Harris ordered the men to mount. He took a moment for a final word with Robert in front of the men.

"Robert, I am leaving you in charge here. You bring Matt in when you determine he is healthy enough for travel. Take the same trail we came out on, if possible. Use your own discretion. A party will return for you once the girl is safely delivered home. God willing, we shall see you at home or on the return trail."

Robert snapped a salute to Harris before the men trailed off into the thick woods. Mark spoke up as the last rider disappeared into the thicket of trees, "Kinda hate to see the boys leave."

"Raises the stakes 'round here, don't it?" Nate scoffed. "Whole damn Comanche tribe could return here if they have a mind to."

"If they do, we're dead, sure 'nough." Mark said. "We cain't defend this campsite with just the three of us."

"Right about that. With the other men, we might've stood a chance."

Robert had heard enough. He said, "The cards done been played. We'll make the best of it. Bitching ain't goin' to help us none. Matt here is goin' to need us to do our best. You two got any ideas?"

They both fell silent. They regretted the appearance of complaining in front of the older man they both admired.

With no suggestions coming from either of them, Robert said, "Ain't no need for us to sit here on our hands. I got several ideas. Mark, you climb to the top of the rock and keep your eyes peeled. You see somethin', git back here and let me know. Nate, you're the scout. Why don't you make a wide circle out 'round the rock and check for fresh sign. That will keep you both busy while I sit here and tend to Matt."

Nate said, "I'd rather be busy out scoutin' than sittin' around on my ass. I'll make a circuit around all these rocks and focus on the direction them bucks went yesterday. Case they're of a mind to return. Likely take all day to do it, but I'll be back 'fore sundown."

He looked down at Matt, still sleeping and oblivious to their conversation.

"He won't be ready for travel today, or tomorrow for that matter."

Robert agreed, "Most likely he will not. You take your time and watch your backside. If you see somethin' bad for us, git on back here. Or if you hear shootin', sneak on back to help out."

Nate went into action and quickly got his gear ready. Mounting up, he seemed content to be moving again.

"See you boys later."

Robert and Mark waved him off into the woods leading to the mouth of the canyon where the Comanche made their breakout attempt. Shortly after Nate rode off, Mark started up the steep incline to the top of the rock.

Robert found himself alone and sitting next to Matt. The camp was still and eerily quiet compared to the thunder of the previous day's fight. The rock stood there, rising sharply above the camp without any of the moaning that had confounded the men before. Robert craned his neck to watch Mark as he neared the last crest visible from the bottomlands. He turned and waved down to Robert. With one last lingering gaze, Mark stepped over the ridge and disappeared from Robert's view.

The silence unnerved Robert. They were more than one hundred miles from Austin, deep in an uncaring wilderness full of peril. The only available help was riding in the opposite direction. The familiar security of well-armed companions was missing. No bantering among the men filled the empty air. A creeping sense of loneliness occupied his mind.

Matt lay out cold to the world, and possibly changed forever. Some head wounds left men a little slower thinking. Sometimes they became a different man in their perception and abilities. Robert expected Matt to live, but a full return to normal was not a sure bet.

Robert preferred to ignore the negative circumstances and scrounged up a dry stick to whittle on as he settled back against an oak tree. From this comfortable position, he could keep a watchful eye on Matt and scan the woods for danger at the same time.

The morning crawled by slowly for Robert as he observed the everyday life of the canyon returning. Overhead, a squirrel bounced from branch to branch investigating the ripe acorns still clinging to the limbs. He released a few that fell bouncing off the saddlebags draped over a log near Matt. The chatter of the squirrels rattled through the treetops as they chased each other up and down the rough-barked oaks. Beneath their overhead antics, an armadillo rooted among the debris on the canyon floor, searching for ants and termites. The poorly sighted armadillo waddled within ten feet of Robert to return to his burrow, secreted in a crevasse beneath a pile of granite boulders. Robert felt his eyes grow heavy in the peaceful cool morning until he drifted into a light trance.

He wasn't sure how long he napped, but he was aware that he was under observation when he started to come around. Cracking one eye open, he peeked over at Matt, who was wide-awake and staring his way. Matt said nothing, but the change in his appearance was obvious. His eyes were much clearer. He seemed to understand where he was, and he opened with a question for Robert that sounded like the old Matt. Strong and to the point.

"You aim to sleep all day?"

"Good to see you too, Matt."

"Yeah, well, you been out for a while."

"Watchin' over you will take it out of a man."

Matt grinned. "Where is everybody?"

"Oh, they're here and there. How are you feeling?"

"Like a horse stomped on my head."

"More or less, one did. You're lucky to be here."

"How's that?"

"You don't remember?

Matt closed his eyes to think back. "Last I remember, Mark was takin' the girl up the rock. So, where is everybody?"

Robert got up and offered Matt a pull from his canteen. Matt slurped the refreshing water, smacking his lips when he was done. He tried to rise, but the pounding in his head started again and drove him back down onto the blanket.

Wearily, he repeated his question, "Where is everybody?"

"Well, right now, there's just you and me. Nate and Mark are out scoutin'. The rest of the men are with the captain, headin' back home."

Matt required a moment to analyze the information. A puzzled expression came over his face. "He left you men behind to nursemaid me?"

"You ain't fit to travel."

"That may be, but what was his rush?"

"Felt he had to git the girl back. Didn't help that Antonio was spooked."

"Spooked?"

"Yep. By the rock. Spirits were talkin' to us last night. That rock commenced to growlin' like nothin' I ever heard before. Was unnerving to the men, and me too. Antonio, bein' of a superstitious mind, took it real bad. Said he wouldn't tolerate the presence of so much spiritual power. And this rock has got 'too mucho' bad spirits for him. It really was somethin' to make a man wonder last night."

"The hell you say. Well, I didn't hear them spirits, but I had some mighty weird dreams myself. Spooked me a little too. Don't rightly know what to make of 'em. I just know I'm glad to be awake now."

"I'm glad you are too. Nate and Mark don't fancy bein' out here a little shorthanded. They got a healthy fear of them Comanche returnin'."

"We gave them a lickin', did we not?"

"Yes, we did."

"Then they ain't comin' back. They'll go home to lick their wounds. Will be a spell before they git the courage to come back for more. That's the ways of the Comanch. We're good for now."

He closed his eyes and rested from the effort of talking. His nose cringed as the pain shot across his forehead. When the throbbing passed, he posed a question to Robert. "Did we lose any men?"

Robert hesitated and let out a deep sigh, "Yes, we lost Lloyd."

Matt's voice grew harsh. "Damn shame. He didn't belong out here. He was too young to die for other men's bad judgment."

He closed his eyes, thinking of the loss of Lloyd. The boy had moved on too soon. The ways of life on the frontier were hard and unforgiving. He felt a heaviness pressing down on him again. Powerless to resist fatigue, he drifted back to sleep, temporarily escaping the burden that the living always carried.

Late in the day, Matt awoke to the sight of the last golden sunlight filtering through the yellow leaves, highlighting them in the brilliant hues of fall. A soft breeze rustled them in a gentle sway that rippled across the treetops like a wave spreading over water. Occasionally, an individual leaf broke free from the branches to flutter aimlessly to the woodland floor, already adorned with an assortment of the colored leaves of autumn. Chickadees whistled their happy song as they completed their daily routines, flitting from tree to tree. A final golden ray of light filtered through the branches and fell across Matt's face, teasing his cheeks with warmth in the cooling evening air.

For a moment, the pain let up enough to allow him to sit up and watch Robert puttering with the fire, adding dead limbs to coax the smoldering embers back to life. Matt whistled softly to get his attention. Robert threw a final log on the fire and turned to face his companion.

"How you doin'?"

"Feeling much better," Matt answered.

Robert noticed Matt's color was finally normal and his eyes clear and alert. The bandage on his head remained clean, with no fresh blood soaking through.

"You ready to ride?" Robert joked with him.

Matt chuckled, "Not yet."

He thought about it.

"Maybe tomorrow. Maybe in the mornin' if we take it slow."

"That would be great. The boys don't like it here too much."

"They're babies. Ain't no damned old spirit going to hurt 'em none."

"Well Matt, if you'd heard what we heard last night, you might change your mind."

"I've heard plenty in my time, and it's hard to believe what you're saying. Grown men gittin' scared over a silly noise. Don't let your imagination git the best of ya."

Robert stepped over to stand nearer to Matt.

"Glad to see you're back to your old quarrelsome self. We didn't know if you'd make it or not."

"Hell Robert, I'll be fine. Head hurts somethin' fierce, but give me a little time. I'll be fine. You can count on it. I got some chores to tend to back home. Gonna take the money that's due me and git them back taxes paid off. That bastard, Colonel Ames, will have to find some other place to steal. He ain't gittin' mine."

On the steep ridge above the canyon, a great horned owl let out three deep hoots announcing that the time to hunt was arriving with the descending dusk. The sun disappeared behind the rugged western ridges, igniting the sky on fire with orange heat reflecting off the feathery clouds that floated above the horizon. A cool wave of air rolled down into the valley as the camp visibly dimmed from the waning light. Another profound set of hoots echoed through the twilight-shrouded woods where so many men had recently died. A sense of sadness permeated the boulder-strewn woodland falling into darkness, ruled over by beasts of the night.

"I'll take it all." Matt spoke with confidence. "I'll take the fightin' and death. There ain't nothin' that compares to life out here in these hills. Indians are fightin' for the same things I want. The freedom to call this land my own. Freedom to roam and do as I damn well please. This is where I feel the most alive. That's a feelin' damn hard to come by. I will keep comin' back out here 'til my legs don't work no more."

Robert stood spellbound by the honesty spilling out of his friend. A friend he almost lost.

Matt glanced up at Robert and said, "Don't forgit, we got a huntin' trip to plan for. You, me, and a few compadres will come out here and live like Comanche. Live like God intended men to live. Free to follow our own wishes. Free of money concerns, and free of the interference of selfish men lookin' after their own damn good."

Robert nodded in agreement. Matt was back. No simple flesh wound would keep a man like him down for too long. Robert felt certain they would be on the trail sometime the next day or two. He noticed a change come over his friend as Matt became preoccupied, gazing over at the small stream of water gurgling in the background.

Matt's voice subdued to a serious tone as he continued, "Just a little business to tend to 'fore we can go off on a lark. I got a few unfinished chores need attention when I git home. Got to git Lee squared away on horse rearing. But that won't be no big task. No sir. That'll be the easy part. Raising horseflesh for spendable cash. That's work a man like Lee is cut out for. The hard part is goin' against a man's natural grain."

He looked up from the creek and slowly surveyed the surrounding woods that brought him such satisfaction to be lost in. He raised his eyes to find Robert listening. He was a rare man. A man he could truly call a friend.

"Yes sir. Some things I've always had a hard time doin'. But now the time has come. It's a job that's got to be done. When we git back to my ranch, I'll see you boys off."

Robert threw another log on the growing fire.

Matt hesitated, thinking through his future course of action.

"Then I got to see to a long-neglected chore. I know my little woman has got her eyes on some new blue gingham cloth that'll make her a nice dress. She'd also like a sit-down meal she didn't have to fix for once. A fresh-sheeted bed would make her happy. She deserves that luxury on occasion. Problem is, that's all in Austin. Sure don't like mixin' with all them people. Guess that's a problem I'll have to git over. Looks like I'm makin' a long overdue trip into town."

<<<<< • >>>>>

Epilogue

Readers who are not familiar with the hills of Central Texas may not recognize the setting for the final scene of the battle with the Comanche. Although the battle description is fictional, the mountains of granite do exist. The largest dome goes by the name of Enchanted Rock and rises 425 feet above ground, covering 640 acres. The area is truly an awesome collection of natural wonders and home to a wide variety of wildlife. Enchanted Rock State Natural Area protects a large concentration of the granite batholiths that dot this expansive area of unique formations.

And yes, the mountain groans.

The Native Americans who made their home in the game-rich area around the rock viewed the pink dome as an area full of mystery. They believed that spirits resided in the rock. Legends told of unusual lights flickering on the surface of the mountain at night. These flickering displays seem to float or move along at random, especially on wet moonlit nights. This natural phenomenon is the reflection of light off feldspar or quartz crystals when viewed at the correct angle. Unfortunately, I have never witnessed this occurrence.

But, I have heard the groaning.

I first traveled to Enchanted Rock when it was privately owned in 1971. I immediately fell in love with the beauty and exceptional qualities of the landscape. The granite hills of the area resemble the Rocky Mountains as close as can be in Central Texas. The attraction I have to the mountains continues to this day, and I am drawn back to "The Rock" several times a year. Do the math and you can see I have been there many times over the years. It never gets old for me.

It groans.

When the rock decides to perform, hold onto your seat. The sound is unlike anything you can imagine. Until you hear it, it is impossible to understand. I

first heard the rock speak on a backpacking trip to the Walnut Springs camping area at the backside of the main rock. It was a warm fall day that saw
rapid cooling in the dry air as soon as the sun dropped below the horizon. I
was alone in the woods and safely secured in my tent when the first murmur
wafted through the trees. Startled, I didn't believe my ears. The book I had
been reading was ditched. Facing the tent door, I was motionless. What I just
heard was impossible. Eerie. I waited in awe.

The rock did not disappoint. A truly wicked moaning commenced with
no let-up. It came from everywhere at once. It rose and fell without a pattern. Several groans emanated at the same time. The grating noise appeared
to come from different portions of the boulders piled on the flanks of the
granite domes. I could not tell where the clamor originated from. It was
everywhere at once. I scrambled out of the tent and approached the most
likely spot of the raspy sound. It was no use. Before I could determine the
location, it stopped. It was over in perhaps ten to fifteen minutes. I still get
goose bumps thinking about the strangeness of the event.

On another trip, the same scenario played out in almost the exact same
way. I was at the pond on the backside of the rock when the now-familiar
noise commenced. Once again, I could not locate the source of the rumbling,
but stood by in awe to enjoy the uniqueness of the experience. Where the
haunting sound comes from does not matter if you are fortunate enough to
experience the phenomenon. It is satisfying in its own regard just to bear
witness to this natural occurrence of unimaginable wonder.

Make a trip in the fall on a warm day with a cool night forecast to
up your odds for an encounter with the spirits. It will be an occasion you
will never forget. The Indians were right to fear the power of the Enchanted
Rock. If you are fortunate enough to hear the groaning, it will be an experience that will connect you with their ancient beliefs in a most powerful way.

Acknowledgments

Writing a book is not a solo endeavor. I owe a deep gratitude to the following gracious individuals for their unselfish assistance. Thanks to Darlene Scott and Vicki Perkins for reading the early rough drafts. To Cyndi Weakley for her keen eye and helpful suggestions. Elizabeth Ann Krouse for insight and encouragement through the editing process. And a final thanks to my son, Philip, for his technical mastery and Lana Castle for her professional word-polishing talent.

Printed in Great Britain
by Amazon.co.uk, Ltd.,
Marston Gate.